PRAISE FOR JOHNNY SHAW

"Johnny Shaw has an incredible talent for moving from darkness to hope, from heart-wrenching to humor, and from profane to sacred. His latest, *Big Maria*, is an adventure story that's equal parts Humphrey Bogart and Elmore Leonard, with just a little bit of the Hardy Boys thrown in. I loved every page."

—Hilary Davidson (author of *The Next One to Fall*)

"[Johnny Shaw] is excellent at creating a sense of place with a few deft strokes...he moves effortlessly between dark comedy and moments that pack a real emotional punch, and he's got a knack for off-kilter characters who are completely at home in their own personal corners of oddballdom."

—Tana French, author of *In the Woods*, *Faithful Place*

"Johnny Shaw calls *Dove Season* a Jimmy Veeder Fiasco, but I call it a whole new ballgame; I enjoyed this damn book more than anything else I read this year!"

—Craig Johnson, author of *The Cold Dish* and *Hell is Empty*

"Johnny Shaw's *Dove Season* may well be the best debut this year. It has the warm wit of Lansdale's Hap and Leonard novels, the effortless cool of Elmore Leonard and just a sprinkling of Crumley's border dust. Here's to many more Jimmy Veeder fiascoes to come."

—Ray Banks author of *Beast of Burden*

BIG MARIA

JOHNNY SHAW

THOMAS & MERCER

Text copyright © 2012 Johnny Shaw

All rights reserved.

Printed in the United States of America.

No part of this book may be reproduced, or stored in a retrieval system, or transmitted in any form or by any means, electronic, mechanical, photocopying, recording, or otherwise, without express written permission of the publisher.

City of Gold

Words by Fanny Crosby, 1875

Published by Thomas & Mercer

P.O. Box 400818

Las Vegas, NV 89140

ISBN-13: 9781612184395

ISBN-10: 1612184391

For
The Fellas

PART ONE: LOSERS

ONE

It didn't take much imagination to guess what the other kids had called Harry Schmittberger when he was a boy. Forty-some-odd years later, the nickname still hounded him.

Deep down Harry knew that if he had been born with a different name, his life would have turned out better. If not better, different. Brock Brannigan. Declan Fisk. Rocco Cabrelli. Brace Godfrey. Names of people real and imagined. Names that conveyed virility and strength and power. Names that affirmed manliness, if not greatness. But like the pitiless parents whom his birth had forced on him, his name was another entry on Harry's growing list of life's unfairnesses.

Harry approached the sometimes-nickname with equal parts hate and acceptance, a perennial throughout his life. As he had moved from school to school then job to job, there was always some jackass who thought he was clever. Some clever jackass who thought he was the first to coin the obvious.

What Harry couldn't figure out at that precise moment was why someone was in his bedroom shouting that name at him. Had he riled anyone recently? Probably, but who could remember? He wanted to sleep, but the angry, loud voice wouldn't let him. The angry, loud voice just kept screaming that nickname. Angrily. And loudly.

"Shitburger!

"Shitburger!

"Shitburger!" the angry, loud voice repeated. "Get the fuck out of my stall."

Harry opened his bloodshot eyes to slits. He wasn't in his bedroom. He wasn't in his trailer. He was somewhere wrong. It was a small room. Not a room. More like a closet. He searched for clues. His eyes alighted on a childlike drawing of an enormous penis ejaculating onto equally monstrous breasts. Written beneath the drawing was a scrawl. "OOOH BABBY." Not the work of a master, drunk-rushed and uninspired, but the anatomy was recognizable. It told him he was in the men's room at the Horseshoe Lounge.

"I got other customers need to use the head."

Harry's predicament quickly revealed itself. Harry had passed out sitting on the toilet mid-crap, his pants at his ankles. If that wasn't bad enough, he had thrown up into his own pants. Chunks of steak and bits of maybe-cauliflower pooled in the crotch of his underwear and spilled into his crumpled pant legs.

Harry mumbled, "I need to chew food better."

"What?" The angry, loud voice grew angrier and louder.

"I don't eat cauliflower." Harry curiously flicked at a white chunk. "Potato?"

"You got like ten seconds, Shitburger. I'm done fucking around."

"I need good, better pants," Harry mumbled. His liquored confusion shifted closer to fear.

"What you need is to get the fuck out of there. The fuck out of my bar."

Harry could not think of an out. He started to cry. Softly at first, but it quickly grew past mere sniffles. He didn't deserve this. Why did stuff like this always happen to him?

There was no sympathy from the other side of the stall door. "You better not fucking be crying."

"I'm not crying. You are." Harry roughly wiped at the tears, stirring them in with the drool at the corners of his mouth. He reached for some toilet paper. The dispenser was empty.

Looking back at the drawing of the dong and boobs, he wondered if people had breast sex in real life or if it only happened in porno movies. He had once found a woman drunk enough to play along, but she had been so flat-chested that he didn't consider it official. In fact it had been a complete failure, with Harry doing little more than dragging his rod across her dry sternum until the Indian burn made him flaccid.

The memory faded back to reality. The drawing in front of him pulsed. The stall tilted. Everything blurred. The ground accelerated toward him.

"Ooh, baby," Harry said softly. And then passed out.

It was only midnight, but Harry's night was over.

He woke propped up against the Dumpster behind the bar. It wasn't the first time that Chico had thrown him out like a sack of garbage. It's like the guy had something against him. At least Chico had left him sitting up. Not quite recovery position, but he wasn't going to choke. That was the ceiling of personal service that the Horseshoe mustered for its regulars.

Someone had pulled up Harry's pants. But from the way it felt down there, nobody had gone the extra mile and cleaned him up. Harry didn't have any friends that close.

He shifted his hip slightly and the stew of semi-solids sloshed in his drawers. He could smell himself over the curdled sweetness of the garbage. It made him sick all over again. Luckily he was mostly empty and only drizzled stringy spit onto the front of his sweat-soaked shirt.

He shut his eyes and leaned back against the warm metal. The night was hot and sticky. He pressed his hand against the ground to push himself up and got a handful of cricket husks. He wiped them on his pants and watched the insect parts drift in the breeze.

Harry's benders had grown progressively more destructive since going on medical leave from his job at the prison. His leg had been mostly healed for a month, but he wasn't ready to go back to work. In fact, he wasn't sure if he ever wanted to go back to Chuckawalla Valley State Prison. On most days it was hard to tell the difference between being a guard and a prisoner. Leaving work only to return to his empty trailer didn't seem that much different than the loneliness of lights-out. At least in a jail cell, you didn't have to walk the length of the trailer to use the can. The work wasn't any different either. The mental gangrene of repetitive busy work ate away at the core of his being. Nobody had warned him that the bulk of the job was paperwork and data entry. He knew he was meant for more than the monotony of a life as a corrections officer.

Harry had gotten the tail end of the dog his whole life. A losing streak that began at birth. But that didn't kill the thin sliver of optimism that he held on to. It was deep down, but it was there. Harry was due. He knew it. You can flip a quarter tails only so many times before heads finally lands. He was better than the other losers in Blythe. All he needed was his shot.

Belching acid, Harry decided that it would be at least an hour before he would be up for the three-block stumble to his trailer at Desert Vista Estates. He tried to manufacture the blissful cliff edge of an alcohol blackout, but was too awake after the commotion inside.

To pass the time, he read the bumper stickers on the trucks in the parking lot. SUPPORT OUR TROOPS. MY COLD DEAD HANDS. LET GOD SORT IT OUT. He counted the Jesus Fish: four. The Calvins Pissing: six. The Truck Nuts: two. Not one COEXIST in the bunch.

Conspiracy Todd's ride was the tie-dyed sheep in the flock of mud-caked and lifted trucks. A Subaru BRAT covered in a psychotic patchwork of adhesive rambling. YOU SHOT JFK. 911CONSPIRACY.COM. THEY CAN HEAR YOU. A yellow ribbon, but instead of SUPPORT OUR TROOPS, Conspiracy Todd had replaced it with ANOTHER EMPTY GESTURE.

As if on cue, Conspiracy Todd's voice erupted from the bar, spitty words seeping through the open windows over the whine of "Every Rose Has Its Thorn" on the jukebox. Time for his nightly rant.

"Government in up to their ears, my friends. Government and the corporations and the media tangled up like pythons in a knot. An orgy of perversions. People don't matter. Not the small people. Not the invisible. Not us, you and me."

"Shut up, you fucking commie." The Horseshoe Lounge's equivalent of civil discourse.

"Such violent ignorance. The product of an American public school, no doubt. Commie does not mean un-American, my denim-clad brother. A Communist is a follower of Marx, Engels, Lenin, and so forth. I subscribe to no single belief. I am a true American trying to show you all—my friends, the small people, the invisible—the truth. The Communists, Fascists, Republicans, Democrats, Viacom, Fox, Amazon, the PTA, Major League Baseball, they're all the same. Don't allow 'them' to turn you into lemmings."

Conspiracy Todd laughed loud and crazy, then stopped abruptly.

"I must call foul on myself. I referenced lemmings. When in fact lemmings—known for jumping off cliffs—never actually did such a thing. The kind of accepted lie I'm trying to unveil. We use that expression, 'a bunch of lemmings.' Animals don't commit suicide. The reality is a Disney movie. A nature documentary. Walt Disney corralled the poor creatures off that cliff, my friends. Murdered innocent lemmings for the sake of the message. The power of mind control. Disney, McDonald's, Coca-Cola—the corporations tell us what to think. Ironic that Disney's head is preserved in a block of ice. Ultimate mind control.

"But maybe we are lemmings. Not because we blindly follow others off a cliff. But because we allow 'them' to throw us off it."

There was no rebuttal. Harry heard only CT's heavy breathing. Horseshoe regulars knew that when Conspiracy Todd hit that certain jag in his monologue, it was best to let him go. CT wasn't your grandfather's hippie. He was two hundred sixty pounds of tie-dye, yoga, and hurt. He was allowed to talk like he did because he was scary muscular and enjoyed giving a redneck beating. If the redneck was lucky. Go too far and you'd end up coyote food. Or so the rumors went. Desert paranoids were a prepared bunch: tinfoil hats and automatic weapons. Conspiracy Todd was their de facto general.

Harry tried to tune out the voices. He tried to will himself to pass out. Nothing doing. The purgatory of one too many, but not quite one enough.

Conspiracy Todd continued. "You let them control you. Let them spit in your face. Let them walk into your backyard and take a greasy shit on your dog. The cities are lost, and small towns are following. Right here in our desert, corporations stole hundreds of billions of dollars' worth of gold from the American people. And none of you even knew you had it."

The word *gold* brought Harry to attention.

"Look it up. Google it. Early nineties, Congress passed the California Desert Protection Act. Sounds great, right? Protect our desert. What could be wrong about that? Everything. The government don't do nothing without a back end. It's always about money. Have you heard of the act? Read it? They know you won't. That's why their reports are ten thousand pages long. You can hide a polka-dot rhinoceros in all that paper.

"Here's how they protected our desert. They made a land swap. In exchange for acres of worthless scrubland to expand Death Valley. A bunch of land that was no good to nobody. Wasn't farmable. No resources. Butt ugly on top of it. The government traded that worthless land for the mineral rights to the Chocolate Mountains."

In his drunken state, Harry was having trouble following the details, but he did his best to absorb the gist of what he was hearing. He wanted to hear about the gold. *Gold* was the kind of word that made you concentrate, even to the rants of a lunatic.

"Here's the scam. Some corporation buys up a bunch of shit land around Death Valley. Then the government passes a bill that says they need those exact parcels. Instead of buying it for the ten dollars an acre it's worth, the government trades the corporation for the mining rights to the Chocolate Mountains. Those mountains are made of gold, my friends. Used to be two hundred mines out there. They say there's hundreds of billions-with-a-B dollars' worth of gold still there. And the government gave it to corporations that I'm sure showed their appreciation to the politicians that drafted the bill in the form of suitcases full of nonsequential bills. That gold was the property of the American people. They legally stole it. That's our gold."

Conspiracy Todd rambled on about the government and the mountains and the gold. And every time Harry heard *gold*, he listened hard. Even when CT went on a long digression about how the CIA made the Star Wars franchise and George Lucas was their shill and possibly an android, he did his best to listen. He had no idea if he would retain anything the next day, but he knew he had to try.

"Our gold," Conspiracy Todd repeated.

Screw that, thought Harry. *That's my gold.*

TWO

The bus had been giving Ricky McBride trouble all week. The overheating and the burning oil were nothing new. The latest headache had the engine stalling whenever the bus dropped below ten miles per hour. It was exhausting having to anticipate every changing light and roll every stop sign, a geriatric version of the movie *Speed*.

As the small problems ripened, Ricky knew that his 1977 Blue Bird CV200 school bus had entered its golden years. But until he could save the money to get a high-end travel coach with a working air conditioner and chemical toilet, he was going to keep the Yellow Bomber on the road with baling wire, duct tape, spit, and prayer. There wasn't anything that hard work and faith couldn't fix. Ricky truly believed that.

At five that morning in the dim light of the not-yet-risen sun, he was trying to patch-weld the radiator and get it reinstalled before his first run of the day. In two hours a couple dozen old-timers would be waiting for him in the parking lot of the Palo Verde Senior Center. He would gently load them into the bus and drive them to another parking lot in Andrade, California. From there the seniors could walk across the Mexican border to buy their cheap prescription drugs. The seniors rode for free. Ricky got paid to make the twice-daily trips by a half dozen of the *farmacias* in Los Algodones on the Mexican side.

He had lucked into both the bus and the gig and needed to keep it going. If the bus gave out, he had no Plan B. He didn't have a whole lot of skills, and it's not like jobs were plentiful in Blythe, California. Everyone he knew was unemployed or picking up low-wage piecework. He knew it was selfish, but Ricky prayed every morning and twice on Sunday for his good fortune to continue. He usually frowned on people who prayed for themselves, but it was really for his family. For his daughter. All his actions, all his work, and all his prayers were for her and her future.

The patch looked good and the radiator was back in place. It had only taken him an hour. He thought about getting back in bed with Flavia. The warmth of her body sounded nice. But Ricky didn't want to chance falling back asleep. He grabbed a cup of coffee and sat on the steps of the trailer.

Desert Vista Estates was the cheapest trailer park in Blythe. And that was saying something. Even with the bargain prices, it never attracted a single snowbird. The winter flock from the north preferred the grassy havens with swimming pools and gravel roads for golf carts. Although some Mexicans lived at Desert Vista, it was mostly white. The Mexicans tended to migrate to Mesa Verde, the other super cheap trailer park on the other side of town.

Ricky wished he could move his family somewhere nicer, but Desert Vista was the only place that he could afford a space for both the trailer and the bus. It was where he was. Where his wife and daughter were. That made it home. He wanted so much more for both of them, but wanting wasn't having.

Ricky drank his coffee and watched the morning pageant. If he had lived in the suburbs, business suits would have kissed trophy wives, gotten into their German-engineered cars, and listened to satellite radio on their commute. But most of the people in Desert Vista were desperately alone, drove beaters or hogs when not hitchhiking, and were unemployed or criminals or unemployed criminals. This morning's procession of lost souls consisted of a couple drunks stumbling home, the sheriff's department dropping off a well-beaten Mexican, and two prison widows on broken heels finishing their kneepad shifts outside the truck stop. The poor women sold their bodies to pay the bills while they waited for their men to be released from one of the nearby penitentiaries. It was a sin, but Ricky found the devotion to their mates admirable, even beautiful. How could any sacrifice in the name of love be wrong?

In the four years that Ricky had lived at Desert Vista, he'd never made the effort to get close to his neighbors. It made it awkward when you shared a beer one day and the next day you caught that same person in your trailer stealing your toaster oven and DVDs. You never knew what kind of mischief a Desert Vistan was into. If someone asked for a ride to the bank, the only good answer was no.

He didn't know anyone's full name. He didn't ask. Paranoid suspicion was a valuable survival tactic. Everyone referred to everyone else by aliases, nicknames, generics (chief, buddy, bro, etc.), or not at all. Most of the time, conversations consisted of little more than a head nod and grunt.

For that reason, he knew most people only by sight. He and Flavia had given each of them nicknames. The Sloth, Albino Wino, Matt Hardy, Roadhouse, and The Kurgan were a few of the men. The Michelin Woman, Fright Night, Goth Betty, and Lucky Tooth were the women. It was a little mean to call them names behind their back, but it's not like he would say anything to their faces. What was the harm?

And just when Ricky thought the train had passed, the caboose arrived in the form of Shitburger staggering toward him with weaving purpose in his half-drunk stumble.

"Morning," Ricky said as he approached Shitburger. He didn't know how loud the pockmarked drunk could get and wanted to make sure he didn't wake Flavia and Rosie. The trailer walls were so thin, it was a wonder they kept out the light.

"Hey." Shitburger swayed, eyes to the ground.

"You okay?"

"I puked my pants."

Ricky was neither surprised nor curious.

Even from five yards, Shitburger's breath smelled like an alcoholic baby's diaper. But that was the prologue. The real odor came from his body. He smelled like a slaughterhouse in summer. Manure and dead beef. Ricky wondered if that was how Shitburger got his name.

"You got a computer, yeah?" Shitburger said.

Ricky nodded and backed up a step, wondering how long he could hold his breath.

"It got websites and that stuff? The Internet, right?"

Ricky nodded.

"I was wondering could I use it for a hour? Got some research to research."

"Everyone's asleep."

Shitburger nodded. "Not now. In no shape. Pants all puked. Soon, but whenever. Later."

"I don't know. I got to work. Then I got things."

"I'll pay."

"How much?" Ricky asked.

"Couldn't be a good neighbor?"

Ricky smiled. "When was the last time you loaned someone a cup of sugar?"

"Twenty bucks. Hour or so. Don't think I'll need more than that."

"Okay," Ricky said. "But you got to wait until I'm back. Around three. Don't come bothering my family."

"Perfect. Three. I got to get cleaned up. Get my beauty rest, yeah?" Shitburger laughed a nauseating laugh until he inadvertently hawked a jellyfish onto Ricky's boot.

THREE

Frank Pacheco couldn't stand a lot of things.

Frank couldn't stand those four old hens. Not even seven o'clock and their piercing laughter grated on his every nerve. Being old don't make you cute, honey. He wanted to tell them to shut up, but that would mean talking to them. That, he couldn't stomach. When they spoke to him, they always reverted to a condescending baby talk that would make a cartoon princess vomit. He didn't know if it was because he was an Indian or they thought he was simple. Probably both.

Frank couldn't stand Blythe. It wasn't that much different from the reservation, but something about the town depressed him. Like most desert towns he knew, Blythe was a sun-faded patch of concrete and dying palms. It felt like it was one good gust away from being swallowed by the sand that surrounded it. Or maybe it had been swallowed and spat out like a wad of indigestible fat. Blythe was the kind of town that you drove past on the highway, hoping that quarter tank of gas would last until a more hospitable stop down the road. Every Tuesday Frank's grandsons drove him down to Blythe from Poston, dropping him off in the parking lot to wait for the Drug Bus with the other oldsters.

Above all, Frank couldn't stand being old. Outside, his body was crumbling, but inside he still felt young and full of adventure. Whenever he saw some hoodlum acting tough, he thought about serving the punk a beating. He had at least one good scrap left in him. He wanted more. He wanted shots of mezcal and cans of beer. He wanted a nice Cohiba. He wanted to bang young quim.

Hell, he wanted to be useful. He was tired of people taking care of him. He wanted anything more than what had turned into a tedious and drawn-out wait.

No matter how many people he had around him, he had never felt more alone.

The Drug Bus pulled up in all its canary-yellow glory at seven on the dot. That was one thing Frank was thankful for. Ricky was always on time. You didn't see a work ethic much anymore, but the big, muscle-bound kid was an exception. He may not have been the sharpest knife in the drawer, but Ricky worked hard and did his best to be polite and helpful.

Frank watched Ricky help one of the hens with her first step. She openly flirted with him. Wet, clumpy lipstick and shameless double entendres. It made Frank sick. Did they think that poor kid enjoyed it?

Ricky smiled when he saw Frank. "Morning, Mr. Pacheco."

Frank grunted.

"You ain't got to act mean around me. I've seen you smile when no one's looking."

"Who said I don't smile? I smile. Laugh, smile, even giggle when I have a mind. Just not this early. All us Indians aren't Iron Eyes Cody."

"Who's that? Relative of yours?"

Frank shook his head and climbed into the bus.

In an effort to be as far away from the hens as possible, Frank sat in the front of the bus across from Ricky.

Ricky took Ogilby Road for part of the way. It took a little longer than the highway and the view was identical, but he knew the old locals preferred it. His passengers liked to be reminded that although the old road might be long in the tooth, it hadn't lost its function if you were patient.

Frank alternated his attention from one window to the other. The Mule Mountains to the west, the Cargo Muchacho range to

13

the east, and the Chocolate Mountains behind them. Mostly rock and scrub, there was no visual difference between the ranges. It all used to be his people's land, but it was hard to lament having something that ugly stolen from you.

"So what kind of Indian are you? There's like a whole lot of kinds, right?" Ricky asked without taking his eyes off the road.

It took a second for Frank to realize that Ricky was talking to him.

"What kind of white are you?" Frank said.

"Gosh. Don't know. Didn't know my parents. Don't even got their last name. Got my first foster parents'. Thinking I'm just regular white, I guess."

Frank nodded. The kid was hard not to like. "I'm Chemehuevi mostly. But all the River Indians got a little of everything else in there. Mojave, Hopi, Navajo. Everyone's mixed red. Some Mexican in there, too. How old are you, Ricky?"

"Twenty-four."

"And you got your own business. Good for you."

Ricky gave Frank a glance and a smile. "I got a daughter. In the first grade. Trying to make things better for her than they were for me."

"All you can do."

"You got kids?"

"I got a daughter myself. Two grandsons."

"I never see your wife. She don't like Mexico?"

"Used to love it, but she passed on. Been gone for"—Frank counted slowly on his fingers—"six years now."

"Sorry. I didn't mean to…"

"No reason to apologize. Used to being on my own."

Frank could remember when Los Algodones was a quaint and quiet border crossing, mostly produce trucks and even mule traffic in town. Now the foot traffic was entirely blue hairs and wrinkled white men. The chipped stucco buildings looked the same, but the businesses inside had changed. They had become doctor and dentist offices, but mostly pharmacies, every other shop competing for the best discount.

Frank went to four different *farmacias* before he found the best price on his cancer medication. He would have to wait until the following Tuesday for the cholesterol pills, vitamins, and less important crap. By then, his casino check should have arrived. The small allotment that he got for being an Indian was just enough to keep him from burning the neon monstrosity to the ground.

The heat and walking took more out of him than he wanted to admit. What was it with Mexicans and their hate for shade? He couldn't remember seeing a single tree in all the Mexican cities he'd ever traveled to. Frank took a break on a low wall and looked over his list. Sweat dripped from his nose onto the folded paper.

Finished with his medicine shopping, Frank wanted to pick up a couple of Cuban cigars with the cash he had left. He wouldn't smoke them, but having them would make him feel good. At the very least, he could chew the ends.

He swayed a little as he rose, light-headed and dizzy. He took a knee. A fifteen-year-old Mexican boy approached and put a hand on his elbow.

"*Está bien?*" the boy asked.

Frank shook the hand away and rose without the boy's assistance.

"*Estoy bien. Yo no necesito su ayuda,*" Frank said sharply.

The boy smiled and shrugged. He hit Frank with a solid right cross to the chin. As Frank fell over the low wall, the boy grabbed for Frank's bag.

The boy was too young to have an effective punch. Enough to knock Frank off-balance, but not enough to hurt him. Frank landed on his ass but held on to the bag, pulling the boy toward him.

Frank got to his feet, ignoring the aching in his hip and knees. The boy continued to pull at the bag. Despite the pain, Frank felt energized. The kid wanted a fight, he'd get the horns. Messed with the wrong goddamn redskin. Frank threw his best haymaker.

And missed horribly. The boy pulled the bag from his grasp and kicked him hard in the stomach. Frank collapsed to the ground with his wind, his pride, and his breakfast knocked out of him.

Frank no longer cared about his bag. All he wanted was air. Sweet, delicious air. Thirty painful seconds later, he had his breath back. His throat tasted like Jimmy Dean and piss.

When he looked up, Ricky stood over him with the Mexican boy's neck tucked into the crook of his enormous arm. The boy struggled but eventually went slack when he realized he was beat. Ricky's size made the boy look small and defenseless. It made Frank feel worthless. This scrawny child had gotten the better of him.

"Got your bag, Mr. Pacheco. You okay?" Ricky reached forward with his free hand.

Frank stood on his own and took the bag from Ricky.

"Thanks."

"You want to get a punch in? I'll hold him still. Sometimes a kick in the butt is the best lesson. Or should I bring him to the cops?"

Frank looked at the frightened boy.

"Let him go."

"You sure?"

Frank brushed off his pants. He wanted to hit the kid. Bloody his face. Beat the youth right out of him. But he knew it wouldn't be satisfying.

"Yeah. No harm done. Let's forget about it."

None of the seniors ever had problems with the border agents when crossing. While buying Mexican prescription drugs and sneaking them over the border wasn't exactly legal, even the

Border Patrol didn't have the heart to stop an eighty-year-old grandma from getting her arthritis meds.

Back at the bus, Ricky finished his head count. Two of his seniors were AWOL, but Ricky wasn't concerned. There were always a few stragglers. He'd give them another fifteen minutes before he went looking.

Frank approached him at the back of the truck.

"Thanks for the help back there."

"Kid sucker-punched you. Next time it will be you that's got my back." Ricky smiled, knowing the old man was embarrassed. He was like a hundred years old. What did he expect?

"Well, that's all I wanted to say. Thanks, Ricky."

"No problem, Mr. Pacheco."

"Call me Frank." Frank walked a few steps, and then turned. "You smoke *mota*?"

"What? No. I mean, not while I'm driving. I mean. What are you talking about?"

"Calm down, kid." Frank laughed.

Frank reached into his pocket and pulled out a plastic baggie. He unrolled it, opened it, and removed a couple thin joints.

Ricky looked both ways and took the joints. He gave them a quick sniff.

"Homegrown," Frank said. "My grandsons are entrepreneurs like you. You ever need more, just ask. We all got a little glaucoma."

"Thanks, Frank."

Ricky put the joints in his shirt pocket.

"You had these on you the whole time? You went into Mexico and back with a bag of grass in your pocket? You could've got caught."

"At my age a little excitement is welcome."

FOUR

"No porn," Ricky said.

"You got a dirty mind and a low opinion. Didn't even dawn on me," Harry said. "Just going to research and get out of your hair."

Harry would have to catch some naked-lady photos when the kid was in the can or something. He needed fresh imagery for his midevening solo. The women in his current stack of nudie magazines had become so familiar that Harry practically thought of them as sisters. His lady lineup had grown pornographically stale, the honeymoon long over.

Harry had cleaned up, but even he was aware of the rough tang of unwashed clothes and alcoholic that rose from his body. If Ricky smelled it, he didn't say a word.

His mind drifting, Harry wondered if people ever lost their sense of smell. Like a deaf or blind person, but their nose didn't work. He remembered hearing that that was one of the things that happened when you got struck by lightning. If you lived. Maybe while he was online, he would find out.

They sat on folding chairs and faced the computer in Ricky's trailer.

"You have about an hour," Ricky said. "When Flavia and Rosie get home, we're done."

Harry nodded. "So how do you work it?"

"What? The computer?"

"I ain't used one much."

"Never?"

"The one at the prison for work, but only to type in names and stuff. Play solitaire. Minesweep."

"Why don't I type? It'll go faster," Ricky said. He was concerned that his trailer might absorb Harry's stink. The sooner he left, the better.

"What if I don't want you to see what I'm looking up?"

"There ain't no secrets online. If it's there on the Internet, anyone can see it. What's it matter?"

"I don't know."

"Look, I can't just explain how to use a computer. Little as I know, there's still a lot to know. It's your call. Either I help or you find some other place to do it. I'm not being a jerk. I don't know how else to help, but to help."

Harry thought about it for a while. He looked at a child's drawing on the wall above the computer. A house and a sun and purple grass in Crayola. He could draw better than that.

"You have anything to drink?" Harry asked.

"Water."

Harry made a face like Ricky had offered him iced urine.

Harry finally nodded. "All right. You help. Look up something called the California Desert Protection Act."

"And my twenty bucks?"

"You want it up front?"

"Yeah."

"Why not after?"

"Because you're less trustworthy than me. Just fact. Ask anyone. People trust me. They don't trust you. If there were a ref or ump or whatever, he would tell you to pay first."

"Fair enough. Probably right." Harry dug in his pocket and handed Ricky a wadded twenty.

Fifteen minutes later, Harry was bored sober. Ricky had found a copy of the California Desert Protection Act online, but it was all governmentese. Who could read all of those heretofores and insomuches?

"Forget this. Can't make head or tail. Search 'gold in the Chocolate Mountains.'" Harry unconsciously whispered, "gold."

"Which Chocolate Mountains?" Ricky asked.

"What do you mean? The ones out here. The Chocolate ones."

"Don't you know nothing about around here? There's two Chocolate Mountains. The ones by the Salton Sea and the bigger ones in Arizona."

"Yeah, but they're the same, right?"

"Nope. Two different states. Not connected. We're actually sitting in the middle between them."

"All I want is the ones with the gold in them."

By the end of their computer research, Harry learned that both of the mountain ranges had gold in them. And the gold was no secret. He also learned that Conspiracy Todd was mostly full of crap, a less-than-surprising fact that he should have taken into account before he had gotten overexcited. Like all Harry's schemes, this one had quickly gone south.

The California Chocolate Mountains were the ones Conspiracy Todd had been referring to. The government had sold the mineral rights to a big corporation for a bunch of desert land. That part he had gotten right. What Conspiracy Todd had failed to mention is that the gold was in the middle of the US Navy Aerial Gunnery Range. A still-bombing-all-the-time aerial gunnery range. The corporation had bought the rights on a gamble. They could only mine *after* the land had been decommissioned. And then cleared of all ordnance. If they ever decided to close the range, it would take decades to make it safe for mining. There were billions of dollars in gold in those mountains, but they would have to wait years and years before anyone could get to it.

The Arizona Chocolate Mountains had gold, too. And it had mines. And miners. People had been finding gold in them thar hills going back two hundred years, since even before the Gold Rush. The Chocolate Mountains had the oldest known gold mines in the West, and Harry was just hearing about it now. Those mines had been tapped out. Harry was only a couple hundred years late.

Harry needed a drink. The whole thing was a wash. Instead of getting rich, he was twenty bucks poorer. He had gotten his hopes up. As usual, reality needed to stomp his groin with its stiletto heel. What had he been thinking? As if one of CT's rants was going to open the door to riches. He felt like a tool.

"You thinking about prospecting for gold?" Ricky asked.

A little too curious, always with the questions, thought Harry. He shrugged.

"Some of the seniors I drive, they go out with their metal detectors. Show me the flakes and stuff they find. Sometimes little nuggets. I could ask where they go."

Harry watched Ricky click from website to website, barely able to retain what he was seeing. There were dozens of gold sites with books and maps and tools and all manner of equipment for sale. If any of those sites knew where the gold was, they would get it themselves. Apparently the real gold came from suckers looking for gold. He wasn't going to be a sucker this time. Not like Amway. Not like those vitamin supplements. Not like all the others. He wasn't going to spend a million dollars to find a thousand dollars' worth of gold.

That didn't make Harry want the gold any less. It was gold. Treasure. Buried treasure. And it was out there. Nothing told him different. Cruel world, he thought. He finally knew what he wanted, but he had no way of getting it.

"You ever heard of Iron Eyes Cody?" Ricky asked out of nowhere.

"Yeah, sure. The Indian who cried at the litterbugs."

"Someone mentioned him today. I wanted to look him up. We done?"

"Yeah. We're done, I guess."

Harry left without thanking Ricky. He had paid him. No reason to thank him too.

Ricky put the crumpled twenty-dollar bill with the rest of the loose bills in the New Bus Fund and put the mayonnaise jar back in the deepest part of the fridge. Only two thousand so far, but the down payment on a new bus wasn't out of reach if he kept doing two runs a day.

He pictured Shitburger out in those mountains looking for gold. Couldn't blame the guy for dreaming. Everyone thinks about winning the lottery, even if they don't buy tickets. It wouldn't even take that much gold to change the life of someone living in Desert Vista. According to one website, gold was over fifteen hundred dollars an ounce. It would take less than a pound to set his family up right. A pound didn't seem like it would be hard to find.

The first thing Flavia said when she walked through the door was "What stinks? You step in something?"

"That guy, Shitburger, the prison guard, the short one with the acne scars, he paid to get on the computer."

"He better not've been looking at naked women. How much?"

"Twenty bucks."

She walked to the cupboard, pulled out the Glade, and sprayed the chemical wildflowers throughout the trailer until nothing was left in the canister.

"Not sure if it was worth it," she said.

"Where's the Rose?" Ricky's eyes watered from the fragrant burn.

"Sleeping over at Anna's. I thought it would be nice for her. She can swim in their pool."

"Your sister spoils her."

"Anna just wants to spend time with her before they move to El Centro. It's only two hours away, but she knows she's going to see her niece a lot less."

Ricky had mixed feelings about his sister-in-law. She helped them out here and there. Almost all of Rosie's clothes were hand-me-downs from Anna's two daughters. He appreciated what she did for them, and there was no doubt Anna cared for Rosie, but it always came with a dash of condescension. Just because Anna married a dentist and they had a nice house, she thought she could look down on him and Flavia.

Ricky wouldn't have minded if Mario the Dentist acted that way. He had earned it, but Anna had married her way there. What right did she have making Flavia and him feel bad? He worked as hard as he could. He fed his family. He kept them safe. Sure, he wanted more for them, but he could only give everything he had. He didn't know how to give more.

"I also thought we could use a night alone, *mi guapo*." Flavia gave him an over-the-top wink.

"Look what I got," Ricky said, pulling the joint out of his pocket.

"Where'd you get that?"

"One of the seniors. Did him a favor."

"I haven't smoked since before I got pregnant. I don't know. I got to work early."

"Think of it as an air freshener."

Flavia smiled. When Flavia smiled, she looked like the girl he had met. The girl who he had fallen in love with inside of a minute. Not the woman who worked too much. Not the woman who was tired all the time. But the woman who was the best mother in the world. The woman who stuck with him no matter what, even when no matter what was a bad idea. When Flavia smiled, everything was right and good.

"Get over here." Ricky took Flavia's hand and pulled her to him.

They got high and made love. Ricky couldn't remember a better night. But later in bed thoughts spun in his head, keeping him awake. That much good in such a short period of time unnerved him. As wonderful as it had been, it was the kind of night that soldiers experienced before they went to die in a war.

FIVE

Harry returned to his trailer and found some cold fried chicken and three beers in the mini fridge. He felt dejected about the gold thing. But what had he expected to find? A treasure map with a big black X-marks-the-spot? Of course the good gold would be hidden or got. Harry hated knowing that there was gold all around him. Other people knew where it was. They were digging it out of the ground. It wasn't fair.

He watched TV as he ate, but couldn't concentrate on the fakey doctor show. It was like a soap opera, the doctors arguing relationship garbage in the middle of an operation. If those were his doctors, he'd give them the business for not concentrating on his hemorrhaging spleen.

Harry needed to do something that made him feel like less of a loser. He needed to get some lady love.

It would have been less work to tug out a hand batch and call it a night, but that would be another compromise, another failure. In the end, it would only confirm the depth of his loneliness.

Harry needed to change his luck. Rubbing all over a lady might not do the trick, but it couldn't do any harm. In a pinch he could always pay one of the women down at the truck stop, but there was no guarantee that would shake his funk.

He couldn't go back to the Horseshoe yet. Chico would be a jerk about the bathroom thing. It was usually a sword fight anyhow. He could try the Indian casino. Get some free drinks at the nickel slots. But there weren't any women there under seventy.

Harry wasn't picky, but he didn't think he could get it up looking down at gray bush hair.

After some thought, it was obvious where to go. Boog's.

He kept it casual with jeans and a Hawaiian shirt decorated with flowers and surfboards. He wetted down his thinning hair and splashed Canoe on his neck and scruff. He wasn't much in the looks department and knew it. A triple threat: too short, too fat, and too ugly. But none of that mattered if you weren't choosy and had a strategy. It's hard to end the night with complete rejection if you're willing to saddle a big lady.

He reached for his gold Saint Christopher necklace but decided to leave it on the edge of the sink. Gold was not his color tonight, and he didn't think he'd need Chris looking over him on this journey.

Boog's Hideout emitted darkness, sweat, and desperation. A concrete bunker with no personality, but in Blythe it was as close to a meat market as you could find. People came to Boog's for booze and sex, which should give a clear indication of the attractiveness of the clientele. The same kind of grim reality as a nude beach. Visions of youthful sexuality immediately smashed by a middle-aged horror show of lumpy grotesqueries.

Boog's was a Tuesday bar. Dead on weekends, but midweek busy. Married people made up a large percentage of the base. Husbands and wives spent weekends with the family, but on a weekday a good excuse could get them out of the house without raising suspicion. Enough time to hit the bar for some quick alley-wrestling. More than once a husband and wife had bumped into each other at Boog's while trawling for strange.

Boog used his bar for band practice, and Harry could hear the music before he opened the door. A fifty-year-old wannabe Lemmy, Boog was the front man for Baculum, a stoner metal band with two basses, no guitar, and a wicked logo. He went by the stage name Oz Penis, and his voice sounded like a gargoyle looks. It never seemed to bother the drunk and horny, and sometimes even brought in a slightly younger crowd.

The bass made Harry's skin quiver when he walked into the humid bar. Baculum was playing an extra-heavy cover of Sabbath's "Hand of Doom." The band wasn't good, but they obviously enjoyed playing, and there was something contagious about music played for the sheer love of it.

Harry let his eyes adjust to the darkness, scoping the possibilities at the bar.

On his second pass, he found exactly what he was looking for: a medium-hot woman with her fat friend. Medium-Hot was a bottle blonde with party-roughened skin and a too-big behind crowbarred into tight jeans. By the way she stuck her bucket out, Harry knew that she thought she was better looking than she was. That would work to his advantage. Her friend weighed at least two bills, but she had a pretty face and the bountiful rump and chestals that came with size.

Harry walked up to the ladies, snapping his fingers and pointing at the big girl. He ignored the thinner woman.

"Where do I know you from?" Harry shouted over the music, examining her face.

She smiled. "I'm not sure."

"Church? Maybe we go to the same church?"

"I'm not really a church person."

One for Harry.

"I'm sure I know you though. I'm Harry." He held out his hand, still ignoring Medium-Hot.

"I'm Tami with an *i*," she said, holding his hand for a second too long, finger flirting.

Two for Harry.

"You're so familiar, Tami with an *i*. I know I know you." Harry took the seat next to her, waving the bartender over. "You want another drink?"

She quickly sucked at the straw of her margarita, nodding and smiling. Harry ordered her another margarita and himself a beer and a shot of tequila.

Three. He was in.

"I hope I'm not taking you away from anything," Harry said, glancing at Medium-Hot for the first time but not making eye contact.

"No," Tami said.

Medium-Hot whispered in Tami's ear and went to shake her backside-and-a-half at the band.

Harry put his hand on top of Tami's. "I'm sorry. Were you with your friend? I didn't mean to interrupt."

"She's usually the one guys hit on. She thinks you're using me to get to her."

"Is that what she said?"

Tami nodded.

"She thinks she's something, don't she?" Harry glanced toward the dance floor.

"You aren't trying to get into her pants?"

"No," Harry said, "I'm trying to get into yours."

That made her smile. She took another drink and put her hand high on Harry's thigh. She squeezed, making one of his balls move involuntarily.

An hour and four drinks later, Harry and Tami were deep in conversation. Some guys try to make ladies laugh. That's fine for a handsome guy, but Harry knew that funny wouldn't get her in the sack. Funny kept you in the game, but funny was for friends. If you want a sure thing, tell a sad story to a fat girl.

They were even drunk enough to dance to some Baculum originals that sounded incredibly similar to the Sabbath covers. One heavy sound that made Harry's jaw muscles hurt, but with titles like "Witches and Wolfbane," "Blood from the Pharaoh's Tomb," and "The Antediluvian Reign of Yog-Sothoth," how could they not have a good time? "You want to get out of here?" Harry said, making his big move.

Without a word, Tami took his hand and walked him to the back door.

The back lot was dark. Couples coupled in the shadows. Harry caught the shapes of a lady on her knees mouthing snake and a bent-over-a-trash-can quickie that sounded like someone was plunging a clogged toilet. As close to love as you'll find in the Boog's Hideout parking lot.

"That's my van," Tami said, pointing to a paint-peeled, mid-eighties Vanagon. She got out her keys and slid open the side door. Harry gave her a playful slap on the backside.

With alarming speed, she turned and slapped Harry hard, loosening a tooth. Her voice scared him. "You hit me again and I'll hurt you. No rough stuff. I'm not playing."

Harry stared at her, feeling his cheek. He was as excited as he was hurt. "I was kidding around."

But Tami was all business. "Are you going to fuck me or what?" she said, pulling her underwear past her skirt and down her chunky legs.

Harry shrugged. "Let's do this."

He unzipped his pants and let them fall to his ankles. Light flashed across Tami's body as she half sat, legs splayed, waiting for Harry to climb that mountain. Harry turned toward the light, hearing a motorcycle. The single headlight blinded him for a moment.

When his eyes adjusted, a big, prison-tatted Mexican stood in front of him. Harry stared at the gothic "13" on his neck.

"What the fuck you're doing?" The inked Mexican spit-sprayed Harry's face.

"I'm just…" Harry stammered.

Over his shoulder Tami screamed, "Fuck you, Nestor. You fucking asshole."

"You're my woman. I'm going to let you mess up what we got? I love you, *princesa*," Nestor said.

"I ain't your woman. I ain't nobody's woman. We done. Harry's my new man."

Harry zipped up his pants and took a step back toward the bar.

"Where the fuck you going?" Nestor and Tami said in unison.

"Back inside?" Harry said, definitely a question.

Tami waved a finger at him. "No, you ain't. I talked to you for an hour. Listened to your boring-ass, bullshit sob stories. You owe me one cock up in here."

"Owe you what? Oh, no." Harry turned to Nestor. "Oh, shit."

"You're dead," Nestor said. His matter-of-fact calmness was terrifying.

Nestor got into a boxing stance. Harry kicked him in the balls. Harry didn't look like much, but he'd lost enough fights to have a few moves. Nestor dropped to one knee. But before Harry could kick him in the head, Tami jumped on his back and clawed at his face. His knees buckled under her weight, and Harry fell face-first in the hardpack with Tami on top of him. He writhed wildly but was pinned.

"You don't hit Nestor," Tami shrieked, pulling his hair toward her. His head followed so far back he thought his Adam's apple was going to pop out.

"I got this, *princesa*." Nestor stood, one hand massaging his groin.

Tami gave Harry's face a slam into the ground and got off him. The release made his body feel weightless for a moment. Harry scraped his hand across the ground and threw a handful of dirt in Nestor's face. He turned and hit Tami square on the nose, knocking her back into the van with her legs up in the air for the second time that night.

It was a decent plan, but not a great one. That was as far as he got. Nestor proceeded to give him a thorough beat-down.

And for the second night in a row, Harry Schmittberger woke up behind a bar, covered in shit. Unfortunately for Harry, this time the shit wasn't his own.

SIX

"Iron Eyes Cody was an Italian."

"Why would you say that?" Frank said. "You like picking fights with old Indians?"

"I read it," Ricky said.

"What lying sumbitch wrote that?"

Ricky stood in front of the open hood of the bus. He toyed with the carburetor, raising the idle while he waited for a couple of seniors to find their way back. They had been gone a little too long and he was concerned. Not about the seniors, but that they might make him late for his next run. In five minutes he would have to head into Los Algodones and find them. Either way, he'd have to book on the drive back.

Frank had walked next to him and leaned on the grille. At first, he had stood uncomfortably close to Ricky and made no effort to start a conversation. After a couple of minutes of silence, Ricky had decided that his research on Iron Eyes was a good ice-breaker. Apparently not.

"It was on the Internet. Says he was a Sicilian. That's kind of like Italian, right?" Ricky said.

"What's a computer know about Indians. Talking out of their holes. Next thing, you'll tell me Tonto was a Chinaman."

"I don't know about Tonto." Ricky felt bad. He hadn't intended to anger Frank. The truth was important, even when it wasn't what you wanted to hear. He tried to change the subject.

"I also read about the gold mines in the mountains around here."

"Computers didn't lie on that, but ain't no news. They been finding gold out here since before Cortés. Indians and Mexicans, it's their gold. The white man stole it, but what didn't they?"

"Cortés don't sound like a white guy."

"White enough to be a thief."

Ricky gave Frank a glance. "All you Indians still talk like that? The white man?"

"You better believe it, kemo sabe." Frank tried to keep a straight face, but a fraction of a smile leaked onto his face.

"You come over here to mess with me?"

"Mostly," Frank said, his smile broader.

"You ever found gold out here, Frank? Keep it stashed in your teepee? Secretly a millionaire?" Ricky returned Frank's smile.

"No, but I know where the gold is."

"Sure you do." Ricky knew the old man was talking lies, but talking about gold was too fun. Everyone should spend some time talking treasure.

"The Big Maria Mine."

Frank waited for Ricky to be impressed, got a blank stare, and then continued.

"They shut down Big Maria in 1903 or thereabouts. Just after the owner was killed in a fight over a fifth ace. Don't know that man's name. Long dead and forgot. The mine went to a relative, some cousin from Philadelphia or Pittsburgh or some city. Fancy Boy set one foot in Picacho—that's the mining town— and all that dust and heat sent him running back to the safety of concrete. He hired a man to run operations at Big Maria. This is where it gets good. That fella—his name I know: a Mister Abraham Constance—was not nearly as honest as our boy from Pittsadelphia thought. After six months Constance told him that he was shutting down the mine. That it was tapped. No more yield. No more gold.

"But it was a lie. A big lie. Still veins of gold up in Big Maria. The shelf everyone had been talking on. Some still do."

"How do you know all this?" Ricky had lost all interest in his carburetor.

"My grandfather worked the Big Maria for Constance. Before and even after it was closed. In those days they only sent Mexicans and Indians into the mines. The Chinese came later. More expendable. Sure as hell more of them. God knows why, but Constance trusted the Chemehuevi best. Only a few people knew that the mining was active. Abraham Constance and his brown and red labor force.

"Then it went to hell. Constance got paranoid. Gold fever, Grandfather called it. The Indians, the Mexicans that worked for him, they started to die off, disappear. Grandfather wasn't having any. He had no plans to wait around to get shot or disappeared. One night he snuck into Picacho, into Abraham Constance's house. Brought his hunting knife. Cut the man open from asshole to eyeballs. Spilled him."

"Jesus." Ricky crossed himself. "Is any of this true?"

Frank ignored him. "Grandfather wanted nothing more to do with gold. One of those old, old Indians that believed in curses and the wind and omens. He saw what gold had made of man. He took Constance's maps and papers and claims. Everything. He put them in one of Constance's lockboxes and buried it.

"From what I understand of the superstitions of my people, I see why he didn't want the papers. But I asked him, 'Why not burn them?' This is what he told me: 'Like a dead Nüwü child'— *Nüwü* is what we call our people—'Like a dead Nüwü child, the unfinished must be buried, or the flames of the dead are sure to awaken the unknowing.' If you understand that malarkey, feel free to explain. Most Indian traditions make no sense to me."

"Where did he bury all that stuff? The papers and maps?"

"He couldn't take the body out and bury it. A townsfolk sees an Indian digging at night, raises questions. He buried Abraham Constance and the lockbox right where he killed him. In the earth under the floorboards of Constance's own house."

"You ever try to find it? You must have."

"Never looked. Far as I know, all those papers, the maps to Big Maria are still there."

"Aren't you curious? I would've dug them up. Went looking for that mine, the gold."

"You and me both, kid. I don't believe all that Indian voodoo, if that's what you're thinking. Gold is just gold. It don't change a man unless he's the kind of man that wants to change. If I could have found them papers, I would have. One problem. My grandfather told me about the gold after the war—'47, '48, thereabouts. Jesus, sixty years ago. The Imperial Dam was built in '42. The town of Picacho, the buildings, everything, they're all under the water of the Imperial Reservoir. And so are Constance and his maps."

As Ricky drove the familiar route back to Blythe trying to make up time, he found himself daydreaming about gold and Indians and underwater ghost towns. It was the kind of thing that children played pretend about. Maybe he and Rosie could build a fort and stir up a story with her dolls. It made him feel like a kid to imagine hunting for treasure.

The mule deer appeared out of nowhere.

As the bus rounded a blind turn, the four-hundred-pound buck ran onto the two-lane road and stopped dead center. Ricky's eyes met the deer's, the animal turning to face the oncoming bus. The deer showed no fear, its serene face challenging the bus to charge.

Ricky had grown up in the country, taught to drive straight if the animal was smaller than a coyote and swerve if it was larger. Unfortunately, swerving and bus don't mix. Ricky knew it but had no choice. He turned the wheel sharply.

A volley of complaints, screams, and a violent snore rose from the seats behind him. Ricky didn't hear any of it over the sound of his own prolonged "Oh, shit."

The bus went off the road, kicking up a cloud of dust as it passed the nonplussed deer. The front tires dipped into a two-foot gully, bouncing everyone out of their seats. The screams rose in volume.

The bus climbed the side of a rocky hill. Ricky fought to turn the wheel back onto the road, his foot above the brake pedal but not pressing it, for fear of losing what little control he had. At fifty miles per hour, the bus raced forward at a precarious thirty-degree angle on the side of the craggy slope. Ricky could feel the upper tires losing their purchase.

"Hold on," he unnecessarily yelled over his shoulder. The head of the bobblehead Jesus on the dash fell off its body and rolled out of sight.

Ricky gripped the steering wheel so hard it felt like it was going to break off in his hands. He ground his teeth against each other and forgot to blink. He could feel the bus tipping, and just ahead he was running out of hill. If he didn't get back on the road, the bus would drop into the next ravine. Could be five feet deep, could be fifty feet. He couldn't see past all the brush and small trees. He couldn't risk it.

Ricky turned the wheel hard left and slammed on the brakes. The rear of the bus fishtailed out to the right as the bus turned to face the road. The giant school bus skidded along the low mountain, turning sideways and perpendicular to the road. Ricky thought the kids called this drift racing. He had seen a special about it on cable. But nobody on the special had done it in a school bus.

The entire world around Ricky sounded like it was falling apart. The crunching and grating of metal on metal tore through the bus, the sound of ten thousand pennies spinning in a dryer.

Ricky flipped the wheel back to the right to try to straighten it out. Nothing doing. The bus had had enough.

An explosive, metallic bang is rarely a good sound.

It would take weeks before Ricky found out all the particulars of what that bang was or what had happened. He only had vague images when he came to. He remembered road and rock and the windshield shattering toward him. He remembered sliding sideways, his left shoulder scraping the open highway. He didn't remember any sound other than loudness. Blood filtered the smell of smoke. He remembered being wheeled into the back of an ambulance. Someone telling him he was going to be okay. Not totally convinced of that statement's truth. He remembered being able to see the bottom of the bus, which he knew was bad. He didn't remember any pain.

And he didn't remember seeing any dead bodies. But that didn't mean they weren't there.

SEVEN

Harry couldn't decide if he looked or felt worse.

Nestor and Tami with an *i* had really tuned him up. Two black eyes. A busted nose, which had been reset and taped with a metal thing to keep the shattered cartilage from sliding down his face. A gap where his two front teeth used to be, two more pebbles in the parking lot gravel. Assorted scrapes, bruises, and cuts. A missing earlobe that had apparently been gnawed off.

That was just his face.

He also sported a couple of broken ribs, a linear skull fracture, and somehow two broken big toes that hurt more than everything else. His butthole stung too, but he hadn't told the doctor and never wanted to know why. He wasn't one hundred percent convinced that there wasn't something up in there, but the truth would eventually reveal itself.

Because of the skull fracture and having been found covered in feces, his doctor wanted to keep him in the hospital for observation. Another couple of nights to make sure there wasn't any brain swelling, infection, or any number of possible complications.

Harry didn't care. He rode his prison insurance. Keep me for the whole month, he thought. The food wasn't no worse than what he ate at home. And although he'd sworn off women after the Tami near-tryst, there were a couple of nurses that were good to look at. Add a drink with a paper umbrella and it would be a sweet vacation.

That is, until his peace was disrupted by a racket in the hall. The quiet of the morning shattered by frantic activity throughout the hospital. Gurney after gurney rolled past his open door. Some empty, some with moaning riders. When the sexy black nurse came to give him his pills, he asked what had happened.

Her face got serious. "Bus crash on the old road. Helicoptered in the bad ones. Just starting to drive in the minor injuries and the dead."

"How many people?" Harry was more curious than concerned. He liked being in the know.

"Dead? Three, four definitely. Only hearing bits on my rounds. A couple more might not make it to tomorrow. That's the word. Everyone on that bus was a senior citizen 'cept the driver. That's a lot of trauma for old folk to take."

Harry didn't care anymore. "Can I get a couple more of those pills, the pain ones? My head won't stop ringing."

"You have to talk to your doctor about any change in your medication."

"Can't it be between you and me?"

"No."

"If I gave you fifty dollars, would you run out and buy me a fifth of Wild Turkey?"

"No."

"A hundred."

"A hundred fifty."

"For that much, you should show me your naked breasts, too."

She cocked her head in that way only a sexy black nurse can.

Harry tried his best childlike smile. "I ain't never seen black ones up close."

She turned and took two steps toward the door.

"Okay, just the booze then."

He told her where his wallet was. Watching her walk out the door with his cash, he wondered if he would ever have enough money to see her naked breasts.

When the man in the uniform who may have been a deputy sheriff or possibly highway patrol told Ricky that three people had died in the bus crash, he was too doped to completely understand. Groggy from the anesthetic from his first operation, he heard the words but didn't grasp their meaning. He knew what dead meant and he understood that there had been a crash. He knew he was in a hospital and that people were helping him. But he couldn't put it all together. He could see all the pieces, but the jigsaw puzzle was still in the box.

Ricky slept through the rest of the day. If he had dreams, he didn't remember them.

By the second day, all drug-induced denial had passed. All Ricky's injuries allowed him to do was lie still and dwell on his role in the crash. Not knowing who Kübler-Ross was, he hurdled anger and bargaining and jumped straight to depression. And blame. And self-pity.

He tried to piece together everything that had happened in those ten seconds. He couldn't help second-guess his reaction time and choices. Had he been going too fast? What if he had braked earlier? Hit the deer instead of swerving? There were so many ifs that could have swung the result in a different direction. Inches and seconds. He had done his best, but his best had gotten three people killed. Three people and counting with Mrs. Apodaca and Mr. Martinez in the ICU.

He tried prayer, but it gave him no solace. The sound of his voice only made him feel more alone.

In his younger days, he had done things that he regretted. But since Rosie's birth, he had done everything to live a Christian life. To have a positive impact on the world. To be good. But trying wasn't enough. Being good wasn't all that mattered. For all the pleases and thank-yous, you could still do damage. You could still destroy. People could still die. And praying wasn't going to bring them back.

No matter what he did, no matter how hard he tried to avoid it, the dead haunted him.

According to the doctors, he would be in the hospital for at least a week. He was banged up from head to toe, but it was his left arm and shoulder that was the major concern. The skin and muscle were worn to the bone from where they had scraped against the tarmacadam. More than half of his deltoid muscle had been erased, shredded into a mutilated tatter of meat. The skin at the edges of the massive wound had been cauterized from the friction. A specialist was brought in to assess how much of the muscle would heal and how much strength and movement he would have. The man concluded that avoiding amputation would be considered a win.

Flavia tried to cheer up Ricky, but sometimes optimism and aphorisms are exactly what one doesn't want to hear. When she had run out of things to say, she would repeat how much she loved him and how she would always stick by his side. Ricky knew she meant it. He knew that it was true, but the truth hurt. He wasn't sure he wanted her to jump off the cliff with him.

"What're we going to do?" Ricky asked her.

"You're going to get better. That's all that's important right now." Flavia cried. She cried for most of the visit.

"I may be out a month. No job. The bus was all I had."

"You'll find something."

"Lot of jobs for a one-armed man. Human slot machine, maybe."

"That's not funny."

"What is?"

It wouldn't take long before the medical bills and the lawsuits and the insurance companies and the cops began their siege. Not right away, but soon. They would wait until he was healthy before they tried to destroy him. They wouldn't want him to trip and break his neck on the way to the gallows.

He knew that he might have to cut Flavia and Rosie loose. It wasn't an easy thought to think. It wasn't what he wanted, but it might be the only way to protect them. If things went sideways, the farther his family got from him, the happier their lives would be.

Knowing this, he couldn't look his daughter in the eye. And nothing hurt more. Rosie was too young to understand exactly what was happening, but she could sense the pain in her father's face. Not his physical pain, but something deeper.

"Don't be sad, Daddy," she said, as if it were that easy.

Ricky ran his uninjured hand through her soft hair and smiled weakly. After he kissed Rosie good-bye, he whispered to Flavia not to bring her by anymore. He might deserve to be punished for everything that happened, but not like that.

Before Flavia left, she said to him, "They led full lives. It was their time. Mr. Jimenez was ninety-two."

She was trying to make him feel better, but somehow that made it worse. These people had survived wars and hardships and their own families only to be killed by an obstinate mule deer and a panicked bus driver.

R icky was wrong. The cops didn't wait for Ricky to get healthier. The blues, grays, and browns of their uniforms stood out brightly against the pea-green hospital walls. The Imperial County Sheriff's Office headed the investigation, but representatives of the California Highway Patrol, the Riverside Sheriff's Department, and the Blythe city cops all felt the need to include themselves. The accident had happened well south of the county line, so there was no reason for any of them to be involved, but everyone wanted the chance to press their hand in the spilled blood.

He did interviews—not interrogations, he was assured—with each agency, answering the same battery of questions. For the most part, his interviewers showed little malice, seemingly sympathetic to the tragedy of the events. The CHP were the exception, displaying dollops of unnecessary arrogance. They probably perceived it as a display of power, but it came off as overcompensation.

While the doctors had worked on him, they had done a toxicology report. Marijuana had been found in his system. While it wasn't proof that his driving had been impaired, it was an illegal substance and complicated things. The impact would be minimal if the authorities pursued criminal charges, but it would be damning in the inevitable civil cases from the injured and the families of the dead. When the lawyers and insurance people finally arrived, they would complete Ricky's destruction that began in the crash.

The long and short of it was that Ricky was not only screwed, but there was no solution. Jail, bankruptcy, even death wouldn't get him out of the jam. It was one hundred percent unfixable. It was hard to wish for a miracle when a miracle wouldn't help.

Frank came to see Ricky. The lines on his face were so deep that Ricky couldn't differentiate between cuts and wrinkles. It didn't look like the old guy had a scratch on him. Ricky guessed that it was some sort of mystical, indestructible River Indian mojo thing. Indians always seemed tougher than regular people.

"Wasn't your fault, kid," Frank said. "Worse driver would've gotten everybody killed. Some things just happen. Hell of a ride you took us on."

"Thanks for coming by, Mr. Pacheco. Glad to see you're okay, but I'm not up for company."

"Don't flatter yourself. I got a biopsy tomorrow on a fresh lump they don't like the looks of. Easier to spend the night. I'm down the hall. And I told you to call me Frank."

"Cancer?"

"Nothing new. Fighting it for years. I'm thinking I can wear it out in the late rounds and win on points."

"If anyone can, Frank."

"Don't mind the cancer so much, it's my daughter needing to take care of me. Do I look like I need to be babysat?"

Ricky shook his head, his mind heading in other directions.

"There was nothing more you could have done. And from the looks of you—wrapped up like Claude Rains—if any punishing is going to happen, that switch has already struck ass."

"An arm don't feel like nearly enough."

"Arm and a leg is more traditional." Frank put his hand on Ricky's good shoulder. "You're a kid. The hell of it will pass. I done horribler things than you, and I've given up on the guilt for those sins long ago. Can't blame yourself for accidents. That's why they're called accidents."

"Tell that to the people I killed."

"You didn't kill 'em. They died. Different."

Ricky looked toward the window in an effort to dismiss the old man. The blinds were half closed. There was no view. Frank finally took the unmistakable hint.

"I'll be by tomorrow. If you're not too glum, we'll play cards."

"I don't want to see anyone. You understand?"

"I understand. See you tomorrow."

EIGHT

The irresponsible combination of painkillers and Wild Turkey kept Harry in a medicated haze but didn't stop his rising boredom. In an effort to liven things up, he roamed the halls in a borrowed wheelchair. He liked the sounds a hospital made: robotic beeps, low moans, foul-mouthed nurses, screaming children, crying mothers, and strange interludes of disquieting silence. It calmed him to hear everything as he floated above it all.

Passing an open door, he spotted Ricky. The big kid was all bandaged up. It didn't take Harry long to do the math. There had been a bus crash. The kid owned a bus. Holy hell. Talk about a bad week. Hospital scuttlebutt put the current death count at five.

Harry rolled into the room. Ricky gave him a blank stare.

"What do you want?" Ricky asked.

"Passing by, saw you. Didn't expect to see anyone I knew."

"What happened to your face?"

"Long story," Harry said. He reached for his missing earlobe and touched the soft gauze taped to the side of his head.

"The wheelchair?" Ricky nodded.

"Just lazy. I can walk, kind of. Toes is broke, so my balance is wonky. They'll heal though. What about you?"

"Mostly my arm. Everything else is supposed to heal. Everything except my life."

"I'd say, 'at least we got our health,' but I'm not that much of a jerk."

Ricky almost smiled, but he pushed it down.

Harry looked over his shoulder, dug at his side, and pulled out his half-empty bottle of Wild Turkey. He took a quick pull and held it out to Ricky. Ricky reached over his body with his good arm, took the bottle, and swigged deeply. They passed it back and forth in silence.

"How about a pull for an old man?"

Ricky and Harry turned to see Frank in the doorway. He wore jeans and a hospital scrub for a shirt. The skin of his neck hung loose without a collar to support it.

Ricky handed the bottle to Frank. He lifted it to his nose, closed his eyes, and let the piquant burn hit his nostrils. He took a short pull. With his eyes still closed in bliss, he handed the bottle to Harry.

"How'd the surgery go?" Ricky asked.

"The piece they cut looked suspect to them. Told me to stay the night. Want to run some tests. Tell you right now, I know what that means. Been living with cancer long enough to know my pluses and minuses."

"Sorry, Frank."

"Tough news," Harry said. He didn't know why, but he immediately liked the old Indian.

"Thanks. Name's Frank."

Ricky spoke up. "I'm sorry, this is Shitbur…I don't know your real name."

"Harry."

Frank and Harry shook hands. Frank stepped back and let out a short burst of a laugh.

"What's so funny?" Harry asked, already laughing a little himself.

"Look at us," Frank said. "You never seen three sadder sumbitches. Ricky wrapped up like a 'gyptian mummy. Harry, you got a metal nose and a face like a jack-o'-lantern in January. Me, I might be pretty on the outside, but I got homicidal lumps uglying up my insides. What's so funny? Not a goddamn thing. Laughing so I don't cry."

Frank let out a big laugh as he grabbed the bottle of Wild Turkey. He took a swig, spit-taking half of it over the front of his hospital scrub.

Even Ricky laughed.

By the time the sun went down, Harry, Ricky, and Frank were solid drunk. Drunk and edging toward maudlin. Ricky had enjoyed that first laugh, but it didn't take long for his guilt to convince him that he didn't deserve even brief happiness.

After they had discussed their various injuries, an uncomfortable silence filled the room. Not knowing each other and having nothing in common beyond their misery, none of them could figure out what to say. They wanted to feel a sense of camaraderie but didn't know how to accomplish it.

Ricky finally found the link.

"Frank knows where there's a gold mine," Ricky blurted out.

"What?" Harry had dozed into his drunk and hadn't quite absorbed what the kid said.

"Well, he doesn't know where it is, but knows how to find it. Kind of."

"Did you say 'gold mine'?" Harry turned to Frank for confirmation. Frank's nod sat Harry up straight.

"Fat Mary Mine," Ricky said. "Ain't that right, Frank?"

"Big Maria. The Big Maria Mine."

"What are you talking about?" Harry asked.

Ricky laid out the abridged version of Frank's grandfather's story. In his drunken state, he got all the dates and names wrong, elaborated on some of the events, and just plain made up a few details. But for the most part, he got the gist of it. Frank was too drunk to correct him, not remembering all the details himself.

"You bullshitting, old man? Or is this on the level?"

"Only know what I know. What my grandfather told me. Truth be told, he may have lied. My grandfather was a bullshit artist. If he didn't outright lie, he was sure to have made up some of it. To an Indian, a good story is more important than any kind of truth."

"You believe him though?"

"I believed all his stories, even the ones I knew were lies. If you don't believe a story, why listen."

"I need odds. What's the over-under that he was telling the truth? Forty percent? At least about the gold and the maps and all the important parts."

Frank gave it some thought. "Fifty-fifty. Maybe closer to sixty-forty against. This is from the man that claimed to have ridden with Hi Jolly's Camel Corps."

"I don't know what that is."

"You never saw *Hawmps!*?" Ricky cut in. "Where's your history? Ain't a lot of heroes from out here. Hi Jolly rode camels for the Army. They got a memorial out near Quartzsite."

"Don't care. Back to the gold." Harry's hands shook from impatience.

"He could've rode with Hi Jolly." Ricky's voice was mostly slur. "When was your grandfather born?"

Harry raised his voice. "Nobody cares. You're saying a coin flip on the gold, though?"

"Give or take," Frank concluded.

Ricky started laughing. His second really good laugh since the accident.

"What's funny? This is serious," Harry said.

Ricky had trouble getting words out. "You're going to look for that gold, aren't you?"

"Maybe," Harry said sheepishly.

"You got to admit it's kind of funny." Ricky tried to stop laughing, but couldn't.

"No, I do not." Harry stood up defiantly but fell back in his wheelchair and decided to orate from there. "I got nothing. Less than that. And it just so happens we have this conversation? That's fate. It's important to recognize these moments. Chances. Opportunities. You don't react, it passes. Times when not doing something is stupider than doing something stupid.

"You're a kid. You'll have other chances. I ain't old like Frank, but I ain't young neither. All that's left for me are long shots and bad gambles. I start turning my back on the two-hundred-to-ones, I might as well pack it in, buy a nice couch and a big stack of pornography, and wait to die."

Ricky stopped laughing. "Sorry. It's the thought of actually doing it. A treasure map hidden in an underwater ghost town that will lead you to a lost Indian gold mine. That's like the back cover of a Hardy Boys book. It's a little ridiculous."

"Ridiculous just means that nobody else has tried."

Ricky drained the remaining drops of Wild Turkey, and the three men talked about gold for the next half hour until Frank and Harry went to their respective rooms to pass out.

PART TWO:
THREE MONTHS DOWN

NINE

Ricky gave Rosie a big hug. Standing at the back door of Anna's spotless town car, he squeezed her against his chest with his one good arm. He dug his nose into her hair. It smelled like baby shampoo and applesauce.

"When are you coming, Daddy?" Rosie asked, but the tears in her eyes told Ricky she knew the answer. Kids were smarter than grown-ups gave them credit for being.

"Soon." Ricky looked away. He hated lying to his baby girl.

She held out the frayed corner of her torn blanket. The faded swath was all that was left of the well-used blanket that she'd had since birth. Rosie called it Manta, the Spanish for *blanket*. Ricky couldn't remember who taught her that word. Probably Anna. Girl and blanket had been inseparable until about a year before. She didn't carry it anymore, but dug it out when she was scared or needed comfort. Ricky struggled to reach for it with his dead, withered left arm.

"What if you want Manta later?" Ricky said, taking the small piece of blanket, but keeping it within reach to give her the chance to take it back.

"You need him, Daddy. Don't be scared."

He gave her one last squeeze and whispered, "I love you," in her ear. She climbed in the backseat. The click of the car door sounded like a cell door clanging shut. Rosie's sad and confused face through the glass crushed whatever hope Ricky had left.

Flavia watched from the driver's seat, her expression sad in its neutrality. They had said their good-byes the night before. There was nothing more to say between them. Words would only tear off the scabs.

Ricky rubbed Manta's worn fabric between his fingers as he watched the car disappear in a cloud of dust. He stared into the vacant space for a moment and then turned to his trailer. It looked different. Dingier, rustier, more broken. He wanted to burn the damn thing to the ground.

Flavia and Rosie had to leave. He knew it. The only way to protect them was through distance. It hadn't been easy to get them to go. Flavia initially refused, but he took it on himself to push her out the door. He had made leaving her only choice. Over the last three months, Flavia had done everything she could to try to help. But with Ricky recuperating and out of work, she was forced to work doubles at the restaurant, and that gave her only enough time at home to watch his accelerated decline. His apathy, self-pity, and eventual drinking all contributed to driving her away. However misguided, in Ricky's mind, the only way he could save his family was through his own self-destruction.

At first they had prayed together, hoping Ricky would find something—anything—that would give him hope. A shred of good news that would show him that he could move forward. Flavia hadn't been able to do it. His daughter couldn't either, and he loved her more than anything. He had lost his faith. And without faith, all that was left was hopelessness.

In the real world, love wasn't a good enough reason to do anything. It was a romantic excuse to make horrible mistakes. The right decision usually hurt. Flavia was willing to sacrifice herself and her happiness, but neither Ricky nor she was willing to sacrifice Rosie's future. When Anna had agreed to take them both with her to El Centro, Flavia finally conceded that it was the best choice.

In El Centro, Rosie would be able to go to a better school, and Anna and Mario could give his daughter a chance. She would no longer be around her crippled deadbeat of an edging-toward-alcoholic father. It had all been discussed with the false truth that as soon as all the legal business was done and Ricky was sober and back on his feet, he would join them. The lawyers had been ruthless, and they were only getting started. The cops weren't any better. There had even been talk of a manslaughter charge. Ricky had dug the hole deep, and this was the last chance for his girls to climb out.

G rowing up, Ricky had never had much. Not much that was positive, that is. He had more than his share of foster homes, bullies, and beatings in his past. And he had always risen above it. For all the pain, the future had offered something better, but optimism came at a price. Hope hurt. Every disappointment chipped away at his belief in the future. After too many punches, no matter how much heart a fighter had, there was a point the poor bastard could no longer stand.

Up to that point, Ricky had absorbed his share of heartache and had never lost hope. His faith in himself and God had kept him going. But the moment he learned that he had killed those people, he no longer felt anything. His faith had been destroyed with his bus and those old people's lives. There wasn't a God that could justify that much hurt.

Three months later, the guilt held strong. The death toll had settled at six. Six fatalities. Six dead human beings. Ricky didn't know the exact number of injured or maimed. The deaths were enough.

R icky sat on the floor of the empty trailer, gutted except for a few empty boxes and stacks of papers and envelopes, mostly unread subpoenas and summonses. Beyond the built-ins, no furnishings remained.

The trailer had been robbed while Ricky had been in the hospital, but luckily there hadn't been much and they hadn't found the cash in the refrigerator. He had given Flavia all the money and sold everything else to give her and Rosie as much as he could. There was nothing that he needed, and he knew that the less Flavia had to rely on Anna, the happier she would be.

The emptiness of the trailer felt fitting to Ricky. A shell of the home it once was.

His eyes found one of Rosie's drawings on the wall. A house and a family. The family in the drawing had a dog. The dog she wanted but never got. It was such a small dream, and yet Ricky hadn't fulfilled one that simple. Ricky cried until his throat burned and his stomach cramped.

He had nothing. His past had destroyed him, his present was bleak, and his future was empty. He didn't even have enough money to get drunk enough to forget.

Frank's daughter, Mercedes, scared the bejesus out of her father. And not just him. She scared the bejesus out of everyone. The fact that she was his daughter didn't allay his fear in the least bit. And now that he was living with her, the dread of her presence kept him in a constant state of anxiousness.

It wasn't anything specific. She had a presence. A refrigerator of a woman, her physical appearance mirrored her immovable stubbornness. Against an unstoppable force of nature like Mercedes, you just did your best to stay out of her way. You run from a tornado, you don't try to stop it from spinning.

It wasn't that she was abusive. Just the opposite. She was attentive and did everything she could to take care of Frank. The problem was that she took care of him with violent fervor. She took care of him whether he liked it or not.

It was one of the bad days. Mercedes wouldn't leave him alone. Ever since he had started his most recent round of chemo and radiation, she had treated him like he was a retarded toddler. He would have called it doting, but it was closer to a prisoner/guard relationship. She never let him alone. No more trips to Los Algodones. Not even a walk in the brown-grass park three blocks away. With her and the scattered neighborhood kids she took care of in the small house, he was constantly surrounded. Yet the more people around him, the more alone he felt. Loneliness wasn't about lack of proximity, but lack of connection.

"Eat your soup," she said, holding the spoon for him. If she said the train was going into the tunnel, she was going to wear Campbell's Chunky.

"I'm not hungry."

"You have to eat. It keeps your strength up." Those were the words she said, but to Frank's ears, he inferred, "Eat or die." Could you effectively stab someone with a spoon?

"Maybe a little bit," Frank said, opening his mouth. He didn't want to get mad or yell. After a dozen spoonfuls, he got up and tried to find an empty room in the small house.

No such luck. Around every corner was a kid or a grandkid or a relative that was there to cadge off Mercedes. The only actual assistance that he appreciated from the other members of his family was the copious amount of *mota* that Mercedes's boys, his grandsons Ramón and Bernardo, supplied him. Mercedes's world lost its edges when Frank could find a quiet corner and smoke his weed.

He put on his cowboy hat and went into the backyard. Caliber, a coyote-shepherd mix, ran up to him and sniffed at his shoes. Frank reached down and patted the dog's head. The dog had gotten big in the five years since Frank had found him. Some bastard had dumped a sack of puppies in the desert to die. Caliber had chewed his way out and lived off his dead siblings until Frank had nearly tripped over him on a hunting trip.

"Good boy," Frank said. Caliber licked his hand and then returned to whatever dog business he had been conducting.

Frank walked toward the giant sawgrass that lined the edge of the yard. Out of sight, Frank dug a joint from under his hatband and lit it. He took a deep drag, held it in, and coughed a little on the exhale.

He was proud of his grandsons. They grew good shit.

Half was enough. He wet his fingers and put out the end before he shoved the roach in his hatband. He had bought the hat when his hair had fallen out. He had always worn ball caps, but they didn't feel right on his bald head. The cowboy hat made him look a little like Eli Wallach in *The Magnificent Seven*. A badass with a big nose.

Walking out from behind the sawgrass, he ran straight into Mercedes. She looked like she had just eaten a raw onion. Frank's knees shook a little. She sniffed the air.

"I'm going to talk to Bernardo and Ramón," she said.

"They're helping how they can."

"They're drug dealers. Their no-good father's fault. I forbid you to see them."

"You forbid me?" But Frank was talking to her back.

She walked back to the house. He had never been forbidden to do something before. He smiled at how ridiculous it sounded, but wondered how idle her threat was. There was one good thing about the cancer. Dying was going to be easier than living with his daughter.

Over her shoulder, Mercedes said, "You have a phone call. Some guy named Harry Shit-something."

TEN

Harry had missed his calling. Even the thought of having a calling had never occurred to him. Turns out he should have been a researcher of some kind. A historian or maybe an archaeologist. Who knew that he had any hidden talents beyond bilking the state out of disability checks and spitting for distance? Even if his newfound aptitude for digging up information was driven purely by greed, it still affected a positive change.

The first time he stepped into the library, he got lost. Too shy or proud or dumb to ask for assistance, he fumbled his way through the small building. It took him an hour to find the right section. And even longer to find any helpful texts.

It wasn't that Harry was illiterate. He read. Working at the prison, he'd often knocked out a Lawrence Block or an Elmore Leonard during a hard day of pretending to work. But those books didn't count. They passed the time. They were fun. They weren't *book* books. Anyone could write them. This research stuff—real books—was more like homework. Or a puzzle. After the first day, he almost said to hell with it. All that reading was dangerously close to having a job.

But he stuck with it, and in a couple months, Harry and the Dewey Decimal System became simpatico. He learned the value of a good bibliography, interlibrary lending, and private collections. One day, he had been so engaged in the history of the All-American Canal that he had failed to take a single drink from the flask he had sneaked into the building. His thirst for knowledge had temporarily replaced his thirst for alcohol.

The work had become important enough to establish new personal rules. No drinking until after six. No women at all. A card-carrying member of the He-Man Woman Haters Club. He even accidentally got in better shape, as the only place to eat near the library was The Juice Shack, a vegetarian meth front. He hated the things they called sandwiches with alfalfa sprouts and tofu "cheese" between two slices of damp cardboard, but the Jack in the Crack was ten blocks away.

After three months of research and careful comparison of modern and hundred-year-old maps from eight different area libraries, Harry determined that Frank's gold mine story, while mostly fabrication, had enough merit for further inquiry. The big news was that he was ninety percent sure he had located the exact coordinates of the town of Picacho. Latitude and longitude to the minute and second.

He found old photos and etchings of the town. Town registries. Censuses. He drew maps and floor plans of buildings from interior photos and descriptions. Oral histories. Written histories. If he closed his eyes he could walk down the dusty main drag of 1901 Picacho, California. He could see the businesses, the wagons, and the people. He could smell the horses and the dust. And the gold.

He knew gold had no odor, but in his mind it smelled the way honey tasted.

The town was well documented, but Abraham Constance was another story. That took some creativity and real digging. First, Harry had to establish that the man had actually existed. A quick scan of birth records verified the fact. Then he had to establish that he had run the Big Maria Mine. Since the claim was under a different name, he had to scour old newspapers. He eventually found three separate articles, including a second-place win in a watermelon seed spitting contest, that listed Constance as a mining foreman.

Finally, Harry narrowed down the home and final resting place of Abraham Constance to four possible structures in

Picacho. It was extremely doubtful that the buildings still stood under the water of the Imperial Reservoir, but anything buried underground might still be under the soil, provided it was deep enough. No reason to believe different. Even if he enjoyed the puzzle, it didn't mean he was doing it for fun. He still needed faith.

He closed the giant, bound volume of *Imperial Valley Press* newspapers from the early part of the twentieth century. Aside from a few obscure scholarly journals he had on back order, there was nowhere else to look. No more research to do. All the books and maps could be returned to their shelves. The next step would be to take the information and actually do something.

Do something? What did that mean? Scuba diving into the Imperial Reservoir and searching the underwater ghost town of Picacho? He wasn't exactly Clive Cussler. What would he need? A boat? Scuba gear? A shovel. A flashlight, definitely. Was waterproof or water resistant the better one?

The sunlight blinded him the moment he walked out of the relative darkness of the library. Realization hit him simultaneously. He didn't know what he was doing. He had never even been on a boat. And scuba diving—that sounded not only hard, but dangerous. He would have to rope in someone to do that part for him.

He hated to share, but he needed other people. It couldn't be done alone. The research, that was a solo deal, but the actual operation was going to be a team effort.

He hit the Horseshoe to think. It was after six, so he allowed himself some celebratory drinks. After a rack of beers and shots, he knew who he had to talk to.

First, Frank. Top of the list. He was an old man, sure. But he was tough as nails and Harry liked him. He liked Frank's grit and no-bull attitude. He would always know where he stood with Frank, and there was something lucky about having an Indian sidekick. Besides, Frank was the one who told him about the gold. He deserved a finder's fee. Ten percent, maybe.

He went back and forth on that big kid, Ricky. He had introduced Harry to Frank. But since that bus accident, the kid had taken a dive into a bucket of awful. Just the other day, he had watched from a distance as the kid's girlfriend and kid drove off.

Harry had seen him a couple of times since the hospital. The kid's arm had healed squirrelly, making him physically lopsided and awkward. He could tell Ricky was drinking every day, the lumpy softening of alcoholism visible in his physique. He looked like a bodybuilder gone doughy.

For the longest time, process servers and guys in suits swarmed Desert Vista. They wandered around the trailer park, always ending up at Ricky's door. A couple of them had gotten rolled and robbed, but that's the risk you take for doing an evil job. The cops were still giving the kid hassle, too.

Even with all that, Harry wanted Ricky to be in on this score.

He had never believed in signs or horoscopes or any of that New Age garbage. But the more he drank and thought on it, the more he knew that the three of them were meant to be together on this. Circumstances hadn't thrown them together in that hospital room on accident. It was destiny.

He'd figure out the next steps when he met Frank. Old men were supposed to be wise, so maybe he'd know the best way to proceed. It was like any big job. It broke down to a bunch of smaller tasks. Every day, every step in the plan, and every task crossed off the list would bring Harry closer to his gold.

Speak of the devil, Harry thought, spotting Ricky in the wine aisle at Blythe Liquor & Bait. Buzzed but not drunk, Harry wanted to pick up a twelve-pack to help him sleep. The world felt out of whack without beer in the fridge.

The kid looked worse than the last time Harry had seen him. Ricky wore a tank top that accentuated his shrunken, burn-scarred left arm. The mottled skin at his shoulder was mostly shiny red tissue and yellow scars. The flesh reminded Harry of the night crawlers in Styrofoam cups on the counter.

Harry wasn't what anyone would describe as a caring person. But looking at Ricky, he felt bad for the way things had rolled for the kid. Only a couple months before, he had sat next to him on the computer, and now he looked broken. Not just the injuries. People got hurt all the time. It was the look in his eyes. The same look he had seen on the faces of prisoners serving long sentences. Like they knew their lives had no purpose.

"Hey, Ricky," Harry said, sidling next to him.

Ricky jumped a little when he turned, almost losing his balance. Ricky had trouble focusing on Harry's face. The kid was drunker than Harry and considerably less experienced at it.

Harry noticed a small swatch of cloth clutched in Ricky's dead, crippled hand. Ricky caught his eyes and moved the hand behind his back.

"What do you want?" Ricky said, returning his attention to the selection of cheap fortified wine.

"Saw you in here, said hello. You doing okay?"

"I look okay, Shitburger?"

Nobody had called him that for weeks. Even more than that, he didn't feel like a Shitburger anymore. Ricky using the nickname bothered him. It wasn't just the word, it was the way he had said it. Like it was supposed to have some hurt on it.

"Heard your lady and kid left. Sorry, man."

Ricky turned to him. "Don't you talk about them."

Harry took a couple of steps back. "I'm not going to lecture you, kid. I like a drink now and again myself. Hell, I'm a little toasted right now. But that's me. It ain't you."

Ricky shook his head and laughed. His laugh was the most humorless thing Harry had ever heard.

Harry continued. "I'm going to see Frank tomorrow. You know, the old Indian. You want to come with me?"

"What do you want?"

"Don't want nothing. I don't know. We're almost friends, kind of, I thought."

"Fuck you, Shitburger."

Harry gave Ricky a hard stare and then a shrug. He walked to the coolers in the back to get his beer. Turning back down the aisle, he saw Ricky stuff a bottle of Cisco Red down his pants. If it hadn't been so pathetic, it would have been funny. The bottle-shaped bulge in his crotch telegraphed "shoplifter."

Ricky walked quickly toward the door. As he passed the cashier, the guy shouted, "Hey!"

But Ricky was already out the door and down the street.

The cashier reached under the counter and pulled out a base-ball bat. He skidded around the counter and headed for the door.

"I'll pay for it."

The cashier stopped and turned toward Harry. He was breathing hard, mentally prepared to give a beat-down. "Motherfucker stole from my store."

"If I pay, it ain't stealing. His wife and kid left him. He's having a bad time of it."

The cashier stared out the open door. His breathing slowed, his anger flattened.

"It was a bottle of Cisco," Harry said.

"Dollar ninety-nine plus tax."

"You were going to take a bat to a guy for two bucks and change?"

"Motherfucker stole."

Harry paid for his beer and Ricky's wine.

The kid had sunk so low that not only was he stealing his drunk, but he was stealing the cheapest booze known to man. If he was going to steal, why hadn't he stolen some of the top shelf, instead of headache in a bottle? Harry remembered the one and only time he drank Cisco. It tasted like a Tootsie Pop dipped in antifreeze. It killed the necessary brain cells but made his fingers go numb.

"Poor kid," Harry said to himself as he walked his beer home.

ELEVEN

They had given Frank a fishing magazine. Probably thought all Indians liked fishing. The last fish Frank had caught was in the frozen section at Albertsons.

He couldn't get past the first sentence. Some article titled "The One That Didn't Get Away." He read the sentence a dozen times. His eyes saw the words, but their meaning never stuck, sliding along the surface of his comprehension. Like he was trying to translate a language he didn't know.

Whether you prefer a baited hook or dry fly, the Desert Southwest offers plenty of wonderful opportunities for catching a boatload of tilapia, also known as "St. Peter's Fish."

Frank read to relax while he received his chemo treatment, but relaxation was near impossible. The thin fabric of the once-plush Barcalounger chafed where his shirt had lifted up. The cold bags on his hands and feet made him shiver uncontrollably. They said they'd keep his nails from falling out, but that didn't make it more pleasant. On top of all that, the treatment gave him the shits, so he was forced to clench his ass muscles for the length of the therapy.

Whether you prefer a baited hook or dry fly, the Desert Southwest offers plenty of wonderful opportunities for catching a boatload of tilapia, also known as "St. Peter's Fish."

He wasn't completely convinced that the old woman in the chair across from him was alive until she threw up on herself.

Whether you prefer a baited hook or dry fly, the Desert Southwest offers plenty of wonderful opportunities for catching a boatload of tilapia, also known as "St. Peter's Fish."

The nurses were pleasant but impersonal. It reminded Frank of when he had worked at the dairy, the same indifferent attitude as putting the milking machines onto the cows. You didn't hate the cows, but you didn't really care about them either.

Whether you prefer a baited hook or dry fly, the Desert Southwest offers plenty of wonderful opportunities for catching a boatload of tilapia, also known as "St. Peter's Fish."

He strained his eyes and brain in an attempt to focus, but that second sentence was as far away as his youth.

Whether you prefer a baited hook or a dry fly...

"Isn't there a cigar store you should be standing in front of?"

Frank looked up to see Harry standing over him. He closed the fishing magazine, its spell broken.

"Find a seat," Frank said, nodding toward a few folding chairs against the wall. After Harry pulled the chair next to him, he handed Frank a brown paper bag.

"Didn't know what to get you, but thought it was right 'cause you're sick, you know, to get a present."

"What is it?" Frank asked, feeling the bag's weight.

"Couple of *Playboys*, a joke book, a flask of mezcal. And a box of Swishers."

Frank glanced inside the bag. "My daughter finds me with any of this, except maybe the joke book, I'm going to catch hell."

"What're you, a teenager? You're scared of your own daughter?"

"Damn right. Built like an angry bowling pin."

"You're old. That gives you—what do they call it—'cart blanch'? You can walk down the street with your johnson in your hands whizzing all over the place. Cops catch you, they'll drive you home. Me, I ain't old enough yet. I'd get arrested after they gave me a blanket party."

"Maybe I'll try that." Frank laughed. "Thanks for the stuff. It's the thought, yeah?"

"What I would've wanted."

"You put some thought into it. That means something. Could've just grabbed some shit at the gift shop."

"There's a gift shop?"

Frank laughed, sneaking a peek at one of the *Playboys*. The girl was completely shaved down there. He didn't like that. Why would anyone want to see a woman's cooch? Those things were scary. He needed a thatch to keep the lady stuff from scaring his willy.

"How's it going?" Harry asked. "I mean all this cancer stuff. You dying or what?"

Frank slid the magazine back into the bag. "Still wake up in the morning. And until the day I don't, I ain't going to complain."

"Need anything?"

Frank shook his head and then gave Harry's face a long read. "You're talking around something. What's on your mind?"

"Straight to it. Okay. I have a question for you. An opportunity. A question and an opportunity."

Frank smirked. "I don't get many of those no more. Opportunities, that is. I get plenty of questions. Most of them from some nurse asking if the medical doohickey that's up my ass is uncomfortable. I am yet to answer no."

"Who knows? Maybe you'll get to like it." Harry smiled. "I'm getting a boat and I'm going to dive down into Picacho. I'm going to dig up that map, those papers your grandfather buried. I'm going to find the Big Maria Mine."

Frank had never laughed harder in his life. Not even when he had been a kid and that mean nun had slipped in cowshit and landed ass-down on a cactus bed. Harder than the time Stink Gillies found out his date to the Harvest Dance had a lady chassis and male plumbing. Frank laughed so hard that he choked on his own spit, bringing a nurse over to him. He dug in the bag and held up the joke book, waving her away. Catching his breath, he looked back at Harry's hurt face and erupted in laughter all over again.

"It's not that funny," Harry said.

After a couple false starts, Frank got it under control. He took a deep breath and wiped the tears from his eyes. He was pretty sure he had shit himself a little. Completely worth it. Harry started to talk, but Frank held out his hand.

"Give me a minute. A full minute. If not, first word you say, I'm going to get going again."

Harry listened to the hospital sounds while Frank took a drink of water. Beeps and typing and gurgling and groans.

Frank spat on the floor. "Okay. Take it slow."

Harry cleared his throat. "I've been researching. A ton of research. The mine exists. Your grandfather's story is mostly true. From old maps, I know the location of the town and have narrowed down Abraham Constance's house to a few possibilities. I can take those coordinates and enter them into a GPS unit. Recreational boats and diving are allowed on the reservoir, so it's just a matter of renting a boat and stuff. It's all legal. No undertow, no sharks, no danger. It either pans out or not, but it only takes a day, maybe two, to find out for sure what's down there. As stupid as it sounds, it's not crazy. We can look where no one ever thought of looking."

Frank stared at him for a moment. "Hell, you say it that way, it's not funny. Almost makes it sound possible. Like it'd work."

"I'm dead serious, Frank. From the go, I ain't treated this like nothing but a job. More serious than any job I've had. The moment I heard about the gold, I knew this was my shot."

"So what do you need from me? Ain't exactly in scuba shape. And I ain't got money to invest, if that's what you're angling at."

"Don't need money. It was your grandfather. His story. You deserve to be in on it. This ain't a one-man job, and I don't know too many people I trust. Thought maybe you might. We could put some kind of team together."

"I got two grandsons that are hard workers and know how to play dumb."

"I haven't figured out hard numbers. Way I see it, you get a percentage, but anyone else gets a flat rate."

"What about Ricky?"

"Yeah, I thought about the kid. I don't know. Arm's all weird. But more, it's his—I don't know—spirit, I guess. Not sure he's up for it."

Frank gave his head a solid shake. "Don't matter. He's got to be in on this."

"You wouldn't recognize him, Frank. He's a mess. His wife left, took their kid. He's drinking more than me. Heard the cops are threatening jail time. Must be like twenty lawsuits against him."

Frank clapped his hands together, giving Harry a start. "Then we help him. Gold is the kind of thing that gives hope. He was there at the beginning. He is part of the team. It's got to be Ricky."

"Quit slapping me."

Frank slapped Ricky even harder. His hand burned red from the force of the blow. Ricky's stubble pierced his skin like a saguaro.

"Stop it."

Frank grabbed the kid by the hair and pulled his head back. Harry handed him a cup of water, and Frank threw the water in Ricky's face.

Ricky's eyes opened wide. There was a crowd standing over him. He recognized old Frank Pacheco and Shitburger. The two serious-looking Indians or Mexicans behind them were new to him. A fresh slap struck his cheek.

"Okay, okay. I get it. I'm slapped. You don't have to do it again."

"You ain't got chairs? I'm an old man."

One of the big Indians or Mexicans exited the trailer and came back with a bucket. He turned it upside down and Frank sat.

Frank looked tired, his skin more ash than rust.

Ricky began to say something, but Frank didn't let him.

"I'm going to talk. You're going to listen. Harry here has a proposal for you. No matter how stupid it sounds—and it's going to sound stupid—you're going to say yes. Got it?"

Ricky looked up at him but didn't respond. Frank slapped him again.

"Yeah, yeah. I got it. I get it."

"Go ahead, Harry. Give him the rundown."

Harry whispered something in Frank's ear. Frank shrugged and turned to the big Indians or Mexicans. "Ramón, Bernardo. Need you boys to wait outside."

They didn't appear offended. The sound of their cigarette lighters fired up the moment they stepped out the door.

"Remember, Ricky, you're going to agree. You're going to do it because I say so. You're going to do it because if you don't, when you've finally finished killing yourself, I'll find your daughter and tell her you drank yourself to death because you stopped loving her."

"You wouldn't do that."

"From what I can see, it's the truth."

Ricky broke down crying. Frank and Harry waited. When Ricky was done, he looked up at them with red, wet eyes.

"What do you want from me?"

Frank turned to Harry. "He ain't going to be able to do squat 'til he's dry."

"Ain't like an everyday drinker can give it up like that. Trust me on that one."

"Sure they can. Just got to have no other choice."

TWELVE

Bernardo and Ramón roughly pulled Ricky from the back of the pickup. They stood him against the rear panel, but Ricky hadn't quite woken and his legs spaghettied beneath him. The Indians looked at each other and let him fall to the ground.

Ricky had fallen asleep on the bumpy ride, one side of his face burned red from the sun. An uncomfortable, prickling heat made his cheek itch. The other cheek had gravel embedded in the skin. His body hurt and his throat scratched.

Ricky scanned the landscape through squinted eyes. Twenty acres of dry wheat fields spread along the base of scrubby desert hills. A small house that looked like it should be condemned was visible past a graveyard of rusted farm equipment. Dogs barked somewhere. Big dogs. A couple of burros watched with more interest than burros should be capable of. There was no shade, and the two big Indians didn't look happy, their smooth, hairless faces dripping sweat.

They each grabbed an arm, fingers digging into Ricky's armpits, and dragged him toward the small house. Ricky didn't struggle. Being dragged was easier than walking, and these guys looked like they could bench a steer.

"Where am I?" Ricky asked.

No answer. Not even a look or grunt. Ricky wondered if he had even spoken.

"Hello?" Ricky said.

Still nothing. But Ricky knew that he had said it, because he had concentrated. He heard the thing he said. He listened and heard. He had definitely spoken out loud.

Up close, it was clear that they were Indians, not Mexicans. Their skin was the same color as a Mexican—not red like people said Indians were—but they had those profiles that looked more natural on five cents than five centavos. He wanted to tell them that they were fulfilling a stereotype through their silence, but he kept his mouth shut. Two could play their game.

The interior of the house fulfilled every expectation that the exterior had established. It looked like a squatter's corner in a condemned building. Mattresses on the floor, garbage everywhere, and three big pit bulls staring and drooling. Squalor with monsters. The big-screen plasma TV on one wall and the leather sofa that faced it were definitely out of place. Just the revelation that the house had electricity was a bit surprising.

It smelled like all the colors of the dog rainbow. Dog food, dog hair, and dog crap. The air should have been desert dry, but it felt damp in the dog stink.

The Indians dropped Ricky onto one of the mattresses. The bigger Indian, who Ricky would eventually learn was Bernardo, leaned in. His voice was deep, each word slow and enunciated. "Do not move. I am very serious. If you move, the dogs will bite you. Maybe they will kill you."

Ricky looked at the dogs. They were looking at him like he was a porterhouse. Like a man-shaped meatloaf. They were not tied. Not even collars. He followed the line of drool from one dog's mouth to the floor.

"Their Christian dog names are Blondie, Angel Eyes, and Tuco. They are hungry. Always hungry," Bernardo said.

"Maybe you should feed them."

The Indian stared.

"How long do I have to stay here?"

"Papa Frank will tell us. We are to keep you safe. We are not to harm you. But we will hurt you."

"Don't harm and hurt mean the same thing?"

"They are different."

"I don't want to know the difference."

"No. You do not."

It wasn't going to be fun for the kid, but Frank knew that Bernardo and Ramón would keep Ricky safe while he dried out. Frank laughed, finding it funny that the kid was going to get sober in the middle of a marijuana plantation. Frank had no idea how much drinking Ricky had been doing, but a little sweat, fear, and pain would clean his system out better than any meeting in the basement of the Baptist church.

While Ricky was at the ranch getting his head straight, Harry and Frank prepared for the dive. It would require a couple trips to San Diego for equipment. They had to schedule the rental of a boat. And they needed some books on the subject of freshwater diving. All said and done, they had no idea what they were doing.

Harry's primary concern was that his last busted-leg check hadn't come from the prison. To that point, his medical-leave money had arrived like clockwork, but it was Tuesday, four days late, and still no check. That was bad. He needed that cash to finance the dive.

"Department of Corrections. Payroll. How can I direct your call?"

"I have a medical claim and my check has not arrived."

"I can help you. Name and ID number."

"Schmittberger. Harold Schmittberger." After he let the female voice complete her giggle, he spelled it and gave her his identification number.

"Okay. It's on my screen. How can I assist you?"

"You owe me a check."

"I'm sorry, Mr. Shitboarder. You are a month overdue for your medical reevaluation. The grace period has expired. You

71

should have received a letter. We can no longer accept your injury claim until a doctor has examined your leg and confirmed that the injury is still negatively impacting your ability to perform your job."

"I was just in the hospital. They were supposed to contact you. I'm still healing. Else why would I go to the hospital?"

"Yes, that shows on my screen, but those recent injuries were not sustained at the workplace. They are unrelated to the compensation that you have been receiving. Only the injury to your leg qualifies you for benefits."

Considering that his leg was completely healed, that was going to be a problem. The teat had run dry at exactly the wrong time.

The voice continued. "I can make an appointment for you. Once the doctor confirms, we can continue your claim, including any retroactive payments. Is Friday morning convenient?"

It had been two brutal days and Ricky hadn't moved from the mattress. His legs had cramped and he had screamed, but he hadn't ventured off the foam island. Ricky discovered two new hobbies: vomiting and sweating. His skin itched, his head pounded, and his bad arm throbbed like the day of the accident. His pinky and ring finger involuntarily twitched.

With the Indians outside cultivating their stinkweed, Ricky decided to test the limits of his tether. To that point, he hadn't wanted to move. The pain had kept him obedient. But he was feeling slightly better. There was a chance that the dogs had grown accustomed to him, maybe even considered him part of their pack.

Ricky stared at his reflection in the dog's black eyes. Dark and carnival-mirrored, but it was him all right. The dog's focus was unnerving. Maybe if he concentrated super hard, he could hone his mental abilities to control the dog's mind. The dog stared back lazily.

Ricky slowly shifted toward the edge of the mattress. With each tiny movement, the dogs' cumulative growl rose in volume. A few inches and the low rumbling sounded almost playful.

A few feet off the center of the mattress and the growl built to deadly. Ricky plopped back defeated. The dogs continued their bored vigil.

The Indians could have at least left him the remote for the TV. It was sitting on the counter across the room. Just far enough to get him eaten. They were supposed to dry him out, not torture him.

He wanted a drink more than ever. Out of habit. Out of need. Out of boredom. He wanted a drink because it was better to be drunk than not to be. Sitting in a hot room all day with three slaughterous dogs baring their teeth and crapping on the floor warranted at least one cold beer and a half hour of *Oprah*.

In two days, Ricky had learned that Bernardo and Ramón were creatures of habit. During the day, they worked in their "wheat" fields. At dusk the truck would drive off. Presumably to head into town and sell some of their "wheat." The Indians would return at night with eighty tacos from Taco Bell, hit the bong, and watch *The Muppets*. The tacos were the only food Ricky ever saw. They fed the Indians. They fed Ricky. They fed the dogs. The four major food groups represented: grease, filler, fat, and fried.

As *The Muppets* played on the big TV, nobody laughed. The Indians got high and appeared to enjoy the show, but Ricky had never once heard them laugh out loud. The dogs watched the TV too. It was the only time they didn't stare at Ricky. They seemed to enjoy the colors and loud sounds, but the humor was clearly too sophisticated for them. The canned laughter from the speakers would have to do for all of them.

From the other end of the room, Ricky was too far to even get a contact high. He wanted to do anything but watch a kids' show that only reminded him of the distance between him and his daughter. If this was part of the healing process, he'd take the wounds.

The biggest problem was that as he dried out, the repercussions of his past rushed back. The dog farts and snoring

Indians didn't keep him awake at night. His conscience did. He had been responsible for the death of six people. Six people had put their trust in him and he had done more than let them down. He had utterly failed them.

What was worse, he had failed his family. He had purposely pushed them away. He loved Flavia and Rosie, he knew that for sure. But it was impossible to be happy, knowing what he had done. Had he protected his family from the attacks by the cops, lawyers, and insurance sharks? Or had he only protected himself from the shame that he felt when he looked in his daughter's eyes?

Night was his best chance to slip out. The dogs slept in shifts, so only one was awake at any time. The Indians' sleep was pot-heavy, dreaming of squaws or arrowheads or—more than likely—Muppets and tacos. Even if one dog attacked, he was sure that the Indians wouldn't let it hurt him too bad. Worst-case scenario, Ricky would make his move and he'd get his leg bitten. Best-case scenario, Ricky could grab the keys off the coffee table, make it to the truck, and escape.

The dog that was watching him, Tuco, was the least attentive of the three. He was often distracted by sounds and movement. Particularly the cockroaches that dined on the growing mounds of garbage. Ricky didn't even know cockroaches could fly until he saw the giant things moving from wall to floor in search of waste. Tuco would lunge at any that got close, but would quickly return his attention back to Ricky. The dog looked confused and disgusted when he caught one and chewed it, but he always went back for more.

Together, Ricky and Tuco watched a particularly juicy roach crawl along the wall. Ricky eyed the keys on the table, calculating the five steps that it would take to reach the couch, the jump over, then the four more steps to the door. He rehearsed in his mind. Jumping the couch between the two sleeping Indians would give him an extra second or two.

The roach crawled down the wall. Tuco licked at his drool, panting loudly. He focused on the insect, no longer interested in Ricky.

Ricky watched the dog. He watched the keys. He watched the cockroach. It was time. Now or never.

The roach flew off the wall. Tuco jumped, trying to chomp it on the fly. Ricky went for the couch, but instead of running he took one awkward step and fell forward. His legs had fallen asleep from being on the mattress for two days. He crashed face-first. His chin hit the ground, his teeth biting off a small piece of his tongue. Blood filled his mouth.

Then the dogs attacked.

The crash had woken up Angel Eyes and Blondie. One dog on each leg, and the other on his bad arm. They bit into him with ferocious abandon, shaking their heads wildly in an effort to rip off his limbs. Ricky screamed, words finding their way through the pain and panic.

"Call them off. Call them off."

The Indians slept soundly. Not even a halfhearted mumble. The dogs bit deeper. Ricky could have sworn that Angel Eyes had reached his femur.

"Bernardo! Ramón!"

Ricky fought the dogs, but their jaws were like bear traps, latched deep into him.

Ricky slowly crawled back to the mattress. He wasn't far, but the weight of the dogs and the excruciating pain made it feel like a lifetime. The moment he was back on the mattress, the dogs stopped chewing and returned to their posts. Tuco licked at the blood around his maw. It looked like the dog was smiling.

"Screw you, Tuco."

The Indians hadn't stirred.

Ricky dressed his wounds with torn pieces of the dog-hair-covered sheet that he had been using as a blanket. Only his left leg was deep enough to warrant concern. After about fifteen minutes, the bleeding slowed.

Ricky laid his head on the pile of clothes he called a pillow. He immediately choked and turned his head to the side, letting blood and saliva drain down his cheek. He breathed heavily through his nose.

While his botched escape attempt had been a complete failure, at least he had agony and the possibility of an exotic infection to show for it.

THIRTEEN

"Look. It's not like I'm happy about this either, but I don't know another way." Harry continued to attack the bourbon bottle.

"You could go back to work." Frank wondered what time it was. He had snuck out of the house and borrowed his granddaughter's Bug to get to Harry's trailer. He wasn't even supposed to be driving, considering his bad eyes and no license. If Mercedes found out he was AWOL and driving at night, he would get a hollering that would shake his brain for a week. Now that she was in the habit of forbidding, would she ground him?

Harry took another long pull. "This is better. Easier. Gives us the money and time."

"I could do permanent damage. Mess it up."

"That's not how this works. If you're fixing something, you can mess it up. But you're breaking something. As long as it's broke when you're done, you get a hundred percent smiley face. A big, shiny A-plus star."

"I could break your leg in the wrong place."

Harry shook his head so hard it looked like it hurt. "You're thinking too much. There ain't no right place. A break is a break is a break. When it's time—and that's some drinks away—you'll bring that snakeskin boot down and the pieces will fall where you break 'em."

"Damn crazy, you ask me."

"Crazy's been working for me lately."

"Stupid's a close second. What if I won't do it?"

"I'd respect that. Kind of a sissy move for an Indian, considering I'm on the receiving end. I can head down to some bar or street corner and find someone that hates me or some meth-head. Either way, the one bone will be two bones by morning."

"And you won't go to the hospital after?"

"Can't. Got to act like it's been like that the whole time. Like it was something they missed last exam. It's only twelve hours. I'm going to get serious drunk. Ain't no amount of pain I can't take for that long with the right amount of booze in me."

"They'll know it's a fresh break."

"As long as it's in the same spot, I'll tell them that's the way it's been. Can't prove otherwise. They'll got to believe me."

Frank shrugged. He didn't want to break Harry's leg, but they needed the money for the boat and scuba rental. If Harry was crazy enough to break his own leg for the sake of the treasure hunt, Frank shouldn't talk him out of it. Hell, he admired the man's conviction. He just didn't want to go to hell for something sinful that someone asked him to do.

He tried to remember his Ten Commandments. Flipping through the list, Frank confirmed that there was no commandment against hurting someone, let alone breaking the leg of someone that asked. As long as you didn't kill no one, assault appeared to be allowed by God.

Harry sat back in the chair in his cramped trailer and held up his bottle. "So have a drink with me. It'll make it easier on both of us. Might even be fun."

Frank tipped his glass and gave Harry the worst fake smile since his eldest daughter's wedding to that Republican.

Three hours later, Harry was slurring, staggering, and prepped for a severe leg injury. Frank hadn't come close to keeping up with Harry's pace, but he was a little drunk. It had been a while. It felt dangerous but good to lose even a little control. He felt younger and—in a good way—stupider.

"I love you, Frank. You're like my Tonto. I'm the Lone Ranger and you're my Tonto. Tonto's horse's name was Scout. Get 'em up, Scout. Used to watch that show. When I was a kid, I'd sit on the floor, eat baloney out of the packet. Watch all the black-and-whites when shows weren't color. Used to be in not color. You're an old guy. Probably watched the old TV shows on the radio. I love you, Tonto."

Frank smiled. He was a couple minutes from breaking the man's leg. Let him have his ramble. Nothing lonelier than a drunk with no audience. Least he could do was give him an ear. Although he could do without that Tonto crap.

"My name is Harold Frederick Schmittberger. But you know what everyone calls me? Shitburger! Or sometimes Shitty or Shits or the Shitburglar. Why are people mean? My name is Harry. Harold. What about Hal? I'd settle for Schmitty. When we find that gold, nobody's going to call me Shitburger anymore. Or Baron Von Shitburg. Or Shitter McShittington. Or Shitsburgh, Pennsylvania. It's going to be Mr. Schmittberger, sir."

"That's right," Frank said, not convinced.

"You're my friend. And Ricky, too. The big, dumb kid. My friends. I love the hell out of you guys. I even like your grandkids. They scare me, pretty sure they want to scalp me, but I know if I got to know them, if they're kin of yours, then we could find mutual interests, things to talk about. I'm sure that I could be friends with them, too."

"They're good boys."

"They like to golf?"

"I don't think so."

"See. There you go. I don't like golf either. Hate it. Don't like playing. Well, I don't know if I do, never tried it proper. Took a dump in one of the holes and passed out pants-down in a sand trap on the municipal course on one of my rougher nights. I thought it was funny, but the cops got no sense of humor. That's why I hate golf. Rather sit in a park and get drunk. All that pretty grass, none of the work. And I can play with my balls in a park, too." Harry laughed his nauseating laugh.

"It's time." Frank felt he had done his duty. Harry's rambling gave him a headache, and he had to get his granddaughter's car back before she got off work at Pollo Loco.

"Time for what?"

"Your leg."

Harry looked down at his leg. "Oh, yeah. I was—we were having such a good conversation. Bonding and all. Almost forgot."

His eyes got red and wet. He stared at the limb like he was kissing his sweetheart good-bye. He nodded his head.

"Let's do this."

The trailer offered little room to maneuver. Harry took the stained mattress off his bed and leaned it against the far wall. He pulled out one of the pine slats and set it to the side. He took off his pants, folded them, and chucked them to the side. He sat on the edge of the bed with the length of his lower leg running over the gap between the slats.

Frank stood over him. He lifted his boot just above the leg.

"Wait," Harry shouted. Frank rested his foot. Harry found a pencil on the ground and put it between his teeth. He clutched the Saint Christopher medallion around his neck and mumbled something.

"What?" Frank asked.

Harry took out the pencil and said, "I'm ready." He bit back down on the pencil.

Frank nodded, lifting his foot.

"Wait," Harry shouted again, spitting out the pencil. "Is this the right leg? I mean, this is my right leg, but is it right. Or my left?"

"How should I know? You said you had a cast. Which leg was the cast on?"

Harry stood up and took a few steps. He mimicked a limp with his left, then his right. "Definitely the right." He sat back down and got his leg in position. He returned the pencil to his mouth.

"You ready?" Frank lifted his boot for the third time.

Talking through the pencil and drooling, Harry responded, "You going to count to three or ten or something? You can count down like the space shuttle. Like ten, nine…"

Frank brought his boot down onto Harry's leg. The snap of the bone and the pencil harmonized. Harry screamed.

Harry's bone was visible through the top of his leg, a splintered pink and white shard. A trickle of blood dripped toward his ankle. Harry's mouth froze in a scream, but only a gurgling sound came out. Tears rolled down his face.

Harry fumbled for his bourbon. He tried to take a drink but poured most of it down the side of his face.

"I'm sorry" was all Frank could get out, staring at the wound.

"Why?" Harry said to him when he was finally able to speak.

"You asked me to."

"Why? Why'd you break my leg?" Harry tried to stand but screamed in pain the moment his foot hit the ground. He fell back onto the bed slats. His rubbery, broken leg bled and dangled off the edge.

"I'll take you to the emergency room. Come on, let's get you to the hospital."

For a long few seconds, Harry said nothing. The look in his eyes told Frank that it was time for him to go.

"You broke my leg, old man!" Harry lunged at him, but was too far away to do anything but fall off the bed.

Frank got out of the trailer, taking each step as carefully and quickly as his old bones would allow. He heard Harry behind him rummaging through his stuff. It sounded like he was dismantling the trailer from the inside.

Frank old-man-ran to his granddaughter's Volkswagen. He looked over his shoulder in time to catch Harry at the trailer door.

He had found a crutch and was maneuvering down the steps. In his other hand was a long samurai sword.

"Aw, hell," Frank said, fumbling with the keys.

"You broke my leg! I break you!"

Harry tried to hop down the last two steps on his good leg, but tripped and landed weird on his bad leg. The sound he made sounded like a pterodactyl getting strangled.

Frank unlocked the car door but stopped to see if Harry was okay. He was worried that he may have landed on the sword.

"You okay?"

Harry's pain-contorted face looked like he was transforming into some kind of monster. With the help of the crutch, he rose.

"Yeah, you're fine," Frank said. He got in the car, locked all the doors, and started the engine.

When Harry reached the car, he crawled onto the hood. Frank punched it in reverse, causing Harry to slide down the sharp arc of the Beetle. His chin hit the front bumper with force. Landing on his bad leg again, pain outranked anger. He threw the katana to the side and cradled his leg like a dead pet.

Frank rolled down the window. "If you scratched Emma's car, expect to pay for it when you're sober."

"You were supposed to be my Tonto."

"You still want a ride to your doctor's appointment?"

Harry looked at his leg and his sword. He nodded. "Pick me up at eight thirty."

FOURTEEN

When Ricky woke up, he couldn't open his mouth. Half asleep, panicked, and confused, he irrationally convinced himself that his lips had been sewn together in his sleep. Clawing at his mouth, he quickly realized that dried blood had congealed and sealed it shut. He pried his lips apart and licked at the red crust, feeling it melt on his tongue.

"You tried to run," a deep, familiar voice said.

Frank sat on a chair. The dogs were gone.

"Where's the dogs?" Ricky asked. His tongue felt like a soaked sponge.

"They're dogs. They need to run around. Do dog things. They're outside."

"They bit the crap out of me."

"That the dogs' fault? That's what dogs do. Your fault for testing the reach of your tether."

"Definitely the dogs' fault. It was their teeth. Your grandsons slept through the whole thing."

Frank smiled. "They love their weed. Makes for deep sleep. Like the way those boys talk. Makes them sound like movie Injuns or retardeds, but it's the *mota*. How you feeling? You need stitches? A transfusion? A hug?"

"I'm ready to go home."

"I been in your home. Ain't much of one."

"Why you doing this?"

"It would bother me when I read your obituary, thinking I could've done something. Can't watch you quit yourself."

"Then don't watch."

"Too late. You're my project now." Frank stood, knocking dust off the thighs of his jeans. "Get up."

Ricky stared at him but didn't make him repeat it. He stood up slowly and painfully. His legs barely held underneath him.

"Where we going?"

But Frank had already walked out the door.

"He was pretty mad last night. Not sure what to expect," Frank said. "Best you go in, test the waters."

Ricky gave Frank a lifted eyebrow. They sat in the Volkswagen in front of Harry's trailer.

"How mad?"

"He attacked me with a samurai sword."

Ricky breathed a short laugh.

"I'm serious."

"I'll go so long as you know I ain't your slave to do whatever you say," Ricky said. But he was all protest and no fight. He got out of the car and walked to Harry's trailer, a limp in both legs that made him walk like he had crapped his pants.

He knocked on the side of the trailer, the tin clanging loudly. He waited, inspecting the tooth marks on his withered arm. The shriveled flesh and atrophied muscles reminded him of chicken skin. He couldn't look at it for long without getting this weird feeling that it wasn't his arm. He banged harder, and when he got no response, he turned to Frank and shrugged. Frank made a turn-the-knob motion with his hand.

Ricky tried the door. Unlocked. He hollered Harry's name as he entered.

Harry was sprawled on the floor of the dark, trashed trailer. There were clothes, bottles, and books everywhere. Ricky watched Harry until he saw discernible breathing. He gave Harry a soft kick in the thigh with his boot. Harry's eyes popped open. Ricky flinched, taking a step back.

Harry slurred a series of sounds that were meant to be words.

Ricky acted like everything was normal. "Frank's out in the car. Told me to come get you."

"Time is it?" The words were garbled but there.

"Almost eight."

"Got doctor." Harry sat up. "Lights."

Ricky found the switch and turned it on. The first thing he saw in the fresh light was the bone sticking out of Harry's leg. The area was bruised black and covered with dried blood. Yellow fat poked through like the foam in a torn cushion.

"Your leg." Ricky tasted last night's tacos in the back of his throat but kept them down.

"Frank broke it."

"Old man don't mess around, does he?" Ricky said.

"Help me get my pants on."

As Ricky got closer, he caught a hard whiff of the earthy rank of Harry's leg and his hundred-proof sweat. It was a nauseating combo pack.

Ricky did his best to get Harry dressed. But he only had one good arm and Harry couldn't sit upright. It made for a lot of clumsy fumbling. Finally, frustrated and impatient, Ricky disregarded Harry's whimpering and jammed his legs into the pant legs.

Frank could hear Harry's screams from inside the car.

After Ricky helped Harry down the trailer steps and into the front seat, he slid in the back himself. The three men sat in silence in the small car. Harry and Frank turned slowly to face each other. Harry took a long pull from a fresh whiskey bottle and belched.

Frank spoke first. "You asked me to. I hadn't wanted to. I tried to talk you out of it. I let you have your one-time fit, because you were drunk and hurt. But try something again, you'll be plenty goddamn sorry."

"If I weren't still drunk, maybe I'd be mad. Screw it, I'll let it go. Be the bigger man. You don't even have to apologize."

"Good, 'cause I don't make a habit of apologizing for things I ain't done wrong. Way I see it, I was helping a friend."

"Hurt like hell."

Frank nodded and shrugged. "Bet it did at that. I might have come down on the leg a little hard. I got anxious."

"The way luck works. It'll all balance out down the line."

"Everything happens for a reason?" Ricky asked.

Harry took another drink. "Yeah. Something like that, but not."

"Don't Indians call it karma?" Ricky asked.

Harry laughed, liquor running down his chin. "That's the other Indians. From India. Like here's a for example, used to see it down the prison all the time. Guy's doing ten years 'cause he robbed a place and shot a guy or something else stupid. He's in prison. But because he's in this bad place, a good thing happens. He finds God or Allah or himself. If the guy wouldn't've been sent down, he'd never got saved."

"But what about the guy who got shot?"

"Exactly. Because he got shot, he probably ended up getting a handie from a hot nurse or something. Don't know exactly, but there is a balance. A natural order."

"What if the guy that got shot died?"

"Not in my scenario. That's a different thing," Harry said, battling to keep his eyes open. "Chuckawalla is medium security. Nobody that killed nobody is in there, 'cept drunk drivers or manslaughterers."

Frank shook his head. "I don't know much, but you don't have a damn clue what karma means."

Harry shushed Frank loudly. "It's like this. Bad things been happening to me a lot and all my life, even worser than usual lately, but there's always something comes out of it. And to get where we're going—heck, we're looking for hidden gold—more bad's going to happen. That's a good thing. 'Cause the way it's tracking, we need to go through the bad and tons of it, if the good is going to be the kind of good that's really good. Ricky knows what I'm talking about."

"No, I don't. Far as I can see, bad leads to more bad."

Harry shook his head. "But it don't. You'll see. My whole life, all the horriblest stuff, it's been leading to now. Or else, it wouldn't be fair. I'm due. It's all leading to something good. Something great. All the truly awful pain I've had to take, that's the balance on the one end of the scale. The good's got to be equally big. It's got to be as big as a gold mine."

Harry smiled, his two front teeth still missing. Frank smiled, too. It was possible. Even a broken clock is right twice a day.

FIFTEEN

"Where are we going?" Ricky asked.

Frank had dropped Harry off at the Imperial Valley Regional Medical Center, and now they were driving through El Centro. The impractical, tall palms that lined the dusty streets offered little shade and no beauty. The emptiness of the downtown felt unnatural, like a movie set in decay.

After Frank parked, he turned to Ricky and head-nodded for him to take a look across the street. Kids were at recess in a playground. Girls and boys in white shirts and black pants or skirts ran and laughed. High-pitched Spanish and English filled the air.

Through some instinctual imperative, Ricky's eyes found Rosie immediately.

Ricky ducked in his seat. "No. Let's go."

Frank didn't say anything.

"Come on, Mr. Pacheco. Frank. Don't do this."

Frank kept his eyes forward.

"She'll see me."

Frank grabbed Ricky by the back of the neck. He leaned in close, their noses almost touching.

"Do you see now? What it's about? It's about that little girl. You don't get your past back, but you got a shot at a future. Not yours. Her future. That's still out there. You got to let that bus crash, the drinking, the self-pity, let it go and start doing right by the people you owe, living people. Debts to the dead don't mean a tinker's damn."

Ricky tried to look away, but Frank held him tight.

"You brought that girl into the world. Now you've abandoned her. Because you're sad? Guilty? Sack up and stop acting the bitch. That's a worse crime than any old bastards that might got killed. Don't matter what you've done to now. You leave that little girl behind, you'll burn in every kind of hell anyone's ever imagined."

"I was trying to protect her," Ricky said, "from the cops and the lawyers and everything they would take."

"You protect someone by fighting. No one ever protected anything or anyone by giving up."

Tears streamed down Ricky's face. He nodded his head. No words came. Frank started the car and drove away. Ricky took one last glance at his little girl.

Frank gripped Ricky's shoulder firmly, fatherly. "We go through our lives, we do good things, bad things. Can't take either back. But we can draw a line. We can say from now on, from this point, I ain't ever going to be a son of a bitch again. She ain't lost yet. You fight, you can have her, your wife, your family back. You going to be a son of a bitch anymore?"

Ricky shook his head.

"You going to draw a line?"

Ricky nodded.

"That's right. Because, kid, there's only one real son of a bitch in this car."

Harry never realized how exhausting sitting in a waiting room could be. He dug through the magazines, but the only function they appeared to serve was as a place to put one's used chewing gum. The kid across from him picked his nose knuckle-deep and stared at him. The guy next to him coughed with abandon, spray going in every direction. It felt like a light rain on the back of Harry's hand, only infectious.

He had been on time, but an hour later the lady nurse at the counter still hadn't called on him. He didn't know he had fallen asleep until he was jerked awake by the sound of his name.

The effort to reach a standing position made him light-headed and nauseous. Half hangover plus half broken leg equaled all awful. Even with the aid of the crutch, every small movement shot electric jolts of pain through his entire body.

After what felt like an epic journey, he leaned heavily against the counter. The lady nurse smiled a well-rehearsed fake smile. It was almost believable.

"Ready for my exam. Leg really needs looking at," Harry said.

"Oh, your examination isn't today."

"Excuse me?"

"Due to a short staff and overscheduling, we cannot perform your examination at this time. The soonest that we can schedule you is—" She typed rapidly into her computer and squinted at the screen. "Three months from now."

"They sent me here. The prison. They scheduled an appointment. The lady on the phone said I needed to come here today."

"Yes. We need a signature from you to defer the examination until we can reschedule. Once we have the signed form and the doctor cosigns, we'll send the completed medical leave paperwork on. After that, there should be no further disruption of your payments."

"You couldn't mail a letter? I had to come in?"

"We require proof of ID, and most patients prefer not to pay for a notary. We've found it easier to have you drop by."

"Easier?"

The throbbing in Harry's leg doubled and made its way into his head. His vision blurred and tilted for a moment, but came back as quickly.

"So you're saying—let me get this exactly right—there is no exam and all I need to do is sign a piece of paper and my money will keep coming until my actual appointment—three months from now."

"That is correct."

"But I—" Harry closed his eyes and bit down on the inside of his cheek. He took a deep breath that didn't help.

"Do you have a question?"

Harry shook his head. "Where do I sign?"

The nurse found a clipboard in a stack and attached a form. She handed it to Harry over the counter. He glanced at the form, and then signed it without reading. The nurse's eyes caught sight of Harry's leg.

"Holy sweet Jesus, your leg."

Harry looked down. His pant leg was stained dark red with blood. The darkness of the blood was surrounded by a halo of some kind of fatty discharge. The sight of it didn't do Harry any favors. He simultaneously vomited and passed out.

Frank chewed on an unlit cigar and Ricky silently scratched at the bandage on his arm. They had been at the hospital so long that it had only made sense to have someone take a look at Ricky's dog bites.

They stood over Harry's hospital bed. Harry's leg was wrapped tight and elevated. His red eyes flitted at half-mast.

"Told you it was a dumb plan," Frank said.

"What're you talking about?" Harry slurred. "The money flow is back on track. Like a charm. Like a lucky charm."

Harry wasn't about to tell them the truth. Nobody had to know the embarrassing fact that his fractured leg had been entirely unnecessary. A minor error in judgment that resulted in two hours of emergency surgery. And a lot of pain. On the plus side, the painkillers they gave him made him feel cozy and warm inside.

"You fixed up now? No worse the wear? Everything back where it should be?" Frank asked.

"Said the break was clean. They reset it, stapled the wound. Should be out in a day or two. Have to change the dressing on my leg regular. Take infection pills. When the gash heals, I turn in the temporary for a plaster cast. I'll let you sign it."

"When do you get money? When can we start?" Ricky cut in.

"That's what I like to hear. Listen to that enthusiasm," Harry said.

Ricky reached into his pocket and pulled out the small swath of cloth that he always carried with him. "I'm ready to find our gold."

PART THREE: HOLY DIVER

SIXTEEN

The small boat drifted along the surface of the water. Scrub and low hills failed as scenery around the dam lake. But the men weren't there for sightseeing. Or fishing, though that hadn't stopped them from bringing fishing gear. There was no restriction against scuba diving. Everything they were planning was perfectly legal. But to Harry, this was his, and he didn't want to advertise. He insisted they appear to be any other fishing boat.

Harry had used his newfound library skills to learn about diving, recreational boating, and other elements of their excursion. He had driven to San Diego for equipment and rented the boat in advance from Bo's Boats, one of two rental places along that stretch of the Colorado River. It hadn't been much different than planning a family vacation or fishing junket. Not that Harry knew anything about either.

The boat was abuzz with activity. Bernardo and Ramón hauled the gear from one end to the other. Ricky organized the equipment as they brought it over. Harry futzed with the GPS unit. Frank worked the rudder, following Harry's shouted commands.

"This is it. Drop anchor," Harry said. "We're right on top of downtown Picacho."

Ricky dropped the small anchor into the water.

"How we going to do this?" Frank asked.

"Figured one of your boys would suit up, hit the water. The suits are weighted. Sink to the bottom, then I can guide them with this GPS thingy as I track against the maps. I paid a premium for them high-tech, full-face masks that you can talk into, like walkies."

Bernardo and Ramón looked at each other, then at Harry. Bernardo spoke for them. "We do not go in the water."

"What?" Harry smiled, but only because he had forgotten to remove the smile from his face.

"I have not scuba dived. Ramón has not scuba dived."

"An excellent opportunity to learn. Who did you think was going to dive? Your million-year-old grandfather with cancer? Me? With a giant cast on my leg? Or was it going to be the shriveled-arm dude? No offense, Ricky. Who, if not one of you two?"

"I did not think of any of that," Bernardo said. "I did not think of any of that, because that was not my job to think of. We are here to lift. Only to lift."

"You're right." Harry felt his rising panic. "We should have discussed it before. Why don't you suit up and we'll forget about it?"

Bernardo shook his head. Ramón mimicked his brother a second later. "I have told you," Bernardo said. "We do not go in the water."

"Frank? Can you talk to them?" Harry's body shook.

But before Frank could answer, Ramón spoke for the first time. He looked down at his feet and spoke softly, but loud enough to hear. "I cannot swim. We cannot swim."

Harry closed his eyes and pinched the bridge of his nose with his fingers. He couldn't believe it. They had come all the way out there and nobody could do the dive. How could it not have come up? Did they want money? Was this a tactic? They couldn't want a cut, because they didn't know about the gold. Unless Frank told them.

"What are we supposed to do? You know how much money I spent? We're supposed to take the boat back? Call it a day?"

"You know what they say about when you assume," Ramón said, still staring at his feet.

"I ask for help and I get the Go Go Gophers. High was bad enough, but stupid and high. I'm surprised you retarded redskins have enough brains between…"

Bernardo didn't bother to let him finish. He picked up Harry, held him over his head like a barbell, and threw him off the boat.

Five minutes later, Harry was back on the boat silently drying his cast. Gooey plaster stuck to the towel. He was lucky he hadn't sunk to the bottom. Harry stared death at Bernardo. The big Indian stared back, daring Harry to speak.

Frank put a hand on Harry's shoulder. "Don't mind the mutiny. You're in charge. What's the plan? We've got to have options."

"There is no plan. That's it. We come back next month when I get the money together again. When my leg is better or we find someone with diving experience. What else can I do? Get some real divers, instead of these…"

Bernardo's look stopped Harry in midsentence.

Harry laughed. "Do you want to fish? We got the boat. We got fish poles. Let's catch some fish."

"I read something about the tilapia being good," Frank added.

"We have no bait," Ramón said.

Harry turned to him, fuming. "The big Indian is right. We don't have any bait. We didn't bring bait. Just another screw-up, brought to you by Harry Shitburger. So we're out of luck on that front, too. Can't even fish. Anyone want to go for a swim? Those of us that know how, that is. Me? I already had a dip, but anybody else?"

"I'll dive."

Everyone turned to Ricky, who picked up a wet suit and held it against his body.

"What?" Harry said. "What did you say?"

"I'll do the dive. I got my legs and one strong arm. It's not like there's ocean currents. Been diving before, too. One time when Flavia and me drove down to Cabo. Been a while, but don't remember it being that hard. I can do it. What have we got to lose?"

Everyone turned back to Harry.

"I love you, kid," Harry said as he stood up and crushed Ricky in a big hug. He turned to the Indians. "Are you two going to sit there or help Ricky with the gear?"

The Indians remained motionless, giving Harry a hard stare.

Frank spoke up. "Okay, boys, you proved your point. Besides, you big baloneys love the Go Go Gophers. Seen a collection in your DVDs."

"Whoopee doopee! We have fun," Bernardo said deadpan. He stood and Ramón followed, picking up the scuba gear.

Ricky pulled Frank aside. "Can you do me a favor?"

"Course."

"Hold onto this." Ricky handed Frank the small piece of cloth, Rosie's *manta*. "I don't want it to get wet."

"It'll be waiting for you. And Ricky?"

"Yeah?"

"I knew you had it in you."

"I ain't doing this for me."

"Exactly." Frank gave him a slap on the back.

Harry wasn't lying. He hadn't skimped on the gear. The full-face mask with the advanced wireless system would allow him to communicate with Ricky underwater. The guy had told Harry it was a twin-hose, open-circuit system with a demand regulator, but that meant nothing to him. He had a GPS unit that would allow him to track Ricky and coordinate his position with the calculations on his maps, both modern and old. He should be able to guide him directly to the most probable locations. Walk the kid right down Main Street.

Ricky felt like a superhero in all the gear. Like a GI Joe action figure. The big one, not the lamer, smaller one. He had the costume and all the hard-to-find accessories. For the first time in a long time, he was glad to be alive. He didn't need a drink. The prep for the dive was rush enough. He couldn't wait to get in the water. Scared and excited.

"Check. Check. One, two."

"Can hear you loud and clear, Harry. Like we're in the same room."

"Let's do this. Any questions about the gear, the plan, anything?"

Harry had his maps out on top of a beer cooler with the GPS tracker and some mapping equipment at the ready. He marked a small dot on the map to designate their current location and had a pen at the ready to track Ricky's movement.

"I'm good."

Ricky walked to the back of the boat. The equipment felt heavy and cumbersome and the flippers were awkward, but he knew in the water it would be different. He checked the pressure gauge. Ricky turned on the headlamp and the flashlight he had tied to his dead arm. He hoped that in the water what little movement his left arm had could be put to use.

Then, as he had seen in countless movies, which was his primary reference regarding diving, he let himself fall backward off the edge.

SEVENTEEN

It wasn't like Cabo. No pretty multicolored fish squirting through the neon reef. No sea turtles swimming along the sea floor. No bikinied wife kicking her flippers ahead of him. No nothing.

Ricky couldn't see squat.

Squinting into the brown water, he was stuck inside a dirt-filled snow globe. His visibility wasn't even five feet. And as soon as he moved in the silty water, the debris he kicked up reduced it to two or three.

"How's it going down there, Ricky?" Harry's voice echoed loud, like it was inside his brain.

"Feels okay, Harry. Still got some 'drenaline, but I'm breathing easy. Water feels good, warmish. Can't see anything though. Super cloudy."

"It might be clearer deeper. Get used to being in the water, then head down slowly."

"This mask is awesome. Like a science fiction. Way better than having that thing in your mouth."

"That's what she said. Over and out."

Ricky let the weight belt do its job and descended slowly. His sense of direction was challenged with no landmarks to guide him, but knowing where down was helped. It was strangely peaceful apart from his breathing and the noises of the apparatus. Nothing to see. Nothing to hear. He could get used to that kind of quiet.

Ricky felt like he sank forever, not able to gauge his speed. He checked the depth, and he had only gone twenty feet. He must have been going slower than he thought or maybe at an angle. As he dropped, the visibility increased, but there was still nothing but silt to look at.

"You're veering west a little," Harry said inside his head. "Try to drop straight down."

"Doing my best."

He adjusted a shoulder strap that was digging into his shoulder. Looking down, he finally saw the lake floor.

"I'm at the bottom," Ricky said.

He reached down, cupped some of the sand, and let it slide through his fingers. It felt cold in his bare hand. A small cloud rose from the floor.

Ricky looked at his wrist compass. "Show me the way."

"Head due east. Maybe thirty yards. That'll put you back below us. You didn't drift that far. Keep your eyes open. See if you see anything towny. Signs. Hell, any wood or brick. Building foundations. Anything with an edge. I don't know what's left or even how close my calculations got us. Look for any kind of marker."

"Roger. Over and out." Ricky was having fun. Considering the last few months, that was monumental.

The lake floor offered nothing for the thirty yards he traveled. He kept it slow, scanning ahead and feeling his way along the surface. Just more sand. He hadn't even seen a single fish. When he finally caught some movement, it was in the form of something scuttling past in his peripheral vision. A fish, a crawdad, didn't matter. Unless it talked and gave directions, it wasn't going to help him find what he was looking for.

"Anything?" Harry asked.

"Nothing."

"Stay east. Dig a little if you have to. Who knows what happens to buildings after they've been underwater for seventy years?"

Ricky continued forward, scanning the ground below him. He dug in the sand, but it clouded his vision, so he stopped. That's when he saw it. Out of the corner of his eye. Bright green in a sea of cloudy grayish.

"I see something."

"What?"

"Looks like glass. Hold on."

Ricky reached for the green sticking out of the sand. He brushed the sand away.

"It's a bottle."

"Could be you're near one of the saloons. Good sign. Means you're in town."

Ricky pulled it out of the sand and turned it in his hand, revealing a Heineken label. Ricky let the bottle drop. It landed with no sound.

"Just some boater's trash. Heineken bottle."

"Out-of-towners. Only a city jerk would drink not-Mex imported and chuck their garbage over the side. Some people got no respect."

As Ricky looked up, something hit his head on the left side. Or more accurately, he hit his head on something. It twisted the mask on his face, a little water leaking in.

"Ow!" Ricky shouted.

"What? What's happening? Ricky, are you okay?" Harry's voice crackled, no longer as clear as before.

"Yeah," Ricky answered. He fixed the mask, and when he was confident that it wasn't leaking, he looked forward.

He had swum right into a building. Or what was left of one. It wasn't much, but it was a short stack of bricks. Enough to represent the corner of a structure.

"I found a building, I think."

"He found a building," Harry said. "I told you, Frank. Give me a second, Ricky. I got to see where you're at."

Ricky ran his finger along the mortar lines of the wall. He swam slowly along what would have been the outside. Reaching a gap which he assumed used to be a doorway, Ricky pretended to knock, then swam into the roofless and almost wall-less structure.

"Maybe the general store. Maybe the claims office. Could have been both. But I'd be guessing. Either way, you're at the west end of town," Harry said.

Ricky brushed his hand on the sandy bottom. Under the sand, he found wood. His fingernail easily dug into it like it was liquid. Small pieces of sawdust floated away. Running his hand through the sand, he found the head of a rusted pickaxe, the handle no longer intact.

"I found a pick. Just the top."

"Okay. I got three possibles for Constance's house. There weren't many private residences, so I've narrowed it pretty good. Head to the northeast. I'll tell you when you get closer."

"Rodger Dodger, Mr. Rogers."

"I think the oxygen is going to your head," Harry said, but he laughed with him.

Ricky held onto the head of the pickaxe, glanced at his compass, and exited the building. He didn't bother to use the doorway, but swam over what was left of the short wall.

"If my maps are worth a darn, you should be heading straight into town."

But Ricky barely heard him and didn't need the newsflash. He was stopped and staring in awe at the town church looming in front of him.

Though he could only see the building's façade in the haze of the water, the church appeared to be almost completely intact. It was a small building with no roof, but the steeple appeared undamaged and there was a wooden cross nailed above the front door. It was the most magnificent sight Ricky had ever seen.

"Ricky? You there?" Harry's voice crackled.

"I've got to check this out."

"What? Do you see something?"

"What day is it? Is today Sunday?"

"What're you doing? What's going on? Remember, you only have so much air. Fewer trips, the better. Ricky?"

Ricky hit the button on the side of his mask and turned off the communication device. The murky silence made his heart skip.

Ricky swam to the church. He pulled at the doors, but they wouldn't budge. A foot of sand blocked them at the base. He brushed the sand away with his hand, shoveling handfuls until the door was clear. He pulled it open and entered into the darkness of the abandoned temple.

Ricky swept the flashlight through the building. Everything was still. The pews, the altar, even one of the leaded-glass windows remained unbroken. There was a spot for a crucifix on the wall behind the altar, but it appeared to have been saved from the flood. In the foggy darkness, the building looked museum-pristine. Ricky half expected to see a congregation face-forward listening to some hellfire and screaming hallelujah.

Ricky crossed himself and awkwardly genuflected before he swam slowly down the middle aisle. It felt funny in the full scuba gear, but this was still a church. It occurred to him that he hadn't prayed since the bus accident.

A bloated book rested on one of the pews, the front board and page edges fish-chewed. Ricky set down the pickaxe and picked up the book. He had assumed it was a Bible, but the faded gilt lettering revealed it to be an old hymnal. The pages floated open, music staves and notes flipping past. The pages stopped where the binding was cracked in the center of the spine. The title of the hymn was "City of Gold."

"You've got to be kidding me," Ricky said.

He looked to the front of the church. For a second he thought he heard an organ. The faint sound of singing children. He ran the light over the corners of the building. But the silent music played only in his head.

Ricky made an effort to sit down, but the cylinder on his back didn't allow it. He returned to the aisle, his flippered feet spread apart for balance. He dropped some weight from his belt until his feet lifted from the floor. He floated upward. For a moment he forgot he was in the water and felt like he was being lifted to heaven.

He scanned the words of the hymn. He looked to his left and right, suddenly self-conscious. Then in the quiet of the underwater chapel, he sang, his voice just above a whisper.

There's a city that looks o'er the valley of death,
And the glories can never be told;
There the sun never sets, and the leaves never fade,
In that beautiful city of gold.

There the King, our Redeemer, the Lord Whom we love,
All the faithful with rapture behold;
There the righteous forever shall shine as the stars,
In that beautiful city of gold.

Every soul we have led to the foot of the cross,
Every lamb we have brought to the fold,
Shall be kept as bright jewels our crown to adorn,
In that beautiful city of gold.

At the end of the song, Ricky reread the lyrics. He closed the book, set it on the pew next to him, and patted the cover softly. He looked straight up into the murk above the roofless church.

"I hear you."

Ricky bowed his head and silently prayed. And for the first time in a long time, he knew that God was listening.

EIGHTEEN

It had been ten minutes since Ricky's communication device had disconnected, and everyone on the boat was concerned. Well, not everyone. Bernardo and Ramón were too high to care. Ricky had plenty of air, but the GPS unit hadn't shown any movement since the silence began. He had not moved at all.

They had no contingency for this kind of thing. He could be stuck, trapped, unconscious, worse. The most they could do was wait impotently.

They had another wet suit, weight belt, a full cylinder, mask, and all the necessary equipment for another dive. But they didn't have anyone that could—or rather, would—do it. So much for the buddy system. Ricky wasn't even supposed to be in the water in the first place.

"Try the radio thing again. Turn some damn dials," Frank said. "Maybe it's on the wrong frequency or set wrong."

"There's only one frequency," Harry said. "It either got damaged or the kid turned it off. Maybe he hit his head again. He sounded a little weird. Like he was confused, asking what day it was. I read about something called nitrogen narcosis. Makes you goofy, like nitrous, laughing gas."

"Has he moved?"

Harry shook his head. "Still in the same spot. Exactly where he was."

"Maybe he found something? Maybe he's digging?"

"Let's hope. I ain't as weirded out by the not talking as I am by the not moving. He could be stuck or knocked out or who knows."

"We have to do something."

"What? We're up here and he's down there. If you got a plan, spill."

"One of us has to go."

"This conversation has been had. The Wonder Twins are scared of the water, I got a busted leg, and you're old as Moses."

Frank thought about it for a while. "To hell with it. Old people skin-dive. I've seen it in travel brochures I get in the mail. Old-lady snorkelers. Like in Miami. Apparently, fogies move good in water. Ricky needs our help."

"Are you serious?"

"I might got cancer, but I'm strong and mean and I could beat your ass, no doubt in my mind. The exercise'd be good for me. Here's what, you fellas tie a towline to my waist. You can drag my old butt back up if need be."

"I love it. Let's do this," Harry shouted. He slapped Frank's back hard enough to hurt.

Frank turned to his grandsons, who were stretched out on the deck. They passed a joint between them and pointed out clouds that looked like penises to each other.

Frank said, "You heard him. Let's get Ricky."

Bernardo put the joint out on his tongue and stowed the roach in his front shirt pocket. He got up slow and wobbly, getting his marijuana legs.

"Wait," Harry shouted.

"What?" Frank turned.

"He's moving. The kid's moving."

Harry showed him the GPS unit. Sure enough, the icon for Ricky was moving slowly east. Bernardo sat back down, relighting the joint. Ramón gave him a light slap on his shoulder and pointed at a particularly phallic cloud. It even had cloud balls.

Harry glanced at his watch. "Now let's hope he remembers to check his air."

Ten minutes later, Ricky resurfaced. The brightness of the sunlight seemed unreal after the relative darkness of the deep lake. He imagined it wasn't that much different from being born.

The first thing he did when he got back on the boat was vomit all over Harry. The abrupt change of environment and the rocking of the boat threw off his equilibrium. It was a new world to him, one that took some adjustment.

Harry shook it off. "You'd be surprised at how often that happens to me. I'm like a puke magnet. Least you didn't take a dump on me."

Harry grabbed the face mask away from Ricky, looking at the communication controls on the side.

"What the hell happened to your walkie thing?"

"I turned it off," Ricky said.

"We thought you were trapped. Hurt. This isn't some toy to tell jokes to each other. It's there to keep you alive. Where's your brain?" Harry's face was beet red, his breathing dramatic.

"I'm sorry, okay? I can't explain, but it was important. It was spiritual."

Harry was about to say something, but Ricky stopped him.

"Let's not waste more time. Get me another tank. I'm ready to go back down. Now I know that we're going to find what we're looking for."

Ricky's excitement immediately doused the flames of Harry's anger.

Harry nodded and walked back to his maps. "Keep the walkie on this time."

While Bernardo and Ramón prepped Ricky's equipment, Ricky gave Frank and Harry a report on what he had seen. Everything after the church. He didn't mention the church. The church was his.

"The water's all filmy and dirty, but when you get all the way down, when you get into the town, it clears up. Like it's saying,

'Come on in.' Amazing how much is still there. Whole bunch of buildings. Most ain't got roofs or nothing, but it's a town. I went inside what was definitely a school. Blackboard, but no writing on it. One building had a sign said it was the post office. And plenty of saloons.

"Like out of a movie. Like it don't belong in real life. When you're up in the higher water, it's hard to tell where you're at. When you close your eyes, there's no up. But not in town. The buildings make you forget the water. It's awesome. Like I'm seeing something no one's seen. A place nobody ain't never gone.

"I was swimming and thinking how special this place is, you know? Maybe when we're all done, I can come back and take Rosie, my girl, down there. Not now, but in a couple of years. When she's older. When she can swim. When she'd appreciate it. It could be our place.

"Anyway, I tooled around. Got the lay of the land. The buildings are built along a line. Outbuildings, or what's left of them, behind. But main buildings right in a row. Show me that map you got there and we'll figure out where that buried stuff is buried."

For the next fifteen minutes, they compared Ricky's visual description, the GPS path that he had taken, and Harry's maps. Harry had been right on the money. The school, the post office, the mill, and a few of the saloons, everything was where Harry thought it would be.

That left the three possible locations for Abraham Constance's house. Now that Ricky had landmarks, he could easily follow Harry's directions. They were confident that once Ricky got back to looking, he would be looking in the right place.

NINETEEN

The first location yielded nothing. The wooden floor of the underwater ruin had given easily, as did the soft dirt underneath. The digging left Ricky in a cloud of gray silica and dirt. After two feet, he hit rock and stopped digging. Anyone trying to hide something in a hurry wouldn't bother with pick work.

Ricky grew comfortable under the water, his movements fluid and his confidence growing. While the gear limited him, he found that it gave him a range of motion different from land. Even his dead arm had some function. He swam past a few buildings, one with a semi-intact porch that looked inviting. He tried to imagine the people that had sat there. Drinking their lemonade or whiskey and gossiping. They were all long dead, but they still had stories to tell.

"You're almost there. Maybe twenty yards. On your left."

"You're really missing out, Harry. It's like another planet."

"Maybe we'll all come back. You know, if this thing works out. Do it in style."

"Do a victory dance right down Main Street. Have ourselves an underwater hoedown at the dance hall."

Harry broke in. "Sure, sure. Keep your eyes out. You're right on it."

"I see the building. What's left of it. Looks like a card house that froze while falling down."

Two of the wood-and-mortar walls had collapsed inward. They had fallen against each other in such a way that one propped the other up. It looked precarious. But the way Ricky figured it, if he didn't disturb it, it wouldn't disturb him. It had probably been that way for decades. No reason to think that today would be the day it fell.

"Can you get inside?"

"I got some angles. Maybe from the top. The center room is right under the busted walls."

"How about the third location? You can always come back if the other building's a wash."

"I'm here. I'm going to take a look."

Ricky swam around the perimeter of the building to get his bearings. The walls, while weathered and chipped, appeared solid enough. The thought of being underneath them still didn't make him happy, but it was a matter of faith. As long as he believed, he would be okay. And at the moment, he felt invincible.

He swam into the collapsing building from above, settling in under the slanted walls. It got deep dark outside of the range of the flashlight. The open area, what probably would have been the front room of the house, was small with only a broken chair tucked in a corner.

As Ricky turned, a school of thick-scaled fish scared the hell out of him. They were the first fish he had seen, and twenty or so swam right at him. A couple bounced off his arms and one off his mask.

"Holy hell!"

"You okay?"

"Fish. Just fish. Ugly things. Came right at me."

"Yeah, there's piranha everywhere down there. Forgot to warn you."

"Seriously? Piranha?"

"Of course not, I'm messing with you." Harry's laughing voice grew muffled. "Hey, Frank. You hear that? Told the kid to watch out for piranha. He believed me."

"I'm going to start digging."

"Come up before we check the third building. Get fresh gear, a full tank."

"Unless I find it here. Then we're done."

"Let's hope."

Ricky had learned through trial and error at the first location. It was all about layers. Remove the sand and dirt slowly. Take a minute to let it resettle. The wood next, either by whole board or cutting through the waterlogged pieces. Finally, dig into the dirt until it got hard enough to no longer make sense.

After Ricky had removed the surface layer of sand, he was surprised to see a rug covering the center of the floor. It was on its last legs, but the faded red appeared bright against the dull grays and browns. The rug disintegrated in his hand when he tried to pick it up, small fibers and string polluting the water around him. The floorboards beneath the rug were wide, and Ricky saw no nails holding them down. Even in the ruined state of the building, it looked like a job unfinished.

As he lifted a floorboard, sand clouded around his ankles. Not from the board, but from behind him. He felt the force of the water on his back pushing him forward like a strong gust of wind. There was no sound, only pressure. Convinced the walls were coming down, Ricky turned in a panic. But everything was still. The wall had moved. It was about a foot closer and the area felt considerably more cramped, but it appeared to have stopped. Ricky waited for a half dozen quick breaths, but nothing happened.

He reached for the next floorboard. As he lifted, he kept his head turned to watch the wall. He picked up the floorboard and set it aside. Sure enough, the wall shifted another foot toward him. He felt the push of the water. Debris flaked and drifted where the two walls touched. Chips of plaster danced. Ricky froze.

He was tired of feeling alone. He needed to talk. "I think if I keep digging, the walls are going to collapse."

"Don't risk it. Check the other place instead. No reason if we don't know it's there. Come back when we know this is the only one left. We'll knock the walls down, move them a piece at a time if we have to."

"I got a feeling. There's a rug. And the boards. This feels right. I'm going to keep going. I'll be careful."

"Don't do nothing a guy in a movie would do. Do what a normal person would do. Nothing stupid or heroic, 'cause stupid and heroic are the same thing."

"Even if it means not finding the box?"

"Well, if it means finding the box, then do whatever you can. No matter how dangerous. The more dangerouser, the better. Take it out of a shark's mouth, you have to."

"Thanks, Harry."

"That's what I'm here for. Seriously, don't be a hero. Nothing's all-or-nothing. We've waited our lives for this. We can wait however longer need be."

Ricky only needed to remove one more floorboard to get a good sense of what was below. He felt confident that if he could remove it without the walls falling in on him, then he could dig without any danger.

If the walls didn't fall on him.

Ricky put his hand on the end of the last floorboard. The moment he moved it an inch, he knew it was holding up the walls. The base of the wall was braced against the board. Or at the least, it was a factor in the wall's stability. He tried to set the board back in place, but the walls started to crack and tumble.

Ricky dropped the weight belt and swam quickly for the opening in the roof where he had originally entered. The walls fell. It looked like they were moving in slow motion. When he thought he was clear, the top edge of the wall caught his legs. The weight of the wall and force of the water pulled him back into the room. Ricky landed softly in the dirt where he had removed the floorboards. He waited for the rest of the wall. He waited for the impact. He waited. Finally, he opened his eyes.

He had escaped being crushed. He was unhurt, but his legs were trapped under a section of wall. He could move them slightly, but not enough to wriggle out. The bigger problem was that he was facedown with the cylinder on his back. Like the inverse of an upside-down turtle, he was having trouble reaching behind his body to remove the debris from the back of his legs.

"Harry? You still there? Harry, you hear me?"

"Still here, Ricky. What's up?"

"Walls fell. Got out, kinda. Then pulled back in. Ain't hurt, but I'm stuck."

"Stuck how? Shut up, Frank. Shut up. I don't know yet. Tell me what you got, Ricky."

"Got some building on my legs. Don't hurt. Hopefully that ain't shock. I think I'm okay. Kind of wedged. Everything moved so slow. Pinned is all."

"Can you unbury yourself?"

"I'm trying, but I got to bend my arm behind my back in this weird way."

Ricky reached his good arm as best he could behind him. He grabbed a chunk of wall and set it to the side. He reached again and grabbed another chunk.

"I might got it. I'll dig as much as I can, then hopefully pull myself out."

Ricky was concerned but not panicked. He had some time. He could do this.

Then he noticed the crack in his mask. It was a visible hairline running vertically along the front.

"My mask is cracked."

"Is water coming in? Ricky, is there water inside?"

"My face is wet, but I think that's sweat. I don't feel water, I don't think, but it's a long crack across the front. I can see it. Thought it was in the water, but it's in my face."

"You need to get back up here."

"Thanks, Harry. I didn't know that."

Ricky continued to move the debris from his legs. He could move his leg a little, which was a good sign. He tried to use his bad arm, too, but even underwater it was too weak to make a difference. Small handfuls at best.

He moved one small piece at a time. Slowly and patiently. He just told himself, do the work. It didn't matter if he was scared. It didn't matter how he felt about the situation. Feelings never mattered. It was always about the work.

When he had removed a considerable amount of debris, he reached over his head with both arms. He dug his fingers into the dirt and pulled his body across the ground. He slid a couple of inches forward, some of the debris settling behind him.

The crack grew on his mask. Or was that his imagination? He thought he felt more dampness on his face. He prayed silently that it was more sweat.

He dug his fingers deeper into the dirt and pulled. His hand latched around something solid. He got a good grip and pulled himself another foot. It was working. With the new purchase, he dragged himself far enough that he could lift the rest of the wall off his legs by bending them and shaking. One flipper was gone. Harry would have to eat the deposit on that. He laughed out loud. His legs were finally free.

"Is that a good laugh or a I've-gone-crazy laugh?"

"Little bit of both. I'm out. I'm coming up."

He looked at his hands to see what they had latched onto. It was a human femur. Ricky let the leg bone drop from his hand. He watched it drift down and land on top of the rest of the human skeleton directly underneath him. Well, most of a human skeleton.

The body had no head.

TWENTY

The three men stared at the metal box on the deck of the boat. The box wasn't large, about a foot and a half square. It was wrapped tightly in leather that had constricted to the sides and corners like taut skin. Out of the water and in the heat of the sun, the leather became brittle and peeled back like corn husk. The straps that held the box closed were chipped and frayed, but the metal appeared to have survived intact with no visible holes. The box had rusted shut at the seam of the hinged lid. There was no lock.

Ricky was still in the wet suit but had removed all the gear. Water dripped from his hair, splashing around his one flipper and bare foot.

After finding the mostly complete skeleton, it had only been a matter of looking underneath the long-dead body. In fact, when he got a good look at the skeleton, he saw the top of the metal box through Constance's ribs.

They continued to look at the box like hounds sussing out a cornered skunk. Excited but cautious. They wanted to get near it but weren't quite convinced of its harmlessness.

It hadn't quite sunk in that they had found what they were looking for. They had done the work, but actually finding it had been closer to fantasy. An object that once only existed in a third-person sixty-year-old rumor now sat in front of them. The potential of its contents was beyond their comprehension.

Up until that moment, the three of them were all on bad losing streaks. Events in each of their lives had plummeted at terminal velocity. Success had become unrecognizable. Good news

practically incomprehensible. For that reason, they had all out-
wardly prepared themselves for eventual disappointment. Even
in the wake of their small victory, they were convinced of defeat.

"Could be nothing in it," Harry said.

"Yeah," Frank agreed. "Or it could be that it's all destroyed
from the water and age. Been down there a long time."

"Or it could be there's stuff inside, but not nothing that does
us no good," Harry added.

Ricky remained silent, his eyes locked on the old metal cube.

Harry gave it a soft kick. It made a hollow thunk, something banging inside it. They all nodded as if that meant
something.

"Ain't empty," Harry said. "Didn't hear no water sloshing."

"We should open it," Ricky said.

Everyone nodded, but nobody moved.

Harry finally spoke. "Need a place we can make sure it stays
dry, no wind. Let's be patient. Do this right. We bring the boat
in. Pack up the gear. Then we hit my place. See what we got."

Ricky went down to one knee and put his hand on the top of
the box. He was surprised by the smile on his own face, but he
couldn't help it. He looked up at Harry and Frank.

"God was with me down there," Ricky said.

After a solemn pause, Ricky smiled and shouted, "We found
the fucking thing." He didn't curse that often, but this was a special
occasion.

Harry and Frank looked at him, surprised. His smile was contagious, quickly turning to laughter. They laughed and whooped
and hollered at the lake around them.

Bernardo and Ramón stared at them. They shrugged, fired up
a joint, and pulled up the anchor.

Frank handed out the Cuban cigars that he had bought
in Los Algodones months before. He had brought them as an
afterthought, as a consolation prize for when they didn't find
anything.

Sitting on the back of the boat smoking cigars with the wind in their faces, they felt like kings. None of them had ever felt like a king before. Not even close. It was a good feeling.

It took longer than they had anticipated to pack the gear and return the boat. Maybe two hours, but it might as well have been a week to Harry, Frank, and Ricky, their excitement percolating.

Bernardo and Ramón headed back to their ranch. They never asked about the box. They had no natural curiosity. Papa Frank asked for help, so they helped. The way they figured it, they got to go out on the reservoir in a boat, which was nice. They had enjoyed the clouds that looked like dicks.

Harry, Ricky, and Frank sat in Harry's cramped and dirty trailer with the rusty box on the cheap folding table.

Frank and Harry had beers in front of them. Ricky settled for grayish tap water. Frank had offered him a beer, making sure that Ricky knew he was only allowed one. A token of celebration. Ricky had refused it. If he was going to quit, he was going to do it right. No need to give him a taste of temptation. One led to two.

Things had changed in the waters of the Imperial Reservoir. Ricky had made a turn. It had become about something else. Too important to jeopardize with drink.

"I sold my torch or I'd cut it open," Ricky said. He looked away embarrassed, knowing that both Frank and Harry had seen him at his worst. Selling his possessions had been the second-to-last thing he had lost. His family being the final defeat.

"Don't sweat it, kid. Wouldn't've worked, anyway. Would've burned everything inside," Frank said.

Harry got up and rummaged through a couple drawers. "It's rust. Doc gave me a tetanus booster for my leg, so I'm immune. Couple of hard knocks with the end of a screwdriver'll bust this sucker wide."

A screwdriver ended up being a butter knife. And a couple of hard knocks turned into a lot of sweating, swearing, and scraped knuckles.

All three of them leaned in with eyes wide when Harry finally wrenched the scuffed and dented lid off the top of the box, his hands stained orange and red from rust and blood.

"This is it," Harry said unnecessarily.

He lifted the lid straight up.

"Holy shit," he shouted, retreating until his back hit the wall.

"Jesus," Frank said solemnly.

"So that's where the head went," Ricky said, then crossed himself. "Makes sense."

"Makes sense? It's a human head," Harry yelled. "Makes sense? Yeah. In a crazy, scalping, murdering Indian kind of way."

"Grandfather must have been very angry. He never said anything about cutting the head off the man."

Harry shouted to the ceiling. "Of course he didn't. He cut off a white man's melon. Don't care how much time has passed, that's a thing you learn not to divulge. Kind of thing, if you're proud of it, you're a certified psycho. Who the hell would brag about that kind of murderous disgustery?"

Harry peered back into the box. "There's a canvas bag under the thing. Ricky, take the head out of the box."

Ricky looked at the dead man's head. He thought the skin would have been dry and mummified, but it appeared moist, soapy. The mouth was open but contorted. He saw no teeth. The eyes were gone, too. The glistening pits stared at him. Wispy hair rested on the top of the head and loose atop the stained canvas bag. There was nothing clean about the cut where the head had been severed. It looked like it had been torn off the man's body. Stringy strands of skin flapped from the ends of the neck.

"I'm not touching that."

"Frank?" Harry said.

"Hell no," Frank said.

Harry pointed at the box. "That's your grandfather's handi-work. You have a responsibility to finish your family business. It's a matter of honor. An ancestral duty."

"Now you're making shit up." Frank said.

"Fine. Let Harry do the sick work," Harry said.

Harry reached inside the box but stopped himself. He got up, opened the cabinet under his sink, and pulled out an unlined plastic trash can. He picked up the metal box and shook the head into the trash, careful not to disturb the canvas bag beneath it. The waxy head landed in the coffee grounds and beer cans with a dull crunch. Loose hairs drifted to the ground. Harry returned the box to the table and the trash can under the sink.

"That's your solution?" Ricky said.

"You want, I could put it on a pole to scare off door-to-door salesmen."

"We should put the head back. It's the guy's head," Ricky said.

Frank nodded solemnly. "A body without a head. That's bad. Old Indian stuff. Grandfather wanted the man to be denied his place in the life after life. Remember, this Constance murdered men for gold and greed. Killed to protect the treasure of the Big Maria Mine. Without his head, he will never rest. We have the opportunity to end his journey. If we don't return the head, his soul wanders, damned. We could be haunted. Or cursed."

"Do you really believe that?" Harry said, concern in his voice.

"No, I'm just messing with you and the kid," Frank said. "The guy sounded like a bastard. Landfill's good enough for me."

Ricky thought about it. What did it matter what happened to the man's body, head, or anything after all this time? God didn't care about a proper burial. His soul was already wherever it was going. Still, a trash can?

"Can we at least bury it?" Ricky said.

Harry rolled his eyes and exhaled loudly. "Okay. I'll take it out to the desert. Put it in the dirt."

Ricky nodded, satisfied. "What's in the bag?"

Harry reached into the box. He pulled out the canvas bag and brushed some loose hair aside. It had some weight. He poured the contents carefully onto the table. Mostly paper, damp but not wet. Old maps, a journal, some loose handwritten pages. A stack of letters tied together with string.

And teeth.

A mouthful of teeth poured out onto the table.

"Jesus, your grandfather was a sick bastard," Harry said. "Another Indian thing?"

"Not that I know of. I'm starting to think Grandfather maybe made up all his Indian legend and lore crap to justify being a psychopath."

Ricky picked up one of the teeth, looking at a filling. "We've struck gold."

Harry reached inside the canvas bag, digging around. "I'll do you one better."

Harry pulled out a nugget of gold as big as his thumb.

TWENTY-ONE

Harry poured the remainder of his beer down the sink and went straight to work. He dug through the old maps and logbooks, carefully separating the pages and scanning them for pertinent information. Ricky was surprised at Harry's quick transformation into studiousness. It was amazing how a chunk of gold increased one's focus. Without any necessary discussion, Frank acted as Harry's assistant. He combed through the book, looking for clues, making notes on a yellow pad.

Ricky wasn't good at that kind of thing, so he tried to stay out of the way. He had never been good in school or with homework or with numbers. He knew how to use the computer, but mostly to look stuff up that he didn't know. He was more comfortable lifting things and fixing stuff.

They took turns holding the gold nugget, and now it sat in front of Ricky on the table, next to a Dixie cup full of black teeth, his chipped glass of stink water, and Abraham Constance's letters.

Ricky flipped through the frayed upper corners of the stack of letters, the return address identical on each: *H. Constance* and an address in Denver. He carefully untied the string that held the dozen letters together. The writing on each yellowed envelope was written in a feminine, old-timey hand.

He opened the first envelope, taking out the tightly folded paper from inside. He had never read someone else's mail, and even this hundred-year-old message felt like an invasion. Very carefully, he unfolded the almost see-through paper. The brittle edges chipped at his touch.

My dearest Abraham...

His mother? His girlfriend? His wife? People wrote so formally back in the olden days.

It is with the greatest sorrow that I write this letter to inform you of the death of your eldest son.

Ricky stopped reading and carefully folded the letter. He returned it to the envelope and retied the string.

He only read the one sentence but had known immediately that it had been wrong. He didn't want to know about Abraham Constance or about the man's family or about the events that brought about his end. The man's head was in a trash can five feet away. He may have been misunderstood. He may have been evil. But no matter what he did and why, every man deserved his secrets.

"I think I got something." Harry stood up and stretched his back. The muted cracking sounded like a string of firecrackers immersed in jelly. He didn't appear excited, but it could have been exhaustion.

It was almost dawn. Harry had worked for hours without a break. Frank and Ricky had grabbed some shut-eye in shifts on Harry's torture device of a couch. Between the sofa springs that attacked the kidneys like prison shivs and the events of the day, neither of them could remember if they had dreamed. But if they had dreamed, they were sure they had dreamed about gold.

Harry spread a map across the dining room table. He had drawn some lines in pen and circled a few areas. Frank wiped sleep from his eyes and joined him. Ricky poured fresh coffee.

"The man kept decent records. He wasn't worried about anyone seeing this. Wasn't in code, pretty straightforward. He had to be able to return to the mine, so he needed a visual map, as well as a regular map. Some of the landmarks will be gone or changed, but between the map and his notes, I think I've got a toehold into finding the Big Maria Mine."

"Show us," Frank said.

"I've still got a ton of papers to go through, so I'm a ways from the exact location. I've definitely narrowed it down to this area of the Chocolate Mountains." Harry drew a circle with his finger over an area of mountainous terrain in Arizona to the east of the Colorado River.

"I thought the Chocolate Mountains were a gunnery range," Ricky said, vaguely remembering when they had first searched online. A million years ago when he had a life and a family.

"You're the one that told me there's two Chocolate Mountains. The California Chocolates are a gunnery range. There's gold and mines there, too." Harry pointed to a spot on the map far to the west near the Salton Sea. "The Big Maria Mine is in the Arizona Chocolates." He pointed back to the circle he had drawn on the map.

"That's a lot of chocolate. Almost the length of the Cal/Arizona border," Frank said.

Ricky laughed. "But at least it's not in the middle of an artillery range."

"Yeah, that's the bad news," Harry said.

"What now?" Frank asked.

"The Arizona Chocolates are a gunnery range, too. Or to be more precise, gunnery *ranges*." Harry reached for another map and spread it out on top. "From here to here. And here to here. That whole area is US Army land. That's the Yuma Proving Ground."

"Proving Ground? What are they trying to prove?" Ricky said.

"That they can blow shit up."

Harry dug through a stack of library books. He was back to drinking beer, having knocked back three in fifteen minutes. "The reason nobody has found that mine is because it's in the middle of a war zone. It sounds like I'm making this up, but I'm underselling the place. You name it, this is where the Army shoots it, explodes it, or throws it out of a helicopter."

Harry pulled out a book and flipped through the pages rapidly.

Frank said, "Okay. They train out there, but not all the time and not in every place."

Harry held up his hand, having found what he was looking for. He read out loud, adding a few of his own personal footnotes. "The Yuma Proving Ground in the Sonoran Desert of Arizona, established in 1943 by the US Army, is one of the largest military installations in the world. In the whole world. At thirteen hundred square miles, it is roughly the size of Rhode Island—of course it is—with multiple variations in terrain. Blah, blah, blah. More history. General whoever. Important training facility. Where is it? This book is a little old and the numbers'll be off, but…Here it is. Get prepared to softly say, 'Holy mother of God,' to yourself.

"With a number of active ranges, over four hundred thousand artillery rounds are fired in any given year. Four hundred thousand. That's more than a thousand a day. An average of one hundred parachute drops a day. I'll repeat, a day. In one day! Thousands of air sorties. I don't even know what a sortie is. Blah, blah, blah. We are screwed.

"Read it yourself. It's like an arsenal for a 1980s action movie. They have minefields, tank courses, artillery ranges, mortar ranges, missile ranges. Missiles. A helicopter range for the choppers to shoot at stuff, including something called the Brimstone missile, which you know kills the hell out of a thing, and I'm thinking with fire. They have a road course running through the mountains for all sorts of badass military vehicles. Do you know what a howitzer is? They're like huge cannons. They got a bunch of those."

Frank tried to bring the tone back toward optimism. "They've got to take time off. Might not be nowhere near the mine."

"Do you read the newspaper? In the last twenty years, we seem to only be fighting in countries that have a lot of desert and mountains and deserty mountains. It's a popular place. And not just for the Army. For the whole world. Sure, the Army's there—but get this—other countries train there as well. Japs, Germans, Canadians, even the Swedes. And who the holy hell are the Swedes fighting?

"For all my faults, I've never been a man that swore." Harry's voice rose. "But our motherfucking gold mine is smack-fuck-ing-dab in the middle of the biggest fucking military jumble-fuck that the fucking free world has ever fucking seen. And also, motherfucker."

Harry got up and paced.

"We get it. What does that mean?" Ricky said.

Frank smiled. "It means we're probably going to die trying to get that gold."

Harry turned to him. "You heard what I said, yeah? And you still want to go?"

"So it's garbage news. A little piss in the picnic basket. But we're here. We got this far. We've held gold in our hands. We can't turn back. We're in this. Why pretend? It might take a day or a week or goddamn months, but we're going to eventually decide to find that mine. Even if it kills us."

"Easy for you to say, Frank," Harry said. "You're dying already. No offense."

Frank gave Harry a hard stare. "Give me a straight answer. You going to forget the gold and go back to your life? Go back to working your shit job at the prison? Are you, Shitburger?"

Harry looked at the trailer around him, walked to the fridge, and took out another beer.

"I hate that name," Harry said, "But that's who I am if I settle for this life. Let's find that mine or die trying. I'm all in."

Frank turned. "Ricky?"

Ricky nodded. "Crazy old man. You go through the trouble to save me from killing myself just to find a whole new way for me to kill myself."

"Things happen whatever way they want to," Frank said.

"They happen for a reason," Ricky said. "Of course I'm in."

Reaching for his cup of dirty water to raise for a toast, Ricky knocked over the cup full of teeth. They spilled over the table and around the gold ingot. They didn't make a pattern and it didn't seem like an omen, but they all stared at the teeth before lifting their drinks.

Frank made the toast. "To Abraham Constance. He may have been a murderous son of a bitch, probably rotting in hell, but without him we'd never have gotten this far."

They touched glasses and drank.

Ricky said, "Don't forget to bury his head."

PART FOUR: STUPID SMART

TWENTY-TWO

If Harry was going to do something stupid, he was damn sure going to be smart about it.

That's why he was sitting in a booth across from Cooker Hobson at a Denny's in Winterhaven, California. As his name would suggest, Cooker cooked. He possessed fairly well-regarded recipes for both baby back ribs and snickerdoodles. His Triple-Layer Carrot-Rhubarb Pie had won first prize at the Carrot Festival in Holtville. Cooker could cook just about anything. But mostly, he cooked methamphetamine.

Harry had met Cooker at Chuckawalla when Harry was a guard and Cooker an inmate. Their mutual hatred for another guard, "Kirch" Kirchenbauer, gave them a jumping-off point to at least a conversational acquaintanceship. Sometimes all it took was a real douche bag to create peace between two less vehement enemies.

Cooker had been clean—or at least uncaught—for a couple of years. He worked short order at the Denny's. In the last year, Harry and Cooker had bumped into each other a few times. Never more than a nod of recognition, but Harry felt okay approaching him. As guards went, he was well liked at Chuckawalla, generous with his porn stash, and always willing to look the other way for a reasonable price.

"Why am I sitting here?" Cooker asked. He hadn't bothered to take off the hairnet that held his ponytailed, graying hair. His handlebar mustache dripped with coffee. It made him look like a walrus coming out of brown water. The world's smallest walrus. Cooker wasn't an inch over five feet, and aside from a volleyball-shaped potbelly, he was skin and bones.

"I need some information."

Cooker gave a look over his shoulder. The restaurant was close to empty.

"You starting a lab? It's a solid investment, Shits. I can help you there, but I got to earn. Mind you, I can't help in person, and you'll want to be careful. I got a book I self-published. It's available on Amazon, both in paperback and Kindle. Everything you need, all the tricks of the trade. Safety tips. Equipment checklists. It's organized good as shit."

"I'm not starting a damn meth lab, Cooker," Harry said, too loud.

Cooker looked slightly offended. "Easy, Shits. Ain't got to act all surprised. That's what I do."

"I'm not starting a meth lab," Harry repeated evenly.

"Then why the fuck we talking? Lunch crowd'll be here soon. You best hurry this reunion along."

"You were in the Army, right? I remember you talking about it."

"I served."

"You were stationed in Yuma?"

"Few months. Not long. Trained there before Iraq. The first Iraq. The righteous one. Desert Storm, motherfucker."

"I need to know about the Proving Ground. Mostly the terrain. As much as you can remember."

"Why you want to know?"

Harry ignored the question. "First, I need to know where the best trails are to reach—"

Cooker interrupted, leaning over the table between them. "I didn't ask *what* you want to know. Only one kind of fucker wants to know what the inside of a military installation looks like. That's a terrorist fucker, motherfucker."

Harry started to laugh and then realized that Cooker was serious. "No, no, no. Back it up."

"You see this?" Cooker said, rolling up the sleeve of his shirt. His skin was blue with tattoos, overlapping three deep in places. But one tattoo stayed pristine on the meat of his forearm. It was a shield or coat of arms with a cannon and a horse on it, a faded yellowish orange. "Second Cavalry. Wolfpack."

Harry didn't know what to say, so he nodded.

"I may be the fuck-up of all fuck-ups. Cooked fatch. Sold it. Been busted. Shit, maybe even killed a couple fuckers. Not much of a crime if they ain't missed. But I'm a goddamn American. And if you're planning any un-American horseshit, any squirrelly Ay-rab horseshit, then you're fingering the wrong hole."

Harry sat back in the booth holding up his hands. "I'm not a terrorist. It's nothing like that. I love my country. I have a good reason. Just can't tell you."

"You can't tell me? Then I can't tell you jack shit. Maybe I'll even call Homeland, see what they think about your unpatriotical Commie questions."

"What could a terrorist do in the middle of them mountains anyway?" Harry realized he was raising his voice. He brought it back down. "The Proving Ground ain't nothing but a place the Army uses to blow stuff up. What am I going to do? Explode something that's already exploded? Or explode it before it explodes?"

"That shit don't explode on its own. You could steal something. They got missiles, bombs, all sorts of death out there."

"That's ridiculous."

"You don't tell it straight, I'm making some government calls. I'm on parole. I need to be talking to a dumbfuck terrorist like I need a second asshole."

"Bird-watching," Harry said.

"What?"

"*Colaptes chrysoides.* The gilded flicker."

"Speak fucking English. You talk more of that foreign shit, I'm going to think you're talking terrorist."

"It's a bird. The gilded flicker is a bird, and the only place that that bird lives is in the Chocolate Mountains. Not near the river. Deep in the mountains."

"And you want to the jump the fence into the Proving Ground to…?"

"To watch it. To see it. To take pictures of it."

Cooker scooted to the edge of the booth. "You are full of some serious shit."

"I'll give you a hundred dollars," Harry said, reaching for his wallet.

Cooker stopped, turning back to Harry. "A fucking bird?"

"It's the truth."

"You know there are minefields and artillery, on top of the heat and the mountains and the rattlers, right? You want to go through all that shit to take a picture of a bird?"

"Not any bird. The gilded flicker."

"Whatever the fuck."

"It's what any dedicated bird-watcher would do. I can't explain, but I need to see it before I die."

"You sneak into the Proving Ground, probably get your wish."

"Not if you tell me what you know." Harry pulled out his map and spread it over the table. "What's the safest way to get to here? That's the best spot for the flicker. Their nesting canyon."

"And you're sure you're not a terrorist? I ain't going to give you directions, then in a couple of months, I turn on the TV and there's a picture of a smoking building and your ugly puss."

"I love birds."

Cooker thought about it for a while. "Fuck that. There's another angle."

They sat in silence for a full minute, Cooker waiting Harry out. Harry finally broke the silence. "Nobody has taken a picture of it in thirty-two years."

Cooker smiled, finally satisfied. "There it is. And you're going to be the guy to get the—what-do-you-call-it—the exclusive. Someone's paying for the bird picture, right? Paying real money. *National Geographic*–type shit?"

"Let's just say my bird hobby is about to pay off."

"How much? Must be a lot."

"Enough."

"Thousand bucks. That's what it'll cost for me to help you find your gilded fucker."

"Flicker. I ain't paying that much. A hundred fifty. To map out a trail."

"Five hundred. But I can't guarantee that shit ain't changed. Been like twenty years. Could be the trails are gone. Could be I send you into the middle of a patrol. Get you more lost than you would be. Or I walk you into a minefield. All I'm saying is: you die, it's not on me."

"I'll take my chances. Two hundred bucks."

"Three fifty."

"Two sixty-five."

"Two seventy five. Up front."

"Deal."

TWENTY-THREE

There's no such thing as a born liar. Although Harry was pretty sure he had met a few women that came close. A good liar was the product of experience and craft, like any true artist. Execution and performance were integral, but it was the construction of the narrative that was the make-or-break. That's where Harry shined. He did his homework.

As he had dug up information about bird-watching, he reminded himself of the components of a good lie: keep your facts straight, details add realism, less is more, truth is stranger than fiction, add a touch of absurdity, you have to believe it yourself.

Nothing helped the success of a lie more than the other person wanting to believe. It could be because they were as gullible as a Mississippi prom queen. Or greedier than an old millionaire's teenage fiancée. But most people believed lies out of sheer laziness. It was easier to believe a person than to challenge them.

Cooker had doubted him at first. But by making Cooker think that Harry was holding back, when Harry finally gave him the "truth," Cooker was primed to believe. Cooker wasn't any different than the other prisoners at Chuckawalla. Another poor, dumb convict.

After Harry gave him the cash, Cooker mapped out the path through the Proving Ground. He had admitted that some of the terrain was unfamiliar, just guesswork, but the trail wasn't that different from what Harry had got from his own best guesses and Google satellite images. It was a strong second vote and cheap for the price.

Harry headed back to Blythe with a rough plan, a preliminary trail map, and a definite destination. And Cooker was none the wiser. Probably forgot about the whole thing as soon as the money got him high.

Cooker didn't believe a fucking word that Shitburger had said. He hadn't trusted the hacks inside, he sure as fuck wasn't going to start now. Bird-watching, his hairy, misshapen ass. Dumbshit couldn't lie worth a damn. Just the same, he was pretty sure Shitburger wasn't no terrorist neither. Whatever his angle was—maybe arms theft and sales—Cooker smelled money. He had two hundred and seventy-five in his pocket. And if Shitburger was handing out three-bills-minus that easy, there was more at the end of that motherfucking rainbow.

Cooker worked the grill on autopilot, cooking up Scrams and Slams, sandwiches, and burgers until the end of his shift. He couldn't stop thinking about the money in his pocket and that map of the Chocolate Mountains.

He hadn't told Harry that during his time at the Proving Ground, he had spent most it gacked out at the Laguna Airfield. Fact was, Cooker couldn't remember shit-all from when he trained there. He did know that the area Shitburger was interested in was nothing but rock. What could be out there?

When Cooker clocked out, instead of heading back to the windowless room he rented in Yuma, he went to the small bookstore in town. Browsing the aisles, he found a map of the area. He stared at the wavy lines depicting the elevations of the Chocolate Mountains, tapping his finger on the spot that Shitburger was trying to reach.

He asked the girly dude at the counter for a phone book, but as soon as it was in his hands, he realized he was in the wrong county. He had nothing else to do, so he got on his hog.

It took Cooker a half hour to find a pay phone once he got to Blythe. Motherfucking cell phones, he thought. Some of us still use dimes. He flipped through the hanging phone book, avoiding the pages that looked like someone had wiped their ass on them. There was only one Schmittberger listed. He memorized the address, but to be double sure, he tore out the page and stuffed it in his pocket.

Ricky waited for the little biker to finish using the phone. Other than a bank over at the truck stop, it was the only pay phone in Blythe. That made it extremely popular, often with a line three or four deep. The worst was when you got behind a guy using all his calling-card minutes to talk to every one of his relatives back in Mexico.

The biker wasn't even using the phone, just reading the phone book, but he had been there first and Ricky wasn't in any hurry. Besides, the guy had that look. One of those little dogs that thinks he's a big dog.

After the guy ripped out a page, he turned, gave Ricky a tough-guy nod, and walked to his motorcycle. Ricky was glad he hadn't rushed him. He wasn't physically imposing in any way—Ricky probably had eighty pounds on him—but there was something about the confident way he carried himself.

Ricky punched in the first three numbers, but stopped when the biker's motorcycle roared to life, massacring the silence in a fifteen-block radius. Ricky waited until the engine had faded in the distance and then slowly pressed the rest of the buttons, reading the numbers off the torn piece of paper in his hand. The electronic tone rang in his ear.

"Hello," a female voice crackled.

"Hi, Anna. Is Flavia there?"

There was a long silence, then an exasperated "Just a minute."

It was more than a minute. Ricky fed a handful of coins into the pay phone.

"Ricky?" Flavia's voice surprised him. She sounded happy to hear from him.

"Hey, baby."

"How are you doing, Ricky? Everything okay?"

"Yeah, nothing wrong. Other than you're there and I'm here. I miss you. I miss the Rose."

"We miss you, too."

"I'm not drinking no more. I'm on a good path. Figuring things out. Believing."

"That's good, Ricky."

"I ain't pressing. I have to earn it. I have to fix what I broke. I know that."

Flavia kept silent.

"I'm doing what I can to make things right. I'm working hard. I got a plan. And faith. It's going to take time, but I'm getting everything back to the way it was. Better even."

"That's good, Ricky. That sounds really good."

"I don't expect anything all at once. You've seen me at my worst. Leaving was the only thing you could have done. I want to see the both of you soon. When you say it's okay. Just wanted to call, let you know that I'm trying. That I ain't given up."

Ricky hadn't realized it, but he had started crying.

"That's good, Ricky." He could hear the tears in her voice as well.

"Is Rosie there? Can I talk to her?"

"She's out with a friend."

"Tell her I love her. Tell her for me, okay?"

"She knows, but I'll tell her. I'll tell her twice."

"I love you, Flav."

"I know. I wish that was all it took. I love you, too."

"Can I call again? Is it okay for me to call like this?"

"Any time, Ricky. I want you to. It sounds like you're trying. No reason I shouldn't try, too."

"I really screwed up, didn't I?"

"Isn't nothing that's broken so bad it can't be glued back together. I got to go, Ricky. Anna's calling me. But I want to talk soon. I want to know you're okay. I love you."

Flavia hung up. Ricky set the receiver back in the cradle and wiped his nose with his sleeve. He dug his finger in the coin return, found a nickel, and put it in his pocket. He started the slow walk back to his gutted trailer with a smile on his face.

Frank couldn't sleep. He thought a nap would give him energy, but he ended up staring at the ceiling. Getting up from the bed in his daughter's house, he felt disoriented and lost. Nothing felt right. Something was off.

He felt hot. His stomach hurt. He needed water. The inside of his cheeks stuck to his teeth. He might puke. Not even halfway to the kitchen, he needed a rest. His ribs felt like they were being squeezed. He thought about calling for help but detested the idea of not being able to do it himself. Defiantly, he made it to the kitchen, dragging his shoulder along the wall and disrupting a framed family photo. He shakily poured a glass of water. Something was screwy inside his body. He shook with chills. He didn't want to bother Mercedes. He wanted to wait, let it pass, see how he felt in a bit.

The water didn't help, most of it coughed back into the sink.

His hand seized and his arm burned with pain. Oh, shit, he thought. I know what this is. He tried to yell, but all that came out was a gurgling sound. He dropped the glass with a loud crash as he fell to the floor clutching his chest.

Frank woke up in the back of an ambulance soaked in sweat and ready to fight. The ambulance guy leaned over him adjusting the oxygen mask. Frank weakly reached to pull it away. With no effort, the guy set Frank's arm back at his side. The man's voice was gentle, like a cartoon bear.

"You're wondering what happened, where you are. You're in an ambulance that is on its way to Palo Verde Hospital. You had an episode."

An episode? What the hell did that mean? He had finished his chemo with a clean bill of health. Cancer wasn't an ambulance thing anyhow. It was more of a kill-you-slowly kind of deal. Then Frank remembered the chest pain.

The bear continued. "A cardiac episode that appears to have corrected itself. However, you needed to be resuscitated, so we're bringing you in for tests. We would have taken you to Parker Indian, but your daughter insisted we drive you to Blythe, where you've been receiving treatment. She was very insistent. In fact, your daughter scared the hell out of Tommy and me."

The guy smiled, trying to communicate that he was joking, but Frank knew he wasn't. Mercedes scared everyone.

"You are doing very well. Your vitals are good and you're in excellent hands. Lie back, get some rest, and try to relax. That's the best thing for you."

Frank stared at the ceiling of the ambulance. Small lights and locked shelves lined the interior wall. The kid was nice enough, but Frank wasn't going to take his advice. He knew if he closed his eyes, he might not open them again. It was a matter of will. It was on him. At that precise moment, Frank decided not to die yet. And as long as he did the work, he would continue to live.

TWENTY-FOUR

Harry set the last letter down on the table. It rested among small confetti chips that had flaked from the edges of the thin pages. Each one of Abraham Constance's wife's letters was a tale of tragedy: a dead kid, a poor investment, a fire. And the final insult, his wife informing him that she was leaving him for his own brother.

Despite what he knew about Constance, Harry couldn't help but feel sorry for the guy. From all evidence, he was a kindred spirit. Another poor chump who had never seen nothing but the short end of the stick. Of course, he had killed who knew how many times for the gold. What was Constance supposed to do? The gold was his chance to balance out the awful.

He looked to the cabinet under the sink. Sorry, Abe.

Harry brushed the paper chips onto the floor with his fore-arm, tied the letters with the old string, and picked up Abraham Constance's journal for a second read. He appreciated the man's all-business approach and penmanship. At points it felt like the words had been written directly to Harry.

From what Harry deciphered, there were roughly sixty pounds of gold unaccounted for at the time of Constance's death. From the simple system used to keep track of the mining opera-tion, Harry gleaned that the gold had been sacked but never exchanged. It could have been bad bookkeeping, but to that point the balance sheets balanced.

After reading the journals and letters, Harry felt like he knew a little bit about Abraham Constance the man. He may have been overconfident, but he wasn't careless. That was too much gold to have sitting around. The only place to safely stow it would have been at the mine. Only a few knew the location, and that knowledge was what sent Constance on his killing spree.

Harry was sure of it. There were sixty pounds of gold sitting in the Big Maria Mine. Sixty pounds. Nine hundred sixty ounces. Sitting there. Waiting for Harry. Calling to him.

Could it be that easy? Follow the rainbow and find the pot of gold? Of course not. Nothing in life was magically delicious. At least not for Harry. He would have to traverse minefields and artillery ranges. The way Harry figured it, if they miraculously reached the Big Maria Mine both undetected and unharmed, it would only be fair that there would be bags of gold waiting for them.

It relieved Harry that they wouldn't have to do any mining. Prospecting had been entirely unrealistic. His only experience with gold mining was the time he had panned for gold at a kiosk in Knott's Berry Farm when he was a kid. The yield had been minimal, a few flakes. A pie tin wasn't going to cut it for this trip.

Just because a person grew up in the desert didn't mean they liked the heat. It just meant that they were too stupid to move to a place where people were meant to live.

Cooker had found shade, but it was still hot as a fresh shit. And boring as fuck. Nothing happened as he watched Shitburger's trailer. Cooker had run out of cigarettes about an hour into watching and now he was jonesing. It was only two blocks to the Circle K, but he had committed. He could hold out, but it pissed him off.

He spat a thick white wad onto the ground. The inside of his mouth was cotton-dry, his lips chapped. His throat scratched and he couldn't stop swallowing. Fifteen more minutes and he'd have to take a break or pass out from thirst. He licked the sweat off his arm to feel the wetness. The salt burned his tongue.

Finally, Shitburger's door swung open and the fat fuck slowly maneuvered down the wooden steps. The cast on his leg gave him a comical hobble. Once on flat ground, Shitburger used his crutches and slowly made his way down the dirt road out of the trailer park. Cooker hadn't bothered to duck for cover, as Shitburger was forced to keep his head down to concentrate on each step.

Cooker waited two minutes and then walked to the trailer. He kicked in the front door with one fluid motion, entered, and closed the door behind him. Unless someone was watching for that brief moment, he was golden. Cooker let his eyes adjust to the shuttered darkness. The only light came from the small hole where the knob used to be. He turned on the sink and drank directly from the tap. The water poured down his cheek and wet his hair. It hurt his teeth and throat and gave him a stomachache. He let the water run over his hands and wrists and rubbed the back of his neck. If he could just find some smokes.

The place was a fucking dump. There was shit everywhere. He had no idea where to start, but there had to be something that would give him a clue about Shitburger's plans. How do you look for something when you don't know what you're looking for? He picked up a stack of books and rifled through the pages. Most of the books were on the history of the area, a couple about scuba diving. Probably junk he was selling on eBay or some shit.

The map that Shitburger had showed him was on the table, the red line that Cooker had drawn still prominent. He had made a few more marks since their meeting, but not much else. Water glasses held down the corners of the map. Three of them empty. One of them had something in it. He picked it up, the map curling in.

Teeth. Who the fuck keeps a cup full of teeth on their eating table? Not baby teeth either, but grown human teeth that had never seen a brushing, black and pitted. Only two kinds of people kept teeth: dentists and serial killers.

The door opened behind him with a creak. Cooker spun, reaching for the hunting knife in his belt. Nobody was there. The hot wind blew the door open a little more. He left the knife in its sheath, laughing to himself. He set the cup of teeth down and flattened out the map. He grabbed a stack of books and jammed them against the door.

Cooker opened drawers, rifling through the worthless contents. He silently prayed to find a half a pack of cigs or the butt of an old cigar. When he opened the cabinet under the sink and pulled out the trash can, he fell back, knocking over the cup of teeth and stifling a scream. A toothless, waxy human head rolled out of the overturned trash can toward him. The soapy goo of the face left a sickly white trail on the linoleum. He kicked it away with his foot.

Cooker had seen plenty that he wished he could unsee. Any man who'd spent time in prison had. But for all his criminal exploits, a human head in a trash can was still outside his comfort zone. Killing a dude was one thing. Keeping parts of him where you lived, slept, and ate, that was psycho shit.

Cooker was growing less curious about the whole thing. Shitburger hadn't seemed like much, a fucking loser. But wasn't that always the guy who they later found out had buried a dozen hitchhikers in their backyard? "He was such a quiet neighbor," they'd say. He glanced at the refrigerator, wondering if it was filled with mason jars and Tupperware stuffed with human organs and severed cocks.

The risk wasn't worth the reward. It was time to walk out of the trailer and call it a two-hundred-seventy-five dollar win. No reason to be greedy.

Besides, he really wanted a smoke.

He soccer-kicked the head back into the trash can and returned it under the sink.

One by one, he collected the teeth, placing them daintily back in the cup. That's when he saw the gold ingot. A big chunk of gold among the scattered molars and bicuspids. He picked it up, feeling its weight. Surprisingly heavy for something so small. He bit it, because that's what people did when they found gold. It left the lightest tooth imprint in the metal. Cooker wasn't sure if that was good.

It took Cooker all of ten seconds to fill in the blanks. Cooker knew why Shitburger wanted to go to the Proving Ground.

He heard the door creak again, but he didn't turn nearly as quickly as before. He had been fooled once, and the gold in his hand was a serious distraction. Then he remembered the books he had placed as a doorstop. The wind wasn't that strong.

Cooker turned and looked up at the big dude standing over him. He had seen the lopsided kid with one bodybuilder arm and one baby arm at the pay phone. What the fuck was he doing in Shitburger's trailer?

It didn't take Cooker long to get an answer. But a boot to the face wasn't exactly the answer he was looking for.

TWENTY-FIVE

Ricky had been sitting on the steps of his trailer when he caught the movement. By the time he turned his head, the little biker had dashed inside Harry's kicked-in door.

His first reaction was to call the cops, but they never took less than an hour to respond to a call from Desert Vista. In a boring town like Blythe, you'd think the cops would be excited to see some action. But after your thousandth tweaker or beaten spouse, the novelty probably lost its luster.

He wasn't sure what he was going to do when he got to Harry's trailer. The guy had rushed in with confidence and purpose, which probably meant he had a weapon. He was a little fella. In fact, it looked like the tiny biker that had been at the pay phone earlier.

Kicking the guy had been improvised, and the violence of the act surprised even Ricky. He felt awful the moment he did it, but if he apologized, he risked looking weak. The guy had broken into Harry's home. A kick was a fair enough punishment.

"What the heck you doing in here?" Ricky shouted.

Cooker tried to uncross his eyes. The blurry guys in front of him were talking. The upside of the pain was that it kept him conscious. The impact had knocked him backward into the table. The rotted teeth were sprinkled on the linoleum around him. His nose was undoubtedly broken, blood flowing like an open tap. He felt it dripping off his mustache. He swallowed the blood that collected in his mouth.

"There ain't nothing to steal here." Ricky took a cautious step toward him.

Cooker had no interest in explaining himself. He rose slowly to a crouch.

"Don't do it, man," Ricky said.

Cooker's vision was clearing. He had to get out of there. Fucking three strikes. One more arrest and he was fucked. He found some balance and rushed Ricky, attempting a tackle around the waist.

Ricky fell back a few steps, but had the weight advantage and easily braced himself. It had been forever since he had been in a fight, but he had the experience of plenty of scraps in his youth. Time didn't diminish certain skills even through long periods of dormancy. Without thinking, Ricky threw hard rights to the liver of the man clutching his waist. The biker folded, leaning his middle away from Ricky's good arm.

Cooker couldn't take many more hard punches. He threw a couple of weak hooks, but was getting more than he was giving. He brought his head up quickly, catching Ricky on the chin.

Ricky bit through his lower lip, tasting the blood and wincing in pain. A thin section of lip hung from his mouth.

The shock of the blow gave Cooker enough time to get his footing.

For a moment, the two men squared off. Both men's faces were covered in blood. They breathed heavy. The peaceful seconds of nonviolence were almost friendly, touching gloves or walking to the dance floor. Then the bell rang in their heads.

Ricky gave Cooker a hard two-handed push to the center of his chest, forcing him stumbling back over the already upended table. Teeth crunched under his skidding feet. He fell onto his side awkwardly but scrambled to a knee.

Ricky took two steps toward him.

Cooker's knife came out in an experienced sweep of the arm.

Ricky scanned the room for an improvised weapon. With his good arm for weight and his bad arm for balance, he grabbed a box of books and threw it at the biker.

Cooker tried to knock the box away, but a brush of the hand wasn't enough to stop the path of forty pounds of books. They crushed him, the corner of the box jabbing his sternum. Another box followed right behind it, landing on top of the last one, knocking the wind out of him.

And another box.

And another box.

Ricky picked up the heavy boxes, lifted them over his head, and threw them as hard as he could, until the little biker was almost completely buried under their bulk and weight.

Cooker gasped for breath, drowning in books. He flailed and pushed at the pages, but more kept coming. Spines and corners bruised his skin. He stabbed with the knife, what little good it did him.

To that point it had been a quiet fight. There had been banging and crashing and furniture breaking, but neither of the men had said much beyond breathing and grunts of exertion. No shouted threats. No angry swearing.

Until the boot came down on his wrist.

"Motherfucker," Cooker yelled, followed by a guttural roar. He struggled to hold on to the knife. Which was a mistake, because it only made the boot come down a second, more destructive time. That's on me, Cooker thought and let his fingers go slack, the knife falling to the ground.

"Do. Not. Move," Ricky said, panting for air. He put his big arm onto his thigh, bending over and catching his breath.

Cooker decided that not moving was a good idea. Not moving hurt less than moving. He closed his eyes and tilted his head back, tasting the blood in the back of his throat. Some might say that it tasted like defeat, but Cooker liked the rare-steak taste. It was the losing that he hated.

Harry stopped as he reached for the knob on the front door of his trailer. He stopped because the knob wasn't there, only a jagged hole. He set the six-pack down and slowly entered.

Cooker was duct-taped to a chair. The chair appeared to be the only unbroken piece of furniture in his home. The table was on its side. His maps and books were everywhere, spines cracked and pages torn. Every surface had blood on it, including a Rorschach on the ceiling. Teeth were scattered across the ground. Interior decoration by way of the Manson Family.

Ricky sat on the kitchen counter holding a bag of frozen peas to his mouth. He nodded at Harry. "I got blood on your peas."

Harry turned his head back and forth from Ricky to Cooker in an effort to comprehend. He picked up one of the damaged books.

"These are library books," Harry said.

"We can tape together the worst ones," Ricky said. When he removed the bag of peas, Harry saw that his lip was shredded and swollen.

"What happened?"

"Guy busted into your place. Kicked the door in. When I found him, he had our gold. Was sitting on the ground, holding it, stealing it."

Harry turned to the biker. "Cooker? What the hell?"

"You know him?" Ricky asked.

"Yeah," Harry said softly, walking to the refrigerator.

Cooker remembered the head in the trash can. His body started to shake, but all Harry had in his hand when he closed the refrigerator door was a beer. Cooker breathed a sigh of relief.

"You got a smoke. I'm dying here," Cooker asked.

"Quit," Harry said.

Ricky pulled Harry toward him. "He knows about the gold. He saw all the maps. He told me that he knows how to get us there. Knows where it is. What we're doing. How would he know all that?"

"I talked to him."

"Without telling us? How do you know him?"

"He was a convict."

Ricky let out an angry laugh. "Why would you trust him?"

"I gave him a bullshit story. It was solid."

"Whatever you told him, it didn't work. Now he knows there's a mine. And where it is."

"You're a really bad liar," Cooker cut in.

"I'm a great liar," Harry shouted.

"Then why is he here?" Ricky asked.

Harry took a moment to think about the question. "What gave it away?" Harry asked Cooker, genuinely confused.

"You, Shits. Didn't matter what you said, I knew it was bullshit 'fore I heard a word. Liars lie. You're a fucking liar."

"You lie to everyone," Ricky reminded him.

"Yeah. You're right. Sorry, Ricky."

"What're we going to do with him? I couldn't figure it. That's why I tied him up. We had our secret, the three of us, now I don't know."

"We can't let him go," Harry agreed.

Harry opened the cabinet under the sink. Cooker watched him pull out the trash can. The three men looked at the dead man's head on top of the trash.

"I thought you were going to bury that," Ricky said.

"Shit on me," Cooker muttered.

"I'm going to," Harry said, setting his beer bottle to the side of the head, closing the cabinet.

"You should recycle that," Ricky said.

Cooker stuttered, tripping over his words. "I didn't see nothing. I don't know nothing. I made a mistake. I'll walk away."

"Don't think we can do that," Harry said.

"I'll help you. I know the terrain. I know military protocol," Cooker said.

"We don't need another partner."

Cooker was desperate. He had gotten greedy and walked into a clubhouse full of sickos. Only a couple of real psychos could look at a head in a garbage can with nonchalance. He was neck-deep in shit. He had to think through how to get out of that fucking trailer alive.

"You don't need to kill me. Killing me would be a mistake." One of Cooker's legs shook uncontrollably.

Harry and Ricky looked at each other. They both laughed a little. Whether nervousness or discomfort, they both simultaneously found it funny that the idea of killing Cooker would come from Cooker himself. The thought of killing him hadn't occurred to either of them.

Cooker went mute. Their laughter terrified him. A trickle of piss soaked his thigh.

"What are we going to do?" Harry said, staring up at the blood on the ceiling.

"Ask Frank."

TWENTY-SIX

"What hospital? For the love of all that is holy, for one second, quit your babbling and talk some sense," Harry demanded.

"You're mean," the high-pitched voice said on the other end of the phone.

"I haven't started, sweetie. You don't start giving me useful information, I'm going to tell you awful truths about Santa Claus, the Easter Bunny, and the Tooth Fairy."

Harry stood at the Blythe pay phone. A line had formed behind him, the nasty looks increasing with each second. He had spent the last five minutes and a pocketful of change gleaning from Frank's five-year-old great-granddaughter that Frank had been taken to a hospital. He didn't know the why, the where, the when, or the what for.

"I have to potty." The voice turned insistent.

"Yeah, so do I, but I ain't announcing it. Let's try again. Is your mother, father, anyone over five there? They couldn't've left you by yourself. Unless they were hoping you'd run off or try to juggle the cutlery, which wouldn't shock me. Who's looking after you?"

"Got to go."

"No. Don't," Harry shouted.

But the sound of the receiver plonking onto a table was her answer. Harry softly banged his head against the wall next to the pay phone as he waited impatiently for the little demon to return. He briefly turned, catching the dirty looks from the people in line behind him. The best he could do was shrug.

It was a long three minutes. She must have really had to piss. The guy with the teardrop tattoo who was next in line shoved him hard in the shoulder, knocking him off-balance. He didn't say a word, but the message was clear.

"Hello?" The little voice was back. She might have only been five, but Harry was sure that she was dumb for her age. He'd had more thought-provoking conversations with fresh turds.

"Thank God. I'm still here. Can I talk to a grown-up?"

"Bye-bye." She hung up.

Harry squeezed the receiver and listened to the muted dial tone. He wished he had the strength to crush it.

"Kids," Harry said and set the receiver in the cradle. He turned and gave Teardrop Tattoo a hard look. Teardrop Tattoo punched him in the stomach out of principle. Harry nodded in agreement and limped back on his crutches toward Desert Vista.

"Frank's in the hospital," Harry reported to Ricky. "What happened?"

"I don't know."

"Is he okay?"

"I don't know."

"What hospital?"

"I don't know. Frank. Hospital. That's all I got."

"Who is Frank?" Cooker asked.

Both Harry and Ricky turned to him. "Shut up."

Ricky paced in the confined area. "I don't know if they got a hospital in Poston. Probably take him to the one in Parker. The rez one."

Harry said, "We can't leave Cooker alone. Take the keys. I'll watch him. I got to clean this mess."

Ricky looked at the keys in Harry's outstretched hand. "I don't drive, Harry."

Harry was about to ask but caught himself. He knew why.

"Right. I got it. I'll bring my books with me. Catch some pages in the waiting room. And if jerko gives you any trouble, gag him."

Hospital rooms were jail cells for old people. The nurses were the guards. The doctor, the warden. Your malady was your sentence. If only Frank could figure out where to dig the tunnel.

Frank didn't like the beds or the pillows. The nurses were okay, but the doctors drove him halfway to apeshit and back. The TV only got XHBC-TV Canal Tres from Mexicali, and between the grown men in childish costumes, the insane cleavage, and the accordion music, he couldn't watch more than a half hour without his brain turning to oatmeal. The guy in the bed next to him was worse off than him. The poor bastard couldn't talk. Instead he made noises that sounded like a duck trying to fuck a whoopee cushion.

The only thing he couldn't complain about was how he felt. In fact, he felt better than he had in a long time. It might have been the drugs. Despite his episode, he didn't feel any more tired than any given day of being an old man. They told him they had a few more tests to run. And after those tests, they told him they had a few more tests. And a few more. A little blood here. A hookup to a machine there. More tests. Monotonous and pointless.

Frank stared at the ceiling. He did the math. It wasn't college calculus. It was simple pluses and minuses. His age was staring him down, and between the cancer and his heart, it was a matter of time before some part of his body quit. Optimism, pessimism, it didn't matter. The machinery was grinding down. He put the over-under at a year. He wasn't sure he was ready. Or ever would be.

"I'd say you're goldbricking, but considering our plans, that would suggest you were actually being productive."

Frank gave Harry a weak smile.

"I drove all over hell looking for you. You know how hard it is to drive with a cast on? Got to drape it over and work the pedals with my left. Pinched a ball when I made a U-turn. Thought you'd be in Parker or the rez. Ended up, I could have walked. Talked to your daughter out in the waiting room. She's a piece of work, that one."

"Don't mess with Mercedes. No joke. She punishes."

"I kind of got that. Wanted to know who I was, how I knew you, why I been calling, and why she never met me before. She grilled me, man. Like a verbal strip search. I told her we were in a book club together. If she asks, we're reading Franzen."

"You are the worst goddamn liar."

"Why does everyone keep saying that?"

"Don't underestimate Mercedes. Moment you turn your back, that's when the tomahawk flies. *Ker-chunk*, right between your shoulder blades."

"We got us a real problem."

"My heart exploded and we have *real* problems?"

"Oh yeah. Sorry, Frank. How you doing? You look fine to me. I mean, as well as a dude as old as you can."

"I'll live. Tell me what you assed up."

Harry took offense that Frank immediately assumed it was something he had done. But considering that it had started with something he had done, he let it go. Harry gave Frank the rundown: his meeting with Cooker, Ricky's battle royale in the trailer, and the problem in miniature biker leather that was tied to Harry's only unbroken chair.

"You don't got many options," Frank said.

"Yeah, I know."

"Can't leave him tied up. Can't let him go. Can't trust him."

"Yeah," Harry said, "I'll do it. I'll kill him."

"Whoa," Frank said. "You jumped to that quick."

"Not so quick. Came to me when I was driving around."

Frank didn't saying anything. He didn't nod or shake his head.

"I'm not saying it's right. Or I want to. But it's what we got. The best solution," Harry said.

Frank held his stare.

"It's our gold," Harry said.

"That's a big decision. Can't take it back," Frank finally said.

"Fucking hell," Harry said, suddenly exhausted.

"You said it."

Harry grabbed a chair and set it next to Frank's bed.

"I didn't bring you nothing this time. Been thinking so much on the gold and this Cooker thing, forgot to bring you a gift. You're in the hospital, you're supposed to get flowers or something. Want me to grab you a burger? Some tamales? Food can't be any good in this dump. I got more girlie mags. Big stack of Mexican newsstand swag. Couple of them so filthy—weird and hairy—I can't look at them no more. But you may like 'em."

"Thanks. I'm good. But if you want to stay for a bit, I'd like that."

Harry nodded.

"The Go Go Gophers come by? If not, I could sneak you some, you know." Harry made the universal symbol for pot by putting his pinched fingers to his pursed lips.

"I'm an old man in a hospital in California. All I need is a prescription."

Harry nodded. They listened to the disgustingly cartoony sounds of Frank's bunkmate.

After a long silence, Harry said, "I'll take care of the problem. I'll take care of it."

"You sure about this?"

"No, but there's no other way I can think of."

TWENTY-SEVEN

"That's my gold. Mine. And no one, not some leather-daddy midget, some Keebler convict, some criminalizing scumsack, is going to stand in the way of my gold."

The slurring, low-rent halftime speech had been frothing from Harry's mouth for the better part of a half hour as he paced in front of his trailer. Paced might be a strong word. It was more of a crazy arc caused by his cast. Through a dry mouth, Harry kept up the banter, hoping that he would eventually forget what the words actually meant.

Harry had sent Ricky down to the hospital to visit Frank. He knew the kid would never go along with murder, not even of a lowlife like Cooker. Easiest way to avoid the conversation was to have it after the fact. Asking Ricky to bury a body was easier than asking him to kill a guy.

Harry took another swig from the paper-sacked bottle of scotch. The more booze he drank, the more the argument made sense. Leave it to alcohol to streamline debate.

"You can do this, Harry. People die every day. This guy is a garbage. What do you do with a garbage? You put it in a bag and leave it on the curb. He's a drug dealer. A scourge. I can make the world a better place. For the world. For me. For Frank. For Ricky. For everyone. He's got to go. So shut your mouth, Harry, and do it already."

Inside the trailer Cooker could only hear snippets of the one-man conversation happening outside. He didn't have to hear much more than the constant repetition of *kill, gold,* and *scum-sack* to know which direction the wind blew. Right up his ass.

He pulled at the tape that bound his wrists, but the kid had used the whole fucking roll. He wasn't going anywhere. He was fucked and he knew it. It was time to prepare for the end.

Cooker's eyes drifted to the cabinet under the sink where that weird, soapy head sat covered in beer bottles and fast-food wrappers. He didn't want to think about what this sick fuck did with the bodies of the poor bastards he killed. He hoped he didn't fuck them. Cooker had avoided losing his ass virginity in the orphanage, military service, and prison, but there was no way of defending his ass after death. It made him sad that this psycho might pluck that flower.

The ranting stopped outside. Cooker closed his eyes to listen. Had Shitburger gone away? What was happening?

The door opened slowly and Harry entered. He kept his eyes to the ground.

"This is it," Harry said.

"Fuck me."

Harry pulled a samurai sword from his closet. He ran his thumb along the blade, yanking it back when it drew blood. He tasted it.

"Salty."

"He's going to what?"

Ricky stood up from the chair next to Frank's hospital bed. His arm got caught in an IV tube, but he managed untangle himself before he ripped it from Frank's body. Frank put his hand on Ricky's arm. He had no grip, but the contact was enough to freeze Ricky.

Frank spoke slowly. "Stay here, Ricky. Nothing for you to get involved in."

"We're in this together. All of us."

"Yes and no, kid. Yes and no."

"What does that mean? I have to stop him."

Frank took a look at the clock on the wall. "Ain't the kind of thing you dilly-dally with. Either done it or he's never going to. Both ways, it's best you stay."

Ricky gently removed Frank's hand from his arm and moved toward the door.

"You shouldn't have let him," Ricky said.

"Come back in here and sit the hell down," Frank said, loud and stern.

Frank's voice was so commanding that it didn't occur to Ricky that there was an alternative to obedience.

"Harry brought this guy in. He made the mistake. He created the problem and he needed to fix it. Maybe it's wrong. Hell, of course it's wrong. But this is our chance. I got no doubt about that. Dumb a plan as we got, we have to see it through. And no matter where it takes us, there's something you got to remember."

"What?" Ricky leaned in.

"Harry is an idiot. Nothing against him as a friend, but he's a goddamn moron. For all the work he's done, for as far as we've got, his ideas are the stupidest I've ever heard. Follow him too close, he's going to stupid you into deep trouble."

"He kills that guy, we can't erase that."

"That's why you have to let him go through with it."

"That doesn't make any kind of sense."

"That wouldn't surprise me. I kind of got lost in the conversation back there. We're talking about Harry and the guy, yeah? I'm on a few painkillers. Have been all day."

"I'm going."

"Let him do it. On his own. That's what I'm saying. When Harry decides to do stupid, you have to let it be Harry's stupid. You have to step back."

"You don't let friends make those kinds of mistakes. This isn't just a law he's breaking. It's a commandment."

"Unless you have a better idea of what to do with this fella, I don't see another choice. Think about your family. That's what's at stake. We got to do what's necessary to get the three of us up those mountains."

"You can't be serious. You're not going anywhere. Look at you. You really think you're in any kind of shape for this trip?"

"I'm going."

"I thought Harry was the moron? And his plan was stupid?"

"He is. It is. But it's one thing to follow. It's another thing to go along. I ain't going to pretend what Harry's doing ain't the right thing. All I'm saying is that we ain't the ones doing it. His mess, his cleanup."

Ricky said nothing, the gears turning in his head.

"I don't know what they got me on, but it's some good shit. What were we talking about? I'm so high."

"There's another way." Ricky took off in a run out the door.

"Please. Let me confess. Listen to my confession."

"Don't make this harder, man. Do I look like a priest? Take a minute. Say your confessing to yourself. I'll give you time."

Harry gripped the sword in both hands, holding it front of his body. Every couple of seconds, he took a practice swing, stopping inches from Cooker's neck. Cooker flinched, his eyes and pants wet.

"Please. Please don't do that."

Harry rested the sword against his leg. "Yeah, right. Sorry. You want me to do a decent job, right? Have to take a few warm-up whacks. Practice swings are going to make it better for both of us."

"Thinking my confession in my head ain't enough. I got to say it. So it's official. Let me say it out loud."

"Yeah, okay. Show on the road." Harry leaned back and took a big swig.

Cooker sucked in snot through his nose, swallowed, and gathered his thoughts. He blinked the tears from his eyes.

"I could've lived better. Done less bad. When I was sixteen, I cut this guy up because he—you know what—I didn't have no reason. I done it because I fucked his sister and he was pissed. I didn't kill him but fucked him up solid. He came at me with a Wiffle bat. Like that could've hurt me. He didn't deserve it. Defending his little sister. She wasn't no more than fifteen. That same year, I cooked up my first batch."

"I don't got all day for your autobiography, okay. I ain't making no documentary movie. Hit the highlight reel."

Cooker broke down crying. "I don't want to die. Don't kill me. Please don't kill me."

"No begging. Here's the best I can do, give you two more sins to talk out, then the confessing is all done. We call it. And no long stories, just the goods."

Cooker nodded, unable to speak, only capable of making spit bubbles from his trembling lips. Finally, he said, "If I only got two, they got to be good."

Harry nodded and set a beer bottle on the counter. As Cooker thought, Harry tried to slice the bottle in half with the sword, but only ended up batting it across the trailer with a loud crash.

Cooker winced at the noise. "Okay. This one time, this trannie blew me and I knew it was a trannie. Like not in the middle, but like before it even started, like the whole time. And this wasn't inside, in prison, where, you know, that don't count. This was at my niece's birthday party in the bathroom. I think it was like the clown's assistant or roadie or whatever. Does that make me gay? It was only mouth sex."

"Of all the stuff you must've done, you picked that? Not really a confession even. More of a clarification. If it was just the mouth, you're cool. We've all been there. Doesn't count, not official. Last one."

"Yeah, the last one. It's bad."

Harry waited, looking at the cut on his thumb.

"I killed a guy for no reason. I was twenty-three. Didn't know him. Didn't rob him. It was late at night. We were the only two people out. Walking. Dark. I saw him and knew I could get away with it, so I did it."

Contemplating murder himself, Harry grew more interested. "How'd you do it?"

"Knife. In the stomach. Over and over and over. Until my whole hand was in his guts. Until my arm was red to the elbow. I think about it and it don't make sense. I'm not that guy, but I am that guy. I did that thing. I was tweaking, but that's no excuse, you know? I don't think he was going to cure cancer or nothing like that, some Mexican, but maybe he had a family."

Harry exhaled loudly. "That's messed up. Least you've made this easier for me. It's go time. If it's any consolation, I forgive you."

Cooker nodded. The confession had given him a level of acceptance that he didn't even know he had in him.

Harry held the sword to Cooker's neck, the cold steel making a sandpapery sound on his neck stubble.

As Harry cocked the sword back over his shoulder, the door swung open with a loud crash. The surprise was enough for Harry to lose his grip during the backswing, sending the sword flying behind him.

Ricky stood in the doorway, his eyes cartoon-wide on the twanging sword stuck in the door, inches from his head.

"Are you out of your mind?" Harry yelled.

"I came to stop you," Ricky said, in mild shock. "I got a better idea."

TWENTY-EIGHT

"Here's the deal. Your granddaddy said you're supposed to watch this fella like you did Ricky. Keep him alive, sober, out of trouble. He'll talk like he don't belong, but you know tweakers. Lies and pity and cowcrap. If you need to, gag him."

Bernardo and Ramón leaned on their shovels, listening to Harry. They appeared to be digging some kind of canal in the front of their property. They were shiny with sweat and red from their natural coloration and too much sun. If one of them held a lace-bodiced woman by the waist, he would be camera-ready for a romance novel cover.

Cooker sat in the front seat of Harry's car. Twitchy and scared, he didn't like the looks of those Indians. For all he knew, the two savages were digging a mass grave.

Ricky sat in the backseat, an eye on Cooker. The dogs barked. He placed a hand on Cooker's shoulder. Cooker jumped. Ricky said, "I hope you like dogs."

"How long do we keep him?" Bernardo asked.

"Until Frank says, I guess. I'm just the messenger. He asked me to drive the guy up here. You been to see Frank yet?"

"Today, maybe. I sent a card and a bouquet of dahlias."

"We. We sent them," Ramón cut in.

"Those are the big, alieny flowers, right? I like those."

Bernardo climbed out of the long hole and dusted himself off, kicking up a thick cloud.

Harry walked to the car and helped Cooker out. He practically had to drag him. Not because he was resistant, but his legs had gone limp from fear. Ramón climbed out of the trench to join them.

Harry said, "If you want, put him to work. He doesn't look like much, but he's wiry strong. Help dig your ditch."

"It is a moat."

"Like around a castle?"

"Yes. Better than a fence. When it is done, we will line the bottom with barbed wire, broken glass, and punji sticks covered in dogshit and Saran Wrap. Then we will fill it with water. Our compound will be impenetrable."

"And piranha fish," Ramón added.

Bernardo rolled his eyes and whispered loudly to Harry, "I joked about piranha, and now he has it in his head. Piranha would be ridiculous."

Harry kept his mouth shut and nodded. He turned to Cooker. "You're staying here. Keep quiet. This could have gone another way, but it didn't. This thing ends right, may even be a payday for you."

Cooker looked at the two big Indians and nodded.

Bernardo grabbed Cooker by the arm and threw him in the hole. Cooker landed awkwardly, twisting his ankle. He looked up confused and had to sidestep the shovel that landed in the dirt between his feet.

"Kind of rough on him," Harry said.

"But alive. That is our only promise. If we are slow to make it down the hill, tell Papa Frank that his friend is safe. We will make him very strong."

It took Bernardo and Ramón three days to finally get down the hill. The moat had consumed them. With the extra labor, they saw the opportunity to exceed their initial completion date. The little biker was a good digger and Ramón was happy. It was the biker, not him, smearing dogshit on the punji sticks.

When they were done, Bernardo and Ramón stood on their roof and marveled at their work. They both agreed that their moat was awesome.

Cooker was happy to be done and back on his mattress surrounded by the dogs. He assumed he had been fired from Denny's by now and his parole officer had made the bad call. He was a wanted man. But every time he thought about that sword to his neck or that head in the trash, he felt lucky. What had they done to make it all snotty like that? How long had they been killing? Why had those sick fucks removed the teeth?

When Bernardo and Ramón finally visited the hospital, Frank wasn't there. According to the hospital staff, he was in room fourteen, bed two. But when they went to the room, he was gone. He hadn't checked out. He hadn't been cleared by a doctor. He had vanished.

Too high to deal with hospital bureaucracy, Bernardo and Ramón did the only thing that made sense. They sparked another blunt in the parking lot, called their mother, and waited for the storm to come to them.

It had been surprisingly easy getting Frank out of the hospital. One switched chart, a change of clothes, and Ricky, Harry, and Frank walked out the front entrance. The glass door even opened for them automatically, as if the building approved of their mission. With Ricky's bad arm and Harry's leg in a cast, Frank actually looked the healthiest of the three of them.

Ricky had been against it. Frank was sick. Frank needed care. Frank needed medicine. He did not need to go. Having him along would make it more difficult. However, in the end, it had been Frank that convinced Ricky.

"I've had it with people taking care of me. People that mean well, but don't bother to ask what I want. Like I'm some child that needs protection. You're asking what I want? I'm telling you. I want to find our gold. And if I die in the mountains, then that's where I die. On my terms. In my way."

Harry took Frank's side immediately, laying out his theories about how apart they were a disaster, but when they were together everything worked. How they were all a part of the same destiny. The three of them were meant to find that gold. Together. Everything had gelled to make it happen. Leaving Frank would be like spitting in fate's face.

Frank was tough. Frank was an Indian. Frank's health wasn't an issue. There was no doubt in Harry's mind that Frank would live to walk into the Big Maria Mine. And walk out with their gold. It was simply their destiny.

Mercedes did not take the information that her father was missing calmly. Her baritone echoed through the halls of the hospital. The nurse at the receiving end tried to stay professional, but the onslaught was unrelenting. None of the witnesses could remember hearing Mercedes inhale. She was all exhale and volume and spit. The poor nurse's crying could barely be heard over the cyclone of words and accusations.

"He is an old man. An old man with a heart condition. A heart condition and cancer. How is it possible that you could lose him? Are you the idiot in charge? The idiot that may have killed my father through your negligence? Or is there a different idiot I should be yelling at?" And it went on and on.

The other nurses came to their colleague's aid. But their numbers only aggravated Mercedes more. Her volume grew and the expression of her outrage shifted to the physical. The head nurse called the police when Mercedes repeatedly kicked a drinking fountain until it disconnected from the wall, shooting water in a horizontal stream across the waiting room.

Bernardo and Ramón knew what came next. They had seen this movie before. They ducked out without any guilt. Abandoning their mother was the responsible thing to do. Someone had to pay her bail.

It took five cops and a few sore groins to wrestle Mercedes to the ground. Her low center of gravity challenged them as much as her surprising hand speed. But even pinned, it wasn't until they cheated by using a Taser that the big woman was subdued.

TWENTY-NINE

Harry would have liked more prep time. But with Cooker under wraps and Frank on the lam, the sooner they hit the trail the better.

It didn't really matter. All the time in the world and they would still be ridiculously unprepared. For starters, none of them were physically ready for the twenty-plus-mile hike. Maybe Ricky. Harry figured that what they lacked in strength and stamina, they made up for in sheer will. That would have to be enough.

Frank tried to help load, but it quickly took too much out of him. So while Frank napped in Harry's trailer, Harry and Ricky loaded the car with all the equipment and provisions that they could scrounge in the limited time. Cases of water and beer filled the backseat. Food raided from the nearest convenience store: beef jerky, Slim Jims, sunflower seeds, CornNuts, bags of chips, Fiddle Faddle, Hostess fruit pies, and a variety of Little Debbie snacks. Camping gear, a tent, flashlights, sleeping bags, and pillows were tied to the roof.

Harry loaded his bag of books and personal items. Even though he wasn't planning on mining, he brought a book along just in case, *Gold Mining and You* by Rufus Blankenship, copyright 1957. It was part of the Junior Woodsmen series, some off-brand Cub Scout rip-off. One of those groups that taught kids good manners, civics lessons, and survival skills for when the bombs finally fell. Harry had never heard of the Junior Woodsmen, although their logo of a Tonto-esque Indian wrestling (rasslin'?) a bear was vaguely familiar. The Indian and the bear weren't just mascots, they also acted as the instructors throughout the book, walking the reader through the easy-to-follow steps to finding gold, although it appeared that the bear did more work than the Indian, who was basically a loafer.

"How are we going to carry all this stuff?" Ricky asked, staring at the overflowing backseat, trunk, and roof.

"I got it covered," Harry said. "Soon as Frank is up to it, we'll pick up the boat."

"Another boat?"

"There ain't any bridges over the Colorado this far north and no roads on the Arizona side that go near where we need to be. We have to take a boat over the river and then hoof it the rest of the way. The river will be the easy part."

Mercedes sat in the holding cell angrier than she had been in a very long time. It felt good.

Everyone has a neutral emotional state. Some people are happy until tragedy befalls them. When the tragedy passes, they return to their natural state of happiness. It's like a default setting. There are happy people and unhappy people. Nice people and assholes. Everyone has a gear they idle in.

Mercedes's neutral state was nowhere near neutral, closer to wrath. She was naturally angry, even if she had spent the last thirty years attempting to suppress it. A volcano building up pressure. A force of nature that could destroy the village below at any moment. In that jail cell, she was dangerously close to another eruption. She was about to go Vesuvius on anyone who got in her way.

She knew the cops were just doing their job. She had trashed the hospital waiting room and goaded them into a fight. But fuck them. Pigs and their power. Fucking hair-pullers, Tasering a lady.

Mercedes preferred Tasers over pepper spray. They might hurt more, but the effects didn't last as long. And you got that weird sexual high from the tingly feeling it left throughout your skin and body. Mace and pepper spray were just annoying.

In her younger, wilder days with the Native American Insurgents for Liberty & Sodality (NAILS), Mercedes had always looked forward to that moment when the pigs arrived at their protests. They would adjust their riot gear and Nazi-walk toward the protesters, batons at the ready. No interest in a fair fight. Just a beat-down they could jerk off to later.

She loved a good fight. It's the whole reason she had joined the movement. She couldn't care less about saving tribal land or better education for Indians or any of that crap. She loved the protesting and the yelling and the fighting and the passion. And the pissed-off-ness. It was the only time she felt liberated.

It had been a long time. She was fifty-two and felt it. After her deadbeat husband disappeared, she was forced to work three jobs to support the boys, sidelining her from any real action. By the time the boys were grown and she had put some money away, the coalition had disbanded and violent protests had gone the way of rotary phones. The complete lack of passion that the eighties and nineties brought, took whatever rage she had left and jammed it deep down. Protests had become nothing but slogans, body paint, and drum circles. She missed the fighting.

Sitting in the cell with little else to do, she thought of the good times. The picket-turned-riot down by Indian Wells over some forgotten land dispute. She broke two ribs there. It still felt worth it as she vividly remembered that rock hitting that pig's face. The UFW strikes in the Imperial Valley when Chavez was at his best. It was a shame that nobody hit scabs with bats anymore. Then there was the sit-in to protest breaking ground for the new prison. That was the time the cop tried to fuck her in the back of the wagon but ended up with a ballpoint pen sticking in his left testicle. It went in like a meat thermometer into raw turkey. She almost started celebrating Thanksgiving to annually relive that stabbing, but as a Native American she just couldn't do it.

Bernardo and Ramón considered leaving their mother in jail. They discussed it. They even made one of those lists that had the pros on one side and the cons on the other. It was close. The cons actually won, but her being their mother and what she'd do when she eventually got out was like a triple pro. They decided to post bail but weren't in any hurry to do so.

Less high, they were better prepared to find out what had happened to Papa Frank. Through a best-of-nineteen series of rock-paper-scissors, Ramón was chosen as the spokesman. He sheepishly walked to the nurses' station, eyes at his feet.

"Excuse me, ma'am," he said, just above a whisper. Women made him nervous, and pretty women even more. The nurse at the desk was a stunningly beautiful black woman.

"Take a number and a clipboard. Fill it out front and back. A doctor will see you as soon as possible," the young nurse said without looking away from her computer screen.

"Excuse me, ma'am," he repeated.

The nurse made a show of it: huge exhale, slow head-turn, dark eyes staring at Ramón, an exhausted "Yes?"

"I do not know if you were here earlier. There was some trouble."

"I wasn't here, but I heard. I'm busy."

"My mother lost her shit. That was my mother. She is in jail now. We are safe."

The woman stared at him, communicating her complete disinterest.

"This is not about her, my mother. She scares me also. But about my grandfather."

"Are you anywhere near the point? Or are we going to go through your whole family tree back to Hiawatha?"

"I do not think we are related. My grandfather was the reason for my mother's explosion. I am not a good explainer. You, the hospital, lost my grandfather. He was here. Now he is not."

She held her stare and then rolled her eyes. "His name?"

"Frank Pacheco." Ramón spelled the last name.

The nurse typed into her computer. Her fingers moved so fast on the keyboard that Ramón was pretty sure she typed nonsense. Women always found ways to get rid of him.

"Mr. Pacheco? He never checked out."

"Yes. He did not check out, but he is also not here."

"Are you sure he's not here?"

"Yes. That was the cause of the commotion," Ramón said.

"Give me one second." The nurse picked up the phone and punched in two numbers. She gave him the world's fakest smile and turned away. Ramón looked back at Bernardo, who gave him an approving nod. When he turned back to the nurse, she had completed the call and was hanging up the phone.

The nurse said, "That was the nurse that works the morning desk. She remembered seeing Mr. Pacheco leave."

"She let him leave?"

"Hospital checkouts are done through billing. She assumed he had taken care of everything. This is not a jail."

"Where did he go?"

"How should I know? Molly said he left with a fat guy in a leg cast and a bodybuilder-type guy with a weird arm. I don't know what that means—a weird arm? Said they made a memorable, funky trio."

"Thank you for your help."

She shrugged.

"You are very beautiful. I love you," Ramón awkwardly yelled and sprinted out the door before she could react.

Bail was set at one thousand dollars. Bernardo and Ramón dumped a pile of crumpled bills on the counter and let the policeman count it. After five minutes of cursing and flattening bills, they were fourteen dollars short. Ramón dropped to the floor, took off his boot, and dug inside. He threw a damp emergency twenty on top of the pile.

The cop took the money and had Bernardo sign some paperwork. He gave him a carbon copy receipt. "You'll need to bring that to the hearing."

"You owe six dollars," Bernardo said.

"What?"

"You needed fourteen more dollars. We added twenty dollars. You owe six dollars."

The policeman paused for a moment and then smiled. "You're absolutely right." He took a five and a one out of the stack of cash. He pointed behind them to the four folding chairs that pretended to be a waiting room. "It'll take about an hour to process the prisoner out. There used to be magazines, but people stole them."

Bernardo and Ramón sat down. Waiting was something they were good at.

THIRTY

It was a bigger boat than the one they had used for the dive. Ricky took Harry's word when he said it was a pontoon boat. Sounded right to him, but he didn't know anything about boats. Ricky wished he knew more things. He didn't think he was stupid. He knew enough of whatever he was doing to get that thing done, but knowing more would be better.

Frank watched Harry and Ricky load the equipment and provisions. His energy and color were better after his nap, but he decided not to push it.

Harry laid it out. "Okay, Ricky. Here's how we do it. You're going to take the boat downriver. We're going to meet you just past Martinez Lake. Frank and I got to pick up the burros."

"I ain't never drove a boat," Ricky said.

"Just like a car," Harry said, then remembered Ricky's thing about driving. "Forget that. Nothing like a car. You'll love it. You and the river. Like Huck Finn."

"Never saw that movie."

"It's a…never mind. Easiest thing in the world. Left, right. Fast, slow. Follow the flow of the water."

"Where do I take it?"

"That's the spirit." Harry set the last of the beer into the boat. He found his backpack and pulled out a map.

"They built a moat," Frank said. "A goddamn moat." Frank and Harry stood in front of Harry's car, hands on their hips, staring at Bernardo and Ramón's new fortification. The moat was six feet wide and ran around the property without a break. Brown water filled the seemingly bottomless construction, a hose feeding a continual stream of water into the makeshift lagoon. The air was thick with mosquitoes and smelled like a septic tank.

"Didn't think they would finish it so fast," Harry said. He kicked a rock into the water. It disappeared in the murk. "Them two braves need to find a couple of squaws."

He walked to his car, leaned into the open window, and honked the horn for the third time.

"I don't think no one's home," Harry said.

"Where's the damn drawbridge?" Frank said.

Harry kneeled and examined the ground. "There's tire tracks going to the edge. Look here. The tracks keep going on the other side. Maybe put boards down and drove on them."

"I'll check this side," Frank said, walking to the edge of the dirt road and scanning the scrub. He kicked at the brush.

Harry searched his side of the road. He yelled back to Frank over his shoulder. "The Gophers going to be pissed we did this without asking? Without them here?"

"Nothing we can do about that. Don't know why they got them burros anyhow. Never let them out. They like feeding them carrots and apples. But other than that, they don't use them for nothing."

"People get attached to their pets."

"I'll leave a note. So they don't think they got stole."

Harry waved Frank over. "Found 'em. There're a couple of thick boards. Under some palm fronds. Look heavy as hell."

"I love my grandsons, but they're children."

The two men dragged one of the thick boards to the edge of the moat. Their first effort to slide it to the other side failed miserably. As the board extended farther, they couldn't handle the weight and the end dropped into the water.

Draining most of their effort, they pulled it back and tried it again. Only faster.

The same result. Only faster. The farther they pushed it out, the heavier it got, and eventually it fell in the water.

"What the hell?" Harry said.

"Maybe one of us has to get in the water. Walk it over."

"Not happening. They were talking about putting glass and booby traps and poo down there."

Frank and Harry leaned their butts on the hood of the car and stared at the moat and boards like they were parts of an ancient riddle. Solve the mystic puzzle and the hidden treasure would be yours.

"It's something simple. Those boys ain't Einsteins," Frank said, pushing himself off the hood of the car. "Come over here. Stand the board on its end."

Harry walked up one of the boards, lifting it until it stood straight in the air. He braced his body against it to keep it from tipping.

"Let it drop. It's long enough. It'll land on the other side."

Harry let go, giving it a soft push in the right direction. The other end of the board landed on the opposite bank of the moat. It bounced but settled, spanning the water. Harry pushed the end of the board until it was straight.

"Nice think-job. Let's get the other one and get this done," Harry said.

Frank leaned in the window of the car. Harry gripped the steering wheel and stared at the moat and the two boards.

Harry said, "I'm not feeling good about this. They couldn't've invested in some wider boards? No wiggle room. I go in the water, I'm going to freak out. The smell is bad enough."

"You're not going in the water. You told me yourself. This gold is your destiny or fate or whatever the hell. This is another test to see if you turn back, but we're only going forward. So quit your menstruating and pull the tampon out. I'll guide you across."

Frank walked across one of the boards to the other side. He gestured for Harry to drive forward.

Harry hit the gas lightly. Frank waved, a little to the left. Harry made the adjustment. Frank gestured forward. The front tires hit the boards. Harry's balls retracted into his body. Frank kept waving him forward. The old man crouched low, hands on knees, looking at the back tires. Harry's car crawled forward.

When the back tires climbed onto the board, he felt the dip of the wood. Inching over the moat, Harry glanced down at the water. He could just make out the sharpened sticks through the swampy water. He could taste the thick stench in his mouth.

After what seemed like forever, Harry felt the back tires drop off the board. He was across. He took a deep breath, having forgotten to breathe on the short drive.

"What'd I tell you?" Frank gave Harry a light punch in the arm through the open window.

"It's going to be a hell of a lot trickier with a horse trailer hitched to the back."

"We'll cross that moat when we get to it," Frank said, walking toward the main house.

Cooker heard the car engine. And then voices. And then footsteps. It didn't sound like the Indians. Had someone come to rescue him? He had been in the room for days with the three dogs. Cooker was starting to wonder if the big Indians had abandoned him now that the work on their moat was complete.

They had worked him like a Mexican. Fourteen-hour days. His hands and feet were blistered and his skin cracked from the sun. He never wanted to see another shovel, taco, or dog again.

The door swung open and an old man walked in. The dogs turned but didn't get up. Cooker spoke through the dry gravel in his throat. "Be careful. These dogs are fucking vicious. One of them bit my leg just because. You got a gun? You may need to shoot them to get me out of here."

The old man ignored him. One of the dogs ambled over to the old man. Frank petted its head and said, "Good boy, Tuco."

"Fuck," Cooker said. "I'm still fucked, aren't I?"

Frank turned to him. "You're lucky, son. Burying you in the desert would've been easier."

"Go to hell, old man."

"On my way. Tell the boys I took their two burros and horse trailer. Bring them back in a week, give or take. You got that?"

"I'm not your message boy. Why should I help you?"

Frank leaned down and whispered something into Tuco's dog ear. Tuco turned to Cooker, a growl rising from deep within.

Cooker's leg started shaking without his say-so.

"Will you please deliver my message?" Frank asked calmly.

"You're taking their burros. Be like a week or so. Got it."

Frank took a key off a hook and walked out. The dogs turned their attention back to Cooker. Tuco lifted his leg and pissed on the corner of Cooker's mattress.

THIRTY-ONE

Ricky turned off the engine and let the boat coast. The current was slow where the Colorado River widened to lake width. It was a beautiful day and with the engine off, the only sound was the lapping of water against the side of the boat. Ricky closed his eyes and felt the heat of the sun on his face. Peace. Quiet. Nothingness.

He was tempted to forget the gold. Forget everything and take the boat south to Mexico and the Gulf of California and right out to the wide-open Pacific. The idea sounded nice at first, pure escape. But the more he thought about it, the less he wanted isolation. He'd had his share. His life was empty without Flavia and Rosie. He was on the road back to his family, even if it was a crazy, winding road.

Ricky opened his eyes and focused on the river. According to the GPS unit, his destination was ten miles away. He turned the engine back on and guided the craft forward, edging closer to the west bank.

Mercedes said nothing in the police station. She didn't say a word on the walk to the truck or the drive through town. Her silence made Bernardo and Ramón increasingly uncomfortable. They knew it wouldn't last. It would turn into something wrong. Just because you couldn't hear the ticking didn't mean the bomb wouldn't explode.

It wasn't until they were on the road to Poston that she finally spoke. Sitting between her two sons, Mercedes's voice was even but strained. "Thank you for bailing out your mother. I will return the money."

"You do not need to. When you have your court date, we get our moneys back," Bernardo said. "If you speak to the hospital. If you say, 'I am sorry,' and explain how they let Papa Frank walk out of there with those men, I am sure…"

Mercedes turned her head so quickly that Bernardo swerved. "Walked out with what men? Who men? What're you talking about?"

"I talked to a pretty woman at the hospital," Ramón said.

"I'm talking to your brother," Mercedes snapped. Ramón shrank from her voice. His immediate instinct was to jump from the moving vehicle. He got as far as his hand on the door handle but stopped himself.

Bernardo nodded. "He does not lie. Ramón talked to a woman. The black lady at the hospital told him. Papa Frank left with two men. We have met those men. They are his friends. Their names are Harry and Ricky."

"How do you know he wasn't taken against his will? He's a sick man."

Bernardo looked at her, not quite understanding. "Friends do not kidnap friends. They help each other. That is what makes them friends."

"Considering that your grandfather may be in danger, you seem pretty sure."

"He is in no danger."

"Bernardo," Ramón tried to cut in.

Bernardo continued, "Papa Frank will show up. I am sure. He was tired of the hospital. He knew you would not let him leave."

"Bernardo"—Ramón looked at Mercedes's clenched jaw and pleaded—"what are you doing?"

But Bernardo was on a roll. "Papa Frank is a grown man. He makes his own decisions. If he wants to go somewhere, he does not need your permission. We are all tired of you bossing us around."

"Oh, shit," Ramón said under his breath.

"Is that all you have to say, Bernardo?"

Bernardo nodded.

"Please pull over."

"Do it, Bernardo," Ramón said.

"Pull over," Mercedes repeated.

"We are almost home," Bernardo said.

"Pull over," Mercedes said, as if all other words had lost any meaning until those two were understood.

"No," Bernardo said.

"Why are you doing this, Bernardo?" Ramón sounded on the verge of tears.

"Pull over!" Mercedes and Ramón shouted in unison.

Bernardo stared straight ahead, pretending to ignore them. To emphasize his disinterest, he whistled the theme song to *The Muppet Show*.

"I am your mother. You will do what I say."

Bernardo closed his eyes. Luckily the road was straight and empty, because he didn't open them for twenty seconds or more. He spoke slowly and definitively. "I will drive you home. Then Ramón and me, we will go to our home. And we will wait to hear from Papa Frank."

Mercedes's face burned red. Her anger grew inside her. She had never hit her children, demanding obedience only through intimidation and fear. While she was known to attack authority figures and inanimate objects with hurricane-like destructive power, she had weaned herself off physical violence to kin long ago. She loved her boys and couldn't imagine striking them. Until that moment.

"Last time," she said slowly. "Pull. This. Truck. Over. Now."

"I will not," Bernardo said.

Bernardo knew he was digging deeper, but he couldn't stop himself. He had seen Harry and Ricky with Papa Frank. They acted like friends. They cared about each other. It showed. Their mother may have had a daughter's instinct to care about his health, but she never seemed to care about Papa Frank's happiness. Whatever he was doing, it was his choice. Bernardo needed to stand up for him in his absence.

A growl rose from deep inside Mercedes. It sounded like a purr at first and then an engine, and then something frighteningly inhuman.

"What is happening?" Ramón yelled.

Not having any recourse, not knowing what to do, and letting her rage completely devour her, Mercedes pounded her head into the dashboard, twice, in rapid succession. Her emotion numbed any pain, but the hard plastic did its damage. Ramón and Bernardo were so shocked that it took three sharp blows of head on car before they absorbed what was happening. Ramón bearhugged his mother, trying to pin her to the seat. She managed to get one more blow in before he subdued her.

Blood ran down her forehead. Her hair had fallen out of its ponytail, and some of it stuck to her face.

Her wail made Bernardo's skin prickle and his ears ring. Completely freaked out, Ramón screamed with her. Mercedes tried to continue her self-punishment, but Ramón held her tight against the seat.

Bernardo wanted to tune it out. He tried. But the yelling and crying and kicking and struggling in the seat next to him was too much. It sounded like a kindergarten class during an earthquake.

He let out an exasperated breath. His mother would always get her way. Her will was inescapable.

Bernardo pulled over to the side of the road.

THIRTY-TWO

Harry sat in his car, deeply concerned that things were going too smoothly. He knew there was supposed to be a point where the bad luck shifted to good, but he wasn't convinced that he had reached the top of that hill.

Getting the two burros into the horse trailer had been surprisingly simple. He had expected some struggle and got none. The burros seemed anxious to be out of their small corral, even if it was into the fresh confinement of the horse trailer.

But staring once again at the boards laid across the moat, Harry had second thoughts. What kind of asshole digs a moat anyway? The boards looked narrower. The moat looked wider. What would happen if one of the tires missed? If the car went into the water? Would he drown? Would he get crushed? Would he die instantly? Or would he survive, only to die of infection after several painful weeks?

Out of all the possible scenarios, there was only one good outcome (he got across) and so many bad ones (a shit-covered spear piercing his vital organs, for example). Everything wrong could happen, so little right. His life story. A crap game played with dice that only had ones and twos on them.

"I don't know if I can do this."

"We had this conversation," Frank said, leaning into the window of the car. "Destiny, all that. Second verse, same as the first."

"I don't know if my body will let me. My leg is shaking. My hands are froze to the wheel. My body, my brain is telling me not to. I'm having a freak-out here. Like a fear seizure or something. Like my body is rejecting me."

"Take a couple breaths."

Harry took three quick breaths. His wheeze sounded like a chain smoker in a Lamaze class. It did nothing to calm his nerves. He reached under the seat and pulled out a half-full bottle of bourbon.

"That's the stuff. Take a drink. A good gulp," Frank said.

Harry took a long pull. Drinking too fast, the bourbon went down the wrong tube. Harry sprayed liquor all over the windshield, the rest pouring down his chin and neck onto his shirt. He coughed, the back of his throat burning with booze and bile. His eyes watered, and heat rose to his face. It took him a solid minute to get the hacking under control. Even then, he felt like shit.

"You okay?" Frank asked.

"Went down the wrong way. Raped my lungs. Maybe it's a sign. The wrong way," Harry said.

"The hell. Sack up, Harry. The closer we get, the more you're going to want to back out. This is the easy part. Everything after is going to be a hell of a lot harder. You do this, you prove you're up for it. You don't get across that water, you don't deserve that gold. Quit acting the pansy, put on your man pants, and let's go."

Frank didn't wait for an answer. He turned and walked over one of the boards. At the other side, he motioned with his hands for the car to move forward.

Harry coughed one last cough and wiped his eyes with the back of his hand. He smeared some of the bourbon off the windshield, not improving his visibility. He reached into the glove compartment and rooted around. Papers, pens, a lighter, a spark plug, a half-eaten sandwich, an apple core, a glow-in-the-dark condom. Where was it?

His Saint Christopher medallion was stuck to a Jolly Rancher. He separated them and clutched the small pendant in his hand.

With hardly a conscious thought, Harry's foot lifted slowly off the brake and the car idled forward toward the moat.

"Nobody dies in a moat. That's not a way people die. Not anymore. Let's do this."

With Harry's maps and the preprogrammed GPS unit, Ricky found the pier easily. The weatherworn wooden structure looked like it had been unused for decades.

Maneuvering the boat against the pier proved to be a challenge, the back end of the boat (aft?) not quite doing what Ricky wanted. But he was in no hurry, so he took the opportunity to learn. On the fourth try, he guided the boat parallel to the pier.

He didn't know beyond squares and grannies, so he tied the boat with a bulky knot that looked like a monkey's shoelace.

After an hour of moving around some supplies, Ricky stretched out on the deck. There were no clouds, only brightness. He closed his eyes and enjoyed the red glow inside his eyelids. The warmth of the sun and the peaceful rocking of the boat made it impossible for him to stay awake. His sleep was fluid and graceful.

He couldn't remember the whole dream. He never remembered his dreams. If he was lucky, he retained scenes and images, but never the whole. He recalled a part of his dream where he was talking to an octopus-like creature with a bird's head. The creature held a candle. It wasn't scary. They were friends. It might have been a birthday candle. In the dream he was getting the creature's permission to go to a surprise party. He wondered what it meant. He didn't really believe dreams meant anything, but he had always liked how excited Flavia would get when he let her interpret his dreams. Maybe he would ask Harry.

He might have remembered more of the dream if he hadn't been jolted awake by a burro licking his face. When a gigantic tongue that smells like fermented cheese wakes you, you tend to lose all short-term memory. At first sight the elongated burro's face made no sense, making him unsure of what it was and what it meant.

The confusion led to momentary panic. Pure reaction. He punched the burro in the side of the head with a sweeping right hook.

Frank had the best vantage point. Everything happened fast, but like an umpire watching a bang-bang play at first base, his mind absorbed and replayed everything to interpret the details.

Minutes before, Frank and Harry had pulled up to the pier with the horse trailer. They saw Ricky sleeping on the deck and thought they'd have some fun. They quietly unloaded the burros—as quietly as one can unload a burro—and brought them over. The burros appeared curious about the boat. As one of them sniffed around, Harry gave it a little push from behind toward Ricky. That's when the donkey licked Ricky's face.

Ricky punched the donkey. The donkey reeled to the side and hoof-kicked Harry square in the nuts. That's what you get for standing behind a donkey. With an echoing scream, Harry flew backward off the pier and into the water. But the donkey wasn't done. It bit Ricky in the cheek. Ricky screamed and grabbed at the animal's face. Harry splashed in the water toward the pier. Frank pulled the burro's reins. Harry climbed onto the edge of the dock. The donkey stepped on Harry's hand. He fell back into the water. Finally, Frank got the donkey under control.

The quiet that followed was tense. Everyone waited for more, the inevitable aftershock after a big earthquake.

Ricky brought his hand to his cheek. The thick teeth of the donkey had done more squeezing than biting. It felt bruised, but the bite hadn't broken the skin.

Frank held the reins on both burros. They skittered on the pier but calmed to the point of control.

"Where's Harry?" Ricky asked. He had been too busy being bitten to hear the splash.

Frank smiled, pointing to Harry at the edge of the pier.

"Give me a hand. My cast is getting heavier," Harry yelled, his wary eyes on the donkey.

"How'd you get in the water?" Ricky asked.

"Stupid thing nutted me in the junk. My boys feel like bruised fruit, my stomach is queasy, and I think I broke my diddling finger."

Ricky and Frank burst out laughing. They knew they shouldn't, but they couldn't stop.

"Yeah, great. Hi-larious. Now will one of my so-called friends help me out of this swamp?"

THIRTY-THREE

"Tell me about the men that took Papa Frank," Mercedes demanded.

They were parked at the side of the road. The traffic was light, so they only got pelted with dust every couple minutes. The boys leaned against the side of their truck as their mother paced in front of them, a drill sergeant at inspection. A small furrow had formed on the ground from her pounding footsteps.

"I do not think they took him against his will," Bernardo said.

Mercedes stopped. "They're with him. They know where he's at. That's what matters. Who are they? Where do we find them?"

"The big one with the littler arm is Ricky," Bernardo said. "Papa Frank had us watch him. A problem with drink. He would not do harm to Papa Frank. Ricky owes him. He appears to be honorable."

"You can't trust a drunk. The other one?"

"Harry. He is not so honorable, a schemer, a planner. Very insensitive to our native heritage."

"He calls us the Go Go Gophers," Ramón cut in.

Mercedes shot Ramón a glance that made three drops of urine leak from his body.

Bernardo continued. "I do not like the one called Harry, but Papa Frank does. The three of them, they are friends. They were on a search. I do not know what for. We went in a boat. They dove in the Colorado River. They found a box."

"What was in the box?"

"I do not know."

"These idiots pull a box out of the water and you weren't curious?"

Bernardo looked at her, not quite understanding. "It was their box, not my box."

Mercedes ground her teeth.

"Do you know where they live?"

"They both live in the same mobile home village in Blythe."

"Take me there."

"We must go by the compound first. Tuco, Blondie, and Angel Eyes have not been fed."

"Your dogs can wait."

"If the dogs are not fed, they will eat what is there. That would be very bad."

Ricky didn't know if all burros were afraid of the water or just these two. He would probably never know. What mattered was the practical challenge of getting two frightened and skittish asses over the Colorado River without incident or injury.

Harry held one by the reins. It whinnied and jerked its head. Its hooves stomped near Harry's feet, scraping against his cast and forcing him to hop out of their way. It looked like they were dancing a jerky shimmy.

Ricky stroked the other burro, but it only reminded the animal that this was the human that had punched its head. Every third stroke, the burro attempted to bite him again. The way Ricky figured it, if the donkey was trying to bite him, it was distracted from its terror of being on the boat.

Harry poked out his head from behind the burro. He yelled to Ricky over the sound of the animal. "Hey, Ricky. How do you stop a burro from crapping?"

Ricky smiled. "I don't know. How?"

"What?"

"I don't know. How do you stop a burro from crapping? What's the punchline?"

"I'm serious. This thing is leaking like a broken soft-serve machine."

Ricky made the mistake of looking. "Thanks for ruining Dairy Queen for me."

"Are they doing any better?" Frank yelled over his shoulder. He steered the boat downriver and toward the opposite bank.

"Who knows," Harry said. "They're not exactly the smartest things. They're calm one second and then they get all squirrelly. Let's just get to the other side."

"How far down?" Frank asked.

"Not far. I couldn't check the Arizona side in person. No roads leading to this dock. Nobody uses it, far as I know. Google showed it was still there, though. Maybe fifteen miles south of Cibola, which we're coming up on."

Harry's burro brayed and kicked at the inside of the boat, pelting man and animal with small pieces of wood and fiberglass shrapnel. The shards made the burro kick more. Harry pulled at the reins, but it kept kicking. A hole formed in the side of the boat.

"Get this boat moving or I ain't going to get my deposit back."

"Maybe if we sang to them," Ricky said.

"Get out of here," Harry said.

"When my daughter throws a tantrum, when she gets out of control, the only thing that calms her is me singing to her."

"That's a little girl. She has a brain. A small one, but a brain. These are manure machines with no brains."

"Don't mean they don't like music," Ricky said.

"You got a better idea?" Frank yelled back at them.

Harry shrugged. "I don't know many songs."

"What songs do you know?"

Harry looked down at his feet and almost inaudibly said, "I know the words to 'Like a Virgin.'"

"Seriously."

"They played it over and over when it was out. Some songs you hate but you know all the words. Heard them so many times they stick. I bet you know the words."

Ricky thought about it. "Yeah, some of them. Flavia loves Madonna."

"Frank?" Harry yelled.

Frank's deep voice bellowed over the sound of the engine, "I came to the wilderness. So now I made it ooh-ooh-ooh."

Then they botched the lyrics together: "If it knew how lost it was. That's how I ooh-ooh."

And as the pontoon boat loaded with three slightly damaged men and two dyspeptic burros drifted down the Colorado River, an almost unrecognizable baritone chorus of "Like a Virgin" filled the otherwise silent desert landscape.

The burros didn't kick once during the song. If you asked any of the men, they would tell you that the singing was a necessary chore and only the burros enjoyed it. They would tell you that they found no joy in it. But men are liars.

"Who is that?" Mercedes asked, standing in the dog-reek squalor of her sons' home. She pointed at Cooker, whom she had almost mistaken for a pile of dirty clothes.

The moment she had seen the moat, she had questioned her effectiveness as a parent. But their living quarters? What had she done to create such childlike offspring? She blamed their father.

"I call him Worky. Sometimes Complainy," Ramón responded, throwing some tacos to the dogs. Tuco and Blondie scarfed them up, but Angel Eyes ate slowly and methodically, dissecting each of his tacos and leaving the lettuce in a small uneaten pile.

Cooker tried to talk through his parched throat. Ramón gave him a can of Mountain Dew. Cooker guzzled the soda but coughed most of it back up in a Day-Glo spray. Catching his breath, he meekly sipped at what remained in the can.

"Who is he?" Mercedes pinched the bridge of her nose, attempting to stave off a headache.

"Another person that Papa Frank was helping. A drug addicted."

"We don't have time for this white trash skitzer. Leave him food and water. We've got to find your grandfather."

"They could be anywhere," Bernardo said.

"I know where they're going," Cooker said through a rasp, his teeth stained neon green.

PART FIVE:
PROVING GROUND

THIRTY-FOUR

Frank, Ricky, and Harry found the decaying pier after a frustrating search up and down the Arizona side of the river. Rotted and covered in high grass, the old pier had little life left. Its ability to support a man's weight seemed doubtful, let alone a burro with a full pack.

"Do you think it will hold?" Ricky asked.

"I didn't get my feet crushed and crapped on for these bastard monsters to drown under a collapsed pier," Harry said.

"Nobody plans for irony, Harry," Frank said.

It didn't take long before the mystery of the pier's stability was revealed. It wasn't scientific, but they got their answer. The moment the boat touched against the pier, the burros' bottled-in fear took over. They leaped over the side rail onto the soggy, rotted wood. Trial by fire. Or rather, trial by burro. The pier held, and the beasts ran for ground. The wood was so soft from age, the burros left hoofprint indentations.

Being the only spry one without a leg cast, Ricky gave chase. Luckily, the burros were weighted down with supplies and only wanted to be off the boat. After some slapstick on the riverbank, Ricky got them under control.

When Frank and Harry found him, Ricky was bent over, forearms on his knees and reins in his hands. The burros chewed on some dry grass, like nothing had happened.

The three men surveyed the terrain. An expanse of undergrowth and dirt led to a group of distant hills and a stunning bajada that would act as their trail into the Chocolate Mountains and ultimately to the Big Maria Mine. They glanced back at the boat and, without any ceremony, began their journey. It wasn't time for words. It was time to hike.

Ricky and Frank each walked alongside a burro, while Harry, due to his leg cast, rode one of the beasts. He had gotten comfortable with one crutch, but hiking on rough terrain was different than carpet. Unless his weight got to be too much for the burro, he would ride. Frank seemed to have a lot of energy, but he could take breaks on the other burro if he got tired.

Near the river, the ground was flat and scrubby, no rocks and little incline. Hardpack, not sand. The donkeys were back to their normal calm selves, having left the terror of the boat. Harry pointed the way, GPS in one hand, folded map in the other.

The base of the mountains loomed ahead, but for now the trail was leisurely. When Frank began whistling "Heigh-Ho" from *Snow White*, Ricky and Harry joined in. The air felt light, the hike easy.

"How many miles?" Frank said. "We should have a goal. Some time or distance. So we know where we're stopping. Or aiming to. Where to set up camp."

Harry looked at his map, adjusting his balance on the back of the burro. "As the crow flies, it's twenty-five or so miles to the mine. But we got some incline and who knows what else. Time'll depend on conditions, the trail, whole bunch of stuff."

Frank nodded. "Then we play it by ear. Keep an eye on the sun. On the terrain. First day'll teach us a lot. We're two-thirds gimp and old man, so no need to push. Ain't in no hurry, right?"

"Let's shoot for the base of the mountains by nightfall," Harry said. "Those hills there. Looks doable. I'm thinking it's going to be four days, maybe five, to the mine. But like you said, no reason to push it."

"So in five days, we're rich," Ricky said to himself.

"Six, tops," Harry said.

Frank laughed. The hiking felt easy with smiles on their faces and gold in their future. Heigh-ho, heigh-ho, it's off to work they go.

After two hours, they hit their first obstacle. As obstacles go, it wasn't much. A loose chain-link fence with one strand of barbed wire curled at the top. A small once-red—now pink—sun-faded sign pathetically tried to send them on their way: GOVERNMENT PROPERTY – LIVE ORDNANCE – RESTRICTED AREA – NO TRESPASSING. Looking down the length of the fence, they could see that the sign repeated its ineffectual command every thirty yards.

"Like they were expecting us," Frank said.

"Probably get hunters, off-roaders, hikers out here. Last thing they need is some idiot getting blowed up 'cause he's in the wrong place," Ricky said.

Harry yanked at the sign a little. "Remind me to grab one of these on the way back."

"What for?" Ricky asked.

"Decoration. Souvenir. Put it in my mansion. Do I need a reason?"

Ricky shrugged and got out the bolt cutters. While he worked on the chain-link, Frank and Harry sat on the ground and passed a bottle of water back and forth. The water tasted like plastic and was already hot.

"How you holding up, Frank?" Harry asked, watching the old man take another gulp of water.

"In the hospital, in town, back there, I was an old man. But out here, on real land, natural nature land, old don't mean squat. I feel right. How about you?"

"Ass hurts like a mother from the riding, but my leg don't hurt."

They watched Ricky work on the fence.

"You think there are sensors or anything like that?" Harry said.

"No. They'd turn 'em off after the fiftieth coyote or mule deer tripped it. They tried that on the border to catch illegals. Damn disaster. Like they forgot it was the wilderness and there was such thing as animals. But I'll betcha the Border Patrol did a helluva job keeping out them Mexican rabbits."

"You're right. What idiot would break into an artillery range?" Harry laughed.

"What three idiots?" Frank added.

"Idiots like a fox." Harry winked.

It took Ricky less than ten minutes to create an opening big enough to get the burros through. While they had gotten some rest, the break had also stiffened their joints.

Ricky and Frank walked the donkeys through the opening. Harry limped behind, his cast misshapen and filthy.

That was all it took. They were in the Proving Ground.

The act of trespassing on federal property felt larger than whatever fine it would cost them if they got caught. That was if they weren't considered enemy combatants, in which case, they were screwed. Guantánamo, here they come. They were at the point of no return. They were breaking their first law.

That is, if you didn't count the assault and unlawful detention of Cooker Hobson. Which they didn't.

Or if you didn't count the marijuana that Frank had brought with him. Which he didn't and the others didn't know about.

Or the extra cargo that Harry had hidden in his bag.

An hour later, they had made no visible progress. They had moved forward a couple of miles, but the terrain and distance from the mountains appeared unchanged. It was the same scrubland, the same desert.

Thunder crashed loudly.

The three men looked up at the sky. At the blue, cloudless sky. The burros danced in place, nervous and twitchy.

The thunder clapped again. Loud but distant.

Then they saw the massive cloud of dust that burst from the side of the mountain in an explosion of rock and earth. It hadn't been thunder. It had been artillery. It was at least fifteen miles away, but the effect of the blast was clearly visible and the sound was shocking, considering the distance.

They watched as the mountain exploded again. The sound took a full five seconds to reach them. The ground trembled slightly.

Nobody said a word, not even the burros. As artillery fire rained down on the side of the mountain, the three men stared open-mouthed at the spectacle. It was beautiful in its way. It was beautiful, the thing that would probably kill them.

THIRTY-FIVE

"Statler and Waldorf are irreplaceable. We raised them since they were donklings."

Bernardo soberly nodded in agreement with his brother. They stared at the empty corral. "Papa Frank will not let any harm come to them."

"I hope they are not frightened. They have not traveled in the world."

"We could not keep them forever. It is their chance for adventure."

Ramón nodded solemnly. "Should we go back inside?"

"If Mother is asking Worky questions, I do not want to be there."

"Poor Worky."

Bernardo found a fat joint in his shirt pocket, lit it, took a monstrous toke, and handed it to his brother. They smoked the joint to nothing, each inhale burning down a quarter inch. Five minutes of silence followed. Then five minutes of drawing pornographic images in the sand with a stick, each image invoking a humorless discussion about how humorous they were. Finally, they reached a strong spell of marijuana-glazed introspection.

Bernardo said, "The moat did nothing. Friends or enemies, they should have been halted by its awesomeness."

"We should have added the piranhas. They are fierce."

"It does not matter what is in the water, if it is easy to cross the water."

Ramón nodded his head solemnly.

"We need something else. Something as awesome as the moat," Bernardo said, "to make our land impenetrable. To make the compound a true fortress."

"Fire?"

"No."

"Lasers?"

"No."

"Snakes?"

"Interesting."

Although a lot of suggestions were considered (including a reluctant veto for spear-wielding apes), they never reached a solution. Mercedes interrupted their battlement conference.

The door of their small house slammed loud enough to make Ramón jump. She didn't look happy, but that indicated nothing. She could have been told that she won the lottery and she'd still look like someone had wiped boogers on her shirt. That was the way her face was. It was a good complement to her angry brain.

The boys instinctively looked for a place to hide, caught themselves, and sheepishly walked toward their mother. Bernardo purposely slowed his pace, forcing Ramón to get ahead of him. Ramón caught on and slowed even more. And like children, the two of them went back and forth until at ten yards away they both came to a dead stop, waiting for the other to move.

"What are you doing? It looks like you're square-dancing," Mercedes said.

"He started it," Ramón said.

"I know where your grandfather is," Mercedes said. "At least, where they are taking him. Do you own camping gear?"

Meanwhile, not back at the ranch.

Harry, Frank, and Ricky were done for the day. It was still an hour until nightfall, but they were tired and didn't want to risk traveling farther and getting stuck in the open. They had stumbled on a perfect campsite.

At first it looked like low hills painted aqua, but as they neared the strange terrain, it revealed itself to be the plastic forms of swimming pools and Jacuzzis. Upside down and stacked haphazardly, the strange forms looked like a 1960s version of a futuristic city. They looked unused but weathered. Large combinations of numbers and letters were painted on the sides of each.

"It's like a swimming-pool graveyard," Harry said.

"What's the military need with all these swimming pools?" Frank asked.

"Everyone likes a pool party," Ricky responded.

Harry knocked on the side of one. A hollow thunk echoed. "Generals, whatever. Ever been on a base? Where the brass live, it's always like a country club."

"We can use them for cover," Ricky said.

He lifted the edge of one of the Jacuzzi forms, the fiberglass structure light enough for his one good arm. He immediately dropped it back in place.

"Spiders. Big ones. Hairy. Ugly."

They explored some of the larger pools that offered access underneath due to their shape, but it only got worse. Spiders, snakes, and in one case, a small family of bats. They unanimously decided to sleep alfresco. In the center of the strange dump site, they found a cluster of tamarisk trees, good enough cover for them and the burros.

Ricky took the packs off the burros and gave them water. If he didn't know any better, he would have thought that the burros were enjoying the adventure. He tried to imagine the journey from a burro's point of view. Maybe he would write a children's book about it when they got back.

From the moment they had heard the first explosion, the air held no silence longer than a minute. For three hours, the men were accompanied by the sound of a steady barrage that appeared to be doing its damnedest to blow the mountain straight to hell.

The ground shook and their ears rang. The burros appeared accustomed to it. But even when the men thought they had adapted, a larger, more dramatic blast would slap their optimism.

Harry gave them the rundown, regularly having to pause for an explosion. "We're way north of the base. There are roads and trails, but we ain't crossed none yet. Up here, as you probably guessed, it's mainly target practice for mortar, artillery, cannons, and, I'm thinking, missiles. Good thing is, when they blow stuff up, they don't want any personnel around. Bad thing, they're blowing stuff up. Might be random patrols, but more likely we ain't going to get within twenty miles of nobody. Here's hoping it's in, out, rich."

Ricky passed out some Pringles and beef jerky. Frank decided not to express his disappointment with the food selection, particularly the sodium content, considering his recent cardiac event. Even with the crap food, he felt better than he had in years. His body ached to the marrow, but it was an honest pain from hard work and grit, not decay.

Harry put two Pringles in his mouth so that he looked like a duck. Frank and Ricky laughed, more nervousness than humor. They had the same excitement and fear as a Webelo on his first overnight camping trip.

The desert night had not yet had its first frost. The air was warm and a little sticky. They laid their sleeping bags in a circle around where a fire might have been.

"What are you going to do with your share?" Harry asked.

Frank answered. "Maybe go on a trip. Always wanted to go to Japan. Travel by myself. I may've been around a while, but I ain't done much. Ain't been nowhere. Ain't seen nothing. I'd like to use some of the money to live the life I got left. I'll put the rest aside for my grandsons. Some money in the bank might keep those two buffalo brains out of jail. How about you?"

Harry smiled. "Get out of the desert for one. Maybe buy a house. Invest in something solid. Mostly I'm thinking about maybe getting one of those mail brides. Like from Ukrainia or Lithuania, out there. I'm figuring with enough money, I don't got to be alone no more. It's a win-win. They get out of the gulag or whatever, and I get to rub uglies with a hot Russian Viking. Or maybe an Asian. Basically, I want to buy a woman."

"We all got to dream." Frank shook his head. "How 'bout you, Ricky? Something a little more grounded, I'm thinking."

"Just want my family back without dragging them down. After I put a little aside for college and school stuff and like that for Rosie, I'll give the rest to the kin of them that died on the bus. Won't bring back their loved ones, but the effort should mean something. Police seem to have backed off. Probably saw no upside in bringing back all that pain. I got a shot. Start over back to where we were. The gold can turn back the clock."

Not able to sleep, Harry stared at the clear night sky. Most people found the great outdoors peaceful. Not Harry. The stars and space creeped him out. It made him feel small. Like a meteor was going to fly out of there and crush him at any minute.

A sound jarred him from his nighttime daydream. The shuffling was somewhere to his right. He leaned on one elbow and in the moonlight he caught Frank searching through one of the packs of supplies.

"You need something, Frank?" Harry asked.

"Where's the toilet paper?"

"I knew I forgot something."

"What do we got?"

"Use leaves."

"We're in the desert."

"We're under a tree."

"This is tamarisk. They got needles. Not leaves. Needles that itch when they touch your skin. Be like sticking cayenne pepper straight up my ass."

"Some people like that," Harry tried to joke.

"I'm not laughing."

Ricky rolled over, slightly groggy.

"Don't use any water," Ricky said. "We ain't got any to waste."

"How many books you bring?" Frank asked Harry.

"The ones I need. Maps and stuff. Too important. Find something else."

"You need all the chapters?"

"You ain't wiping your ass with a library book. That's against the law."

Frank dug through the supplies, weighing each object's wipeability. He glanced at some socks and underwear but threw them back. Frank triumphantly held up a *Playboy* magazine. "Got it."

Harry shook his head. "No. That's a collectible. That's for morale."

"I'll wipe my ass with the articles." Frank grinned, rolling it up and putting the rest of the gear back.

Something in the pile caught Ricky's eye. "What's that?"

"Nothing," Harry said.

"Smells like cologne," Frank said, reacting to the strong smell of aftershave. He bounced the bowling-ball-sized object in his hand, feeling its weight.

"What is it?" Ricky asked.

"It's mine. It's nothing." Harry stumbled to get to his feet, but exhaustion and the cast slowed him down. Ricky stood and took the wrapped object from Frank. He held his face away as he peeled off the sweatshirt. He looked more disappointed than horrified at the human head in his hands.

"Why does it smell like perfume?"

"I soaked it in aftershave. Canoe. We were going to be in the sun. I thought it'd be better."

"Is that the goddamn head? That's the goddamn head. What the hell, Harry?" Frank shouted.

"Why'd you bring it?" Ricky asked.

"Bad juju." Frank gave himself the sign of the cross and spat on the ground. Ricky had never seen that combination but was inclined to do the same. It looked like it warded off something.

"I'll dig a hole," Ricky said.

"We can't bury it here," Harry said, "the middle of nowhere. We need to bury it at the mine."

"What's the difference?"

"The difference between burying him and throwing him away. At the mine, he'd be where he was meant to be. Here, he's garbage. I've read his journals and letters and papers and stuff. He did tons of bad, but as much bad happened to him. Who's to judge? He's the reason we're here. He's one of us."

"No, he's not. He's a head. The head of a dead thief and murderer."

"He's part of this group. Another loser. Just like us. We owe him. He left the gold for us to find. Don't matter if it was his ruthlessness or his greed or his stupidity, it only matters that he did those things so we could be here. All that bad created this opportunity. We owe some thanks and a little respect."

"Horseshit," Frank said. "Get the shovel."

The sound of helicopter blades ended their argument. The rotors were quiet. But in the silence of the desert, it might as well have had a bell tied to its collar. Ricky dropped Constance's head, rushed to the burros, and grabbed their reins to make sure they didn't spook. Harry crawled to the head. He brushed off some dirt and cradled it in his arms. Frank stood still, the *Playboy* still rolled up in his hand.

The helicopter was there and gone in seconds, receding into the night. The craft was at least a mile away, but it was enough of a reminder of where they were and the dangers they faced.

"Keep the damn head," Frank finally said. "I ain't got energy to argue. I'm an old man and I got to take a shit."

THIRTY-SIX

The hills were alive with the sound of music.

Unfortunately, the music was Metallica's "Leper Messiah," not Rodgers and Hammerstein. And instead of Julie Andrews whirling atop an alpine rise, there was a Humvee throwing donuts in a low valley. To complete the chaos of the tableau, the soldier at the wheel intermittently fired a pistol out the window at Lord knows what.

On their bellies, the three men peered over the edge of a cliff down at the canyon floor. Ricky had tied the burros to a dead tree fifty yards behind them. The Humvee drove in tight circles between two groups of low hills: the hills where they were at and the hills where they needed to get to.

"The Hummer's the troll and we're the Billy Goats Gruff," Ricky said.

"I don't know what that means," Harry said.

"It's a kids' story," Ricky said.

"Nobody read me stories when I was a kid."

Frank patted Harry on the back. "Life's tough, Harry. The troll wants to eat the goats. The goats want to get across. That's the troll. We're the goats. I'll tell you the whole thing before you go nighty-night."

No other vehicles were visible and the Humvee appeared to only have one soldier in it. One soldier with a seemingly bottomless supply of ammunition and no knowledge of how brakes worked.

"That guy's drunk," Harry said.

"Or crazy," Ricky countered.

"Maybe crazy, but definitely drunk. I know drunk, and drunk is when shooting at stuff sounds best. You know how when you get high and Nacho Doritos sound better than a lady hole? Or at least as good? Shooting at things, firing a gun at cans and bottles and signs and furry animals, that's the Doritos of alcohol. GI Joe down there, he's wasted. I'm thinking tequila. Definitely not red wine. Red wine makes you more stabby."

"Don't soldiers come in groups? Like troops or units or divisions? That guy's alone," Ricky said.

Frank spoke up. "Yeah, and I'm pretty sure his detail wasn't to drive in circles and shoot in the air. Whatever that guy's doing, he's off the rez."

Harry nodded. "Not much we can do. Too far too walk around. We're going to have to wait him out. If he's shooting-at-demons drunk, he'll pass out soon. Especially in this heat."

It was midmorning and already in the high nineties in the shade. If there had been shade. Other than the one dead tree, the hills were bare and rocky.

"Shouldn't take long. Once he passes out, we'll stroll right by him."

Three hours later, the guy was still driving in circles and shooting out the window. He had made a leap from Metallica to Pat Benatar, but other than that, very little had changed.

He stopped the vehicle once. But the men's optimism was immediately shattered.

The three men watched the soldier exit the driver's side with a bottle in one hand, pistol in the other. He holstered the gun, unzipped his pants, and like a human funnel, attempted to pour alcohol through his body. He put the bottle to his mouth, lifted it vertically, and chugged as he pissed. He finished the bottle long before the piss. In fact, he made it all the way through "Hell Is for Children" and the very beginning of "Heartbreaker" with a steady stream. Upon completing his micturition, he gave the bottle a long stare and threw it down into the evaporating puddle of urine. Then with great ceremony, he saluted, withdrew his pistol, and executed the bottle at his feet.

He returned to his vehicle with the slow gait of a man who had murdered his best friend.

Then it was back to driving like a maniac and shooting willy-nilly, the somberness of the moment having passed in the moment it took to start the engine.

The three men watching on the hill were sunburned, sweating, and an hour past irritable. The ground felt like a griddle. Small flies stuck to the sweat on their arms and made them scratch uncontrollably. The water they drank to stay alive was excruciatingly painful on their cracked lips.

Harry strategized. "Screw this guy. Let's go. He says a word, one word, we mess him up. I don't give a dog turd he's got a gun. I will kick me some butt."

"He's got to run out of gas eventually. Gas and ammo," Ricky said.

"Those beasts got massive gas tanks and better mileage than you think. And the US Army ain't never had no shortage of ammunition," Harry said.

"We ain't got a choice," Frank said. "We try to go around, who knows if there's even a way. And the last thing we need is a confrontation. Remember what happened with your buddy Cooker. We got to stay on the trail. Go down into the valley and then back up through there." He pointed across the valley at a cut in the hills that looked like a natural switchback.

"How long we going to wait?" Harry said.

"Long as it takes. Impatience will always screw you. I'm the oldest, wisest, and least healthiest. If I can take it, you young 'uns can, too."

It ended up taking another forty-five minutes. The Humvee rolled to a stop, the engine dying. Nothing for five minutes, and then the soldier got out, kicked one of the tires for about a minute straight, and shot six holes in the front windshield. He stared at the vehicle like it didn't make sense, took off his boots, shirt, pants, and underwear, and fell into a fetal position in the shade of the Humvee.

"Get the burros," Frank said.

The three men's eyes never left the sleeping, naked soldier as they led the burros down the hill. They moved tentatively, ill at ease. The trail came out onto the valley floor about fifty yards from the dead Humvee. In single file, they made their way across the wash.

One of the burros brayed loudly. The men stopped, but the soldier didn't move. When their hearts slowed to a reasonable rate, they continued.

Everything was hunky-dory until they reached the middle of the valley. Halfway between the two groups of hills, fully exposed and out in the open, the soldier rolled over.

Ricky, Harry, and Frank froze. They held the reins of the burros tight, pulling the beasts to them, brushing them lightly to calm them. Time stopped. It wasn't the movement that spooked them most. It was the soldier's face.

His eyes were open. He stared right at them. Unblinking, unmoving, and intense. Ricky felt like the soldier's eyes were boring into him.

"What do we do?" Ricky whispered. "He's looking right at me."

"Nothing," Frank said. "He ain't looking at nothing but whatever he's dreaming. His eyes just opened. He's out."

Harry leaned down, whispering. "We better hurry. In this heat, his eyes are going to dry out or a fly's going to land on his eyeball, and it's going to wake him up. We don't want our mule train to be the first thing he sees."

They picked up their pace and walked the burros the rest of the way. When they reached the switchback, they looked back at the sleeping soldier. He was in the same position. His eyes were still staring at the nothingness of the valley. But if you asked Ricky, he would have sworn that he had seen a smirk on the man's face that hadn't been there before.

They climbed the switchback and hiked into the far hills until they were out of sight and safe. As safe as one can be in the middle of an artillery range.

Darkness came a lot quicker than they had expected. They had lost most of the day waiting. To compensate and make up time, they tried to hike by the light of dusk. But after the third time Frank slipped on a rock, they quit for the day. They stopped in a flat but rocky area. They hadn't passed cover in a while and would have to hope for no air patrols.

They kept the banter to a minimum and did their best to sleep, but the barrage of artillery fire started up again and continued through the night. Louder, closer, and more imminent. The ground shook and flashes of light appeared in their peripheral vision. The men slept in ten-minute increments. A reminder that the challenges that they had faced were nothing compared to the ones on the trail ahead.

THIRTY-SEVEN

The small, leaky rowboat landed on the Arizona side of the Colorado River. The first light of morning gilt the ridges of the Chocolate Mountains with a faint orange glow.

It was Cooker's third trip over the river, and he couldn't feel his arms from the shoulders down. Between the current and the quantity of shit the two braves and the squat squaw packed into the boat, it was a wonder they hadn't sunk. The rim of the boat never seemed to get more than an inch above the water level. For all his rowing, the boat only crept inches at a time. The shoveling that he had done on the moat had toned his arms, but this was still brutal.

Cooker dragged the boat to the shore and looked at all the crap—not including the three heavy-ass Indians—that he had hauled over the water. Packed into backpacks, plastic bags, and canvas satchels, there was camping gear, canteens and bottles of water, a small amount of food, a coil of rope, some flashlights, assorted tools, toilet paper, and a couple of rifles.

Cooker sat on the ground and lit a cigarette. It almost made him puke, but after he caught his breath the light-headedness turned pleasant. He reached for a bottle of water, but the line-backer lady who he'd learned was named Mercedes kicked his hand. He shrugged, accustomed to the abuse. He watched the Indians do a shoddy job of covering the rowboat in brush.

"We brought too much, Mother," Bernardo said. "We cannot carry all this without burros."

"We have a burro." Mercedes pointed to Cooker. The smile on her face brought back the fear she had induced back at the compound. "We each carry a backpack. Tie the rest to his body."

"Worky is surprisingly strong," Ramón noted.

"Oh, fuck that," Cooker said. "I can hear you, you know. I ain't hauling all this shit nowhere."

"You are our prisoner. You must do what we say. It is the rules," Ramón said.

"I have to do jack shit. I have to sit right here is what. Smoke cigarettes and count the grains of sand. I rowed your fucking boat. I showed you the way on the map. I'm done."

"We made a promise to Papa Frank that we would watch you."

"That don't mean I got to carry everything. You guys are like three times my size and ten times stronger. Why do I got to be the one?"

Bernardo and Ramón looked at each other and shrugged. "I do not know. You just are. You are Worky. You work."

Mercedes walked to Cooker and knocked the cigarette from his mouth with a hard slap. "Enough sass. Or do you need me to repeat all the possible—yet equally painful—fates for your testicles?"

Cooker picked up the cigarette, took a deep drag, chucked it back on the ground, and stood. "Load me up, you fucking savages."

After forty-five minutes, they had made little progress. Cooker's body was so *Beverly Hillbillies*-ed with gear that only his face and the bottom half of his legs were visible. He trudged along the rocky flatland, driven by will and Mercedes's goads.

"I have to rest," Cooker said through raspy breaths. His stride moved as much to the side as forward, the Walmart waddle of a four-hundred-pounder.

Bernardo looked behind him. "I can still see the river. I can see the boat. We have traveled nowhere."

Mercedes hit Cooker in the legs with a switch she had fashioned from some chaparral. "If we're going to catch up, we can't slow down. We need to speed it up."

Cooker's wordless answer came in the form of collapsing onto the ground. His hands never rose to break his fall, his face handling that job. Luckily for him, he had passed out before the impact occurred.

"Is Worky dead?" Ramón asked.

Mercedes gave him a kick to the calf. His body bucked a little. "We should turn him over. Could drown in the dirt."

Bernardo rolled him onto his back. Or rather, he rolled him onto the stack of backpacks and gear tied to his back. He looked like an overturned turtle with his arms, legs, and head suspended above the ground. Blood ran down his cheeks from what looked like a broken nose. Pebbles stuck to his face.

Ramón snapped his fingers in front of Cooker's face. Bernardo poured some water in his mouth. Cooker woke up, choking and swearing.

"Worky lives," Ramón said.

"Okay, we'll each take a few packs. At least until he gets some energy back," Mercedes said. "Men are always weaker than you want them to be."

"I worry that Statler and Waldorf are frightened. They have never been on their own," Ramón said to his brother.

They had redistributed all the gear and were making good progress. They had crossed the cheap fence and entered into the military complex. Mercedes mumbled something that sounded like, "None of this their land. Every right to go where we want."

"I am sure they are okay," Bernardo said.

"I love them," Ramón said.

"I know, Ramón. I do, too."

"Sweet Jesus," Mercedes said, "they are donkeys. You two need to meet some girls. Find wives."

Bernardo and Ramón looked at each other and shook their heads in the same way a teenager does when their parent uses the phrase "the bomb" (as in, "Was band practice the bomb?").

The distinctive thump of helicopter blades rose in the distance.

"Lie down. Everyone. On the ground," Bernardo yelled.

Ramón reached into his backpack and pulled out a huge tan tarp that was painted to look like the rocky terrain of the desert. Cooker and Mercedes were on their knees, Bernardo joining them. Ramón shook out the tarp like a laundered sheet and threw it over them. Bernardo and Mercedes each grabbed a corner, pulling it taut.

The four of them stayed facedown on the ground and listened until the sound of the helicopter receded into the distance.

Mercedes smiled and nodded. "You learned things growing that ditch weed."

"We do not grow ditch weed. We grow quality," Bernardo said.

"I'll be the judge. Torch some up. Might take some of the ache out of these bones," Mercedes said.

Bernardo and Ramón looked at their mother, at each other, and back at their mother.

"Don't act so surprised. I was a radical. It's part of our culture. Are you holding or not?"

Ramón nodded and pulled a big blunt out of his front shirt pocket. "I never knew you were radical."

THIRTY-EIGHT

"You boys lost?"

Ricky, Harry, and Frank looked up at the silhouette standing over them, the morning sun at the man's back. The glare of the light didn't allow for details, but the outline of the pistol in his hand was unmistakable. It gave focus to the situation.

The man didn't wait for an answer. "Sorry to wake y'all. Don't like it myself when someone disturbs my slumber. No nodding back off though. I ain't a snooze button. Not going to get your asses back up in seven minutes. I got a gun. Alarm enough. It's time to wake the fuck up."

The men sat up, alertness coming quickly. An armed man will do that.

"You best stay put. If you got to move, scratch your balls, stretch, I'd suggest doing it on the slow side."

Harry said. "We're hikers. Hiking the Cargo Muchacho Trail."

The man squatted down on his haunches, the pistol draped casually over one leg. With the sun at a fresh angle, the man became immediately recognizable. His face was blistered and burned red, but it was the drunk driver/shooter/soldier from the day before. His face was lean, his cheeks hollow. His eyes were bloodshot, deep-set in their sockets. His all-purpose redneck accent gave him away as a hillbilly of sorts, from the South or maybe the Ozarks.

The soldier laughed. "That right? Never heard nothing about a Muchacho Trail. Cargo Muchachos, the mountains, heard of them. They're in California. You're in Arizona. On Army land. You're lost as shit, trespassing, and in all kinds of trouble."

Harry tried to bolster his lie. "That's impossible. We followed the maps. Maybe you're the lost one."

"I might be lost, but I know where I'm at. You boys have seriously shit the bed."

"We got GPS."

"Then it's broke."

"Secondhand, maybe. But it works fine," Harry said.

Frank cut in. "We never passed any signs or fences. Are we really on a military base?"

"Not so much a base, but US Army property. Yep, you're there."

"You're sure?" Frank said.

"Positive, sir. You want to know why?" The soldier smiled. His smile was villainous. The kind of smile a circus clown would have, if the clown was a serial killer preparing to castrate you. He held the smile, and then repeated the question. "You want to know why?"

"I'll give. Why?" Frank said, waiting for the inevitable bad news.

"You boys didn't just make your camp in the middle of the Proving Ground. You made your camp in the middle of a motherfucking minefield."

Harry, Frank, and Ricky quickly looked around at the rocky ground surrounding them, their eyes frantically looking for some evidence to support the soldier's claim. But for all their concentrating and squinting, they couldn't see anything.

The soldier picked up some rocks off the ground. One at a time with delicate precision, he would lift a stone in front of his feet and set it to the left of his knee. Slowly and precisely. The clacking of the stones the only sound. With each stone, the pile beside him grew a little larger. When he had cleared the area, four small metal spikes were visible sticking out of the ground.

"Seriously?" Harry said. "Those things are all around us?"

"Is that thing live?" Frank asked.

"Only one way to find out." The soldier smiled that smile.

"Why is there a minefield with live mines?" Harry said. "They let soldiers train near live explosives?"

The soldier shrugged. "Maybe 'cause it was dark or y'all are stupid, but the sign that you walked past, it says, 'Danger, Live Ordnance, Mine Testing Range.' They ain't training no soldiers, they're testing different kinds of land mines. Blast mines, fragmentation, flame mines, bounding ones, chemical mines, the whole megillah. Trying to discover all the different ways to blow up the enemy. You and your mules just made yourselves the enemy. Don't know how you made it smack-dab to the middle without exploding yourselves up, but I wouldn't bet on that kind of luck getting out."

Ricky spoke for the first time. "You made it to us. You walked through the minefield without getting blown up. You must know where the mines are."

"I'm US Army trained, son. I can get you out of here the way you came."

"You followed our tracks," Frank said.

"What if we don't want to go back that way?" Harry said.

The soldier picked at a flaky piece of sunburned skin on the side of his nose. "Now why wouldn't you want to go back the way you came? Seems like a group of lost hikers would want to get themselves unlost."

"Can you get us to the east edge of the minefield?" Harry said.

"Our friend has been in the sun too long," Frank cut in. "We'll go back the way we came."

The soldier held up his hand. "Might be time for me to call the MPs. Let them work out this situation."

"You ain't going to do that," Harry said.

"I ain't?"

"What're you doing, Harry?" Ricky said.

"You're not," Harry said, and then mimicked the man's accent. "You want to know why?"

The soldier looked at his pistol, then back at Harry, waiting for the answer.

"Because you're like us. Not where you're supposed to be. Because, I'm guessing, your orders weren't to get drunk and shoot at bottles and demons. Because you're just another fuck-up. Join the club. And because—like every other son of a bitch on the planet—you like gold."

The soldier studied Harry's face. His expression made it look like thinking hurt.

After what felt like forever, the soldier stood, saluted, and announced, "Specialist Third Class Clement Harwood. Call me Wood. I'll listen to what you got to say."

Wood turned out to be a good guy. A crazy son of a bitch, kind of scary, definitely on the edge of cracking, but who wasn't when it came down to it. His demeanor was even more off-putting. His crazy didn't manifest itself in twitches and nervous tics, but in an unnatural calmness that felt cold and passionless.

Harry gave him the spiel, a kinda-sorta version of the truth. The short version he told Wood was that they had discovered a map to a gold mine. None of them had anything to lose, so there was no point in trying to stop them. If Wood let them on their way, Harry promised to make it worth his while. Or if he was so inclined, Wood was welcome to join their excursion, offering a full share.

Wood listened, a smile at the corner of his mouth. He didn't seem to care about Harry's explanation. He appeared satisfied enough that he was accepted by them and that they were looking for gold and going toward the explosions, not away from them. That was the point that he found the most intriguing. Something he wanted to be a part of.

Now that he had new friends, Wood was anxious to tell his story. It was like he had been waiting in the desert for someone to come along and listen. Maybe a spirit guide or a vision of a mystical Indian was closer to what he was expecting, but he settled for three yahoos in a minefield.

"It probably looked like I'd lost my shit. All that shooting and driving and hollering. And I know there's going to be hell to pay if I decide to go back. Don't yet know if anybody knows I'm gone. They will though, when my division gets back.

"I'm supposed to be war gaming with the rest of them. Before we left, I called my wife. Did I tell you I'm shipping out in two weeks? There's that there, which is what I joined up for, but also damn scary. These games, they're like a dress rehearsal for the real thing. Crazy that wars actually happen in the world, you know. Real ones. Not just in the movies or PlayStation. So I call home, see if I can get Sherry to come out, say good-bye. Sherry, that's my wife, she tells me she's banging my brother and she's faxing the divorce papers and do I know the Army's fax number. Barely says hello, like she's in a big hurry. Oh, did I mention, she's pregnant with his kid. She says my brother told her to tell me that he's sorry and feels real bad, but it's love and what're you going to do when it's love?

"After that, I'm half expecting her to hit me with a list of shittier shit. Waiting for the other, other shoe to drop." His voice became falsetto. "Wood, yeah, your mama and your dog, they been having an affair, but it went south, and they made a suicide pact and killed themselves. And that rib shack you like, Bones and Marrow, it closed."

He squinted up at the sky. "I figured I had a couple choices. And all them choices involved this here pistol. I could eat it. Pull the trigger and that's that. But I weren't raised to take my life. I could head back to Beckley, shoot the whore and my ex-brother. But by the time I got there, I wouldn't be killing mad no more, and then I'd just be an asshole. My mama'd never forgive me either. And punching him in the face or taking a bat to her Ford Fiesta wasn't going to take away them bad feelings.

"So I skipped out on my company, grabbed too much booze and a shit-ton of ammo, and shot my pistol until there was no more shooting to be done."

"Make you feel any better?" Ricky asked, genuinely interested.

"Yeah. It was like a little mad, a little hurt went away every time I squoze off a shot. Like I was killing all that shit.

"Fuck her, you know. They deserve each other. My brother's dumb as a box of hammers and she ain't no rocket surgeon. Used to be something to look at. But after we got married, she put on eighty pounds. In my brain, she was the fuckable girl behind the counter at the DQ. The one with an ass like a plum making Blizzards and shit. Should've known when I met her mama. The big, fat acorn didn't fall too far from the big, fat tree. And just so you don't get the wrong picture, she didn't put on those pounds in five years or after a kid or nothing. No way. Took her like six months. Ate like she was getting paid. She'd go through like three bags of Funyuns in a day of couching it. She was on her way to being like the lady a county over that fused to her sofa. It was fucked up, but I was still loyal."

Harry said, "Sounds like you're better off."

"You'd think. But with her at home, it made it easier to ship out to fight. I didn't want to go back home. I don't know if I knew it, but I was more readier to go to war than back to her. Now that I got choices, I'm scared to shit. Like I got this fresh start, new horizons, you know, and now some fucking Ay-rab is going to blow my guts out my asshole."

"Once we get the gold, you can go wherever you want. Mexican border's right there. We all deserve a fresh start," Ricky said.

"I should get a gun. Sounds like good therapy," Harry said.

"You boys want to shoot a little? After I get us out of this minefield, I'll let you pop off a few rounds."

"If you don't know where the mines are, how are you going to get us to the other end?" Frank asked.

"It's fifty, maybe sixty yards to the perimeter. The things ain't invisible. Long as we're in no hurry, I can get us there safe. I think."

THIRTY-NINE

Sweat stung Ricky's eyes. He blinked and shook his head. He wanted to wipe it away but didn't dare release his grip. His good hand gripped the burro's reins tightly, his dead arm weakly holding the burro's mane. The animal seemed to have ceded control, but you could never tell when a burro was going to get independent. Ricky kept his body close, feeling the animal's heat through his clothes.

Frank walked behind, guiding the burro with Harry on it. Ricky could hear their breathing, but he wasn't about to look back. He concentrated all his attention on the man that was guiding them through the minefield. On Wood. On his feet.

Every step they took was a gamble. Before that morning, Ricky had thought the bus crash was going to be as close to death as he was going to get. At least until he died. But that brush with death lived in his past. It was only something he looked back at now. Standing in the minefield, he could see death in his present and future. In seconds, it could be over. The reaper's breath was warm on the back of his neck.

Wood turned, giving the small caravan a smile. "We don't get it right the first time, we'll just try again."

Only Harry laughed, all nerves. "Great. A comedian."

Wood said, "Follow my steps best you can. It's all about the mules. I'll go slow. Try to give the area a sweep to make sure it's wide enough for them. Try not to shit your pants. You boys got nothing to worry on, I been trained by the United States motherfucking Army."

Wood gave them a loose salute, took two steps, and exploded.

Ricky had no idea where he was. There was sky above him and what felt like rocks underneath him. The world felt quiet, although he couldn't know that with all the ringing in his ears. He turned his head to see what dead looked like. Just more rocks. Maybe he wasn't dead. It didn't look like heaven or hell or any-place in between that he'd ever imagined or heard described.

His head pounded and his body ached, making it impossible to think. He couldn't remember what had happened. The moment before that moment. That is, until he looked down at his body and saw the blood and bits that soaked his torn shirt. His skin under-neath was black and dirty, strips of skin like loose fabric. He felt his face, and then stared at the dark blood on his hand.

He was cut and bruised and burned over the whole front of his body. Most of the blood must not have been his, but rather some of what remained of Specialist Third Class Clement Harwood, Wood to his friends.

Ricky stood up and wiped the blood out of his eyes. Nothing felt broken. He looked over the ridge at the minefield below, the east edge at least forty yards away. The open field was empty, save for a small crater and half a dead man. All that remained of Wood was his head and torso. His legs, all the way to the hip, were gone.

How had Ricky gotten out of the minefield? The last thing he remembered was Wood saluting. The blast must have knocked him unconscious. Had the explosion thrown him all the way onto the hill? That seemed impossible, outside of a cartoon. It was the wrong direction, to boot.

Where were Frank and Harry? Maybe they brought him there. But then, where were they? Where were the burros? There was only one crater in the minefield and only one corpse.

"Hello," Ricky shouted. "Harry! Frank! You out there?"

His voice echoed down below. The volume burned his throat. But when you hurt all over, it's easy to ignore one of many pains. He shouted their names until he couldn't.

The yelling made him light-headed. He sat down on a rock and put his head between his legs, steadying his breathing. With his eyes closed and the silence of nature, he suppressed his rising panic.

The peace was shattered by artillery fire on the side of the mountain. Compared to the sporadic mortar fire on the previous nights, there were no breaks between the explosions. No gap longer than five seconds. Just a steady barrage that sounded like the end of the world.

Ricky sat up and watched the dusty clouds rise on the side of the mountain, close enough to shake him.

He tried to pray, but the sheer enormity of the sound made it impossible to concentrate.

"Stop it! Just for one second, stop it!" Ricky screamed.

The artillery stopped.

"I'll be damned," Ricky said.

Something moved out of the corner of his eye. He turned in time to see the burro run into a narrow pass between some craggy rocks fifty yards to the east.

Ricky didn't hesitate. He ran in pursuit, shaking his dizziness with only partial success. He stumbled forward, using his hands as much as his feet. He reached the rocks where he had seen the burro, the ground too rocky for tracks, but there was only one direction the animal could have gone.

Ricky raced up the narrow trail. It was essential that he caught the burro. At that moment, it was everything. If he could find the burro, he would be connected again. Ricky picked up his pace, his feet racing forward and his good arm pulling at rocks. He slipped, his scrapes opening up, but he quickly got to his feet.

Rounding a bend, he ran straight into the burro's back end. His feet slipped out from under him and he landed on the rocks hard.

But he had found the burro.

Sitting on the ground and staring up at the animal, he couldn't help but laugh. The ass's ass knocked him on his ass.

His laughter didn't last long.

FORTY

Ricky chalked up the burro's quick halt to the species' natural unpredictability. At least, until he looked through the burro's wickets and saw the real reason.

"You've got to be kidding me," Ricky said under his breath.

A cougar stood in the middle of the trail, motionless save for its eyes and its flicking tail. The big cat's eyes moved from Ricky to the donkey.

Ricky rose to his feet slowly, gently stroking the burro's haunch.

"Easy. It's as scared of us as we are of it." But as he said it, he knew that was malarkey. There was nothing about the cougar that looked scared. Desperate, maybe. Hungry, definitely. The animal's ribs were clearly visible. The starving animal was deciding what was the appetizer and what was the main course.

The cougar growled. A low rumble that Ricky felt in his chest. A line of white saliva ran from the animal's mouth to the ground.

Everything was still. Ricky knew that the moment anything moved all hell would break loose. He stood as still as he could for as long as he could. But the burro wasn't down with that game plan.

The burro reared up and kicked wildly with its front legs, even though the cougar was ten yards away. The cougar responded by rushing at the burro and pouncing onto its neck.

Ricky screamed in a pitch he didn't know was in his register. In retreat he only got as far as falling backward on his ass again. The donkey jumped and thrashed, limited by the narrowness of the trail. It kicked with front and back legs, frightened and crazed.

The cougar dug its teeth and claws into the neck of the burro, bracing itself for the wild ride.

As Ricky rose, he got tagged by a back hoof in the midsection. The blow folded him in half, his wind gone and his ribs cracked.

The burro broke the mountain lion's death grip and threw the cat through the air. Gracelessly it bounced off a rock wall, and unlike Ricky had been told as a youth, it didn't land on its feet. It landed awkwardly on its side and rolled to a skidding halt. That wasn't going to stop the hungry animal though. Hurt and pissed off, the cougar rolled and rose to its feet.

The burro, unable to turn around, backed away from the cougar, walking right over Ricky. One hoof dug into his leg, another completely crushed his dead arm. He was already in so much pain from the kick in the gut that the additions barely registered.

Ricky quickly realized there was nothing between him and the cougar. The cougar seemed aware of it, too. Why tangle with the crazy thing with hooves, when there was a soft, bloody snack right in front of him?

God's design had definitely failed Ricky at this point. What Ricky would have given for some claws, fangs, talons, or, at the very least, anal scent glands. Advanced reasoning and opposable thumbs did little good in a head-to-head scrap with a cougar.

The cougar stalked slowly forward. Each step landing softly and quietly. Ricky had never felt defeat as strongly as he did at that moment. All Ricky could think to do was close his eyes. He was done. He accepted it. He just didn't want to see it happen. He would rather spend his last moments thinking about his daughter.

"I'm ready," Ricky said.

A loud growl and strange, fleshy chunking sounds followed. Like the sound of a paper cutter trying to slice a brisket. The cry of the cougar reached a deafening pitch.

Ricky opened his eyes in time to see the cougar fall, bloody gashes in its side. The animal struggled to its feet but fell immediately back down. As scared as he had been, Ricky felt bad for the cougar as it took its final breaths. Blood and guts soaked the ground.

The last thing that Ricky remembered before passing out for the second time in one day was the image of Harry covered in blood from head to leg cast. Harry, standing over the dead animal, holding a samurai sword, and yelling, "Fuck you, cat! Fuck you, cat!"

Ricky jerked awake, but Harry quickly pinned his shoulder to the ground. He was so weak, he didn't bother to resist. "Don't move. I patched you up. Don't want you to mess up all my work."

"Where are we?" Ricky relaxed, the pain reducing his desire to stand.

"A cave. Somewhere in the middle of downtown nowhere. Frank's here. He's sleeping. Both burros are tied up. Here for the night. Taking a personal day after all the excitement."

Ricky let his eyes adjust to the darkness. They were in a low cave. The ceiling was about four feet above them and covered with daddy longlegs spiders. There were so many, it made the rocks look like a breathing sweater. Looking toward the dim twilight at the mouth of the cave, he could see the burros. One stood, licking the bite and claw wounds of the other burro that rested on the ground. It wasn't clear if the animal was trying to help or if it liked the taste of blood. Frank snored somewhere, but Ricky couldn't find him.

Harry went back to work on Ricky's wounds. "Frank snores like a hungover pig, but it's good he's sleeping. That minefield took some years off all of us. I thought he was going to have another heart attack, a stroke, something. Surprised I didn't have one. He only got his color back an hour ago."

"What happened? Back with Wood? Can't see it."

"This is going to hurt," Harry said, pouring vodka onto Ricky's torn chest. After Ricky got all his screaming out, Harry took a gulp of the vodka and helped him fill in the blanks.

"After Wood stepped on a landmine—wasn't his week—boom, everything happened at once. The air was all dust and black smoke and like a bloody red mist. We should've let the burros go in front of us. Not that I would've wanted them blown up, but better than what happened, yeah?"

"How did I, we, get out of the minefield?"

"Fate, maybe. Mostly luck. The mine explodes. Your donkey bolts, dragging you like a rag doll. You were probably unconscious, out from the blast, but still holding on to the reins and mane. Good grip you got, even your little arm.

"You should kiss that burro on the mouth. It made a beeline for the hills. Easy as you please, ran right out of the minefield."

"And you two?" Ricky asked.

"Our donkey took us on Mr. Toad's. Where yours went straight for the hills, ours jumped all around. Heeing and hawing and kicking. In a minefield. I grabbed its mane and held on, cussing and crapping myself. Frank wasn't as lucky. He had the reins wrapped tightly around his hands and it kind of dragged him here and there. He never got under its hooves, but still, it was a lot of thrashing around for an old man.

"Bad luck to be in a minefield. Good luck to get out. How everything's been since we started. Step back, step forward. We're here. We're closer. We're alive. Frank cussed me out, says it was because of Constance's head, because I brung it. Bad luck charm. Or maybe the head was the thing brought the good luck part of the deal, you know? Our talisman.

"When the donkey finally stopped its spaz, Frank and me were in the hills. Frank was scraped and bruised, could hardly breathe. He really didn't look good. I set him down, gave him some water, and went looking for you. Grabbed the sword to use as a walking stick and scrambled through the rocks best I could. When I found you, that lion was bearing down. I had a good angle."

"Thanks for that," Ricky said.

"I went ninja on his ass. Stupidest thing I've ever done. Jumped off those rocks and started slicing and dicing. Thought about taking a bite out of its heart, 'cause it seemed like what you're supposed to do, but the thought passed."

"You risked your life for me, Harry."

"I wouldn't've if I'd've thought about it. Get some sleep. Let's hope tomorrow is less eventful."

Frank woke in the middle of the night. From dead sleep to wide awake. He squinted at the deep darkness of the cave and tried to make out shapes. Without anything to look at, he was left with his thoughts.

There was nothing quite like watching a man explode and surviving a minefield to stoke the coals of one's introspection. And Frank had to admit that being alive felt better than it had in a long damn time.

Nobody was taking care of him. He was taking care of himself. Nobody was telling him what to do. He was making his own decisions. And most importantly he had something to look forward to in his future, erasing the bleakness that every man faces at the end of his life. Death wasn't nearly as welcome a guest as it had been a few weeks back. It was good to be alive, no matter how short-lived life might be.

Frank reached out and touched the cave wall. He let the spindly legs of hundreds of spiders tickle the back of his hand.

FORTY-ONE

"We are lost and we are only getting more loster," Ramón said. He glanced at the sun and wiped the sweat from his face, wishing he was a lot stoneder.

Mercedes violently shook her head. "We are Native Americans. Proud Chemehuevi. We cannot get lost. Our blood is never lost. Our souls are never lost. We are connected to the land. One with it. We are the land with feet."

She held her arms to the side, her face to the sun. "Guide us, Mother Sun. We're your wandering children. Show us the way."

Bernardo leaned in to Ramón and asked, "Did you give her more of the weed?"

Ramón nodded. "A little bit. It calms her down."

"And crazies her up. Do we have enough for three?"

"I have one pound of the Purple Peace Pipe and a half pound of the Oliver Stoned."

"That will have to do," Bernard said gravely. "If she gets paranoid, that is on you."

Mercedes waved her arms at the rocky hills that surrounded them. They had hiked up the mountain into the deep grooves of the bajada. Without a horizon, all sense of direction was gone. "If our Mother Sun cannot tell us the way, then our white man will. He knows this land. The foot's on the other foot. The white man will guide the Indians."

Cooker chucked his pack to the ground and sat on top of it. "Sorry to shit in your teepee, Fatahontas, but I got no idea where we're at. I might've at one point, but now I can barely tell which way is up. No point in walking in circles. Sun's low, too. It gets dark in this maze, we're likely to walk off a cliff. The big, dumb brave is right. We're motherfucking loster than shit."

"Get up!" Mercedes yelled, taking a few steps closer.

He shook his head, squinting at the sun and pointing. "Once that sun is gone, it's going to be Pin the Tail on the Asshole, all blindfolded and spun around. Ain't going to see nowhere from nothing. Just because I've been doing what you say don't mean everything you say ain't stupid."

Bernardo stepped between them. "Worky has a point. We make camp here."

An hour later, the four of them sat in the dark. A debate had erupted and quickly ended about starting a campfire. Ramón was disappointed. He had brought the fixin's for s'mores and had his heart set on them. Their loss. More for him later. They were left with the country dark, their aching shoulders, and each other.

"How does this end for me?" Cooker asked.

Bernardo answered. "It ends good. You return home. Your addictions are gone and you are a better man."

"Addictions? I ain't addicted to shit. I cooked but never took. Except to test."

"It is a disease. The first step is to admit that you have a problem." Bernardo took a huge drag on a massive spliff and passed it to Ramón, who nodded in agreement.

"It is all about boundaries and self-control. Just say no," Ramón said. He inhaled deeply on the joint.

"Papa Frank is trying to help. You will thank him when you see that he has saved you."

"Saved me? Motherfucker kidnapped me. I've been telling you, you fucking morons. Your Papa Frank is keeping me on ice, because I know things he don't want no one to know. Shit, he obviously don't want you to know."

"I know things," Ramón said defensively.

"I know where Frank is going—you know that—but I also know why he's going there."

Mercedes stood up, dusted the dirt from her backside, and stood over Cooker with her hands on her hips. "He was taken by two men. Dragged against his will into these mountains."

"Don't think so, honey," Cooker said, making a bad decision by following with a smirk. When Mercedes kicked him in the leg, he acknowledged to himself that that one was on him.

"We have no secrets. My father tells me everything," Mercedes said.

"Sorry, lady, but if he didn't tell you about the gold, then he didn't tell you shit."

Mercedes opened her mouth to speak, but Bernardo got in before her. "What gold?"

"They got a map, the three of them. From the look of it, they killed some dude—cut his head off—to get it. That's what greed does to a person. They find that gold, they ain't sharing. Your Papa Frank, he's like their leader. Kidnapped me. Lied to you. He's got gold fever."

"My father does not lie to me," Mercedes said defiantly.

"How much gold?" Bernardo asked, ignoring his mother.

"Maybe why they dove in the reservoir," Ramón added.

Bernardo shook his head. "Obviously. That is where treasure maps are. There was probably a pirate ship or something down there. How much gold is there, Worky?"

"I don't know, but it has to be a lot to hike straight into a fucking artillery range, yeah?"

Mercedes sat back down. "Doesn't change a thing. We're finding your grandfather and bringing him home. Gold, silver, diamonds, what does it matter? He is an old man. A sick man. And he needs me, his daughter."

Nobody said anything else. But that didn't mean they weren't thinking. Thinking about gold.

FORTY-TWO

The sign read WELCOME TO BAGHDADVILLE.

"What now?" Harry said.

The three tired men and their burros stood in front of the makeshift sign. The rocky trail had opened up into a paved road. The craggy hills to a high plain. And in the center of the plain, past the sign, there was a small village of about twenty buildings. A wood and plaster village. Deep-black asphalt roads led into the town from four directions.

There was no movement or activity. No clouds of dust or smoke. Not even a bird in the sky. They listened for engines or voices, but it was impossible to hear anything over the mortar barrage in the near hills.

"We shouldn't risk it. Let's go around," Frank said.

"I don't see no one, nothing," Harry said.

"It's a town. Whyever it's out here, it's for people. Might not be anyone this moment, but they'll show up eventually."

Harry said, "We go around, it'll take a day, maybe two. And we still got to cross those roads. I don't know if you noticed, but none of us is any kind of shape. The mine is over that rise."

"We get seen, we get caught, it's over. We rush it, we screw ourselves."

"We go through the town," Ricky stated with authority.

They both turned, surprised. Ricky had been quiet since they had found him. "Don't mean to vote against you, Frank. But look at the terrain. Going around, we'll be just as out in the open. At least in there, there's places to hide. And Harry is right. We're beat-up. Maybe a place to fill our water. We're running super low. It's worth chancing it."

Frank looked Ricky up and down. He was a mess. His whole body was a giant scab, some of the black from the explosion still embedded in his skin, and the burned bits were pink and yellow. Harry had told Frank that he was pretty sure the kid had some broken ribs, too.

Frank nodded and walked past the sign. The three men headed down the road into a town that shouldn't be there.

None of the men had been to the Middle East. Hell, none of them had been to the Midwest. It didn't matter. Walking into the town, they were convinced that they were getting an accurate taste of a Middle Eastern village. The attention to detail was impressive. All of the buildings had Arabic signs and advertisements in the windows. There were benches and chairs in front of a few places. The buildings looked authentic, like on CNN footage. But without people or animals, Baghdadville had that spooky ghost-town vibe of a place that had been evacuated quickly.

Ricky cautiously walked into one of the buildings, expecting to find wood frames and dirt floors like a movie set, but it was a regular room. Fully furnished with a worn table and old chairs and Arab pop music posters on the wall. Dishes on the table. A few oil drums felt out of place, but Ricky figured they had tons of oil over in Arabia, maybe so much the Arabs kept some in their homes. At closer inspection, the chairs weren't old, but made to look that way. He thought it was called *distressing*. Like the fake bricks on the wall of an Italian restaurant or the rocks at Disneyland.

It was the cleanliness that gave it away. It was all too new. It usually only took the desert a matter of weeks to age a thing. The sun, the wind, the sand, all merciless. The only age these buildings showed was a new kind of old. Like seeing the seams of the latex on an actor's old-age makeup.

"Let's take a look around. Find some water. Anything else useful," Harry said.

"Don't push it. Get in, get out," Frank said.

"Ain't nobody around, Frank," Harry said. "And I'd rather get caught than die from thirst."

Ricky jumped in. "Place ain't big. Got to be water somewhere."

They led the burros through a wide door into one of the buildings and tied them up. The burros seemed pleased with the shade. As a reward, Ricky gave each of them a PayDay candy bar, which they downed without chewing.

The three men walked down the freshly paved street, each carrying as many empty water bottles as they could. Their eyes darted around for any sign of movement. They had to rely on their eyes, as the artillery fire drowned out most sound.

Inside the next building they found a big open space with a kitchen. The faucet yielded no water and the stoves no heat. It was like an Iraqi model home.

Next to the building was an outhouse that had no smell. Harry peered down the hole and took a big whiff. "Sucker's fresh. You fellas look around. I'm going to christen this barge."

"Grab the toilet paper when you're done," Frank said. "Miss July chafed my backside."

Harry smiled. "Two rolls. Now you glad we came to town?"

"I'll be glad when we're at the mine. Until then I'm sticking with ornery." Frank gave Harry a wink to tell him there were no hard feelings. "Enjoy your shit."

After a failed door-to-door campaign to find water, Ricky and Frank were ready to give up. Each interior was no different from the one that preceded it. The same faux-weathered furniture and nonfunctional fixtures.

"Got no reason to believe that if we keep looking we're going to find anything different," Frank said.

At that moment, the artillery fire in the distance stopped. They both jumped. They had become so accustomed to it that the absence was jarring. But it wasn't replaced by silence. It was replaced by what sounded like giant pots and pans clanking together. Ricky and Frank turned toward the sound.

They watched with horror as an M1 Abrams tank rolled through the intersection thirty yards in front of them. A perfect parade side view of a vehicle they had only seen in movies. It was beautifully frightening. As quickly as it had appeared, it was gone.

Frank and Ricky ran as fast as their battered bodies would take them.

Harry sat on the Army-issue toilet seat and wiped his ass with the Army-issue toilet paper. He was going to have to break it to Frank softly that the Army TP wasn't any less abrasive than the magazine. Maybe the government thought a sore ass made a meaner soldier.

His thoughts were interrupted by gunfire. Automatic weapon fire, to be precise. It was so loud, so close, that it sounded to Harry like it was inside the outhouse with him.

Being in the single-most defenseless position, Harry did the only thing he could think to do. Panic. Losing all control of logic and filled with small-animal terror, he pulled up his pants and pushed at the outhouse door. It didn't budge. He threw his body at the door, coming close to dislocating his shoulder.

He screamed through tears. He was trapped. The gunfire drowned out his wailing. It sounded like a war outside. He decided to hide in the outhouse rather than attempt an escape. Only one hiding place in an outhouse. He looked down into the deep hole where he had just deposited a considerable load.

"Why do I always end up covered in shit?"

The door swung in quickly, hitting him in the back and almost knocking him into the hole. He caught himself. He threw his hands over his head and turned. "Don't shoot. Don't shoot."

"Time to go," Frank said to Harry, grabbing him by the shirt and pulling him out of the outhouse. Ricky stood over Frank's shoulder.

"They're shooting" was all Harry could get out.

"Fake bullets. War games. Army's on the other side of town playing soldier. We can't get shot, but we can get caught. Got to get back to the burros. Hide and pray."

Harry nodded stupidly, still in a daze. He reached back to the outhouse and grabbed the two toilet-paper rolls. He wanted to salvage whatever pornography he still had. He stopped and swung the door open and closed. "I get it. It opens in."

FORTY-THREE

They made it back to the room with the burros without incident. That was about the best news they could report.

Outside, the gunfire continued. The mortar fire on the mountain started again to the east. And the metal grind of tanks rolled through the streets. They knew they were the sounds of pretend war, but they weren't any less enveloping and frightening than the real thing. Especially for civilians in a piss-poor hiding place.

They didn't have a choice. Waiting was their only option. If Frank, Harry, and Ricky tried to leave Baghdadville, they would be seen on the open plain. They had to make do with where they were and what they had. Suck or no suck.

The stairs leading to the second floor were wide enough for the burros. The men tugged on the reins to get the beasts to climb the steps, but the animals would take a step, think better of it, and back up, forcing the process to start over. It was as if God was directing an amateurish and perverse interpretive dance through the burro.

There was so much noise it was impossible to gauge its direction. There was no close or far away. Only loud and louder. The mortar on the mountain was the farthest but the loudest. It was like drowning in sound. Underwater without a sense of up or down.

Harry sat on the fifth step of the stairs pulling at the reins of the immovable burro. The animal's neck stretched, but its feet remained rooted to the floor.

"I'm going to kill you. I'm going to chop you into little donkey pieces. Climb these stairs."

"Maybe we should leave them down here," Ricky said.

Ricky had tried to help by pushing the burro's ass. But the first time the burro threatened to kick, he backed off. The pain in his ribs reminded him how stupid it was to stand behind a burro.

"We don't get them upstairs, might as well stay down here, too. They find the burros, won't take another minute, they'll find us," Frank said.

"They got to want to go," Ricky said, reaching into the burro's pack. He pulled out a handful of candy bars.

Ricky opened up a PayDay and held it in front of the burro. It tried to take a bite, but he pulled it away, walking backward up the stairs. The burro didn't move for a few seconds, as if it knew it was being tricked. But its desire for candy outweighed any insight a burro was capable of, and soon both burros were standing on the landing of the second floor happily eating their peanutty reward.

With the burros as hidden as they were going to get, the best Harry, Frank, and Ricky could do was sit on the floor with their backs to the wall. Adrenaline dip, the heat, or plain boredom, it could have been all three, but within fifteen minutes the three men were sound asleep.

While outside, the war raged on.

Ricky woke to the sound of voices. He froze. How long had he been asleep?

He turned. Frank and Harry slept soundly.

The voices were close, but how close?

Frank let out a sharp snort that sounded like the first tug on the cord of a chainsaw. Ricky put his hand over Frank's mouth. Frank's eyes opened in brief confusion. When he locked eyes with Ricky, he calmed. Frank woke up Harry in a similar fashion.

The gunfire had died down, though occasional bursts could still be heard. The voices grew from murmurs to words. Getting closer. But not as close as Ricky had first thought. Outside the building. Not inside. Not yet. Two voices, but no way to know how many people.

Ricky closed his eyes, held his breath, and listened.

"Quit dragging your ass, Larios. Why you always last? Is it a Mexican thing?"

"I'll show you a Mexican thing, *pendejo.*"

"I'll pass on that."

"Let's find a place, dig in. I'm tired of all this walking."

"That what you going to say to Hajji? Don't shoot me, bro. My feets hurt."

"Fuck you, Gung Ho. You really think we going to learn something today going to keep us alive over there? If we ain't learned it yet, we ain't gonna."

"Ten minutes. But only if you got a cig for me."

"Done. I know how much you brothers love menthols, but alls I got is Marlboro Reds. Man smokes."

"I got your man smoke."

Laughter followed. The two talkers and two other men. Four men total.

Upstairs, the three men and two burros listened to the boots on the concrete floor below. The men entering the building.

Ricky's stomach turned pukey. His skin quivered. Curious, one of the burros took a step toward the stairs. Ricky rose and tiptoed to the burro. He pulled a candy bar out of his pocket and fed it to the animal. The other burro took a step forward. He neighed, but it was drowned out by a fortunate volley of gunfire. Ricky took a deep inhale and quickly found another candy bar.

The voices continued below.

"You going to see your lady before we ship out?"

"Coming out Wednesday. You?"

"Wednesday, too. With my boys. Going to take them to the old prison in Yuma."

"I've done that. Cooler than you'd think. Takes like an hour. Can't kill a day, but it's educational and shit. Wouldn't've wanted to be a con back then."

"You hear that?"

Ricky was pretty sure he was going to throw up. He stroked the neck of the burro and waited for the sound of boots on the stairs. Frank and Harry sat resigned to their fate, both of them shaking their heads in disgust. Nothing left to do but get caught. No excuse or flash of cleavage was going to get them out of this speeding ticket.

The burro took a step away from the stairs. Its hooves clopped on the hard floor. To Ricky, the steps sounded like explosions.

No voices from downstairs, but the distinct sound of a rifle being engaged. Then all hell broke loose.

The mad cacophony of gunfire and yelling sounded like a thousand people fighting in a closet. Boots shrieked and skidded on the floor. The words, mostly four-letter, echoed in shouts. At least six distinct voices fought for dominant volume above the pounding report of assault rifles.

The volume was so abrupt, Ricky felt like he had been socked in the stomach. He wanted to cry and puke and run at the same time.

When the ruckus and gunfire finally stopped, it was followed by laughter.

"I think we're all dead."

More laughter and a few playful fuck-yous.

"I'm calling bullshit on you, fucker. You shot me after I killed you. Where's our observer?"

"Taking a leak. How we going to tally this?"

"That was fucking nuts. My ears are still ringing. Can't hear a fucking thing. Why didn't you dumbfucks wait until we were outside?"

"We didn't know you were in here."

"Sure we did. It was strategy. You trapped yourselves. If we're the insurgents, we're going to motherfucking insurge."

"Why couldn't it be like regular laser tag without the sound? My head is pounding."

"Supposed to ready us for live fire."

"What the fuck do we do now? We're all dead."

More footsteps.

"What the hell? You couldn't wait until I was done pissing?"

"Some fucking observer. All you observed was your wang."

"Let's head back. Maybe the monitors on these things can tell us who killed who when."

"I definitely killed you, fucker."

"Zombie kill. You killed me from beyond the grave."

And with that, the soldiers left. Their voices, laughter, and boots grew fainter.

Ricky swallowed the bile in his throat and turned to Harry and Frank. They both shrugged.

"They're gone," Ricky whispered.

"Even the US Army can't mess with our destiny," Harry said.

"Dumb luck," Frank said. "Nothing but dumb luck."

"You say tomato." Harry laughed. "Eventually you're going to see. Destiny, luck, fate, three sides of the same coin."

"A coin only has two sides, Harry," Ricky said.

"Heads, tails, and the side. Sometimes a coin lands on its side."

FORTY-FOUR

Ramón tapped Bernardo's head with the tip of his boot. Bernardo grumbled and swatted lazily at the foot but didn't wake up. Ramón stepped on one of his brother's fingers, slowly putting pressure on it and grinding it into the hardpack. Bernardo woke abruptly, squinting up at Ramón and pulling his finger from under his foot.

"Why step on fingers?" Bernardo put his finger in his mouth, immediately removing it and spitting out dirt.

"Worky is gone," Ramón said. "I looked all over. In the rocks. Up there. Over there. I thought he was taking a dump, a squirt, but I am now sure he bolted, because…" Ramón trailed off, chewing the inside of his cheek.

Bernardo sat up, knowing the news was bad. "Because why?"

"Because unless you have candy in your pocket, he left with all the food. And some of the water. And the good flashlight. And my baseball cap. And some other stuff."

"Did he take the *mota*?"

Ramón shook his head. "It is in the bag I use as a pillow. So there is a bright side."

Bernardo nodded. "Does *she* know?"

"About the weed or Worky?"

Bernardo stood up. "I better tell her."

Mercedes listened to Bernardo with a surprising amount of control. When he was done, she clapped her hands together loudly, rose, and collected what was left of their supplies.

"Let's catch that thief. Can't have gotten much of a head start. Only been light for an hour."

She dropped to a knee and ran her hands along the dirt and gravel. She sucked a finger and held it in the air. She closed her eyes and sniffed loudly. Finally, she picked up a small stone, popped it in her mouth, rolled it around, and spit it out.

"What are you doing?" Ramón asked.

"Our people are the best trackers in the world. It is a talent imbued within each and every one of our tribe. It does not need to be learned. It is in our blood. We hunt the signs, track the thief, and get our stolen supplies. Then we continue on to find your grandfather."

"We are not doing any of that. And I am very positive that tracking is something people do learn," Bernardo said. "And none of us, including you, were ever taught that skill."

"Don't turn your back on your heritage, son. We are a proud people."

"We cannot track shit, mother."

Mercedes turned her head sharply.

Ramón let out an involuntary whimper. "Do not do it, bro."

Bernardo stepped forward. He spread his legs wide as if in preparation to withstand a heavy wind. "This trek is over. We return west, back to the river, back home."

Mercedes faced Bernardo. "Do. Not. Talk. Back. To. Me."

Bernardo looked up at the sun in exasperation. "Mother, Ramón and I have heard your shouting our whole lives. Yes, we are frightened of you in town, but no longer in the middle of the desert. We are trespassing on Army land. We are lost. We have no food. I will play the mother-son game when I cannot die from it. Until we have cement under our feet, I am the decider."

Mercedes fumed but remained silent.

Bernardo turned to Ramón, who looked like he was waiting for a balloon to pop. "What supplies do we have?"

Ramón couldn't stop staring at Mercedes. He was transfixed by how red his mother's face had become. The color of a dog's pecker. If steam was ever going to come out of a person's ears like in the cartoons, now was the time. He didn't want to miss it.

"Ramón!" Bernardo barked.

Ramón snapped out of it. "We got all the *mota*. Two jugs of water. Some supplies. But no food that I saw. None."

"We are not done talking." The quiet words leaked from Mercedes's mouth.

"Yes. We are," Bernardo said. "We go while we still have sun to follow. If we head west, we will find the river."

Mercedes turned abruptly, picked up her blanket, and folded it.

Ramón walked next to his brother. "I would not sleep, brother. You may wake up dead."

"With no food, we cannot waste time."

"We can forage."

"It is all rocks and dirt. We cannot live on spiders and thorns."

"What about the *mota*? We could eat it. Like a salad."

Bernardo nodded. At the least, it would make the hike painless.

FORTY-FIVE

"Up there?"

Frank shouted over the mortar fire that blasted against the mountain. The mountain that Frank pointed at. The mountain that the trail led to. The mountain that was made out of explosions.

Frank rubbed his eyes as some dust drifted down. "You didn't say nothing about mountain climbing. That's really steep. I'm an old man, for Christ's sake."

Harry waved his map. "I didn't know. A map is a flat thing. There's squiggly lines for mountains, but how do I know from how high? It ain't a pop-up book."

Frank snatched the map from his hands. "You see the numbers next to the squiggly lines? Jesus. The artillery, that's a big thing, but I was prepped for that. Been looking at it, hearing it. But mountains? Might be too much."

Harry looked stung, like Frank had bad-mouthed his mother. That was, if Harry had had anything but loathing for his mother. "The mine is on the other side of that rise. There's a trail. No climbing. Like walking up stairs. Rocky stairs."

"Rocky stairs that someone is trying to blow up."

"Nothing can stop us, Frank. We'll make it. Destiny, like I've been saying. We're here. And there's been all kinds of chances for this to go sideways. Darkest before the dawn, right? This is our last test. Or one of the last. No promises on this being the last one."

Frank laughed. "Yeah, no more tests when you're dead. I learned that from cancer. Only, when you got cancer, pieces of you ain't flying through the air in all different directions."

Ricky walked between the two men, holding his arms out as if stopping a brawl, though the men had shown little anger and were ten feet apart. "We got to decide next. Is this the only way?"

"Only way I know."

"Can't do nothing about the height, but we can wait until they stop bombing."

Frank shook his head. "What happens if we get halfway and it starts up again? Or the trail farther up is covered in rocks and we can't get though? That trail has taken damage, I'm guessing. It only takes one mistake. But that's not my problem, it's the climb. This old body is having trouble walking. I slow you down, I stop, could get you boys killed. Can't live or die with that."

Frank walked away and pretended to do something important with one of the burros.

Harry turned to Ricky. "You two stay here. I'll go and see if the mine is there. If the gold is there."

"You said it yourself. There's something about the three of us. It works when we're together. Let me talk to Frank."

Harry nodded. He found the flattest rock he could and unfolded the map on top of it. Ricky walked to Frank who stared at the explosions on the mountain and stroked the neck of the burro.

Frank spit on the ground and spoke slowly. "Looking up at that damn mountain. At all that violence and smoke. It's like looking at death. Like I'm seeing the end."

"We'll wait until it stops."

"That ain't the thing. I'm ready to face them explosions. Family, friends, life. Couldn't give two shits. It's a sad day when you realize your life don't matter."

"You matter. You're just questioning your faith."

"I'd need faith to question it. When you're young, your life is all future. Dread or excitement, you're looking forward. But when you get old, it all switches to the past, about what's behind you. What do you do if you don't like what you've done? You can't look to the future for atonement, because the only future you got is nothingness."

Ricky shook his head. "If you don't believe in anything, I don't know, you have to find a way to believe in something. Even Harry believes in destiny or that dead man's head or whatever."

Frank laughed. He picked up a black rock and rubbed the charred ash off it, until a smeared brown showed through. "It's not like old age, a long life, makes you somehow satisfied. I'm not explaining good. I'm not saying I don't care if I live or die. Only a crazy person wants to die. Getting old turns death into that next-door neighbor you hate, but you've learned to make peace. I do care about living. It's that I ain't got much living left. I'm looking up at an exploding mountain and I want to live. And it's the worst fucking feeling in the world.

"I thought this adventure would give me something more than the gold. Not meaning, but something. Maybe it has. It's been good to be on my own. Friends. The chance to get a win at the end of a losing season. Going through an artillery range to get to a gold mine is the single stupidest thing that I've ever done. Gloriously stupid in a life where I wish I had done more stupid things. I guess when all's said and done, I'd rather die with my idiot friends than in bed wasting away. It's what we came here to do. If I die trying, at least I die trying, right?"

"So you're good to go?" Ricky asked.

"I may be a lot of things, but I ain't a man who lets down his only friends. But I'm serious, my body is broke. We need to move fast up that hill. If I slow us down, I could kill us all. And if my choice is let you down or get you killed, I know my call."

"I got an idea," Harry said, hobbling to the two of them. "I need my katana."

There might be a doctor who would approve of using a samurai sword to remove a leg cast, but the world is full of quacks. The hygiene alone was suspect, considering the amount of dried mountain lion blood and hair still caked to the blade of the decoration/weapon. But there was no stopping Harry once he got the idea in his head.

"We need that burro for the supplies, and with the rest of the supplies on the other one, there's only room for one rider. My leg is healed enough. Not all the way, but enough to walk."

"What if it isn't?" Ricky asked.

"Then I climb back on the burro and we try it that way. Same difference. But we got to go all four of us."

"Four?" Ricky asked, and then got it. "Oh, the head."

"So who's going to help me jam this thing down the leg hole?" Frank asked.

They didn't help jam anything. They watched as Harry slid his sword into the opening at the top of the cast and started sawing at the inside.

"It feels pretty spongy. All my sweat made it sloppy on the inside. Gooey from the dead skin and filth, it won't take long."

"I feel a little sick," Ricky said.

"Lot of give in there. If we had water to spare, I'd pour it down there to help break up the rot and plaster."

"Seriously, Harry," Ricky pleaded, "stop describing."

"Careful not to cut yourself," Frank added.

"Really? I hadn't thought of that. Hey, what does this remind you of?"

Harry grabbed the handle of the katana with both hands and stroked it up and down in a not-so-subtle jerking off motion.

Ricky covered his mouth. "I can smell your leg. Jesus. It smells like the inside of a rotten pumpkin."

After fifteen minutes, the sword dug a small crack in the side of the cast. Harry set the sword down and pulled at the opening to make it wider. Scraps of plaster broke off in his hand. He threw them to the side.

"Almost got it."

Harry pulled the remaining part of the cast off like a boot. His leg had atrophied and the skin had taken on the color and appearance of rice pudding with hair in it.

Frank said, "Talk about a farmer's tan."

"Can you stand?" Ricky asked.

Harry stood slowly, putting his weight on the leg. He winced with the first step, but after a wide circle, his stride became more confident.

"I ain't going to run no marathon, but I can do this."

They waited an hour until there was a lull in the Army's effort to destroy the mountain. Considering the amount of explosive activity over the last couple days, fifteen minutes seemed like a reasonable amount of time to guess it was a dinner break rather than an overlong reload. After all the noise, the silence was disarming.

The sun set behind them as they did their best to hurry up the trail toward the scarred blackness. The burros did their best on the rough, rocky trail but were forced to move slowly, their footing unsure. Ricky pulled the lead burro, the animal sensing the danger and fighting with every step. The burro moved forward, but it clearly wasn't happy about it. Harry followed, leading the burro with Frank and the remaining supplies on it.

The air was cool and smelled like a battlefield. Ash and powder, but without the death. The quiet reminded them that they were in nature. That the mountain had been there long before the Proving Ground. And for all the Army's efforts, the mountain would be there long after they were done assaulting it. Down below, they could see the lights of a few vehicles, a helicopter in the distance, and the city of Yuma and what might have been Mexicali far away on the southern horizon.

"Let's beat the darkness," Harry said.

"And the bombing," Frank added with a surprising amount of humor in his voice.

The sun was gone, but they still had the light of dusk to guide them. The trail hit a crest one hundred yards ahead of them. They had climbed for about a half hour. Slow progress, but no danger.

Harry looked at his GPS and a small notebook as he walked. His limp had become more pronounced as the hike continued. He looked up from his notes. "After the crest, it's within a half mile. The trail will drop. It looks like it opens up a little. When the trail opens, the mine's around there."

They began to believe that they were going to make it. But, of course, that good feeling couldn't last forever. In fact, it lasted another two minutes.

Fifty yards from the crest, a fresh volley of artillery struck the mountain above and behind them. All around them. Intense light blinded them. A shower of rock rained down. It sounded like all noise combined.

Ricky no longer had to pull the burro. It took off. Right over him, trampling him and dragging him until he let go. As Ricky rolled, holding his already battered ribs, he watched the burro climb the trail. There was a brilliant flash of light, and the burro was gone in a cloud of debris.

Everything got a lot more confusing after the burro exploded.

FORTY-SIX

The intensity of the barrage was beyond anything the men had ever experienced. Its brute force had no place in the natural world. A lightning storm or tornado paled. It was like being inside a comet. Light strobed so quickly that their eyes never fully adjusted. Larrups of sound assaulted them, any silence between explosions lost in the ringing and humming that filled their near-bleeding ears. Chaos overwhelmed all senses.

Ricky scrambled to his feet, forgetting the pain in his side. Not conscious of what he was doing, only doing it. He ran in the direction he was facing, beyond rational thought. He tripped on the rocks as he moved up the hill and over the crest, the mountain exploding around him. Large chunks of rock showered down on him, cutting his back and head, knocking him off-balance, but he kept forward through will and terror. Even as the world exploded, Ricky had no quit. He couldn't have explained why. He couldn't have told you where he was going. He couldn't have told you if he believed he would ever get home. He couldn't tell you anything. He could only run.

For Frank, running wasn't an option. He was at the mercy of the burro between his legs. The burro had taken off up the hill, faster than he had thought the animal capable. The burro passed Ricky in a clumsy run with Frank holding on for dear life.

Frank had no idea where he was heading. The world was never steady enough for him to get his bearings. He thought they were on the trail, but the burro was at a full gallop, stampeding solo in animal panic.

In seconds, the exploding artillery was behind him. The light and sound continued, but he was out of the range of the explosions. His shadow cast before him with every blast. The burro didn't slow, transporting him farther from the danger. He laughed and shouted.

"That's right, you bastards. You Army sons of bitches. Try all you want, you'll never kill a mountain. And you'll never kill this crazy Indian."

He laughed and cursed the bombs and praised the burro. He threw out his doubt and retrieved his faith tenfold. He believed every word that Harry had spoken about fate and destiny and all the rest of that horseshit. Maybe it was shock, but he hadn't ever felt happier than that moment.

That is, until the burro unexpectedly tried to make a steep rise and threw Frank.

Frank landed hard on the rocky earth. He felt the warmth of blood on the back of his head, and thought it was funny that he was sleepy with so much noise around him. He wanted to stay awake until the end of the party, but the ball would have to drop without him. Everything went fuzzy, then dark.

Unlike Frank and Ricky, Harry didn't run. He didn't panic. He didn't do much of anything. He watched the show and did nothing. He didn't even move. Harry stood on the trail and stared at the beauty of the explosions that surrounded him. The white fire of the blasts grew like flowers, etching his vision with light. When he closed his eyes, he could still see their shapes. Like dahlias, he thought. He reached into the top of his shirt and pulled out his Saint Chris pendant, gave it a kiss, and put it back.

Harry had talked big about destiny and fate when the world was quiet, but raining artillery could shake most men's faith. The fury of an aerial assault had a way of spreading doubt along with shrapnel. Not Harry. His belief never faltered. He knew he was okay. He was more concerned about his leg as he started the painful slump up the hill.

Harry held his hands to his side like he was walking in the rain, letting the dust and gravel play on his skin. A large rock struck his good leg, but he ignored the sting. He smiled and walked peacefully up the trail. He hadn't gone crazy. He was terrified of dying, but he knew it wasn't his time. He sang "Singin' in the Rain" at the top of his lungs.

And then silence. The artillery stopped. Harry stopped singing.

The darkness was abrupt. Harry couldn't see a thing, blinded. He took short, careful steps as his eyes adjusted and the stars filled some of the shadows in his path.

He didn't see Ricky or Frank. They had disappeared quickly when the artillery had begun, moving quickly up the trail and out of sight. Harry smelled the dirt and smoke and powder. It was sweet but burned his nostrils and made his eyes water. He wanted to sit but knew he needed to keep moving. He was tired and his leg hurt like a bastard.

He tripped on something close to the crest. Leaning down, he felt its wetness and what smelled like barbecue and singed hair. He knew immediately it was some part of the burro. He was glad it was dark. He wasn't interested in finding out what part.

"You deserved better."

Harry found Ricky about ten minutes later. The big kid was walking in a wide arc, stumbling over the rocky terrain, visibly dazed.

Ricky squinted through the darkness at the approaching figure. He shouted over his own ringing ears, "How'd you get out of there?"

"Walked. Told you, I wasn't up for a marathon, so I took it slow."

Ricky's breathless laughter filled the night. He laughed until he started coughing. Harry sat down in the middle of the trail. Ricky joined him, lying back on the rocky path.

Ricky wiped his mouth with a tattered piece of his torn shirt. "I thought we were going to die."

"Yeah."

"I'm glad we didn't."

"Yeah."

"We got to find Frank. I think he made it out on the burro."

"If we made it, he did too. As horrible as that was, the fact we're sitting here is proof of some kind of magic. Don't worry. We'll find him and the burro and Constance. He was with Frank."

"God brought us here."

"God, juju, voodoo, I don't really care. As long as we stay alive and get rich."

"We're here because he wants us to be."

"Whatever you say. I can't walk no more. Why don't you pray for Frank? We'll find him at first light."

FORTY-SEVEN

Frank's head rang. And his back, eyes, ribs, and ass weren't exactly keeping quiet either. The sharp rocks that he had fallen asleep on dug into him at odd angles. He made a weak effort to sit up, not getting far before everything tilted. Frank puked in his lap. He stared at the vomit, hoping that all that red was from the Red Vines he had been eating.

The sun hadn't yet risen, but it was light out. The rocky terrain that surrounded him looked like another planet.

He gingerly touched the back of his head. The stickiness that matted his hair reminded him of the night before. Explosions and burros and screaming. The fear and panic and looming death. The beginning came back to him better than the end. Yet here he was. The death not so looming after all. The burro was gone. But he was alive and he'd take that.

Then it occurred to him. Where were Ricky and Harry?

He tried to ignore the pain behind his eyes as he dug his heel in the dirt and rose to standing. He was twenty yards off the trail. Using the light on the horizon as his guide, he faced west toward the artillery range.

His first step was a failure. He fell on the rocks, cutting both his hands. But thinking of his friends, he quickly rose and carried his body as fast as his old legs would take him.

Following the rough trail, Frank found Ricky and Harry asleep in the middle of it about twenty minutes later. They were scraped and bloody, but their chests rose and fell, so he knew they were alive.

As he awkwardly leaned down to wake them, something moved out of the corner of his eye. Something on the horizon. Something living.

He turned his head quickly, but nothing was there. Had it been a man? An animal? Had he imagined it? He was sure he had seen something. Then again, considering what his body and mind had been through, his sanity wasn't an absolute.

With his eyes on the horizon, Frank kicked Ricky's boot lightly. Ricky's eyes opened, taking a moment to adjust. He smiled.

"You're alive," Ricky said.

"Don't feel like it," Frank said. "How's he?"

"Same as us," Ricky said. He stretched, but yelped and popped back upright when his back cramped.

Frank turned his head quickly. That movement again. This time, he caught the shadow of something up the trail. It disappeared behind a rock before he could identify it. But there was no mistaking this time, he had seen something.

"There's something over there."

Ricky turned. "I don't see nothing."

"Behind that rock."

"That's probably why I don't see it. What is it?"

"Something. I don't know. A person. An animal."

"I'll take a look."

Ricky picked up a rock and stood. He held his lower back for a moment, but shook off the pain. Ricky and Frank walked cautiously up the trail, keeping their eyes on the big rock and waiting for disaster.

Ricky whispered, "Should we holler out? If it's a patrol, don't want them to get trigger happy, shoot us."

"They saw us already."

Ricky got ahead of Frank, taking charge. He reached the big rock and looked back at Frank, who was only halfway up the trail, huffing and close to collapse. Ricky pointed and finger-mimed that he was going to look around the rock. Frank nodded.

Ricky slowly moved around the large rock and came face-to-face with a gigantic head and huge eyes that made him fall backward. He inadvertently screamed, "Monster!"

The burro made a scream-like sound and took off in the opposite direction.

Ricky turned to Frank. "It's the burro. Our burro."

"Get him. What're you doing? Get him. It's got all our stuff," Frank shouted, trying to pick up his own pace but falling down instead.

Ricky nodded stupidly, got to his feet, and took off after the burro. The animal stayed in his sights. It alternated between running and walking, keeping just enough of a pace that Ricky couldn't gain ground. It was like the animal was leading him somewhere.

The trail wound downhill, growing narrower with sharper turns. Jagged walls of rock jutted out on both sides of him. The burro dropped in and out of sight as Ricky moved as quick as he could down the snaking path. Gravity did most of the work but took away most of his control. He was falling on his feet down the side of the mountain. If he tried to stop, he would eat a mouthful of sharp rocks.

Ricky called the burro and whistled, but he didn't know the animal's name and was too out of breath for reasonable volume. His mouth tasted like stomach acid and his vision turned yellow, but he kept on after the stubborn bastard. He felt like he was going to pass out, but he'd keep running until he did.

Frantic, Ricky turned a corner. The trail opened into a small depression with high canyon walls. A small valley hidden within the mountains around him. There didn't appear to be any outlet. The end of the trail.

The burro was tired, trapped, or done screwing with Ricky. It chewed at some chaparral that had struggled to survive, mostly dead and brown. The plant's efforts at life were for nothing as the burro ate any green that remained.

Ricky walked slowly to the burro, put his hand on its side, and bent to catch his breath. He spit on the ground, laughed, and gave the animal a friendly pat. He found a canteen in the burro's pack and downed the water until his stomach hurt.

"You're a jerk, but I'm glad you're alive."

Ricky found a shallow bowl in the pack, poured some water into it, and held it for the burro to drink. The burro lapped at it viciously. When empty, Ricky refilled it and the burro drank more.

Ricky lay down on his back. He looked up at the bright blue of the morning sky. It took him five minutes to catch his breath. He hadn't realized how out of shape he was. His body ached all over.

"Where are we?" Ricky said to the burro, not expecting an answer.

Strangely, he got one.

"We're at the Big Maria Mine."

Ricky turned to see Harry and Frank standing at the trail-head, the only entrance. They were taking in the walls of the mountain valley.

"I don't believe it," Harry shouted. "We made it."

FORTY-EIGHT

They held out as long as they could, but the hunger pangs grew increasingly painful. The hiking and the sun had escalated their discomfort, abdominal cramps, and complete lack of energy. When they finally decided to eat, they had already given up hiking and lay prone on the ground. Mercedes, Ramón, and Bernardo consumed all of the marijuana in one sitting.

Half an hour later, they were higher than they had ever been. And for the boys, that was saying something.

"I am going to wait here for my spirit guide," Ramón said, draped over a large rock in an awkward position, one leg on the ground, the other sticking straight out. "I hope it is an eagle, but a wolverine would be equally awesome."

"There are no wolverines in the desert," Bernardo said, staring intently at his own hand. He liked the swirliness of the lines. They were swirly.

"Not real wolverines. Spirit wolverines."

"Even spirit wolverines do not travel this far south. If we were in Nevada, but not here."

Very swirly.

"You are right. What about spirit spider monkeys?"

"Now you are speaking of awesome."

"Quiet," Mercedes shouted. "Be quiet."

Bernardo and Ramón lazily turned to their mother, who was attempting to stand on her head.

She said, "Our lives have been turned upside down, so to see right side up, we must adjust our point of view."

Over-adjusting, she landed hard on her back. Bernardo wanted to return to the magical wonder of his hand.

"Can you hear it?" she asked, ignoring any pain.

Bernardo shook his head.

Ramón nodded. "I think I do."

"It sounds like the inside of a dishwasher. The ocean in a shell. You can hear it? I think it's my brain sounds." She sat up quickly, eyes wide and head darting around. "Where are we?"

Ramón shrugged. "Desert. Mountains. Papa Frank and the Army, something. Was he drafted? That cannot be right."

"I am very high," Bernardo stated. "Yet still, I wish I was higher. Because only then could I eventually become the highest. I am taking a nap."

Bernardo woke up three hours later. It took him more than a minute to put together where he was, why, and what it all meant. He was still high, but closer to a run-of-the-mill Muppets night than an all-out Phish show. He craved tacos, but that would have to wait.

Shadows passed over his face. He looked up expecting birds but instead witnessed a dozen paratroopers gliding through the air, briefly blocking the sun. They were a considerable distance away, chutes open, moving gracefully through the air. Bernardo watched them disappear over the other side of a rocky hill.

They had traveled by the sun, but were as lost as they had ever been. Bernardo had enough rationality to evaluate the dire nature of their current situation. He gave Ramón a kick in the calf and shook Mercedes awake. "Get up. Grab your shit. The bullshit is over."

Mercedes and Ramón looked around confused, but the expression on Bernardo's face quickly sobered them up.

"I want to hear nothing. If we do not get serious, we will die. Or worse, get arrested."

They did their best to head west, but a half hour into their hike, clouds filled the sky. Winding through the mountain path, they were still lost. They continued forward, but to what or where they didn't know.

Bernardo led the way with a general's gait, marching forward, challenging Ramón and Mercedes to keep up.

A brief celebration followed when they reached the bottom of the mountain and entered a large flat plain. If just for the change of scenery, the transition was a minor victory. If they kept the mountains behind them, the plain would lead to the river.

"We are almost out of water," Ramón said, shaking their last bottle, half full.

"It will have to do. We cannot make water," Bernardo said.

Mercedes gently put her hand on Bernardo's forearm. Her voice was small, her head down. "I'm sorry."

That stopped Bernardo and Ramón in their tracks.

"This is my fault. I'm sorry."

Ramón looked at Bernardo. "What is happening? Are we supposed say something? I'm scared."

"It is nobody's fault. Although Worky has some explaining to do. Your doings were out of respect for your father. We, out of respect for our mother," Bernardo said.

"And our burros," Ramón added.

"It will take more than a bad nature hike to hurt this family." Bernardo almost smiled, but his face didn't know how.

"Do you forgive me?"

"You are forgiven," Bernardo said.

"Yeah," added Ramón.

Mercedes flinched from something landing on her head. She held out her hand. A fat raindrop landed in the center of her palm.

In seconds, it was pouring rain. Plump drops pounded down in sheets. They opened all their bottles and held out their hats to catch all the water they could. The containers filled up quickly.

The ground turned to muddy clay. When their feet sank above their ankles, they searched for some kind of shelter.

Ramón led the way as they slogged through the mud as quickly as they could. They headed back in the direction of the mountain, hoping for a cave or at least solid ground.

"This could flood really quick," Mercedes yelled over the torrent.

"Do you see anything?" Bernardo yelled.

"I cannot see past the rain," Ramón said.

"What is that?" Bernardo asked. But not in time.

Ramón ran directly into a metallic wall. It made a loud gong over the drumming rain. He bounced back and onto the ground with a muddy splash. Bernardo walked to the wall and ran his hand over it, squinting at the chipped metal siding.

"It is a bus. A school bus."

Not caring why there was an abandoned school bus parked in the middle of the desert, they ran inside. Bernardo swallowed cobwebs as he made his way down the aisle. He swept them to the side and spit them out. Water dripped from his hair and body. Ramón and Mercedes followed, shaking themselves off. Ramón shook some of the mud from his body.

"You two okay?" Mercedes asked.

Bernardo and Ramón nodded. Out of breath and out of ideas, they sat in silence, listening to the plinking of the rain on the metal roof. In other circumstances, it might have been a pleasant sound.

FORTY-NINE

"So where is the damn thing?"

Frank stood in the center of the small bowl looking up at the walls of the cliffs. "If the mine is here, if we're there, where is it?"

The three men didn't try to escape the rain. They sat it out uncovered for the twenty minutes of its fury. Now soaking wet, they wandered around the strange circular valley with the high canyon walls.

"I don't know, but it's here," Harry said, frustration in his voice. Not the first or even fifth time the question had been asked and answered.

"Shouldn't there be an opening, a door, maybe a sign? If the mine is here, wouldn't there be—I don't know—a mine?"

"This isn't some riddle, Frank. I'm not screwing with you. It's old. It's hidden or buried or something. But according to everything, all my research, all the reading, it's here. Or around here."

"Is it here or around here?"

Harry looked up from the damaged GPS unit that he had been attempting to repair and stared at Frank. "How do I explain better than 'I don't know'?"

Ricky looked at the walls of the valley, ignoring the two men. He spoke as much to himself as Harry and Frank. "It looks like a crater. Where we're at. Not like a natural valley, but a crater. Like on the moon."

Harry and Frank stopped what they were doing and looked at the walls. They craned their necks taking in the circular, crater-esque shape of the depression.

Ricky continued. "Maybe this is an old crater, like one that was made billions of years ago, like by the meteor that killed the dinosaurs."

"Wait a second. You believe in dinosaurs?" Harry asked.

"Sure, who doesn't?" Ricky said.

"But you can't believe in both God and dinosaurs," Harry said.

"Why not?"

Frank broke in. "Considering that we're standing in a military test range, I'm going to go out on a limb and say this crater was made by a missile of some kind. Which means it wasn't here when the mine was here. It was made after the mine was abandoned. The Army blew up your goddamn mine, Harry."

"Shut up, shut up, shut up." Harry threw the GPS unit onto the ground. "When are you going to finally trust me? We made it this far, and I'm still riding the high of being alive. We crossed a minefield, a fake city at war, and an artillery barrage, and we lived. We should've died last night, the day before, and the day before that. All of us. But not one of us did. What are the odds? We've been tested and tested and tested. This is our ninth life. Not the time to quit. That gold is here and it is ours.

"Maybe a missile made this crater. It'd be like the government to screw us without us knowing it. And maybe the mine entrance was here and now it ain't. Means the entrance is gone. Don't mean the mine is gone or the tunnels got filled up. If we're standing on the mine, then we're standing on the gold. Mines don't go side to side, they go down. We want that gold, we dig."

Frank shrugged and walked away, but that was enough for Ricky. He nodded and pulled a shovel from the burro's pack.

Four hours later, the three men were tired beyond the limits of exhaustion and in the worst moods of their lives. Which was a real milestone, considering that their lives hadn't exactly been all rainbows and blow jobs to that point.

That's what four hours of digging hardpack and rock will do. Digging a hole to find another hole and finding nothing. Not even a clue to make more digging seem worth it. Each muscle ache ripped at what little faith each man had left. They had been beaten and battered and had asked for more, but gotten a whole lot of nothing in return.

The artillery started up to the west. Far enough that they were confident that they were at a safe distance, but close enough to make them wince with each explosion. The ground shuddered, and their memories of the night came back with each strike.

The interior of the crater was roughly fifty yards in diameter. Each man picked a spot and dug. After an arbitrary depth, the digger moved on and tried another random spot. After four hours, the area looked like a battle zone, foxholes spotting the landscape. The burro watched curiously, sniffing between holes for anything edible. It licked at pebbles but let them fall off its tongue.

Frank had stopped digging an hour earlier. He lay on his back in the bottom of one of the holes. The damp soil felt good, but he couldn't help feel like he was lying in a grave. Even through the exhaustion, it was hard to be at ease when someone could cover you with dirt at any moment. When he saw Ricky standing over him, his heart skipped a beat.

"Jesus, Ricky."

"Didn't mean to scare you. Had to talk. What're we doing here? We going to keep digging until we can't dig no more?"

"I'm already there. I got the heart to dig, but not the heart."

"You need water."

Ricky handed Frank a canteen. He glanced over to Harry, who was digging feverishly. His form was awful, but his frantic enthusiasm made up for it. He dug like the Tasmanian Devil cartoon ran.

After Frank took a drink, he said, "Harry believes that as long as he keeps forward, he'll reach the finish line. But everything isn't always in front of us. You can only pound your head into the same wall so many times. Sometimes forward ain't nothing but an empty hole."

Ricky shrugged. "We made it here. It feels really close, you know?"

"You're right. Don't listen to me. What do we got to lose? I'm just tired, kid. Don't mean to be the voice of shit."

"I've been praying. We'll find that gold."

"You prayed for gold. What does God think about that?"

"I prayed for my family. The gold is part of that."

"A small part."

"Hey!" It was Harry.

Ricky turned and Frank sat up, peeking over the edge of his hole. Harry's head and shoulders were visible from the top of the four-foot-deep hole on the other end. He was waving frantically.

"I think I found something. The ground is different here. Like the soil's darker or—it's just different."

The burro wandered near Harry, sniffing and kicking at the pebbles near the hole.

"Might be nothing."

Then the burro disappeared. Ricky had been watching the burro as it walked by Harry, and then it was gone. In a cloud of dust. Poof. Running it back in his mind, the animal hadn't so much disappeared as dropped. Like the ground swallowed it up.

The three men stared in silence at the spot where the burro had been. The only sound, pebbles and rocks clacking together. And then a thud and a loud bray.

Harry turned to Ricky and gave him the saddest look Ricky had ever seen. "That's not good," Harry said.

And then he disappeared, too.

FIFTY

All Harry could see was nothing. Darkness surrounded him. He hadn't lost consciousness, but the blackness didn't quite convince him that he was awake either. The fall had been a jolt of intense confusion that felt like he had been spit into outer space. For a terrifying couple of seconds, he thought he was blind. The relief was monumental when he finally looked up and saw the light from the holes thirty feet above him. The holes that he and the burro had fallen through.

The walls of the pit had slowed his drop as he careened down the narrow channel. His landing had been unexpectedly soft. It hurt, but he had been surprised at the amount of give. There was an advantage to a life of misery, at least when it came to pain. He had absorbed worse many times before.

It took him a minute to gather that he had landed on top of the burro, the animal breaking the majority of his fall. Harry's still-healing leg stung from where his heel had hit the hard surface of wherever the hell he was. That leg was never going to heal right.

A voice shouted from above. "Harry!" It was Ricky. "You okay?"

The kid sounded frantic. But Harry would probably be a little freaked too if someone just disappeared. Someone and a burro. Standing there all lah-di-dah, then like a crummy magic trick, presto and gone.

Harry saw the silhouette of Ricky's head above him. It made the opening look like a cartoon eye.

"I'm alive," Harry yelled through some pain. "Better be careful. Else you'll be down here with me."

"You hurt?"

"Don't fall in, kid. Seriously. You'll land on me."

"I'm on my belly. Frank's got hold of my foot. It feels stable where I'm at. You hit like a tunnel that was covered up."

Frank laughed. "I always get the shaft."

"I'll take it from the lame joke that you're okay."

"I don't feel too hurt. Unless it's one of those internal spleen-related injuries that kills you two days later."

He pressed a hand against the belly of the burro, pushing himself up to see how well he moved. He stopped and held his hand against the coarse hair, feeling its stillness. "Think the donkey's dead. I don't hear or feel no breathing. I landed on him. He's warm. If he ain't dead, he's super messed up."

"There should be a flashlight in its pack. Or a lantern, if it ain't got broke. Maybe, hopefully some rope."

Harry rolled onto his stomach and climbed the side of the donkey, feeling for the heavy bundles. He ran his fingers over the animal's body, trying to figure front from back and top from bottom. His hand finally found the canvas of the pack and dug inside. He dug through clothes, candy bars, and Abraham Constance's head. Eventually his fingers wrapped around the familiar cylinder of a flashlight.

The light hurt his eyes, and the first thing Harry saw was the twisted neck and grotesque expression of the poor, definitely dead burro. An unexpectedly high-pitched noise leaped from Harry's mouth. He had a new image for his nightmares. The burro's tongue sagged between its blocky teeth. The animal's eyes stared glassy and empty and sad.

Harry pointed the light in the other direction.

"What do you see?" Ricky asked.

Harry broke out laughing. "I told you I'd find the mine. Harry Schmittberger delivers."

"We really found it," Ricky said through a laugh of his own. "The mine, not the gold." Frank didn't mean to be negative, but he was tired and felt like hell. His skin crawled in an odd way and his hands buzzed. He was ready for a bed and a shower and a meal.

The two of them sat in the shade with their backs to the wall of the crater. They both stared at the hole. The sun had dipped lower in the sky, the cooling air pleasant.

"Every step, we get closer," Ricky said. "Don't matter the next screwed-up thing that happens."

"But there's always something. Notice that. We're at the mine, for all the good it does. We can't get down there. Harry can't get up. The burros are dead. Even if we find the gold, how are we going to carry it?"

"Just another obstacle. I don't know how to get down there or get Harry up. That's a tricky one, but we'll figure it out. The supplies are in the burro's pack. Most of the water and food, too. We don't figure it, we're as screwed as Harry. I tried having him throw supplies up, but it's too far for him. The guy's got an arm like a girl. He couldn't get a water bottle even halfway. He's got the rope, too." Ricky stood and paced.

"Maybe the tunnels, the mine shafts lead to a way out," Frank said.

"Harry wandering in the dark? Last thing we need is for him to get lost. Or hurt. How stable is the rest of the mine, right?"

Frank stared at his shoes, smiled, and asked, "How far down is it, did you say?"

"I don't know. About twenty-five feet. Maybe a little more."

"I got an idea. Hope you're not shy."

Pain shot up Harry's leg. He put more weight on it. Harry wasn't going to let something as ordinary as a not-quite-healed broken leg stop him. His curiosity and greed drove him forward. It wasn't about getting out of the mine. It was about finding the gold. If he found it and died, at least he'd end on a victory. The next sucker would find his smiling skeleton guarding the hidden treasure. Although, how can you tell if a skeleton is smiling?

He took delicate steps down the mine shaft, throwing the light from the flashlight in front of him.

Timber supports were visible every six feet, some in better condition than others. He could see areas of the tunnel that had partially caved in, rocks forming in piles. At the end of the visible light in one direction, it looked like it might be completely blocked. The more Harry studied the condition of the construction, the more the possibility of complete collapse loomed. Maybe it wasn't the best idea to explore.

"Harry! You there?" Ricky's voice shouted from above.

"Where am I going to go?"

"I'm dropping down a line. Tie the rope to it and I'll draw it back up."

"I didn't think you had anything that'd reach."

"We figured it out."

Ricky and Frank stood in their underwear and laceless shoes. They double-checked the knots on the makeshift line made from their clothes, socks, belts, a handkerchief, and shoelaces. They had discussed tearing the clothes into strips but decided that should only serve as a last resort. They couldn't remember which burro had carried their extra clothes. Nobody wants to be stuck in an artillery range in only their tighty-whiteys.

"Think it'll reach?" Frank said.

"We can get a couple more feet with our underpants if we need it."

Frank looked down at the sagging elastic of his underwear. "Let's hope it doesn't come to that."

Ricky got on his belly and snake-crawled to the edge of the hole. Frank stayed behind on his hands and knees, feeding their clothes-rope one foot at a time. Ricky dropped the end into the hole, guiding it down. It grazed the side of the narrow shaft, dropping dust and pebbles into Harry's face. Harry shook the dust off, holding his hands up for the line.

"Can you see it, Harry?" Ricky said.

"Another ten feet."

Ricky looked back at the other end. They looked like they were going to have enough.

"You naked up there? I knew you guys partied."

"We got our underwears on," Ricky said.

"Sure you do," Harry said with a laugh.

Ricky felt a tug on the line and gripped down on the leg of jeans. "Don't pull hard. I don't got much slack. I drop this thing, we're done."

"Sorry. Got excited," Harry said. "I'll tie the rope on."

Ricky waited, gripping the clothes too tightly, his knuckles yellow against the sunburned red of his hand. He felt the weight of the rope.

"All yours," Harry shouted.

"I'll pull it up. We'll tie it down. Get you and the stuff," Ricky said triumphantly.

"What're you going to tie it to?" Harry asked.

Ricky turned and scanned the crater, as he carefully pulled up the line. The entire area was flat and treeless and rockless, with a whole lot of nothing but the holes they had dug. There was nothing to tie nothing onto nothing.

FIFTY-ONE

"I can't hold your weight," Frank said.

"Yeah. I know." Ricky's head hurt from the thinking.

Frank and Ricky lay on their backs and stared at the scattered clouds in the dying light. They didn't want to leave Harry in the mine overnight. They had about an hour to decide their options before it would be too dark for safety.

"I can't climb down a rope," Frank said.

"Yeah. I know." Ricky needed an aspirin, but of course the aspirin was in the burro's pack. And the burro was down in the mine with Harry. And also dead, not that that impacted the effectiveness of the aspirin.

It was like a puzzle. A brainteaser. It was like that game with the farmer and the fox and the chicken and the river. He couldn't remember how it went, but he did remember that he hated that game. The whole thing was stupid. Why would a farmer want to get a fox across a river? The farmer would shoot the fox and then bring the chicken and the feed over. Or was it a dog? It might have been a snake.

"Ricky, you still with me?" Frank's voice snapped him back. Thinking had always slowed down Ricky's thoughts.

"Let's talk it out," Ricky said. "The two of us, we can lift Harry and the supplies out of that hole. Right?"

"Sure. You're strong. I bet you could do it yourself."

"Okay. That's a start. We drop down the rope. We get the supplies. We get Harry up here. Then it's all three of us. And all our stuff. Nobody's trapped. That puts us at square one. But we're trying to get to the end of the maze, not the beginning. We could leave Harry down there. Let him roam around, see what he finds. He's already down there."

"It's going to be dark soon."

"Mine's dark no matter what time," Ricky said.

"He can't get far on that leg."

"I should be down there. You think you two can hold my weight? You don't got to lift, just keep the rope steady."

"Borderline. If we brace ourselves, tie the rope around our waists, maybe. We outweigh you, right? But what's the difference? Then you're in the mine, not Harry. Same difference."

"Totally different. I can get around. Like when we went diving. Same thing, but no water. Even with my arm, I can climb up and down the rope probably. I can move through the mines or shafts or tunnels or whatever they're called. And we don't got to worry about Harry getting hurt or trapped."

Frank turned his head, looking at Ricky's profile. "Yeah, we don't got to worry about Harry. Don't mean something can't happen to you. You hurt yourself, a rock falls on you, a cave-in. Hell, a spider bite, whatever, you're screwed. Anything happens so you can't climb the rope, we can't get you back up, you die."

"The gold's down there. Someone's got to get it. I got the best shot. And I got faith in God and gold and my family and that weird, soapy head and everything else to know that I'll be safe."

"That don't comfort me. Faith is the surest way to get killed. You can believe, but don't forget to watch your ass. Something happens, I'm going to feel like hell for not talking you out of this."

Harry was the last thing they pulled up. They had lifted all the supplies first, which had been considerably lighter and less squiggly. Harry wasn't a tall man. But what he lacked in height, he made up for in density. Ricky couldn't tell if he was getting weaker or if Harry was made out of some kind of fatty metal.

As the remainder of the sun disappeared, Ricky and Frank pulled Harry out of the hole. A one-armed guy and a sick geezer weren't the optimum pairing, but inch by inch with sweat pouring from their faces, they found a rhythm.

Ricky lifted with his good arm, but couldn't hold the weight with his bad arm. At first, the rope slid and burned through the weak grip of his withered hand. So Ricky pulled Harry up a foot, and Frank would use what strength he had to hold the rope steady for the second it took Ricky to readjust his good arm. They repeated the process dozens of times. It was slow, hard work, but after fifteen or twenty minutes, Harry crawled toward them, clawing at the dirt and looking back at the hole.

Exhausted, each man found a spot against the crater wall farthest from the two holes. Harry parceled out the food. It wasn't exactly a feast, but one could do worse than a bag of chips, a box of Hostess CupCakes, and a handful of Fruit Roll-Ups. Water had never tasted so sweet. Frank rolled a joint, lit it, and passed it. Ricky didn't see the pot as a breach of his sobriety, like taking a doctor's medicine.

After one hit of the pot, they all broke into simultaneous laughter. No one had said a thing. It was just one of those synchronous moments when the three men were all thinking the same thing, seeing things the same way, seeing the ridiculousness of their situation, the ridiculousness of everything.

The joint got passed until it was almost gone. When it was little more than a quarter inch, Frank popped it into his mouth and swallowed.

They had almost forgotten where they were, sinking into the illusion of a weekend camping trip or overnight hike, but the beating sound of a helicopter returned them to reality. No one bothered moving. There was no place to hide and unless the helicopter shined a light directly on them, they weren't going to be seen.

The chopper flew straight overhead, its lights streaking the sky and its blades thumping out the silence. The men watched it recede into the distant night sky.

Finding a comfortable position, Frank squirmed on his back and stared at the infinity of stars in the sky. The Army appeared to be taking the night off from its usual barrage—maybe it was a holiday. No bugs or birds or other sounds of nature dampened the silence. It remained desert quiet. Peaceful in a land for war.

While he may have had his doubts at moments, Frank was glad he had gone on this stupid adventure. The gold was a screwy goal, but Harry and Ricky were the only real friends that he'd made since his closest buddies had died.

When his best friend Chocho had died in '03, he had been the last of the gang to drop dead, leaving only Frank. Frank had felt completely alone. He and Chocho had known each other since grade school. Even in adulthood, they rarely went a week without at least talking on the phone. That relationship was special, but also unrepeatable. So he never tried. He went lone wolf and repelled everyone except his family. And they repelled him.

Sure, they loved him, but Christ, they weren't his friends. Mercedes was protective, but intolerable. The boys were dutiful, but adolescent and always high. Not exactly the makings of anything more than grandfatherly time, the bond more spit than glue.

And then Ricky and Harry came along. Crazy, stupid, and tragic, but kindred spirits. Three men with nothing to lose. What would he do with the gold? Who cares? Give it away. But he hoped for Ricky and Harry that they found something. They deserved it.

Old age was odd. Frank never felt like he was very good at it. Didn't want to be. Funny how when an oldster does something a young man would do, it's either cute or pathetic. Screw them. Quiet hospital beds are for quitters. I'll do what I do. I'll take the rocky earth as my bed any day of the week.

A good boxer steps it up in the later rounds. He doesn't let up. Those are the most difficult, they take the most endurance, but they are the rounds that win or lose the fight. Frank was going to keep swinging until the final bell. Frank was going to shock Death with a Ron Lyle haymaker and then kick him in the sack when he was on the ground. If it's ever okay to fight dirty, it's when you're fighting for your life. *So bring it on, you bony son of a bitch. Death don't confront me none.*

FIFTY-TWO

"What is that sound?" Bernardo rose to one elbow in the aisle of the school bus. Tiny spiders scattered like dust motes around him. He shook his hands and arms, more spiders drifting to the bus floor.

"Some kind of machinery?" Ramón sat up on the bench seat. He licked his lips and tried to spit, but nothing came out. His dry mouth tasted like cabbage and broccoli left in the sun.

They got to the window at the same time, rubbing the greasy residue until they could see shapes.

"Is that what I think it is?" Ramón said.

Neither Ramón nor Bernardo had ever seen a tank before, but they had read enough comic books to know that that was what they were looking at. Bernardo thought a tank would be bigger, but it was big enough to be scary.

"What is it?" Mercedes sat against the back door of the bus, her legs splayed in front of her.

"A tank. An awesome tank," Ramón said.

"Get down. Did they see you?"

Ramón and Bernardo ducked. The grinding clank of the tank grew closer and then stopped. The idling engine grumbled ominously outside. Nobody moved, waiting for some sort of clue as to the best course of action.

Mercedes poked her head up to look out the window. "What's it doing? It's sitting there. Don't they have someplace to be? Something to blow up?"

Ramón lifted his head to the bottom of the window to take a peek. "The cannon part is turning toward us."

"This is bad," Bernardo said. "They are target practicing and this bus is the target they are practicing with. We must run. Now."

Bernardo scrambled to the front door and hit the hardpack at a sprint. He tore around the side of the bus, getting as far away as he could. After a moment, Bernardo looked back. Ramón was right behind him. Mercedes was not. She was nowhere in sight.

The cannon of the tank pointed directly at the bus.

"Where is she? What do we do?" Ramón stopped and watched the tank.

Bernardo stopped as well. "Mother will be fine. She just—"

The cannon fired. The sound was huge. The bus didn't so much explode as leap off the ground. Not high, but when a bus jumps five feet, it's still impressive. It looked similar to when Bernardo and Ramón would blow up cans with firecrackers. No fire, just destruction and volume.

"Mother?" Ramón said, looking first at the mangled metal of the bus, and then at the tank. He charged the tank. A twenty-second sprint cleared the distance. He clamored up the side of the hulking machine and banged his fists on the top hatch. He clawed at its edges, trying to pry it open with his fingers.

Bernardo walked in a daze toward the blackened husk of the school bus. There was some smoke, but no fire. Reaching the edge and kicking at a chunk of twisted metal, he turned to the tank. He watched Ramón jump up and down on top of the hatch, until it opened and sent his brother flying backward.

Bernardo approached the tank. A blond man in a strange uniform popped out of the hatch, his gaze darting between Ramón and Bernardo, bewildered.

"You killed my mother," Bernardo said.

"No one was to be here. Who are you? Does your tribe live in these mountains?" the blond man said through a thick accent. It was less exaggerated than the Swedish Chef on *The Muppet Show*, but Bernardo was sure it was Swedish.

"You killed my mother," Ramón echoed.

The Swede turned to Ramón, who had fallen to the ground. He was covered in dirt and rising to a knee. Bernardo rounded the side of the tank as the man jumped down between them, his hand on the holster on his hip.

Bernardo held up his hands. "Going for that gun—even thinking about bringing a firearm into this—would be a mistake, Drago. My mother was in that bus."

"Our mother," Ramón yelled.

The Swede said, "You are to put your hands above your heads until I assess this situation."

"Are there more of you in the tank?"

The Swede didn't answer. Bernardo gestured with his chin to the hatch. Ramón nodded and scrambled up the side of the tank. When the Swede went for his sidearm, Bernardo was on him. With nothing but a tight squeeze of the wrist and a turn, he had the poor guy up against his own tank, disarmed and embarrassed.

Ramón leaped before he looked, dropping straight down into the tank. Bernardo held the gun to the Swede's back.

"Ramón?"

Ramón's voice echoed from inside the tank. "There is no danger."

"How many are there?"

"Three. They will be no trouble."

"How do you know?"

Ramón popped his head out of the hatch and tossed Bernardo a can of beer. "It is just one other Aryan and two ladies. You know, sexy ladies. Ladies of the night for having sex with."

Bernardo gave the Swede a look.

The Swede shrugged. "Lars and I were in Yuma and we met—I don't know their names. They said the tank made them, uh, horned. We commandeered one of our vehicles to—for a tour."

"Our mother is exploded because you were trying to impress a prostitute."

"They were excited to be in the tank."

"Prostitutes do not need to be impressed. Prostitutes need money."

"Was your mother really in the bus?"

"She sure was." But that wasn't Bernardo's voice. Or Ramón's. They both turned to see Mercedes standing between the tank and the bus, her hair smoking a little and her face blackened on one side. She looked like some kind of crazy demon. Which wasn't too far from the truth.

"You are alive," Ramón shouted.

"These the bastards that tried to kill me?"

"I can explain," the Swede said, fear creeping into his voice.

"How did you...?" Bernardo asked.

"Went out the back door."

Mercedes walked to the tank and ran her hand along the exterior. "So we're saved, right? I told you Indians couldn't get lost. What country are these Nazis from?"

FIFTY-THREE

Frank must have died at some point during the night. No last words. No ceremony. No nothing. Just an old man going to sleep and staying asleep. Business unfinished. The end at the middle. The world continuing on as if nothing had happened. His final breath had gone completely unheard.

Ricky zipped Frank into the sleeping bag to keep the insects away. Some industrious ants had already staked a claim, but Ricky brushed them off with his hand. Harry drank from his flask and said nothing. It didn't seem fair to either of them. Frank was supposed to die after they found the gold, not before. Frank's death didn't jibe.

Ricky talked to talk, lost in the loss. "How did he look last night? He looked good, yeah? He was tired, sure, but no more than you or me. Maybe he was hurt more than he let on. Acted tough for us. Frank never complained. Never."

Ricky placed his hand on the sleeping bag and said a silent prayer. Harry dropped his head but didn't close his eyes. He watched Ricky's lips move silently. Eventually, Ricky said "Amen" softly and stood.

"Damn" was all Harry had in him. No other words felt right or necessary. This was new to him. Not the death. He knew his share of dead people, but he had never cared enough about a person to care if they had died. He'd known the old man was near the end, but that wasn't the same as seeing him no longer as a human being, but a limp collection of skin and body. Harry was sad to the bone. Sad for someone other than himself for possibly the first time ever. He wanted to kill God, or someone God loved, show him how it felt.

Harry didn't know how to deal with those feelings. He wanted to be alone. Harry limped the perimeter of the crater until he was at six o'clock to Frank's body's noon. He slid down the wall and put his forehead to his knees. He didn't know if he was going to cry. He didn't know if he had it in him. He didn't know anything anymore.

Ricky watched Harry, letting him experience the death in his own way. Ricky believed in God's plan. Frank was a good man. God was fair and good, he knew it. It was sad, but Frank was in a better place. Ricky believed it. He had to and he did.

A silent, mournful hour later, Harry rose from his seated position and approached Frank's body. He ceremoniously took off his Saint Christopher necklace, unzipped the sleeping bag, and placed the necklace inside. He nodded sharply and closed it back up. Ricky walked up behind him.

"We have to carry him back," Ricky said.

Harry rose, his eyes never leaving the body.

"It's too far without the donkeys. We have to leave him here. Bury him. Leave a marker. Tell his people. They can come back for him, if they want."

"It feels wrong."

"You bet it does, kid. Wrong in every way. But sometimes, wrong is all you get."

"Like we're abandoning him, you know?"

Harry nodded.

Ricky said, "Okay. We bury him and head back first thing to tell his family."

"After we find the gold, you mean," Harry said, knowing that wasn't what he meant.

Ricky shook his head. "Frank is dead, Harry. That's the end of our adventure."

"No, it isn't. The gold is here. Frank dying changes things, sucks, but it don't end them."

"Yes, it does. We bury Frank and go home. This whole plan got him killed. We have to live with that."

"Don't you dare put that on us. We didn't do jack to get Frank killed. Some cancer or heart thing or whatever disease he caught did. He was a grown-up who understood what risks are. We headed into a missile range. He wouldn't've come if he wasn't ready to kick."

"Even if I wanted to stay," Ricky said, "we can't get back up and down the mine with two people. It's a three-person deal. The gold is as far away as when we were in town. It's time to go home."

"What if I figure a way?" Harry said.

"That's not really the thing."

"What if I figure a way to get in and out of the mine? Will you stay and help me get that gold?"

Ricky looked over at the sleeping bag holding his dead friend.

Harry kept up the pitch. "One. No. Two days. Give me two days. We don't have the gold in our hands by then, we pack it in and head down the hill."

Ricky thought about it. He thought about his family, his wife, and his daughter. As much as he wanted to be home, the gold still mattered. He wanted to go back winners.

Ricky gave an almost imperceptible nod. "One day. That's all. I don't think we have enough water for two days and the trip back. Even now with two people."

Harry nodded and clapped his hands together, no idea how he was going to get them in or out of the mine. He needed inspiration. That one-day deadline would pass quickly. He had to figure something out.

Ricky and Harry set Frank down gently in the pit he had been resting in the day before. The same pit that Frank had imagined as his grave had become just that. Some might have found it funny, but the irony would have pissed Frank off. Irony is only amusing when it happens to someone else. Death isn't funny to the dead. It's rude.

Ricky pulled Rosie's *manta* from his pocket. He gave it a kiss, slid onto his stomach, and slipped it into the sleeping bag with Frank.

"Protection for your journey," Ricky said softly before standing. "We should say something."

"You're the Goddy one. I wouldn't know where to start," Harry mumbled. He knew if he talked in his regular voice he would cry. He didn't want the kid to see that.

"Bow your head."

Harry decided to believe in God for the next ten minutes, so long as it meant that God would hear whatever prayer Ricky prayed. He would believe for Frank. After that, he'd go back to atheisting. He let the shovel fall to the ground.

Ricky took a breath and exhaled loudly. "Lord. As we lay Frank Pacheco to rest here in the beauty of the Arizona desert, please watch over him and take care of him. Frank was a good man. A caring man. A father, a grandfather, and a friend. And while I'm not sure whether he believed in you or in a group of Indian gods or animals, I know he was a man of faith. He would not have come out here unless he truly believed that there was more than what he could see. His belief in this trip and his friendship is all you need to know to know Frank as a man. While your rules are strict, your love is endless. I put my faith in you to do right by Frank. Lord, you always know the right thing. This one is easy. That's all. Amen."

Harry nodded, stared into the grave, and then picked up the shovel.

Ricky found a spot on the other side and sank his shovel into the soil.

"Wait," Harry said, running to the bags and stacks of supplies.

"What's wrong?"

"Nothing," Harry said. "Might as well bury two birds under one stone."

He held up the wrapped head of Abraham Constance.

"I'm not sure you're supposed to put two people in the same spot. Won't that be confusing if someone comes back for Frank?"

"It was his mine, too," Harry said.

Dropping down to his stomach, Harry gently rested Constance's head in the vicinity of Frank's chest. It toppled to the side. Harry tried to roll back in place, but it fell to the other side. Harry left it.

He pushed himself to his feet, giving Frank and the head a final look. Both covered and wrapped, it looked more like they were burying old clothes than one and one-fifth of human being. It was disturbing how quickly a person became a thing.

Ricky dropped his first shovelful of dirt onto the body. The pebbles and dirt sounded like hard rain from inside a canvas tent.

"Wait," Harry said, eyes filled with mischief.

"Second thoughts on burying the head?"

"Frank can still help."

FIFTY-FOUR

Covered in dust so fine and faded it looked like ash, Harry and Ricky shovel-patted the earth above Frank's grave. Not a word had been spoken as they had done the work. There was nothing to say. The finality of the moment said it all, and it ate deep at both of them. Nobody should have to bury their friend.

They stepped back and examined their work. The thick rope looked strange, like a dead vine, rising out of the ground in the center of the fresh dirt.

Against Ricky's initial protests, Harry had tied the rope around Frank's waist and ran the rope up, bracing it with small rocks as they buried him. The way Harry figured it, Frank's weight and the depth of the hole should easily hold Ricky's weight. He could use the rope to enter the mine and climb out. Ricky thought the idea was a desecration of Frank's body, but Harry argued that Frank had agreed to help and he would have been happy that even death hadn't kept him from fulfilling his obligation. After all, Frank was still in for a share of the gold.

Ricky finally ceded out of exhaustion and the certainty that he would eventually lose the argument. He felt the need to protest, but it was like defending against ten shouting men. No matter how many verbal punches he landed, eventually it would be him on the ground bleeding from the nose and ears. That's what arguing with Harry was like.

"We still have daylight," Harry said. "You want to give the mine a go right now? No time like the present. But you're the one down there, so it's your call."

Ricky looked at the hole. He should have been excited, but he wasn't. He was ready to return to Blythe, but he had made a promise to Harry. And to himself that he would see this thing through to the end. Even if Frank wasn't there to bolster his confidence, it didn't mean he couldn't hear the old man's voice in his head. If he was heading down the right road, he was going to have to keep his promises. Stupid or not.

As Harry prepared the rope and the supplies, Ricky ate the last of the Slim Jims and drank a Red Bull. Not surprisingly, the combination hurt his stomach, and his esophagus felt like it had been scoured with oven cleaner.

Three flashlights (because two extra is better than one extra), two full canteens of water, a small spade, a big knife, thick leather gloves, three lighters (same logic as the flashlights), a candle, and some granola bars for energy. It was the kind of list that an eight-year-old would make before running away from home or camping in the backyard. Might as well pack a few comic books and a Game Boy.

"You hear that?" Ricky said. He stopped digging through the remainder of the supplies. He held a roll of their pilfered military toilet paper with his head cocked.

Harry looked up quickly. "What? Someone coming?"

"No. It's quiet. They haven't blown nothing up. There hasn't been any explosions. Not for a while. Not all day so far. Not last night either. The longest they've stopped since we started."

"Maybe today's a holiday. One of the lame ones you forget. Columbus or Arbor or Flag Day. Even the Army takes a day off."

"I don't think that's true. One Army guy? He takes a day off. But the whole Army? They don't take vacations. Or else the bad countries would invade."

"Maybe the howitzer is on the fritz. I'm sure there's a reason. Don't worry. None of the bombing or mortaring or missiling is happening east of the ridge. If they stopped, they stopped bombing over there. And if they start up again, they'll start up again over there."

"Maybe they're re-aiming. We're in a crater, right? Maybe that part of the mountain has seen enough. Need to fallow it like farming."

Harry spoke as soothingly as his rasp would allow. "Calm down. Yeah, we're in a crater, but looks like it's been a long while since this area took damage. There's plants growing. The bombing is west."

"The same direction to get back."

Harry smiled and nodded. "And we'll crap our pants and jump off that bridge when we get to it. Right now, let's enjoy the peace and quiet."

"Got thoughts in my head about getting in that mine and all them explosions starting again and it caves in on me. I can imagine it, and the idea of being buried under the dirt and rocks and stuff makes my stomach real queasy."

"That's probably the Slim Jims."

"I'm not joking."

Harry gave Ricky a manly pat on the shoulder. He couldn't think of anything else to do. "I thought you were the optimist? God's watching over us, right? Or at least, he's watching over you."

"God's watching over all of us, sure. But believing that God has a reason for doing stuff don't mean that everything is going to turn out the way I want. Means that I believe it's going to turn out the way he wants. No optimism there."

"He's got you this far, hasn't he? And if you die, you're going to heaven, right? It's a win-win. Gold or heaven."

"I can't talk about this with you. You have no faith. You talk to me like I talk to Rosie about Santa Claus, and that ain't what it is."

It took Ricky a couple of dangerous near-misses to get the hang of climbing down the rope with only one good arm. But once he figured how to dig the toes of his boots into the rope, he caterpillared down: feet then arm then feet and so on.

Four feet from the bottom, he let himself drop. The ground felt good. It made him feel like the first of many possible dangers had passed. Like the first level in a video game. He removed his backpack and turned on one of the flashlights, letting his eyes adjust.

"Everything okay?" Harry's voice echoed down from above. "Careful you don't trip on the dead donkey."

Ricky tripped on the dead donkey.

"Thanks," Ricky said, slapping the dust off his pants. The cloud of fine dust diffused the flashlight beam that pointed down the mine shaft.

"Good luck," he heard Harry say as Ricky waded into the blackness.

FIFTY-FIVE

Darkness had never frightened Ricky. Even as a child, he had been at ease in dark, confined spaces. When you're a foster kid, you get used to hiding. Hiding from "parents" or "siblings" or "uncles" or any number of other forced family that claimed they were there to help. It occurred to Ricky that God may have given him a childhood under houses and in closets for the necessary strength to walk down a one-hundred-year-old mine shaft without superstition or fear.

The wooden braces that supported the rocky ceiling looked weathered but strong. The shaft he walked down felt unchanged, untouched, from the time it had been mined. After thirty yards, he found himself below another vertical shaft. A wooden ladder rose up the narrow opening. He pointed the flashlight into the darkness, but the light only rose ten feet before it hit rock. The opening had been sealed for a time, possibly by the same explosion that created the crater.

How many openings led into the mine? How large was the mine? From the description that Harry had gleaned from Constance's journal, it hadn't sounded like a big operation. Harry claimed that the gold had been mined, bagged, and left for them. The way Harry described it, the gold should be waiting for them near the opening. But which opening?

Ricky's plan was simple and stupid. Walk around until you trip over a big bag of gold. He couldn't think of a better option.

Harry hated waiting. He paced and fidgeted until his leg burned. In an attempt to get his stress under control, he did push-ups for the first time since guard training. He had despised them then, too. After four pretty good ones, his back dipped and his arms shook. Maybe he would use the gold for a gym membership.

The sound of helicopter blades began as a low hum but built quickly to a thump. Harry scrambled to his feet and moved to the nearest wall of the crater. There was no real cover, so the best he could do was press himself against the limited shadows. He held his breath and waited for the helicopter to pass.

It didn't. He couldn't see the chopper, but the sound of the blades indicated that it was hovering. What was it waiting for? Had they seen him? He hadn't actually seen the helicopter, so it couldn't have seen him. But this was an Army base. Who knew what kind of technological wonders they had? Had stealth technology gotten so good that the Army could make their vehicles invisible? It sounded like the helicopter was right overheard.

He wanted to take a peek. See if he could catch a glimpse of chopper blade to reassure himself that it was a regular helicopter. But he didn't dare move. He pushed his back as hard as he could against the rocky wall, sweat dripping down his face and cooling his arms. He felt sick and had to piss really bad.

Harry closed his eyes and took a stab at praying. It seemed to work for Ricky, so what the hell.

"Here's the deal. Even though I don't really believe in you, and feel kind of ridiculous for talking to myself, I need a solid down here. Not so much for me, but for the kid. As much as I want that gold, I'm feeling good about getting this far. Gold is better, but, you know. Thanks, if you had anything to do with that. But, man, you blow it for the kid, you're going to lose him. Kid lost his faith once, don't dick him over again. That bus accident was bullshit, by the way. That's all. Amen, Mother Mary, all that other jazz."

And as if on cue, the helicopter blades receded, and it was silent again. The sound only a bad memory. Though the rhythm of the blades continued to beat in Harry's pounding head.

To be on the safe side, Harry waited five minutes before he dared move. Blocking the sun with his hand, he combed the sky and saw nothing, only puffy, gray clouds on the horizon. He took a long piss and a longer exhale.

Ricky wondered how long he was going to trek through the mine before it was time to call it a day. Obviously, finding the gold would be good, but there had to be a stopping point if he didn't. He wasn't worried about getting lost. Straight ahead had been his only choice so far. In movies, mines were complex mazes, but apparently in reality it made more sense to dig in one direction. The only crossroads he had encountered was the spot where Harry had initially fallen in. That appeared to be the primary entrance.

One long tunnel with nothing in it. Not even a remnant of the old mining operation. No picks. No shovels. No helmets with those lights on them. No lanterns. No nothing. And especially no nothing that looked like gold.

It occurred to Ricky that someone could have found it before them. A lot of time had passed. A worker that had escaped Constance's murderous spree? Maybe Frank's grandfather lied and came back for the gold. What were the odds that they were the first to set foot in the mine in all that time? The military could have found it and swept the area on a routine patrol. There must have been surveyors—whatever they did—out here at some time. Ricky was starting to believe that this wild-goose chase was more of a snipe hunt.

He had to focus. He wasn't coming back down here ever again, so he might as well suck it up and make his search a thorough one. Complaining never did no one no good. He got on his knees and swept the ground with his hand. The dirt was cold and as fine as sifted flour. If this place was untouched, of course a whole bunch of dust would have settled and accumulated on the mine floor. Maybe covering stuff from seeing it easy. He should have brought a broom. He brushed away the dirt anywhere the ground appeared uneven. For thirty minutes, he crawled up and down the mine shaft and searched near the walls but found nothing but rocks.

On his hundredth rock—he had kept count to maintain his sanity—Ricky decided that due diligence had been achieved. He was calling it empty. There was nothing to find. Nothing in the mine. He had searched every direction until the mine had ended or become impassable. He had kicked every rock and examined every small bump in the path. There was nowhere else to look.

He returned to the dead donkey and the rope, unsatisfied with this as the end of the adventure. Frank dead and no gold. Was life that anticlimactic? Ricky decided that it was. Life wasn't stories. It was a gift without a ribbon.

Ricky tried to find the bright side, but it's a weak consolation when the high point of your day is that you weren't buried alive.

Ricky double-checked the saddlebag of the donkey to make sure that Harry had gotten everything. Of course, he hadn't. He had half-assed it and only got the supplies from the easy-to-reach top bag. He could see the full and bulging saddlebag pinned under the donkey's flank.

Knowing that some important tools for survival were possibly inside, Ricky stepped back and tried to figure out how best to get to the bag. The donkey was too heavy to lift, but maybe he could move it. He unhitched the saddle and then wedged himself between the donkey and the wall. He put his back to the donkey and pushed with his legs against the wall, the donkey sliding away from him very slowly. The sound of scraping skin made the inside of Ricky's cheek itch. He held on to the bag, doing his best to keep it stationary while the dead donkey inched away. He kept at it until his aching legs were straight and the donkey was as far as he could push.

Standing, Ricky held the ache in his lower back, his legs wobbly underneath him. He shook it off. Picking up the saddlebag, he was surprised to find a couple small leather bags underneath it. He didn't remember ever seeing them. They were old and brown, weathered and chipped. Like they had been there for a hundred years.

"No. That easy?"

Ricky dropped to a knee. Picking up one of the bags, he immediately felt its weight.

"Lord God in heaven."

The rawhide drawstring was knotted tight. He dug in his pocket for his knife. After some struggling and sawing and even frantic biting, he got the bag open. He shoved the knife in the opening, lifted it out, and held the flashlight to the blade. At the end of the knife was a small mound of dull yellow granules. Not exactly yellow. Gold.

The donkey had fallen on top of the gold. It had been at the entrance to the mine the entire time. Just like Harry had thought.

"Wish you could see this, Frank."

Ricky's eyes welled up. He clutched one of the bags to his chest like you would a newborn and wept openly. He thought of Flavia and Rosie and everything that led to that moment. The pain he had endured and the pain he had been responsible for. There was still work to do. The gold didn't fix everything. He knew that. But finding the gold was good. It was. Finding the gold was better than not finding the gold. He knew that for sure.

There were four small bags. Ricky guessed that each one weighed around twenty pounds. He tried to do the math in his head, but all he could do was the simple times tables. Four times twenty. Eighty pounds of gold. He didn't know how many ounces that was or how much gold cost per ounce or any of the other numbers. Not important. The only thing he needed to know was that eighty pounds of gold was eighty pounds of gold.

R icky tied the first bag of gold to the rope. He gave it a hard tug to test the old drawstring's ability to hold the bag's weight. "Pull her up. Your brain's going to explode when you get it in your hands, Harry."

For a moment, the bag didn't move, hanging in space. Ricky squinted up the mine shaft at the darkening sky. Then slowly the bag rose and ascended up and out of the hole.

Harry's hearty "Holy hell. It's heavy!" echoed into the shaft.

"Send the rope back down," Ricky yelled up. "There's more. Gold, Harry. We found it. You, me, and Frank found the gold."

The rope dropped down, brushing the shaft and enveloping Ricky in dust. He tied another bag to the rope, careful with the old drawstring. Harry pulled it up, and then dropped the rope back down. Ricky tied on the third bag. He noticed that he was whistling a tune. Ricky didn't know he knew how to whistle.

The drawstring and canvas of the fourth bag were too badly damaged from Ricky's knife and teeth to tie it safely to the rope. Ricky found a jacket among the supplies. He put it on, stuffed the damaged bag into the interior pocket, and zipped it to his neck.

"I'm coming up," Ricky yelled.

He gave the rope a hard tug to remove any give.

"Brace it. You don't got to pull. I'll climb."

Harry didn't respond.

Ricky used his feet and legs to brace himself around the rope and his good arm to pull up. He moved at a snaillike pace. For ten minutes he inched up the rope. Then a strange thing happened: he felt himself being lifted. He gripped the rope tightly and enjoyed the ride.

He had no idea where Harry found the strength to pull him up. Maybe in his excitement over the gold, he had gained the adrenaline and strength to lift him. Ricky held on, proud of Harry. He was really moving, the hole above him getting increasingly closer.

Ricky's excitement was immediately shattered by utter disappointment.

When he surfaced, he saw the truth of Harry's remarkable strength. Harry wasn't even touching the rope. The unlucky bastard sat on the ground with a gun to his head. Six guys in fatigues pulled Ricky out of the hole. The gold sat on the ground in front of Harry, who stared sad and longingly at the old, weathered bags. He lifted his head and met Ricky's eyes.

"Sorry, kid."

The moment couldn't be experienced silently. Ricky needed to say something that fully expressed his reaction to the tableau in front of him. He found the perfect word.

"Motherfucker."

FIFTY-SIX

Ricky marched behind Harry as they descended the hill. The hike felt considerably shorter without the donkeys, the bombing, or the anticipation. The expectation of gold was now dread, and apparently dread sped the clock. Also, the soldiers holding guns on them knew where the hell they were going.

The hike would have been pleasant if they hadn't been at gunpoint. Three men took point in front of them, while the other four soldiers were somewhere behind, rifles pointed to the ground, but no less frightening. None of the men had directly threatened Ricky or Harry. They hadn't treated them poorly in any way. In fact, they had said almost nothing. Everyone involved seemed to be acutely aware of the whos, whys, and whats of the situation. Words would be redundant.

Ricky and Harry weren't restrained. Whether out of compassion or practicality, it wasn't immediately obvious. Probably the latter. At the roughest points in the trail, the men needed their hands to navigate the craggy rocks. With no reason to assume that Harry and Ricky were armed, the soldiers hadn't even bothered to frisk either man. Ricky took some pleasure in knowing that he still held one of the bags of gold inside his jacket.

The thought of running never occurred to either man. Where would they go? Fighting, running, or protesting would be nothing but wasted effort. They were caught, and they accepted it.

Ricky felt a drop of rain on his cheek and looked up at the darkening clouds. The cool breeze felt good on his sunburned face. The drops were large but sparse. They stopped as quickly as they started. The desert soil drank up the water. Ricky had become so accustomed to the bombing and mortaring that he initially took the thunder and lightning for another barrage. But the beauty of the flashing lightning felt peaceful compared to the unnatural destructiveness of the man-made explosions.

"Need to double-time it," one of the soldiers said behind Ricky. "Last thing we need. To get caught in rain. This trail goes muddy, might as well be a Slip 'n Slide."

The soldiers in front picked up their step to just shy of a jog. Ricky and Harry tried to keep up, but Harry's limp slowed them. The shoves at their backs and the occasional shouted expletive did little to quicken their pace and even less for their balance and desire to comply.

"Move it, shitheads. What you slowing for? Keep moving."

Finally, Harry hit his wall. He tripped and fell, and rather than get up, he stayed on his ass and flipped off the soldiers. Not a general sweep of the middle finger, but individual attention to each soldier present. "For all my faults, I try to keep my language clean. Working in a prison, never wanted to sound like those animals. But you've brought me to it. Fuck you. And fuck you. And you, you over there, fuck you. I ain't going another step. I'm sitting here. Come rain, shine, hurricane. If the sky shits scorpions, I don't give two and a half shits and a pint of piss. I ain't moving. My ass and this rock, consider them in love, married, and honeymooning. Oh, and you, in the back. Fuck you, too, brotherfucker."

Ricky sat next to Harry and crossed his arms defiantly. Ricky vowed to take Harry's side no matter how stupid, stubborn, or painful. They had nothing left but each other.

"Harry's right," Ricky said. "What can you do? There's nothing to threaten us with. I'm tired. I'm hurting. And I can't care."

The soldier that appeared to be in charge at the mine—the one who had held the gun on Harry—stood over them. He was a fit Mexican American kid who didn't look a day over twenty. None of them did. He looked up at the sky and then slowly back to Ricky and Harry. "Sirs, it's important that you get up. For your own safety."

"No," Harry said.

The soldier's jaw muscles contracted. He spoke so slowly, each word felt like the last one until the next one came. "You need to get up. You stay here, you'll get struck by lightning. And if we're here, we're going to get hit, too. Once the lightning finds us, we're all going to get stung. We were told this thunderstorm was going to land hard."

Harry answered. "It look like I give a rat's about lightning? Or rain? Or you? Why don't you run along? We'll meet you down there, you're so scared."

"I read somewhere that when you get struck by lightning, you lose your sense of smell. Is that true?" Ricky asked.

"That's funny. I read that, too. Looks like we're going to find out," Harry said.

The soldier's face made his restraint look painful. He kicked Harry's boot with his steel toe. "Get up."

"No."

Kick. "Get." Kick "The." Kick. "Fuck." Kick. "Up."

Harry spit on the soldier's boot. "That's five times you kicked me. The last one hurt a little. One more and you're looking at a lawsuit, maybe a court-martial. Army hates bad press. I got witnesses, rights, all that. Back off, Gomer."

The soldier laughed. "You are one hard-assed hard-ass. Time it takes arguing, you end up getting your way. You got five minutes. Rest your feet. Catch your breath. How's that?"

"That wasn't so hard." Harry smiled, and nudged Ricky.

The soldiers huddled ten yards from Ricky and Harry. Harry could hear the murmur of their voices but couldn't make out the words.

"Last chance to get our story straight," Harry said. "Honestly, I think the only crime we committed—at least the only provable one—is trespassing. Don't mention Frank. We stick with we got lost and we'll walk away with a wrist slap."

"What about the gold? We got lost and stumbled on gold? That's our story?"

"That's our story. Don't got to be true, so long they can't prove it's false."

Ricky watched the huddled soldiers talk. On two separate occasions, one of the soldiers glanced back at Ricky and Harry. His eyes were vicious, his sneer sinister.

"We ain't getting no slap on the wrist," Ricky said.

"Trust me. I know the law good. I can talk my way out of this. I got a gift."

"You ain't looking at it. Think about where we are and what's happening." Ricky shook his head. "They ain't arresting us. They got sixty pounds of gold or something like that. What's that? A million dollars or whatever the math is? They turn us in, they got to turn in the gold. Because we'll tell whoever, the authorities, we found it."

"Closer to two million," Harry said solemnly, and then jumped back to reality. "If they want the gold, they'll let us go. Not like we can go to the police on them."

"I think that's what they're talking on. If they should let us go," Ricky said. "Or if they should leave us out here. You know, kill us."

Harry didn't say anything for a moment. He calculated the odds. Then softly, as if the sums added up and he didn't like the answer, "Dang."

The rain started again, heavy drops spotting the ground and picking up quickly. Ricky and Harry ignored it. All that heat and sun made the water welcome. Getting wet was the least of their worries.

"Eight guys killing two is bad business," Harry said. "That's a conspiracy. One of them could eventually talk. Haven't they seen movies? Someone would ask where they got the gold. Or their guilt would get to them."

"Might be true, but they're not that ahead in their thinking. They're here, that's then. They got a pile of gold and barely trust each other. Means they're definitely not trusting us."

The soldier in charge adjourned the meeting and approached Ricky and Harry. Water dripped from the brim of his cap as he stood over them. The rain was really starting to come down.

"It's time to go. Don't give me a hard time. I'm telling you, it's too dangerous. Not just lightning. Rains going to wash out the trail, we're not careful."

"Are you going to kill us?" Harry said.

The soldier blank-stared him for ten seconds. "The vote was four to three. I'll tell you how you did when we get to the bottom of the hill. I'd hate to ruin the surprise."

FIFTY-SEVEN

Harry wasn't going to take no for an answer. On the walk down the hill, he went to work on the leader. With the rain pouring in sheets and the men sliding and sinking in the mud and wet sand, Harry negotiated and bargained and talked as if the sheer quantity of words would be enough to sway the soldier.

"Keep the gold. That's a given. Sure, we found it. Worked our asses off. You don't even know the hell we've seen. Unfair, but hey, that's life. Only children and twats think the world owes them a fair shake. Damn near got killed, but to the victor goes the spoils."

The Mexican soldier stopped in his tracks. "How'd you know my name was Victor?"

"What? I didn't. No. That's just a saying."

The soldier laughed. "I'm fucking with you. A joke. You think I'm retarded or something?"

The ground leveled out but remained extremely slippery. Nearing the base of the large bajada, the group of men slid more than walked. Three Humvees were parked in the deep mud of the plain thirty yards in front of them. Harry and Ricky would learn their fate soon enough.

Harry kept up the word barrage. "I respect that you voted. I got to accept the outcome. That's democracy. That's the goddamn American way. How it works. Guy you voted for may not win, but the people have spoken. But not telling us where we stand, that's just cruel. Making us wait, kind of a dick move."

The soldier gave him a glance, blinking the rain out of his eyes. "Don't you have any hope?"

"Hope ever do you any good?"

The soldier leaned in as if telling Harry a secret. "You're right. You know, I'm sorry. Really. Didn't think of it as cruel to not tell you. My bad on that one."

"Whatever," Harry said. "What happens now?"

"When we get to the Hummers, you're going to die."

Harry gave a small nod, all out of words.

"Didn't tell you up on the mountain—didn't kill you—'cause we didn't want to carry your asses down. Being practical."

"Not that it's important now, and I sure don't want to undermine your leadership skills, but it would've been just as practical to have left us up there."

"Might've raised more questions. Drone spotted you. That's how we found you, you know? Didn't stumble on your shit. They know you're out here. Couldn't pretend you don't exist. Our orders were to retrieve you. Not our fault if you died in the process of being apprehended."

"You believe in hell?" Harry said, mind racing to find the exit. There was always a way out, but sometimes the door wasn't obvious.

The soldier shook his head. "Lived in this desert too long to believe there's anything worse."

Harry turned to Ricky, who had been watching and waiting, somber and silent. Harry gave him a slow shake of the head. Ricky nodded and shrugged.

"Can I take one last look at the gold?" Harry asked.

"How long did it take you guys to find it?"

"Our whole lives."

When they reached the Humvees, rather than rush into the dry safety of the vehicles, the men stood in a semicircle facing Ricky and Harry. The soldier in charge broke himself off from the group. Apparently he wasn't the type of military man who left the important work to his inferiors.

"The both of you," the soldier barked over the rain and lightning. His tone turned formal, as if a ritual was about to be performed. "Come with me."

"Give me a second here." Harry held up a hand and turned to Ricky.

"It's been a pleasure, kid. I don't got many friends. And never had none like you and the old man. Least we found the mine and the gold. That's something, yeah? Really all I wanted. Spending it probably would've ruined it. Feels like we lost, sure. But it wasn't a blowout."

Ricky shook his head. "God has his plan. Even if we don't understand, this is where we're supposed to be. I'm glad we met. I'm glad we're here. And whatever happens next is whatever is supposed to happen next. I made a friend. That's not a small thing."

They shook hands and stared at each other silently.

"You guys ready?" the soldier said softly. He actually looked touched by their exchange, as he lifted his sidearm from its holster.

"The gold?" Harry asked. "One more look?"

"Yeah. That's right. I'm not a complete bastard." The soldier opened the front passenger side of the nearest Humvee, reached inside, and picked up one of the leather bags. He handed it to Harry, who used his body to protect it from the rain as he opened the drawstring. Ricky leaned in with him for another look.

Harry said, "Wish it smelled like something, you know? Gold should smell like flowers or a vagina, something distinct so you know it's gold. Looks mostly like dirt, but it's still the most beautifullest thing I've ever seen."

Harry tied the drawstring of the leather bag tight. When he looked up, the soldier was pointing the pistol two feet from his forehead.

"Let's do this," Harry said, closing his eyes. Ready for the bullet and the end that would follow. He hoped there was more than blackness.

But instead of a gunshot, a strange voice shouted through the downpour. Scratchy and desperate, like a cat having sex with its tail in a door.

"Jesus Christ. Thank fucking God. I'm saved. Lord, I am saved."

Harry recognized that voice. He turned and saw Cooker in a loincloth made from a bandana and a T-shirt knotted together. His wild, long hair stuck to his tattooed chest and arms from the water and mud that covered him. He stumbled forward, like a movie mummy with one hand in front of him.

"I've been walking and hiking and climbing all over. In a line. In a circle. For a while in a hexagon. A pentagram. Like a rabbit in a maze. Lady in the labyrinth. Ants ate all my food when I slept. I ate meat from a dead lion, but that made me puke. I was so hungry, I almost ate the puke. This rain is the first water I've seen in a day. It's hard to drink the drops, but the puddles taste like shit. Another day and I'd be dead."

"Halt. Stop right there," the soldier commanded, turning his pistol to Cooker. The other soldiers lined up next to him and aimed their rifles and side arms at Cooker as well.

Cooker held both hands up. "Whoa there. You can't shoot me. You're saving me. You don't strangle the kitty after you get it out of the tree. I'm the kitty."

"They were about to shoot us," Harry said. "I don't think they read the rules."

Cooker stumbled toward them, his face unable to hide his curiosity and confusion. "You're soldiers. Sworn to protect the citizens of the United States of motherfucking America. I'm one of them citizens. And I need protecting."

"Stop where you are or my men will be forced to open fire. Do not take another step or I will have to take it as a sign of aggression."

Cooker stopped, his feet sinking slowly into the mud. He looked tinier than ever. He looked like he was shrinking. He breathed hard, chest rising and falling dramatically.

"I'm a US Army veteran, motherfuckers. Lower your weapons. You should be saluting me, not pointing rifles at me."

"Don't move, Cooker. They mean it," Harry shouted.

Upon hearing his name, Cooker turned to Harry. "Wait a minute. I know you, you son of a bitch."

Cooker absentmindedly took a step toward Harry. One step too many.

The men opened fire.

Harry couldn't tell which soldier fired first. But with all the excitement of the moment, it took less than a second for everyone to join in. The light was more blinding than the sound deafening, muffled by the rain.

As if controlled by a puppet master having a seizure, Cooker's body jerked and danced unnaturally. Each time it looked like he was going to fall, the force of the bullets lifted him back up. Just long enough to literally tear him in half, center mass disintegrating until he was two, and then a sloppy pile of man on the ground.

Harry didn't waste any time. He dove into the open door of the closest Hummer and scrambled over the passenger seat, feeling for the keys in the ignition. No such luck. He looked back, assuming Ricky had followed, but the kid was nowhere to be seen.

He frantically dug around the car for keys or weapons, but found only a pack of gum and some bottles of water.

Through the open door and pouring rain, Harry watched the soldiers slowly lower their weapons. He could just make out the looks of amazement on each of their faces. The product of their participation in the absolute destruction of a human being. Military training and television did little to prepare one for an honest-to-God slaughter. Slowly the shock wore off.

"Just as screwed," Harry said, watching the men turn toward him. Two of the soldiers pointed, and the others moved toward the Humvee, lifting their weapons to their shoulders.

That's when their world went sideways. Harry saw the strange darkness grow behind the soldiers, but he didn't know what it meant. It was a looming darkness that got darker and bigger and louder as it grew nearer.

Then it happened.

A wall of water crashed against the side of the Hummer, slamming the passenger door closed behind Harry with its force and moving the vehicle sideways across the mud. Harry unconsciously put on his seat belt.

When rain in the desert falls too quickly and the ground has no time to absorb it, a flash flood is created. The position of the Humvees was essentially at the mouth of the temporary river, where all the water from the mountains flowed onto the plain.

Harry screamed to scream, not caring that no one could hear.

The soldiers immediately disappeared in the rising force of the flash flood, some sucked under, others swept into the distance along the brown foam. A leg, a hand, a head bobbed briefly, but soon only molten mud and thrashing water remained.

The Humvee continued to be pushed along at the whim of the rushing water.

Harry clutched the steering wheel, knowing that all he could do was ride the flood. The Humvee tilted, picking up speed in the accelerating current. The roar of the world was deafening. Like he was inside a washing machine or in the middle of a boiling ocean.

Harry watched in amazement out the mud-spattered windshield at the two other Humvees on their sides, moving slowly ahead of him. Insanity's regatta. The soldiers were gone, victims of nature. Finally it occurred to him that Ricky was out there, too. He hadn't seen the kid since right before Cooker got blasted.

Poor kid, Harry thought. He just wanted to help his family. He was the best of the three men. But the torrent wasn't there to punish people, it just was. A raging river was apathetic to the moral fiber of any person in its path.

Harry let his body relax as much as he could. He remembered reading somewhere that the best thing to do in a car accident was to let your body go slack. Tightening up caused more injuries. Panicking would do him little good. He took huge breaths whenever he took in air, just in case the water got high enough to get inside or the Humvee capsized.

By the time it was all over, Harry would only remember the event as an idea, the individual seconds so traumatic and chaotic that they were beyond concrete memories. He didn't know how long the water had carried him or how far, he only knew that it did. And that he had lived through it.

Harry ended up at the muddy edge of the flood plain that had formed in the small valley. The rain had stopped and the water had receded or sunk into the ground, leaving thick black mud. The Humvee had sunk deep enough to block the doors.

He was alone and cold and wet. But when he finally had a chance to evaluate his situation, he saw the bag of gold. He had held on to it when he had jumped into the Humvee. He had instinctively kept his grip on the bag, the drawstring wrapping itself between his fingers. For all the tragedy and chaos, he had survived with at least some part of the reward intact.

Harry climbed out of the driver's window and sank knee-deep into the muck as he tried to take his first step. He slogged forward as best he could.

He couldn't really describe his mood as happy. Not with Ricky and Frank dead. He couldn't tell you if it had all been worth it.

Harry scanned the horizon, nothing but desert and mud. The light of dusk gave the landscape an orange glow. He kept on through the mud, walking in the direction of the setting sun. Heading west. Heading home.

PART SIX: ODDS & ENDS

FIFTY-EIGHT

Harry sat in his car outside of the modest white stucco house. He watched the little girl ride the brightly colored plastic toy tractor around the brown lawn. The girl's name was Rosie. He knew that. Ricky had said it enough times. But for the life of him, he couldn't remember the name of Ricky's wife. Some Mex name, but he couldn't come up with it.

He sat in the hot car for twenty minutes. He knew he was stalling.

The *Imperial Valley Press* had run the story about the tragic flash flood inside the US Army Proving Ground. It had shown pictures of the seven soldiers who had died. They all got hero's funerals. They hadn't found any other bodies, but they hadn't been looking.

Harry knew it was a straight-up miracle that he was alive. Not just surviving the flood, but the trek home, the whole damn trip. Covered in mud and broken by physical exertion, he had walked without pause back to the Colorado River. It was another five hours in the dark until he found the boat. That had been three days ago. Three days during which he had done little more than sleep.

Harry didn't look forward to informing Ricky's lady that the kid was dead, but that was one lie he couldn't tell. The truth was the only way to deliver her share.

He took a swig of bourbon from his flask, popped a breath mint in his mouth, and got out of the car. He ambled slowly to the front door, his leg still hurting with what was probably a permanent limp. The little girl stopped the tractor and watched him. He gave her a wink. She gave him a smile.

Luckily, there were no steps, the front door at ground level. He knocked, then took a step back and waited. The door opened. Ricky's wife stood in the doorway. Harry wished he could remember her name. He gave her a grin, realizing that he had never noticed how good-looking a lady she was. Good for the kid.

"Hello, ma'am. I don't know if you remember me. My name's Harry Schmittberger. We never really met, but I lived in Desert Vista in Blythe, where you used to stay. People used to call me Shitburger. That's how you'd probably know me. Shitburger." The name still stung.

"That's awful. People can be so cruel with their names," she said.

"I'm thinking about changing my last name. Been feeling like a different person."

"How can I help you?"

"This is yours," Harry said.

He held out a small metal box that he had found at the Goodwill in Blythe. It was decorated with a bird and some flowers, but mainly he got it because the lid was good and tight.

"What is it?"

"Something that belonged to your husband. We had a business arrangement. That's his share. Actually, it's more than his share, but he earned every bit of it. You can use it better than me. It's a long story. Details aren't important, but you should know that everything Ricky did, he did for you and your little girl. He went through hell, but I ain't never seen a man so devoted to people he cared for. He inspired me to look for what he had."

"Nice of you to say, but—"

"Please take the box, ma'am." The ache in his arms told Harry that he was still extending the box out to her. "It's a new car, your kid's college fund, more. It's what Ricky gave everything for. You have to take it."

"If it's Ricky's, you should give it to Ricky. He would—"

Harry didn't let her finish. "Wait a minute. What do you mean, 'give it to Ricky'?"

"Unless you're in a hurry."

"He's here?" Harry found himself walking into the house past her, craning his neck toward the back rooms. She didn't try to stop him.

"He's in the back. Sleeping."

"Ricky's alive? He's here and alive?"

"Maybe you should tell…" But she stopped midsentence when she saw Harry was crying. Smiling, laughing, and crying. Harry dropped to one knee, a hand on the armrest of the nearest chair.

"Are you okay?" she asked.

Harry nodded his head, and then looked up through wet, red eyes. "Can I see him?"

Ricky woke from the sound of the bedroom door opening. He thought he was still dreaming when he saw Harry standing in the doorway wiping at his face. It had to be a dream, because Harry was dead. He had died in the flash flood. Ricky sat up and blinked himself awake, but Harry still stood there.

"Is that really you?" Ricky said.

"I was going to ask the same thing. I thought you was dead."

"Far as I knew, you were the dead one."

"Guess we're just two zombies."

"How?"

Harry gave him the rundown. The flood, the Humvee, the wild ride, and the hike back. Truth really was stupider than fiction.

When Harry was finished, he asked, "I had the Hummer to protect me. How did you get out?"

"Don't know. Soldiers opened fire and I took off. I was running and what I figure must have been the first wave of water smacked me hard in the back. Knocked me out cold. Don't know how long, but not long, I don't think. I woke up wedged between some rocks just above the waterline. Best I could figure it, the water swept me up and brought me to this small patch of higher ground. When the water went down, I looked for you. No such luck, obviously. You'll never believe what happened next."

"I'm at the point if you say a UFO picked you up, I'd believe it."

"Not far from the truth. Not a UFO though. A tank. And who was driving? The Go Go Gophers, Frank's grandsons. With their scary mother."

"Get the hell out of here."

"That's why that little biker was out in the desert. The one they shot up. Jesus, that was horrible. They followed us, look-ing for Frank. But they got lost, and somehow come across some Sweden soldiers in a tank. Seems these two Swedens had a couple of Mexican hookers with them, so they weren't exactly ready to turn anyone in. They gave us a ride to the road. The inside of that tank was cool, all sorts of switches and stuff."

"Did you tell them about Frank?"

"Had to. Soon as the mother knew who I was, she threw me against the side of the tank. Strong, lots of upper-body strength. She held me there, screaming, 'Where's my father?' in my face. I was scared, I'll tell you. Just blurted out, 'He's dead.' She looked at me for a long time. I told her that Frank had passed away in his sleep. Craziest thing, she nodded and got real calm. Said some-thing like, 'Then it's time to go home,' and that was that."

Harry shrugged. Nothing sounded crazy to him anymore.

"In fact," Ricky said, "it wasn't until I told Frank's grandsons that I owed them for their burros that they showed any reaction. I've never seen two men cry harder."

"Been thinking about that myself," Harry said. "I made some calls. Got a guy that's going to sell me a couple of donkey puppies to give them. Figure we can't bring 'em back theirs, but we can do that much."

Ricky said, "If you thought I was dead, what made you come by here?"

"Came by to drop off your share."

"What are you talking about?"

"Haven't you known me long enough to know that I always got another trick up my pant leg? I keep it next to my penis. I never let go of that bag of gold."

Harry set the metal box on the edge of the bed next to Ricky. He opened it. Inside was the leather bag.

"That's most of it. For you and your family. Put some aside to buy the donkeys, and I'm going to give some to Frank's people. I only kept a little for myself."

Ricky laughed.

Harry continued. "More I thought about it, the less I could think to spend it on. I didn't want the gold nearly as much as I needed to find it. You got important stuff. Real stuff. Use that money smart. In fact, let the lady spend it, instead of you."

Ricky kept laughing, almost uncontrollably.

Harry chuckled. "It's not that funny."

Ricky reached under his pillow and pulled out another leather bag, now inside of a gallon Ziploc freezer bag. "There were four bags in the mine. This one was in my coat."

"Holy mother," Harry said.

Just then, Rosie ran into the room and climbed onto the bed, hugging her father.

"Who's he?" Rosie asked, pointing at Harry.

"This is your Uncle Harry. He's family."

Rosie held her hand out formally to shake. "My name is Rosie."

"It's nice to meet to you." Harry took her hand and gave it a soft squeeze. She shook his hand up and down in an exaggerated manner. "What do you want to be when you grow up, Rosie?"

"I'm not never going to grow up," she said.

"Good for you, kid," Harry said.

ACKNOWLEDGMENTS

First off, I would like to thank everyone at Thomas & Mercer and Amazon Publishing for all their hard work on the book. Specifically, I'd like to thank Jacque Ben-Zekry and Andy Bartlett. You two made the process easy.

Huge thanks to Michael Batty—not only a great drinking buddy and one hell of a writer, but one of the best first readers on the planet. Ain't no one I'd rather talk story with over a few beers. (Michael writes as Bart Lessard. Check his stuff out.)

The acknowledgments for my first novel were written so early on that I didn't have an opportunity to express my gratitude to certain people. A big thanks to the following authors, who didn't know me from Adam but agreed to read *Dove Season*: Ray Banks, Bill Cameron, Sean Doolittle, Craig Johnson, and Charlie Stella. All class acts.

I'd also like to thank all of the independent bookstores that stocked *Dove Season* (and that I hope are carrying this book), especially my local mystery bookstore, Murder by the Book, in Portland, Oregon. They didn't have to, and they did, and that's a big deal to me.

Finally, thank you to my beautiful and talented wife, Roxanne. You might not be able to tell through all the swearing and violence in my books, but everything I write is a love letter to you. I would be lost without you.

Big Maria was written at Beulahland in Portland, Oregon.

ABOUT THE AUTHOR

Johnny Shaw is the author of the novel *Dove Season: A Jimmy Veeder Fiasco* and editor of the online fiction quarterly *Blood & Tacos.*

Johnny received his MFA in screenwriting from UCLA and over the course of his writing career has seen his screenplays optioned, sold, and produced. For the last dozen years, Johnny has taught screenwriting. He has lectured at both Santa Barbara City College and UC Santa Barbara.

Johnny lives in Portland, Oregon, with his wife, artist Roxanne Patruznick.

Made in the USA
Charleston, SC
03 October 2012